PRAISE FOR THE ONE APART

"An outstanding, well-detailed story that is hard to put down, evocative, thought-provoking, and filled with surprises and hope... *The One Apart* is very highly recommended ... Expect far more insight from this read than most, tempered with a purposeful saga to keep readers thoroughly engrossed to the end."

— *Midwest Book Review*

"Avery breaks the laws of nature and lifts a veil ... Sophisticated ... Masterful ... The work of a conscientious and gifted writer."

— *Readers' Favorite*

"Our reality is only the tip of the iceberg ... *The One Apart* is a story heavy with emotion ... A unique tale that rewards readers who take the journey."

— *Entrada Publishing*

"A perfect blend of realism, fantasy and deep spirituality ... Fascinating and compelling ... Illustrates the power of compassion and empathy ... A poignant and satisfying conclusion ... This book will stay with you long after you finish it, a hallmark of excellent literature."

— *Chanticleer Book Reviews*

"A fascinatingly intricate narrative that will captivate readers from beginning to end ... Avery draws the reader in to learn and discover more ... Readers of any age, from teenagers to those more seasoned, will appreciate the masterful narrative that Justine Avery has superbly developed ... *The One Apart* easily garners a five-star rating and will divulge more insight and perception each time readers explore its pages."

— *Seattle Book Review*

"Masterful ... A powerful psychological conflict that draws the reader irresistibly ... [Avery] demonstrates great mastery, creating worlds that readers will love to explore."

— *Readers' Favorite*

"An extraordinary concept ... A fascinating plot with a convincing portrayal of characters ... This is the book you should be reading."

— *San Francisco Book Review*

"Beautiful, emotional, and intense ... The novel twists perceptions of the real world and other, unknown dimensions ... The story dives deep."

— *Foreword* Clarion Reviews

"The story itself is fascinating... I was caught from page one, and the pace never slowed ... A unique perspective on the subject of what it is to be human, to grow up, and what comes after."

— *Manhattan Book Review*

"I was immediately drawn into the novel and felt a connection with the well-developed and relatable characters ... Compels the reader to open his mind to understand the full depth of the story and the world beyond our reality here on Earth. The themes of love, acceptance, true friendship, and kindness emanate throughout as Avery masterfully tells this unique journey."

— *Tulsa Book Review*

"Highly original with several unexpected twists ... An engaging story that will have readers cheering for [Tres] and his family."

— *Blue Ink Review*

"Recommend this book to anyone who can read ... You can't miss this."

— *Stuffed Shelves Reviews*

"A compelling story ... Seamless way in which the supernatural and the normal blend together ... The conclusion to the story was incredible."

— *Readers' Favorite*

THE ONE APART

JUSTINE AVERY

SUTEKI
CREATIVE

Cover copyright © 2018 Oishii Designs

ISBN-13: 978-1-948124-00-3
ISBN-10: 1-948124-00-9
ASIN: B076B7RDWY (ebook)

For Devon,
who made me fall in love with stories all over again

This is not the real reality.
The real reality is behind the curtain.
In truth, we are not here.
This is our shadow.

— RUMI

PART I

BEGINNING

Non nobis solum nati sumus.

— WE ARE NOT BORN FOR OURSELVES ALONE.

1

––––––––––

MEMORIES WASHED OVER HIM IN A FLOOD OF CASCADING IMAGES. Sharp, flashing scenes stabbed at his awareness.

The onslaught pursued his consciousness, ramming him with a barrage of every experience from countless lifetimes.

With a white-hot blaze across the screen in his mind, realization became revelation.

Tres remembered *everything*.

2

SANCHA HIKED UP HER OVERSIZED DENIM OVERALLS AND THUMPED down the hallway of the only home she knew. The wooden floorboards creaked beneath her swollen, bare feet, sounding the warning of a pregnant teenager on the move.

She tugged at a dark auburn ringlet springing into her green eyes. "At least I still look cute—from my neck up," she said, flinging her ponytail over her shoulder in defiance as she turned her attention to navigating the stairs.

SANCHA SHUFFLED into the kitchen and around her mother's broad body leaning over the stove.

"*Please* eat your breakfast today, Sancha," Maria said, carefully weaving her tone.

"Good morning, *Mother*," Sancha said, over-dramatizing. She yanked open the refrigerator, let out a sigh, and slammed the door closed again.

"Eat, please," repeated Maria, setting a plate of hot, nutritious food on the chipped Formica table.

Sancha slid her feet across the linoleum and planted herself in a chair, resting her chin on her hands. Even the wafts of heat from her favorite foods offended her sensitive nostrils. "But I don't *feel* like it," she whined.

Maria turned around, matched her daughter's frown, and raised the stakes with one arched eyebrow.

Sancha picked up a fork and swung it at the offensive meal with full flare. Her scowl swallowed up a forkful of runny scrambled eggs.

Maria sighed with relief and turned to address the dirty dishes. "Any day now," she said. "And it'll all be over."

"I'm not keeping it! I *told* you!" Sancha shrieked, pounding the tabletop with her fist.

"I didn't mean—" Maria stood alone in the kitchen, listening to her daughter stomp up the stairs again.

SANCHA LET the tears stream only after her bedroom door closed behind her. Her chest heaved with each sob, making her feel more vulnerable than ever.

Her future flashed before her eyes: snapshots of a rundown apartment, her hands covered in calluses, tasteless food on paper plates, the shrill cries of demanding babies surrounding her, smelly diapers piled in every corner—and no friends. It was the most damning life any teenager could conjure up.

She'd been dragged out of school—and her social life— kicking and screaming. She missed Carol the most, the one person in the whole wide world she could tell everything to —*everything except this*. Sancha felt more alone than she ever thought possible.

In school, around her friends—especially those pointless teachers and piles of meaningless homework—she never had to *think* about anything at all. Now, she had so many thoughts swimming around her head, she almost choked on them. They were impossible to ignore, just like all the questions and all the doubts—and the *life* growing inside her.

She longed for a way to make it all just go away. And she wished she'd never let that blue-eyed stranger *touch* her.

3

TRES FELT HIS BODY ABRUPTLY DROP AROUND HIM WITH overbearing weight, encapsulating him once again.

The mental images, the overpowering memories, finally faded. Only an ominous stillness remained.

Every cell within him began to twitch, infusing with energy —even as he felt immobile. Every joint, tendon, and bone ached under the pressure of being *alive*.

A deep sadness engulfed him. He pondered possible reasons. And, just as quickly, he was distracted by the presence of his own simple thoughts.

Thoughts. He realized his own *thinking*.

This mind—certain of its own newness—desired to explore, feel, do, *be*. Tres opened his eyes—*tried* to open his eyes. He found his eyelids fused shut.

He opened his mouth. Thick, warm syrup seeped inside his swallow. Intense fear washed over him, even as he knew exactly where—and how—he was.

Oh, no.

Tres was aware, more aware than any had ever been. In this moment, he knew everything—and yet, *nothing*.

He was *beginning* again.

4

"Aaaahhhh HHHHHH!" Sancha's pain developed its own voice to commemorate the culmination of the last thirty-nine weeks of her life.

Maria sat at her side, holding her hand tighter than Sancha squeezed hers in return. The doubt and fear on Maria's face confirmed for Sancha that she definitely wouldn't live another minute.

"Aaaaaaeeeeeeeeekkkk!" Sancha ripped her hand out of Maria's, yanked herself upright, and lurched forward to glare at the head of the attending doctor nestled between her open thighs. "What in the hell are you doing down there?" she spat like a girl possessed.

Stunned into silence, the fumbling doctor tried to retain composure. He glanced at the attending nurses standing on either side of him.

"*I said,*" Sancha wailed, "what the hell are you *doing* down there? Do you even *know* how to get this thing out of me?"

"Sancha!" Maria snapped, clamping her daughter's hand in hers again. She swiped at the sweat on Sancha's forehead as if to erase the cause of the outburst.

Sancha glared at her mother, blaming her for everything she'd suffered throughout the past school year.

The doctor spoke with renewed calm. "Sancha, we're doing the best we can. I've been with you through all of this. Just trust me, and *relax*. This baby won't be ready to be born *until* you're relaxed."

Sancha detested the way Dr. Phillips adopted a fatherly tone. She didn't remember her own father. She definitely didn't *need* one now. "Through all of *what*? Where were *you* when that man got me pregnant?"

Maria's palm clamped over her daughter's mouth before it could fire one more scathing shot. Sancha wriggled her head back and forth, realized her mother intended to keep the hand glued to her mouth, and succumbed. She closed her eyes, and her strained muscles started to relax.

"That's it..." The doctor's voice grew distant as another wave of unbearable pain consumed Sancha entirely.

5

THE MEMORIES CLUNG TO THE BACK OF TRES'S MIND: THICK, RICH with detail, and waiting to overpower again. Only the over-whelming impression of pure sensation kept them at bay.

His heart beat in short, sharp bursts. Every bodily part felt alive in the rawest sense. All senses absorbed information at once, none demanding priority over others.

Everything at once. His aged identity—fraught with an unnatural expanse of knowledge—attempted to describe his predicament.

He could not imagine how any one being survived the experience of becoming completely *new:* a blank sheet of mind space gradually filling to form an utterly individual identity.

But *he* had survived this. He'd survived *before.*

So many befores.

How many? *Ages.* How often? *Eons.* His awareness answered before his human brain could venture to calculate or summarize.

Too much. So many. All around.

The torrent of flashing images poured over him—through

him—yet again: the perfect storm of every and all prior experiences.

Nooo...

6

SANCHA'S DROWSY HEAD ROLLED FROM SIDE TO SIDE AGAINST A clean hospital bed pillow. She forced her eyes open, one at a time. Remembering her predicament, she squeezed her eyelids closed again and promised herself she would not open them until she was home in her own bed. She'd just wait out the end of the terrible dream.

Sharp pain suddenly skewered her abdomen, stretched down through her pelvis, and culminated where mounds of gauze and padded underwear wrapped around her. She winced at the agony and her own sense of dread, abruptly aware she'd never be the same again.

"Sancha..." Maria's voice was gentler than Sancha remembered hearing it before. "Sancha, dear..."

"Can we go home now?" Sancha said, still refusing to open her eyes to reality.

"Sancha, you have to heal a bit more. Remember how hard all of this was on your body. And," Maria drew a deep breath. "There's... the *baby*."

"It's not mine! I don't want to ever talk about it again. It didn't happen! Don't say it!"

The entire maternity ward seemed to quiet.

Maria spoke, this time as if she'd just conferred with a much higher authority. "Sancha, you must see *your baby*."

Sancha's face twisted in a grimace; her hands formed fists. "No! I'm giving it away! I don't want to see it! It doesn't exist! Give me those papers! Let me sign the papers!"

She collapsed against the hospital bed again, out of breath and out of pleas. Maria reached out to wipe a strand of damp hair from Sancha's forehead, felt her daughter relax at her touch. She stroked her hair as she did when Sancha was so much younger—which didn't seem all that long ago.

When she found the right words, Maria spoke. "I will only ask you for just one thing ever again. I want you to see this child before it leaves our lives. You..." Maria's voice broke before she finished her statement. "Sancha, you *need* to look at this baby before you... just *look* at him."

Him. The single word affected Sancha deep down in a place she didn't know was there. The sound of the syllable warmed her ears, caused an ache in her chest, made her pouting bottom lip tremble. A *him* had come out of *her* own body.

"It's..." She clamped her eyes shut tighter still, but she couldn't keep the welling water from seeping out of them. Her hands clenched the blanket on either side of her, entwined it around her fists.

PATTERNS SWIRLED above in a whorl of blurred color. Tres blinked. Focusing his newly developed lenses or manipulating his occipital muscles into a squint was impossible.

He lay helpless, only able to exert his own will with subtle, undisciplined movements. The agony of his confinement in a casing he couldn't control was dulled only by his gratitude for his newfound sight. He consoled himself with the mesmerizing hues and colors hovering overhead, watched them roll into one another and reshape into new patterns.

His new ears struggled to register the sounds converging and crumbling all around him. His consciousness managed to decipher desperation, complacency, excitement—all suspended in the air. He added his own curiosity and enthusiasm to the atmosphere.

He waited—few other choices available to him. He absorbed and translated all available sensory information.

Then, the moments unfolding became wholly familiar: little bundles of packed revelation to unwrap. Each held the potential for any combination of the full spectrum of all possibilities.

A bubble of wordless sound escaped from his mouth. Anticipation enveloped him, expanding into a complex form he hadn't known before.

He wept with complete recognition. Moisture threatened to disable his limited vision.

So many. So much. Now again. Again.

A CASUAL KNOCK pre-empted the arrival of an attending nurse. Sancha heard the sounds of a metal cart rolled in, its wheels locked in place at her bedside. She took a quick puff of air and released it as the knuckles of her fists began to turn white.

She heard a rustling of linens, then Maria leaning toward her from her chair on the opposite side of the bed.

Something heavy and warm was laid against Sancha's arm.

"Sancha..." Maria pleaded this time. "*Please.*"

Sancha squirmed against the uncomfortable pressure on her arm.

"I can't let you live the rest of your life," Maria whispered, "knowing you never even *saw* him."

Sancha swallowed. Her breathing quickened. She rolled her lips between her teeth. And she opened her eyes—as slowly as humanly possible.

The brightest pair of crystalline blue eyes stared back at her.

They blinked tenderly, giving away how new to blinking they actually were. Their steady gaze pierced straight through to something rooted within Sancha.

The eyes blinked again, temporarily cutting off the intense connection before opening again to resume it. Sancha rested on her bed in silence, mesmerized by the novice rhythm of blinking resembling Morse code.

Every muscle in her body relaxed. Her mouth began to form an unthinkable smile. She couldn't help herself.

The baby—*her baby*—beamed at her with his big, round eyes and flooded her with the total contentment and perfect peace that wafts only from brand-new life.

———

TRES NESTLED INTO THE SOFT, warm cradle. He blinked to clear his eyes, hoping to hone their focus. He blinked as his only way to communicate to this new world and convey his extreme gratitude, acceptance, and wholehearted joy.

He blinked with the love of a timeless soul in greeting to his mother.

7

Tres strained—willing every muscle—in yet another unsuccessful attempt to squeeze all his pudgy fingers into a tight grip. His O-shaped mouth opened and closed like a fish gulping oxygen bubbles in water. He gurgled his frustration, spittle oozing from the corner of his newborn mouth.

Unable to reach, grasp, or even roll over, he was trapped by his own rotund, untrained form, even as his newborn brain rapidly developed. The limitations of cell reproduction, tendon growth, and even his small size stifled his physical ability while his brain charged with electric pulses, new synapses, and mental connections at an exceptional rate.

His body grew unbearably slowly; his mind raced to adapt, process, and encompass the timeless, intangible knowledge contained in his consciousness. He fought to contain the awareness and capacity no one—before Tres—had ever suffered.

The overwhelming presence of lifetimes of information and experiences seeped into his awareness yet again, threatening to suffocate him and burden every aspect of beginning anew.

Against all dignity, he finally permitted his own insufferable child identity to cry out.

THE FIRST WAIL startled Maria from exhaustive slumber in the comfort of her own bed. The pitch vibrated windowpanes throughout the old house.

She rocketed from beneath her quilt, fearing the absolute worst as she reached into the bedside bassinet. Her grandchild, nearly blue in the face, grimaced between tear-soaked cheeks. He drew in quick gulps of air, preparing for another outburst.

Maria's warm hands smoothed his fine hair. She dabbed at his dripping nose with the sleeve of her flannel nightgown. Still, the baby wouldn't be soothed.

The next shrill spilled over with otherworldly heartache no other could ever comprehend.

"SANCHA!" Maria burst into the far bedroom—wailing child in her arms—and lurched at her sleeping daughter, grabbing her arm more tightly than she intended. "Sancha, he won't take the bottle. He won't calm down. You have to—"

"Mmmnnn."

"Sancha! Your baby *needs* you."

On cue, the confirming shriek sliced through the night, stabbing at the teenager's fragile disposition.

"Aaahhh!" Sancha screamed back. "Make him stop!" She covered her ears. "It hurts!"

Maria wedged the baby into the bedcovers piled next to Sancha's chest and jerked on the chain hanging beneath the lampshade. The burst of soft light reflected from the wet, newborn face. Sancha's hands slid from her ears as her attention fell into the depths of the twin oceans of her son's eyes.

She reached for the tiny body, drawing it closer. Mesmerized by one another, mother and son communicated without words or emotions—promising volumes.

I'M SORRY.

The words echoed in Tres's mind. The thought began to drum, lighting up and fading again like a flickering neon sign.

So sorry... for your pain... for my existence... for all that I have done and ever will do.

His bodily, biological confinement threatened to consume him completely. He whispered to his beleaguered brain, spoke to the life force within his swimming cells, and urged his vital processes to carry on.

I can wait. I can, he urged himself to believe.

8

AFTER THEIR FIRST NIGHT AT HOME, SANCHA INSISTED HER CHILD lie at her own bedside. Each night, she'd wake between dreams and reach for him, pulling the wheeled bassinet nearer. She stroked his cheek before her smiling face rose into his view beneath a halo of sleep-tousled, auburn hair—an angel of light appearing from the depths of the surrounding darkness.

Tres's body slept; his consciousness, never. Alert to all, he never missed a moment of his mother's presence or attention.

She reminded him of someone—of so many. He would never tell her.

Sancha was different, *significant*. He knew it long before he realized that *he* was.

9

MARIA SQUINTED WITH SUSPICION AT THE PAIR OF CHILDREN huddled together in the corner of the cold examination room. Her daughter and grandson pawed and fawned over each other as if they were the only two on Earth.

Sancha rocked the one-week-old baby in her arms, continuously cooing. As she stuck her tongue out with delight, the baby promptly imitated the gesture with an added deluge of spit bubbles.

Dr. Phillips knocked before entering and greeted all three visitors with a professional smile. "How are we today?" he asked, planting himself down on the wheeled stool in the corner of the room.

Sancha—lost in the enjoyment of her newfound friendship —left social etiquette to her mother.

"We're just fine, thank you," Maria answered.

"It looks that way," Dr. Phillips observed. He thumbed through the forms attached to his clipboard. "I see you've moved your appointment ahead of schedule. Is there any specific concern or...?"

"Yes," Maria answered, returning to her visual study of

Sancha and baby. "Well, no, but the little one is... he's really... very *quiet*." Her forehead wrestled worry lines.

"Quiet?" The doctor almost chuckled. "Every now and again, the quiet types are born, babies that are just *content*—easy to please!" He smiled in Sancha's direction before adding, "And you two should consider yourselves very lucky."

Maria pursed her lips. "He doesn't cry."

"Well, some babies—"

"No, he *hasn't* cried—at all. Not since the first time."

"That is... well, no, that's not normal. All right." Dr. Phillips wheeled over to Sancha. "Let's have a look at..." He leaned back to read the label on the file peeking from beneath his clipboard. "*Baby Boy Rivera?* You haven't named him yet?"

Sancha peeled her gaze from her baby, looked at the doctor, then at her mother.

"No," Maria answered. "Not yet."

"Well, you're going to have to decide soon then. Your week is almost up. We'll be calling you to get that birth certificate finalized and registered."

Maria nodded, her concern for the baby greater than her disappointment in her indecisive daughter. Dr. Phillips proceeded with the examination, carrying out every standard test without a single sign of complaint from his infant patient.

"He's fine," Sancha declared, thrusting her arms out.

Dr. Phillips returned the newborn to his mother's arms, not failing to notice the baby's instant recognition and ease.

"Yes, he seems just fine. I'll send his blood sample to the lab."

"He didn't even cry when you pricked his heel." Maria said.

"That does happen—sometimes. It's rare, but—"

"Something's not right," Maria mumbled as Sancha resumed gurgling at her baby.

"Ms. Rivera, try not to worry unnecessarily. Everything looks great at this point, and his development is right on schedule." He flipped through the file again. "In fact, his motor skills and reflexes are actually a bit advanced. Your grandson's developing well. He'll be up and around, getting into trouble, and talking a mile a minute—in no time."

10

"HE NEEDS A NAME," MARIA SAID, POURING SCRAMBLED EGGS onto the plate decorated with a face of bacon strips.

Sancha stared at her plate. "He *has* one," she said.

The hot iron skillet slipped from Maria's hand; she sighed her relief as it landing safely on the stove burner. "What... did you decide?"

"I didn't." Sancha prodded at her eggs, recovering her bacon art one eye at a time.

"I thought you—"

"He has one *already*. I just don't know what it is."

Maria's subconscious almost recognized the truth in the statement before it was buried by her conscious again. "Don't be silly. Did you choose a name? If not, I will have—"

"No, you will *not*," Sancha ended the conversation.

———

IN THE FENCED back yard Maria referred to as "the garden" sat a rusting swing set for two: Sancha's favorite spot in the whole world. Swinging there—in and out of the shade of the broad-reaching maple tree—seemed to slow time and shoo away all teenage troubles.

"I have to name you," she called out to her bright-eyed baby resting in a basket nestled in the grass below her. She swung her pale legs to propel herself higher into the morning sunlight, her glittering hair swirling around her. "But you won't tell me what yours is," she pouted.

Her polka-dotted summer dress fluttered in the breeze as her legs scooped up another pocket of air. "I guess you can't," she concluded on a downswing. "Yet," she shouted into the air.

She dug her bare heels into the dark soil and slid to a stop. She leaned forward, her hands still holding tight to the chain-link as she contemplated the tiny creature that still seemed like a daydream.

"So... what do you want to be called *for now*?"

Her son's vibrant, pink mouth formed patterns of O's.

"James?"

He only stared.

"Joshua? I love *Josh-u-a*," she cooed.

"Probably not a J name. Albert?" She giggled.

"Oh, why can't you just tell me?" Her renewed pout prompted a blink in return.

Sancha slipped off the smooth wooden seat of the swing and crouched over her baby. She stared into his eyes, searched for what she couldn't find the words for.

Tres... tumbled through the thoughts of the one given many names.

I am Tres, every cell in his body verified.

Never recorded, never spoken aloud, the single symbol of his self-identity was his alone. He was sure of it. He *felt* it, even as it surfaced from the single sealed precipice of his awareness.

Tres... of the ages. Tres... of countless lives. Tres... the afflicted.

Without warning or invite, the memories returned—never just one, always all.

No... no... no more. Don't... I can't...

First, pain. Then, suffering—followed by the sheer force of subconscious suffocation.

Mind collapse. Memory overload.

Fading... fading.

I...

THEN, "*AARON...*"

Her voice seeped into his subconscious slumber with more tenderness than it had ever held before.

"Aaron..." snaked its way between jagged remnants of memory—strong and soothing, sure and true like a beacon of light promising safe passage to shore.

Take my hand, the spoken syllables urged.

Tres reached.

———

"HELLO, *BABY,*" poured like love from Sancha's lips as her small body leaned over the basket, her knees stained green in the grass.

"*Aaron.*" Her eyes smiled along with her mouth. "Do you like it? I think you do," she whispered with motherly assuredness—her first.

She kissed his blushing cheek; his eyes widened. "My little

gift, my *miracle*." She lifted the basket toward the blue sky above and spun, her toes digging divots in the dirt.

Aaron reached for the plump clouds, grasping at life itself, never wanting to let it go.

PART II

ENDURING

Festina lente.

— Make haste slowly.

1

"No! I don't *want* to!"

Aaron watched his mother throw her arms up in the air with theatrical opposition.

"Don't you miss your friends?" Maria tried next.

Sancha's stare fell to the ground. "Sometimes."

"I'm sure they'll be excited to see you too."

Predictably unpredictable, Sancha's temper renewed. "No one even *called* me while I was out of school all year!"

"Well, they were busy... doing what teenagers do. And you should be too."

Aaron wriggled helplessly in a bundled blanket on the living room couch. The natural fear of abandonment rose to catch his breath even as it surprised himself. He was *too old*—but vulnerable yet again.

The newborn hung on every word, soaked up every admission. In so little time, he knew both of his caretakers so very well.

Sancha's fiery eyes flared. "*Maybe*, if I *had* a phone, my friends would've called me."

"We have a phone."

"*I* don't have a phone! And everyone else in *the world* does!"

"You know we can't afford such things. Now, *bite your tongue,* Sancha."

The teenager shot out an exaggerated breath of temporary resignation and retreated to her baby's side. "*You* don't want me to go, do you?"

"It will be good for you," Maria said. "For *both* of you." She reached into the laundry basket for another cotton onesie to fold.

Sancha turned to scrutinize her mother, unaware she'd be pushed onto the school bus the very next day.

2

SANCHA RESTED HER CHIN ON HER FOLDED HANDS AS SHE SAT AT A desk at the back of the classroom. Not a single student spoke to her; most of her classmates didn't even seem to remember her. In her own environment—the playground of her innocence— she was now a stranger.

Everyone seemed to *know* something, something they didn't dare speak. Even her former teachers glanced at Sancha as if searching for some physical sign of her social pariahdom— almost effective enough to drive Sancha to seek out its symptoms on her own skin.

When the bell rang, signaling the end of fifth period, Sancha gathered her belongings and raced out of the room, away from her agony. It was Carol, her closest friend of all, who appeared next to her at her locker and dictated the tone of Sancha's remaining high school experience.

"You're not one of us—anymore," Carol carefully pronounced beneath her upturned nose. Her unblinking eyes corroborated.

"What... what do you mean?" Sancha asked in a tiny voice.

"You're..." Carol huffed and replaced her neutral expression with a more sinister one. "You *know*," she said.

"But I—" was all Sancha managed to plead in her most submissive tone.

"It's just *gross*," Carol said.

"*Carol...*" Tears began to well in Sancha's eyes.

Carol turned and sashayed away. "How *could* you!" she spat over her shoulder from a safe distance.

AARON BALANCED on his perfectly round belly, rotating left and right, taxing his just-born limbs, urging his body to accept his commands. He spun on the blanket on the living room floor and admonished himself for not being able to do more.

His giant blue eyes met Maria's.

She held his stare, studying him in silence as she sat in the tattered rocking chair in the corner. Aaron looked away, concentrated on opening and closing his hand, folding and unfolding his plump fingers at varying rates.

Maria leaned back and returned to her crocheting. *Baby booties,* Aaron guessed. *Impressively intricate work,* he recognized without the ability to compliment.

He gurgled, practicing vowel sounds within cheeks too tight and saliva-soaked for speech. He kicked at the air behind him, lashed out at his bodily confinement.

"I *know*," Maria said.

Aaron lifted the weight of his head to meet his grandmother's gaze again.

She cocked her head to the side, noticing his timely response. "There's something *different* about you," she said.

Aaron blinked away his fright—and hopefulness.

"I *will* protect my daughter," Maria warned.

She began to rock, her fingers manipulating the crochet hooks with absolute accuracy while her formidable gaze clung to every action of the infant before her.

———

SANCHA SPENT sixth period wondering if her former friend's final words referred to Sancha's unmentionable sexual act itself—or her socially unacceptable choice to not share the original secret with her best friend.

Sancha leapt onto the bus at the end of the day, clinging to her books and all her girlhood dreams.

3

———

WITHOUT THE PRESENCE OF SANCHA'S ENERGY, THE FAMILY HOME was devoid of joy, moaning with every creak. Each passing day of her first week away at school stretched longer, lonelier.

Disconnected from Sancha, Aaron felt even more weak and alone. The spark of life in Sancha was his lifeline. She tethered him to patience and serenity—to sanity.

And Maria continued her analysis of her grandson with the wariness of a woman who'd suffered vast heartache herself. She caught his every movement, recorded his every infant inflection. She judged all—relentlessly.

———

BY THE END of his week alone with his grandmother, Aaron decided on an act of both defiance and amnesty: the affectation of a smile. The grand gesture was a huge physical achievement for him. And it was *not* received as the gift of good will that he intended.

"*My God!*" Maria's large hands covered her open mouth, then reached for her heart. In pure distress, she glared at the infant. Then, she spoke with calm accusation.

"It's too soon."

Aaron's aged awareness detected words of warning—perhaps, even friendly recommendation.

"*Impossible,*" she whispered. She leaned forward and reached for him. Her fingers forced the corners of his tiny mouth to lower again.

Aaron submitted, committing the lesson to memory.

SANCHA RETURNED home from school in silence, uncharacteristically closing the heavy front door softly behind her.

"How was school today?" Maria called from the kitchen.

There was no answer—no movement at all. Maria glanced into the living room to confirm Aaron's safety, then scurried to the entryway. Sancha sat on the bench seat near the door, her head lowered, her soft locks hiding her face.

"Sancha, what is it?" Maria knelt before her daughter and lifted her chin to reveal her face, devoid of expression. Maria couldn't decipher her daughter's needs, and that upset her most of all. "Please. Please tell me. Sancha, what is it?"

Sancha slowly shook her head. "I can't. I can't go back there."

"Sancha—of course you can. Whatever it is, it'll pass. Your friends have missed—"

"No."

"I'm sure the teachers are just—"

Sancha shook her head again.

"Sancha, what happened?"

Sancha stared at the tops of her shoes. "I can't... go back."

In her daughter's tone, Maria heard the devastation—the

collapse of all the strength and optimism of youth. And that was all she needed to know.

"No," Maria promised. "You're not." She lifted Sancha's chin again. "You've done nothing wrong. Do you understand?"

Maria wrapped her daughter in the security of her embrace, granting her the forgiveness the world outside refused to give her.

———

HOLDING AARON TOO TIGHT—HIS little face damp with her own tears—Sancha sought all the comfort she never asked for through all her teenage struggles.

"What do I *do* for the rest of my life? I was gonna be something. I was..."

She released the compressed bundle in her arms and looked at the tiny face tucked inside.

"Where did you come from? I mean, I know but... why me? Why was *my* life supposed to change? I'm not strong enough. I'm not smart enough. I don't really know what to do, but now, I can't imagine *not* having you."

Sancha stroked her baby's cheek. "You're so... *perfect*. Just perfect. All the things I'm not. Everything's new for you, all ahead for you. You can do anything you want—anything at all." She didn't realize her own smile; Aaron did.

Looking into his eyes, she asked, "What *do* you want to do, Aaron? What do *you* want to be?"

She lost herself in a pleasant daydream: the dream of a possible future much wider than she ever dreamed for herself before. She imagined the life her child might live.

AARON GAZED at the face of his mother, appreciating all the finer points of her beauty, within and without. And he remembered mothers past—even those that had abandoned him and those he lived entire lives without knowing. In that moment, he felt the warmth of the collective motherly support of all mothers.

It emanated from Sancha. So young and unknowing, she was the mother burdened with the oldest child ever to exist.

And she was the one who drew Aaron from his own past, giving his *present* an allure he desperately needed to find. For Aaron, *right now* brimmed with the abundance of all his lives.

4

SANCHA CONTINUED HER SCHOOL ASSIGNMENTS AT HOME WEEK TO week; she read every text and spoke every subject to the newborn always at her side. Aaron's amusing, unwavering attention transformed the most dreaded assignments into a game. Sancha quizzed him, waiting for his chubby arms and fingers to wave and wiggle—seemingly randomly—in response.

ONE AFTERNOON, Maria encouraged Sancha to set aside the schoolwork early; Sancha was more than happy to oblige. She skipped out the back door and into the sunshine. Maria planted herself at the dining room table among the abandoned textbooks, and eyed Aaron as he rested in his baby seat perched on the chair next to her.

"She's outside now. We're alone," she said to her infant grandson.

Aaron blinked, his little leg kicking as his bare toes curled and released.

Maria nodded and picked up the open book before her. She

read aloud, "The en... *enco-mi-enda* system of colonial Spanish America... most closely resembled the European practice of..." She looked directly into his eyes, then continued, "A... absolutism. B... primo... *geniture.* C... patronage. D... manor... ial-ism. E... nepotism."

Maria squinted at the big blue eyes staring back at her. "Tell me."

Aaron blinked rapidly—three times. Then, he blinked again.

Maria tried to conceal her sudden gasp. She quickly read aloud, "Which of the following was an important virtue in Confucianism? A... warlike prowess. B... filial piety. C... public charity. D... poverty. E... manual labor."

Maria found Aaron's gaze diverted by a flickering reflection of light on the ceiling. She tapped his forearm. "Answer me."

He returned his attention to his grandmother. He blinked twice. Maria nervously adjusted herself on her chair.

She rested the still-open book on the table and picked up another. She eyed Aaron, then read aloud, "A number—n—is increased by eight. If the cube root of that result equals negative zero-point-five, what is the value of n? A... negative fifteen-point-six-two-five. B... negative eight-point-seven-nine-four. C... negative eight-point-one-two-five. D... negative seven-point-eight-seven-five. Or E... four-hundred and twenty-one-point-eight-seven-five."

Aaron blinked three times—without hesitation.

Maria's lower jaw fell; the textbook trembled in her hands. "You can't possibly..." she stuttered. "Okay, okay... Sancha has been repeating these questions all afternoon. You..." Maria rummaged through the tabletop clutter, uncovering an unopened book. "You have not heard from *this* one."

She opened the textbook to a random page. "The Earth," she read, "has a radius of six-thousand-four-hundred kilometers. A satellite orbits the Earth at a distance of twelve-thousand-eight-hundred kilometers from the center of the Earth." She drew in a deep breath and continued, "If the weight of the satellite on Earth is one-hundred kilonewtons, the gravitational force on the satellite in orbit is..." She confirmed she still had Aaron's attention. "A... eleven kilonewtons. B... twenty-five kilonewtons. C... fifty kilonewtons. D... one-hundred kilonewtons. E... two-hundred kilonewtons."

Aaron began to blink.

"No!" she shouted, freeing one hand from the heavy book and reaching toward him. "Show me."

Aaron's tiny brows curved; he looked at the large hand poised before his face. His arm lifted. His hand wrapped around Maria's finger. His fingers squeezed hers once, then a second time.

Unmoving, Maria stared at the baby before her, then finally pulled her hand from his grasp when it was absolutely apparent he would not squeeze her finger again.

Her shaking hand covered her mouth. Then, her head shook slowly side to side. "No," she whispered between her fingers.

She slammed the textbook shut, and rose to her feet with unusual speed as Sancha ran inside with a big smile.

"It's such a beautiful day!" she sang.

Maria forced herself to nod and gather herself. "Clean up this mess. Dinner will be soon."

MARIA NEVER QUIZZED AARON AGAIN. She preferred to be well outside of earshot whenever Sancha pored over her schoolwork with her cooing companion within arm's reach. Instead of intervening, Maria prayed with more passion, every night before going to bed.

"Grant us, Lord, Thy protection. And in protection, strength.

And in strength, understanding. And in understanding, knowledge. And in knowledge, the avoidance of judgment. And in the avoidance of judgment, the cleansing of true acceptance. And in true acceptance, the serenity of peace. And in the serenity of peace, the love of all existences. And in that love, the love of spirit and all creation."

5

AARON, DRESSED IN MORE LAYERS THAN USUAL, WRIGGLED IN HIS infant seat set on the kitchen table. Maria muttered a checklist to herself as she stuffed a diaper bag to overfull, her purse and coat hooked in one arm.

Sancha peered into the kitchen, her eyes still struggling to open to the new day. "What's... going on? Are you..." she began as her just-awake brain began to register her observations, "taking him somewhere?"

Sancha slid across the floor in her socks and locked her grip on the handle of the infant seat. Aaron happily waved a fist in the air, unaffected by his grandmother's rushing.

Maria stopped in place, clasped her hands together, and announced, "He's going to daycare."

"What!" Sancha swung Aaron and the seat off the table and into her arms.

"I think it's best," Maria offered, her voice revealing her exhaustion.

"No! He's just a baby!"

"He'll be fine. The ladies in the facility know how to care for infants."

"What? Those old hags at the daycare at the *factory*? The ones that used to make me do all the work for them when you left *me* there?"

"Sancha, it's a very good facility. We're lucky to have it at all. If I actually had to pay for—"

"You're not supposed to *take* him anywhere—whether it's free or not! Aaron's supposed to stay here—at home—with *me*!"

"I have to return to work. We can't afford—"

"Go! Go back to work! Leave *my baby* alone!"

Determination overrode Maria's sympathy. She reached for the handle of the baby seat.

"Take your hands *off* him!"

"Sancha..." Maria forced her voice to soften. "You're acting *crazy*. Nothing's going to happen. Aaron will be fine. And, when I return home from work, he'll be with me."

Both held fast to the seat hanging between them.

"You don't trust me," Sancha said. "You don't think I can take care of my own baby."

"That's not true. I know you can. I've seen you learn to do everything to care for him—and quickly. It's just not... *I don't want you alone with him*." Her final sentence rang with a strange tone.

"I've *been* alone with him! All the time!"

"Not *all day*. And not without me here."

Sancha remained silent, her expression knotted in confusion.

"He's going with me," Maria continued. "We'll be back at three-thirty. I expect you to have your schoolwork finished by then."

Tears welled in Sancha's eyes as she succumbed, out of arguments.

"Let go," Maria ordered. "I won't let anything happen to him. You know that."

Sancha's fingers opened; her hands returned to her sides, smoothing the flannel of her pajamas. Her chin dimpled as tears began to slip down her cheeks.

"Aw... THERE HE IS!" The manager of the on-site daycare facility reached for Aaron. She pulled him out of his carrier and held him in the air for inspection—quickly recovering as she forgot to support his newborn head and neck. "What's his name?" she asked, feigning interest.

"Aaron."

"Ah, little Aaron: the big surprise!" she cackled, drawing the attention of the two daycare employees chatting over their morning coffee in the corner, oblivious to the children in their care.

Maria frowned, resisting the urge to respond.

"Well, we're very glad to have him here. And... good to see *you* back, Maria. You really took full advantage of your employee health benefit, didn't you! Lucky you, sneaking that one past HR." The manager continued to focus only on Aaron like a wolf anticipating its next meal. "Well, you already filled out all the paperwork," she continued, "so, it's off to work for you then!"

Maria followed the woman's outstretched arm directing her toward the exit.

"Oh, we're going to have *so* much fun with you!" the woman squealed as she dangled Aaron in the air.

"If..." Maria spoke up, "if you have any trouble at all, don't hesitate to come get me." She received no response before the bell sounded the five-minute warning for the start of first shift. Reluctantly, Maria hurried toward the hubbub of the factory floor and the sea of industrial sewing machines.

"LOOK AT YOU," the daycare manager spoke to Aaron in his grandmother's absence. "Aren't you *pretty* for being a little bastard."

Aaron wriggled against the biting, bony hands under his arms, defenseless.

THE FLUORESCENT BULBS overhead cast a bluish white haze over Aaron's surroundings, emphasizing the static coldness and cruelty he detected. It hovered all around, hungry to swallow his newborn body whole.

The glassy eyes of his captor were mirrors reflecting his fears and the enduring aches of bygone lives. Her eyes offered no view into a fellow soul, no salvation or temporary pacification. They were webbed with their own suffering.

A child's spontaneous shout clawed at Aaron's hyper-sensitive ears. Disorganized noise rose and fell—twisting, torturing, building with the din from the factory floor resonating all around. The room began to spin around Aaron, provoking nausea, stirring every complex emotion.

He closed his eyes, clenched his fists, tensed every muscle in his small body, and screamed out with full operatic authority.

"JUST TAKE HIM!" the daycare manager screeched at Maria as she wagged her finger at Aaron. "We can't accommodate his sort here. This is not *that* kind of facility. You're going to have to find a more suitable setting for him—someplace equipped for... for children like *that*."

"But... I don't understand," Maria said. "If there was any— he's such a *good* baby. You should've just come for me and—"

"I have, haven't I?" the woman snarled. "No, we're just not able to offer care for special needs cases. It is not our responsibility to deal with *problem* children. You'll have to find another facility."

"But I can't afford... this is an employee *benefit*." Maria adjusted her tone. "There's just some kind of misunderstanding. Maybe he's just coming down with something. Is his temperature normal?"

"We are not a *medical* facility!"

"Well, you must be prepared to care for sick children or minor accidents!"

"Of course, but that is not the case with *your grandchild*, is it?" The manager's eyes protruded from her head.

"I'm sorry," Maria tried. "I just don't know what you mean. He's never been left with strangers before but—"

The woman flung her hands onto her hips. "He's unfit for daycare—just *unfit*."

"I'll just visit HR and have a discussion with—"

The woman's fingers batted a dismissal. "You can do what you want, but I'll just write a full report of your grandchild's *unsuitability*."

"He's just a baby!"

The manager's neck craned toward the daycare employees tuning into the argument. She retreated behind her desk, and leaned toward Maria. "There's something *wrong* with him. Some kind of... *disability*. You know it, and I know it. Don't embarrass us both by denying that and turning this into a bigger issue than it has to be."

Any remaining softness in Maria's demeanor disappeared. "That is just *not true*," she said, picking up her grandson and his belongings and hurrying out the door.

6

"Remember to never leave him out of your sight," Maria hurled at Sancha between gasps of air, "unless he's secure in his infant seat or his bouncer or—"

"I *know,* Mother!"

Sancha stroked the fine, golden hairs on Aaron's head as Maria hesitated at the front door before leaving for her shift.

"I can't take any more time off of work, Sancha. If I do, they'll—"

"You're driving me *crazy!*" Sancha erupted, closing her eyes tight to achieve a yet higher volume.

"All right, all right. He *is* your child. It's just—"

"I know how to do *everything.* You've drilled it all into my skull." Sancha's fingertips pressed at the side of her own head. "It's impossible to forget!"

Maria nodded. "It's just that, sometimes, unknown things can happen that you just can't prepare for."

"I will call you ASAP." Sancha looked at Aaron again. "I don't want anything to happen to him either."

Maria's chest expanded with a large breath, then she

grabbed her keys and left Sancha and Aaron alone—completely —for the first time.

"Finally," whispered Sancha, her eyes bright with anticipation.

THAT AFTERNOON, Maria reached her doorstep in record time, just fifteen minutes after the bell sounded the end of first shift. The weight of her worry sounded in every heavy footstep as she rushed through the doorway.

"Where is he?" Maria asked, still gasping for air when she spotted Sancha sitting before the television set in the living room.

"Aaron? He's outside," Sancha answered without redirecting her eyes.

"He's what!" Maria disappeared through the back door with uncommon speed.

"He loves it out there!" Sancha shouted as the screen door snapped shut.

Maria found Aaron lying in the sunshine, his tender eyelids closed, his body nestled in the baby basket. "Too much sun for a baby!" she screeched as she carried the basket inside and laid it gently on the rug. Aaron opened his eyes to meet his grandmother's.

"I don't think—" Sancha mumbled, her own worry surfacing.

"He could be sunburned!" Maria reprimanded.

"But he—"

"Why isn't he inside with you?"

"He doesn't like it. He doesn't like TV. He loves watching the clouds."

"Well, you're not supposed to ignore him. He's your child! Did you even play with him today?"

"Of course, I did," Sancha quietly answered. "I thought… I thought he might like seeing things moving on the screen or something—I don't know—but he didn't like it. He got all—I put him under the clouds. They make him happy."

"Huh? He shouldn't have even noticed…" Maria's nagging suspicions piqued again. "What was on the television?" she finished.

"Nothing—normal stuff. He just freaked out," Sancha answered as a matter of fact, sitting on her knees next to Aaron.

"Freaked out?"

"He looked all crazy—like he was scared."

"He cried?"

"No—you know he doesn't cry—he got sad."

"What do you mean he was *sad*? How—" Maria recognized the pointlessness of her questions even as she tried to ask them.

"It wasn't good. I had to get him away—and I did. Didn't I, Aaron?" Sancha leaned over the basket, smiling at him.

Aaron gulped at the air, his chin tickled by the popping spit bubbles.

Maria's brow furrowed, her hands still on her hips. "What else happened today?"

"I learned he *loves* ice cream!" Sancha announced with enormous pride.

"You're not supposed to feed him—" Maria pressed her palms to her forehead. "*Jesus.*"

"What?"

"Never mind. He seems to be okay." Maria looked at Aaron. "But there could be a frightening mess in his diaper." A hint of a smile appeared on her face. At Sancha's sudden distress, Maria laughed and let go of all the worry she'd carried all day.

MARIA SAT in her rocking chair as the sun sunk into the horizon, observing the interaction between her daughter and grandson. She regarded every glance exchanged, every flash of nonverbal communication.

"Mm-hmm," Sancha nodded at Aaron, his head lifted toward his mother's voice as he lay on his belly on the living room rug. "You know what's best for you," she said as she met his grasping fingers with hers. "You know lots of things, don't you?"

A knot of uneasiness formed in Maria's chest. "Sancha," she called.

Sancha's attention remained fully devoted to Aaron. She nodded toward his uplifted eyes.

"Sancha?" Maria tried again, raising her voice.

A chuckle erupted from Sancha while her eyes remained locked with Aaron's. "You're full of strange things," she said only to him, as if in response to some unspoken statement Maria was not privy to.

AARON CONSIDERED CRAWLING, THEN CHOSE TO SKIP THE expected pageantry in favor of his own freedom. As soon as his infantile muscles developed the strength to support his upper body in a sitting position, he pulled himself to standing. Then, he made his first steps within minutes. Few steps were required to teach his legs to walk and accommodate perfect balance.

As soon as he walked, Aaron longed to run. The lengthier stride proved too much for such an untrained body, but every fumble and fall ushered new excitement as it promised that full mastery of his infant body was just within his grasp.

No one could have imagined such physical feats for an infant —months, even a year, too soon—nor did Aaron allow them to witness such miracles. He practiced only when alone—or so he thought.

IT WAS Maria who felt compelled to check on her grandson one morning during her weekday routine. On impulse, she casually leaned around the corner to peer into the living room from the doorway.

There, along the length of the rug in the center of the room where he'd been rolling on his belly the evening before, her infant grandson calmly *walked,* placing one foot in front of the other as if he'd been doing it all his life. Maria witnessed it all: the careful stride, the resultant fall, then the immediate return to a standing position followed by more steps forward. Aaron didn't hesitate; there was no sign of an infant's awkwardness at all.

Maria immediately denied the scene, pulling herself back into the hallway. She opposed the possibility of an infant exercising calculated, purposeful *self-instruction.* She refused the observation of a baby laboring toward a *known* result—as if he was aware, in advance, of the intuitive *feel* of walking.

Maria leaned through the doorway again; she observed the impossible—*again.*

Her presence was noticed. Aaron promptly fell on his bottom but failed to appear surprised or discomforted. Only a pout—reflecting very *adult* disappointment—appeared on his plump face.

Maria turned and walked away, her disbelief controlling her body and extracting her from the situation her mind needed to reject.

THAT EVENING, Sancha and Aaron entertained each other on the living room rug while Maria focused on her latest needlework project, crochet hooks rapidly working the silken yarn piled in her lap. She interrupted their play once she lost all ability to remain quiet, almost admonishing herself as she spoke.

"Why don't you encourage Aaron to sit up on his own?" she suggested, her eyes still fixed on her crochet work.

Sancha continued to tickle Aaron under his triple chin, delighting in the smile he flashed in return. "No..." she cooed at Aaron. "He might hurt himself."

"You should encourage him. He won't have any reason to learn if you don't push him—just a little bit."

"But it took *forever* for him to even smile!" Sancha complained.

Maria glanced up, then returned her attention to the spirals of sky-blue yarn flying between her fingers. "You never know," she said, attempting a playful tone. "He might even be ready to walk."

Aaron rolled his head in his grandmother's direction.

"No way!" Sancha screamed with excitement. Lowering her voice, she reminded, "But Dr. Phillips said that he won't be able to walk until—"

"Nonsense. Every baby is different—we all learn at our own pace. Why don't you help Aaron sit up—right now—and see what happens?" Maria's crochet project was finally set aside.

Sancha glanced from her mother to her son. She slipped her hands beneath Aaron's arms and lifted him.

"That's it. See? He looks quite comfortable," Maria encouraged.

"He looks wobbly."

"Why don't you try lifting him to his feet?"

"But he's *never*—"

"*Give* him the chance. He only needs to learn what *you* want him to do."

Sancha's delicate features contorted as she processed her mother's words. "Okay..."

She tentatively lifted Aaron higher, her hands still secured beneath his arms. He rocked back and forth on his toes, his eyes wide.

"Now, let go."

Sancha tightened her grip.

"He'll be fine," Maria reassured her. "His diaper's all the padding he needs."

Sancha predictably disagreed. Still, her fingers lifted from Aaron's back, and she closed her eyes as she fully released his body.

Aaron dropped to his bottom with a weighty bounce.

Sancha immediately wrapped her arms around him as she spewed apologies, unaware she was the only one in the room in need of reassurance.

"Do it again."

Sancha glared at her mother. "No! He's not ready."

"*Again*."

Sancha's green eyes gleamed with the hint of approaching tears, but she did as her mother insisted. She held Aaron before her, balancing him on his teetering legs and tender feet.

"Let him stand."

Sancha let go, and Aaron remained standing. His blue eyes recorded his mother's response, his stance unwavering.

"Oh, my gosh! Look at him! Look at him! He's standing! Aaron!" Sancha squealed.

Aaron began to sway, leaning on one leg and slowly tipping to one side. Sancha reached for him, prompting her mother's reprimand.

"No. Let him be. If you expect him to fall, he will."

As they continued to watch, Aaron completed the turn and took his first step—his first *sanctioned* step. Then, he took another—and another. Sancha stared with incredulity as she watched her own child walk across the living room rug.

Then, he *ran*.

Sancha and Maria held their breath, stunned—the sight too much, too soon.

"*Aaron*," Sancha whispered—just before she experienced the profound sensation of her own child running into her arms.

Mother and son embraced for the first time. Sancha's tears released as a small slice of her adolescence slipped away, replaced with a new, more mature depth of emotion.

Even as Maria's mind filled with more questions than answers, her own tears came as she witnessed the pure, unadulterated bond between mother and son.

And Aaron's little heart raced, his small body teeming with the adrenaline of newly granted freedom.

8

Dr. Phillips dangled his stethoscope before Aaron's eyes. "He doesn't seem to be reaching for objects yet, but that's not too much of a concern at just three months."

"That's because he doesn't *want* it," Sancha snapped. She anxiously wiggled in a metal chair in the corner of the examination room as Maria glared at her.

"Does he try to grasp for things at home," the doctor asked, "when you're playing with him?"

"No, he doesn't *try*," Sancha answered. "He just takes whatever he w—"

"Shh!" erupted from Maria.

Sancha retreated, her body relaxing as she looked down at her lap. Maria offered an excuse for her daughter's outburst, but too late. Dr. Phillips was already intrigued.

"I'm sorry, Sancha, what were you saying?" he asked.

"Nothing," she chided.

Maria offered, "He's developing at his own pace," and punctuated her statement with a nod.

"Of course," Dr. Phillips agreed. "Still, he didn't even seem to be tracking the stethoscope with his eyes. We should schedule a full examination of his sight."

Sancha couldn't contain herself. "He just doesn't *care* about your stupid—"

"Try it again," Maria intervened, addressing Dr. Phillips.

"Excuse me?" he asked.

"The test—the stethoscope. Try it again."

The doctor followed the order, and Aaron acted precisely how his grandmother insinuated.

Dr. Phillips relaxed as Aaron clumsily waved an arm and opened and closed his hand sporadically. "Ah, that's just wonderful—exactly as he should. The little guy must've been teasing me!" His audience ignored the joke.

"That's good. That's very good," he continued, glancing at the checklist attached to his clipboard. "Any other developments? Is he raising his own head yet?"

Mother and daughter remained silent in solidarity.

"Well, that's fine. I'm sure he will be soon, and how exciting that will be!"

Sancha didn't wonder why her mother never told her that Aaron's development was so advanced. She just beamed with motherly pride.

WEARING HIS YOUTH AS A DISGUISE, Aaron had all the time he could wish for to observe, ponder, deliberate, and approach *this* life with precise determination. He raced with abandon within the walls of the family home, exploring every corner—a toddler by talent but not yet in age.

Still, for the majority of each passing day, he only sat and observed, pretending to play as a child should. And he listened, archiving everything. Over time, Sancha and Maria unwittingly revealed themselves fully to the child in their midst—with every emotion expressed, confession made, or thought said aloud. There were no household secrets but those left unspoken—Aaron's included.

In stark contrast with his own capability, he chose not to speak, not to utter a single syllable. He was well aware of the consequences of what one single, spoken word might reveal.

Though there were worlds of ideas to share, vast volumes of information and infinite theories and unnamable concepts to counter with, formal communication could spark a bonfire—a signal to all, known and unknown, that he—this *one*—did not belong. Silence was his shield.

Aaron had everything to say. And so, he was left with nothing to say at all.

9

As soon as Aaron revealed his ability to run, he made it obvious that he was done with diapers. He climbed onto the toilet seat and shrugged off any assistance. Without any conscious decision or awareness, Sancha and Maria began entrusting Aaron to tend to all of his own needs, leaving him largely unattended.

When Maria did seek out her grandson's whereabouts, she would find him building an intricate structure with found objects or simply staring out of a window, pondering the passing clouds. Rarely, did she find herself surprised—which surprised her most of all.

By four months old, Aaron fed himself, ignoring all textbook dietary recommendations and feasting on the full variety of solid foods. He selected the clothes he wanted to wear each day. He was granted his own bedroom and a twin-size bed suitable for an adult.

He napped like a cat: any time, day or night, and without delay. Just as naturally, he chose when to play, when to be read to, and when he wanted to venture farther from the house— even if still confined to the baby stroller for the benefit of any prying eyes. The baby—with his focused attention and meaning-packed gaze—made it clear when and if he wanted or needed anything at all.

And neither Sancha nor Maria dared question the regular occurrence of fortuitous incidents in their lives. Just as Maria grieved over the vacuum cleaner finally falling to disrepair, the next hopeful attempt to use it revealed its unexpected revival. It worked just as well as new. Minor electrical issues disappeared as quickly as they were discovered; recurring repair issues suddenly fixed themselves. Even household plants seemed to flourish under a green thumb that neither Maria nor Sancha had. Each minor miracle was accepted in stride—too precious, too timely, and too numerous to question without risking appearing ungrateful to the powers that be.

AARON GREW into the toddler with the steadiest stride, the surest self-confidence, the easiest nature. In the security of seclusion, he blossomed, unhampered by the outside world and uninfluenced by any—other than the two who could never comprehend but would always make every effort to nourish his individual nature.

And he continued to wait out the minutes—wading through the necessary circumstance of infanthood. He filled every second with activity, every moment with mental exercises demanding his complete attention. If he didn't, his *pasts* would overpower him.

Each new day that he breathed within his *present* body, he was reminded of all those he'd occupied before. Every moment, Aaron battled the predicament of his own identity, struggling for the stability and survival of his own sense of self. Until he was freed from childhood, he remained an anomaly without answers —a soul, he felt, without salvation.

He continued to race—from being held accountable for what he never asked to have bestowed upon him. He ran from the hauntings emerging from the shadows of his mind, always nipping at his heels.

10

When Aaron was five months old, Maria found him sitting among piles of forgotten books knocked from the built-in shelves behind her rocking chair in the living room. One of the lengthiest titles lay open across his lap as his bright eyes followed each line left to right.

In that moment, Maria's mind first wandered to how she'd always wished Sancha was more interested in reading—then it nearly toppled her with the realization that her very young grandson *was*.

"*Of course* you can," she said aloud.

Aaron looked up at her, awaiting her appraisal.

Maria nodded as she walked toward him. "Yes, you should read—of course. What better way to pass all the time?"

Crouching beside her grandson, she thumbed through the titles of curled-cornered paperbacks and few hardcovers. "Just my old books from school," she apologized. "Some from Sancha's classes." She lifted the cover of the book resting across Aaron's legs. "The Encyclopedia Britannica? That has to be really out of date." She smiled. "No one's even opened a volume in *so long*."

She studied the face of her grandson; she always felt reassured by its innocence. "You're going to need more, aren't you?" she asked, pulling herself to her feet again.

Aaron blinked at her, his blue eyes almost smiling.

Maria determined it was time to renew her library card—even felt a bit of a thrill at the idea. Even so, the bitter taste of fear—for little Aaron, for the future of their family—stung the back of her tongue.

"Mom," Sancha called out as she swung through the kitchen doorway, hair swaying behind her.

"Mm-hmm," Maria answered as she fussed over multiple saucepans on the stove.

"Isn't it too early for Aaron to *read*?"

"Never too early to read!"

"You know what I mean." Sancha toyed with the salt and pepper shakers on the tabletop. "Aren't you supposed to learn in school?"

"School is just a *program*: a schedule, a formality. Learning happens at its own pace. It doesn't matter how soon Aaron's reading. You should be very proud of him."

"I am. It's just," Sancha huffed, "I don't want him to be *weird*."

Maria swung around with a sauce-covered wooden spoon in hand as her daughter's lengthy whine ended. "Don't you ever call him weird or anything like that!" Maria drew a deep breath. "Your son is special."

"I know, I know." Sancha's expression blended confusion with failed comprehension. "It's just... *how* did he learn to read?"

"I suppose," Maria struggled to explain, turning her back on her daughter again, "by listening to you read to him."

"Yeah, I guess. He *is* super smart." Sancha's motherly pride returned, replacing her fear.

"Yes, he is."

Sancha slid to the doorway, stopping as soon as her mother spoke again.

"Sancha, don't worry. Don't be... afraid."

"I'm not," Sancha answered too quickly, then stared at the toes of her socks. "But what if he's—sometimes it feels like he's *smarter* than me."

Maria nodded, her lips pressed together. She offered, "He's... *more* than either of us."

Their silence hung heavy in the room until the weight was lifted by the rattle of a pan's lid dancing on a cushion of steam.

"But he needs us," Maria concluded for both her daughter and herself. "And we're going to be here for him, aren't we?"

Sancha nodded with full youthful conviction, adding her commitment to her mother's, neither knowing what their commitment would one day ask of them.

11

SUMMER RETURNED, SETTLING FIRMLY IN THE BACK GARDEN AND warming the soft soil beneath Sancha's bare feet as she pushed Aaron in his favorite swing. She answered his silent plea to go higher, higher, and up into the web of lower branches of the maple tree, peaking his flight path with a cool shot of shade.

Together, they reached the same conclusion—with shared reluctance and without words. It was time for Aaron to go out into the world, even at such a young age. He needed more; he needed what came next.

A WARM AFTERNOON rain began to fall when the familiar puttering of the family car's engine announced Maria's arrival after an extended mid-week shift. Sancha skipped up the back steps and swung open the screen door, leaving Aaron slowing to a stop as he lifted his open mouth to the sweet drizzle already wetting his face.

As Maria opened the front door—her orthopedic shoes squeaking over the hardwood floor—Sancha greeted her with respectful silence. She watched her mother tuck her keys and purse back into the drawer in the sideboard and remove the plastic rain cover from her cropped coiffure.

Maria lifted a weary smile. "Have a good day?"

Sancha nodded, beaming a brighter smile to hasten her mother's evening renewal. Maria raised her eyebrows, granting Sancha the permission she waited for.

"He needs to go to school." Sancha's smooth diction reflected the maturity she acquired over the last year. "I've taught him everything I know."

The statement rang true, even as Maria accepted she'd never realize the full extent of its meaning. She countered, "He doesn't adapt well with—"

"He'll be fine," Sancha returned with conspicuous certainty.

"How do you know?"

"He'll try very hard."

Maria nodded. "It won't be easy—for any of us."

"We know, but he needs to—"

"*We* could teach him—here at home."

"No. He needs to... do the *normal* things."

Maria found herself nodding. "It will cost. A lot."

"How much?"

"A *lot*."

Sancha looked to the floor for a solution.

"You'll have to go work," Maria decided, regretting the fact as much as she feared Sancha's response. "But I don't want you to get behind in your own schoolwork. You're almost finished and—"

"I won't—I promise. Aaron doesn't want me to either."

The statement momentarily stunned Maria. She shook off her discomfort, her voice wavering as she suggested, "You could get a part-time job. Maybe—"

"I'm not flipping burgers!" Sancha shouted, her inner teenager re-emerging.

"Well, there are other things you can—"

"I can work with you!" Sancha's heels lifted off the floor as she suppressed her urge to jump up and down with her sudden excitement.

Maria chuckled. "It's not easy work, Sancha. And I don't know if there's an opening, especially for someone with no experience. They wouldn't offer you the usual rate—probably minimum wage. And the other ladies... they aren't exactly welcoming."

"I don't care. You're okay with them; you're always going on and on about how funny they are. I wanna work with you!"

"Okay, Sancha. I'll ask at the office—but I can't guarantee anything."

Even with her concern for her daughter's ability to adjust to such an environment, Maria felt a small thrill at the idea of having her near.

12

As the calendar marked the last month of heady summer, Maria rested against the frame of the back door and peered through the screen, drinking in the healing, humid air while watching her daughter and grandson at play. She savored the languid Sunday's serenade of birdsong and the laughter of loved ones, despite her awareness that such peace and absence of care wouldn't always be as plentiful.

Sancha chased Aaron around the swing set, the length of her well-worn summer dress waving behind her. Aaron squealed, turning on his heels to chase his mother in turn. He giggled without reservation as he ran past her, racing circles around her.

"Sancha," Maria called out. "I want Aaron to help me with dinner."

"Really?" Sancha shouted as she slid out of Aaron's reach. "Did you hear that, Aaron? I'm off the hook!" Then, to her mother again, "Right now?"

"Yes, please."

"All right," Sancha whined. "You better scoot," she instructed Aaron, patting him on the back of his shorts as he ran past her.

He stretched to reach the handle of the screen door, his

grandmother turning it for him. "Would you like to help me with dinner?" she asked as he walked inside. He blinked in reply. "Well, there's something I'd like to talk to you about first," she said. "Let's go upstairs."

IN AARON'S BEDROOM, overlooking the back garden where Sancha meandered as she searched for the recent late-summer blooms, Maria sat on the edge of the bed and stood her grandson before her. She looked into his eyes—subconsciously searching—and drew a preparatory breath.

"It won't be long now," she said, resting her hands on his small shoulders before her self-consciousness compelled her to remove them.

"Your mother's coming to work with me—soon—and you'll be going to nursery school."

Aaron continued to stare, wide-eyed and accepting.

"It will be—well, we'll just see." Maria urged a smile onto her face. "And that's what you want?"

Aaron's cool blue eyes blinked at her.

"Then..." A single nod punctuated a deep breath as she said, "It's time for you to speak."

Aaron blinked rapidly in succession. His small chest heaved.

"You have to fit in with the other children," Maria explained, "the best that you can."

Aaron's narrow lips squeezed together.

"Do you understand?" she asked.

Aaron blinked his answer again.

Hopeful, Maria waited. She released a long breath, then lifted herself from the soft mattress. "Good boy," she said and walked toward the doorway.

Before leaving, she turned to him again and found him

standing just as still. She extended the invitation once more, with her eyes only.

Aaron's mouth opened slightly, then closed again. Maria frowned and turned away, the ruse of dinner forgotten.

Then, the sound of a brand-new voice sent a shiver down her spine, raising the tiny hairs on the back of her neck.

"*Thank you,*" her grandson spoke with the clearest delivery, the most articulate inflection. The two words burst with almost infinite meaning.

Maria blinked at the moisture in her eyes; a few tears escaped. She nodded her reply, sensing the pointlessness of her own words.

Removing herself from the room and her grandson's view, she leaned against the wall in the hallway for support. More tears fell—the first for as long as she could remember. She cried her relief; she cried her gratitude for the brief but monumental gift.

And she cried to release the full weight of her guilt, for every minute she'd carried and concealed the notion that her own grandson, perhaps, would be more properly cared for by an entirely different family.

SANCHA AND MARIA chatted over dinner at the kitchen table while Aaron fed himself with the deliberation and tidiness of an adult and listened intently to the comforting melody of their flowing speech.

"I can't wait to go to work with you," Sancha mumbled through thick-sliced ciabatta covered with lashings of butter and roasted garlic.

"It's not going to be like you think," Maria warned. "It's very hard work, and you'll have to learn quickly or—"

"I will." Sancha said, oozing with adolescent confidence. "It'll be fun... sitting around talking all day, using the big machines, making things."

"You'll get bloody fingers."

"Hmm?" Sancha hummed behind lips sealing in a mouthful of lasagna.

"Your fingers. It's dangerous. You'll stab yourself a million times before you get the hang of it."

"What?"

"The needle. They're industrial machines—faster and more powerful than what you used in home economics. And a lot more dangerous." Maria instantly regretted her honesty. "I'm sure you'll get the hang of it," she added with a smile.

A laugh fell out of Sancha's mouth along with red sauce. "You're just playing with me!"

Maria answered with a blank stare.

"Wait—you're not joking?" Sancha questioned. "I'm really going to be *bleeding*?"

"Guaranteed—until you get the hang of it. Just... try not to get too upset when it happens."

"What do you mean?"

"Well, a lot of the new girls, they can't stand the sight of blood."

"A finger prick? I can handle that."

"I remember the time you tried to slice the end of your finger off with the paring knife when you were chopping onions."

Sancha swallowed. "That was... a lot of blood."

"Imagine stitching your finger to the material you're sewing —and having to *un-sew* yourself."

"Mom!" Sancha's fork dropped against the edge of her plate. "That can't happen! Can it?"

"It does—all the time—but you're going to be careful, like I taught you."

Sancha stared at her plate, slowly chewing again. "Maybe I *should* work at Burger King."

Aaron giggled.

"Oh, you think that's funny?" Sancha beamed in his direction.

Aaron smiled, lifting his fork to his mouth.

Sancha returned her attention to her own plate, the smile falling from her face. "Do you think," she directed to her mother, "I'll work there forever?"

"Of course, not. We do what we have to do. And then, there will be plenty of time for you to do whatever it is you really want to do."

"I don't know what I really want to do." Sancha swiped the prongs of her fork around the remaining lasagna on her plate.

Aaron glanced at his mother before turning to his plate again. Maria studied his movements for a moment before reaching for the pan of lasagna to offer second helpings. Sancha shook her head, drawing swirls of sauce at the edge of her plate.

"Don't play with your food," Maria said.

"What if I never know what I really want to do?" Sancha asked. "What if *this* is all there is?"

"Don't be silly. You have your whole life ahead of you. And you have a *son*."

Sancha nodded. "I know but—"

"You do what you *have* to do. Then, the rest works itself out."

"But..." Sancha whined against her mother's certainty. "You don't *really* know. You have no idea. You say stuff like that all the time. It doesn't *mean* anything. It doesn't *help*."

Sancha slid her chair back from the table, digging another trench in the linoleum. She stood, glaring at her plate.

"Sancha, finish your dinner."

"I'm not hungry."

"Sancha, sit down. Please."

"Fine." Sancha dropped herself onto the chair again, crossing her arms.

"I know it's hard," Maria said. "Do you hear me? I *know* it is. We didn't ask for..." She glanced at Aaron as he focused on his own careful eating. "We can't choose everything that happens in life, but that's okay. Everything's *going* to be okay."

"But how do you *know*?"

Maria shook her head, then offered, "Because I'm old. Because that's just the way it always is. You make do—people do all the time—with whatever life throws at you. And, you always come out okay in the end."

"What Maria speaks..." interrupted a voice Sancha had never heard before—a child's pitch, smooth and rhythmic, "is true... *Sancha*."

Aaron's speech was the most unique Sancha or Maria had ever heard—his pronunciation alone, *beautiful*. Both stared at the source of the small—but authoritative—voice sat between them. Their mouths were agape, eyes wide with disbelief. Maria's began to smile.

"Aaron..." Sancha whispered.

"Hello, *Mother*," he said, adopting childlike exuberance.

13

Aaron continued to guard his identities as much as possible, preferring not to speak, not to share, not to open up too much. He avoided revealing anything that may frighten those who cared for him. He feigned naivety until he almost fooled himself.

He remained characteristically pensive: intrigued but cautious, exhilarated yet restrained. The battle between his two selves—the new and the extraordinarily old—rapped at the protective mental barriers he'd built over the first year of his life.

Maria reached for Aaron and adjusted the collar of his new shirt. "How does that feel? Too tight?" He shook his head and looked up at her with the unassuming face of a child.

"I'm worried," she blurted, against her better judgment. "I still don't know—it still feels silly to talk to you as if you're not a child. I don't really know if you understand or—"

"I understand," Aaron answered with an adult's self-assurance.

It wasn't often the words that her grandson spoke that astonished Maria. It was always their tone, the manner of delivery, the impression of the speaker behind the child's voice.

Maria looked over her shoulder, confirming they were alone together. "I have questions," she said, lowering her voice. "I don't know if I—" She nodded in answer to herself. "Maybe I shouldn't know the answers."

Aaron blinked.

"Maybe we shouldn't have given you so many freedoms. Maybe we should've raised you differently." Her fingers stopped fidgeting at her grandson's neckline; she almost smiled. "Listen to me... full of worries."

Aaron spoke to her discomfort. "He who is not satisfied with himself, will grow. He who is not sure of his own correctness, will learn many things." He remained still and calm as he stood before her, as though she was already familiar with the vastness of his nature and the breadth of his thoughts.

Maria's hands dropped to her sides, and she knelt on the floor before him.

"I don't know who you are," she said. "You're my *one-year-old* grandson, and... I have no idea *who* you are."

Aaron's small body tensed.

"But I *know,*" she said, "that you belong to us, that you're part of us—somehow, for some reason. And, I know... you are *good.*" Her hands tugged at the hem of his shirt. "And that's enough for me—for a grandmother—for now." She forced a smile and patted his waist.

"But I also know," she continued, raising herself to her feet, "that you must fit in *here.*" The word struck Maria as more foreign than her open admission of her grandson's uniqueness.

"Look at these," she said, handing him two thin workbooks. "I picked them up from the library. *These* are the words you should be using—whenever you're outside this house. When you're home, you are... yourself. Out there, *these* are your words."

Aaron nodded, opened one of the books, and began to memorize the vocabulary of children.

———

MARIA TRUDGED up the staircase with a basket of neatly folded laundry perched on her hip. With each creaking step, she detected a peculiar cooling effect, just enough to prick at the hairs on her forearms and at the nape of her neck. She paused, balancing her weight on two steps.

Most windows in the house were open to the outside weather: thick with the desire to rain but offering refreshment within the stifling heat trapped indoors. Room to room, the air was tolerably warm and muggy—except along the staircase at the center of the house.

Maria proceeded, confirming the lowering temperature as she stepped higher. Its lowest point was at the top of the stairs, just outside Aaron's bedroom.

The feeling wasn't of cold but only of certain chill: an invisible and slight icy sheen woven into the surrounding environment. Maria rested the laundry basket on the landing, then stepped through the doorway to her grandson's room.

"Aaron, are you..."

He raised his head to meet her gaze, the child's reader resting open on his lap. Maria scanned the room; she found no reason for the odd sensation she felt.

"I must be working too hard," she muttered as she retrieved the basket and continued down the hallway.

WHEN HIS GRANDMOTHER was out of view, Aaron turned his small head to the side and gazed over his shoulder—at the empty corner of his room, that wasn't empty.

14

"It's our big day! Are you ready?" Sancha directed at Aaron. He replied with a smile and a blink.

"Don't frighten him," Maria said, pulling on her own jacket after zipping up her grandson's. "Aaron, you remember your words, don't you?"

He nodded.

"Good, very good. We wouldn't want—"

"Mom! You're gonna scare him!"

Maria offered Sancha a smile, then knelt before Aaron, her grandmotherly concern overriding all. "And don't... do anything *helpful*—at nursery school. You know what I mean, don't you?"

Aaron blinked.

"Nothing. Just *play*. Play all day. And use your voice—just a little bit."

"Mom, you're gonna confuse him! He's a *kid*! He knows how to be a kid!"

Maria passed a final, meaning-packed gaze to Aaron. "All right then, we better get going."

LITTLE SOPHIE'S SPROUTS burst at its seams with children under the ages of five or six. The academically-acclaimed compound consisted of one main building painted in bright red, a large, fenced play yard, and several manufactured buildings—all linked by a web of pathways.

Hand-in hand, Sancha and Aaron filed through the parking lot toward the wide-open doors of the main entrance. Maria hurried behind, toting less childcare supplies than the other adults but many more concerns.

The owner of the nursery school greeted them with open arms beneath a smiling, mature face framed with over-dyed, brass-colored hair. "Welcome! I'm Sophie Sheridan." She bent forward to address Aaron. "It looks like it's *someone's* very first visit. And you must be..." she teased as she nodded her acknowledgment to Sancha and Maria. "I'm good at this. Let me guess... *four* years old?"

Sophie held up four fingers for Aaron's benefit; his tiny eyebrows raised. Sancha looked to her mother.

"He's just over a year, actually," Maria said.

"*One* year?" Sophie repeated.

"Yes, I called last week, and we discussed the possibility of—"

"Oh, yes, yes." Sophie stood upright, her hands still resting on Aaron's shoulders. "You'll have to forgive me. Most parents assume..." She smiled at the toddler with his perfect posture and calm self-assurance. "Well, we'll just get to know this little guy..."

"Aaron," Maria offered.

"*Aaron*—a bit over the coming weeks and see if he belongs in one of the older classes—perhaps." Sophie leaned down to direct her words to Aaron again. "For now, we just want you to *be yourself,* have fun, learn a ton, and we'll take it from there."

Aaron's eyebrows remained raised as he studied the older

woman's face, then smiled at her. Maria forced a polite smile while Sancha displayed her frown with pride.

"He's *smarter* than—" Sancha defended.

"Oh, I'm sure he is. All of our little sprouts are." Sophie winked at Aaron. "We just want to make sure Aaron—like all the others—is exactly where he needs to be to suit him best."

Sancha relented to silence.

"Want to see your class then," Sophie asked Aaron, "and meet the other children?"

He only blinked in reply. "He's very excited," Maria answered for him.

Sophie squinted at him for a moment before taking his hand to lead him through the entrance as Sancha and Maria followed.

After following a short maze of hallways, the door to the luminous classroom lay wide open before them, revealing a veritable circus of rampant children. A few leaned precariously against the scattered infant furniture, one screamed under the deluge of his own tears, most others crawled across the carpeted floor without aim, and nearly all were over-wrapped in thick diapers.

"Da-da," one infant dressed as a boy babbled at the feet of his apparent father.

Aaron's face revealed a hint of uncertainty as Sophie led him to a circular rug in the corner of the room where the other children had already tossed every colorful book onto the floor. The child to Aaron's left finished saturating one corner of a cardboard book with his own saliva and continued his focused work on the second.

Maria searched the room for any toy or tool that might be of remote interest to her grandson's unique intellect. Only a computer sat on the teacher's desk, off-limits to the children.

Aaron sat on the floor as expected of him and crossed his legs beneath him, his hands neatly clasped over his lap.

Sancha whispered to her mother, "I don't think this is gonna—"

"We'll give it a try," Maria said. "It's what he wanted. We'll see how it goes."

Sancha nodded, blew a puff of air from her mouth, and looked toward Sophie.

"Well, everything we need is taken care of already," Sophie said, "so you're welcome to stay as long as you like before your little man is ready to begin his first day with us." Her smile was large and genuine.

Maria knelt before her grandson. "All good?" she whispered.

Aaron blinked.

"I hope..." she said, "Well, we'll just see you very soon. Okay?"

Aaron released a reluctant smile and watched his mother and grandmother leave with the same lack of enthusiasm. He was alone again—alone with the world to explore, alone with his thoughts.

"I WORRY ABOUT HIM," Sancha admitted, sitting uncharacteristically still in the passenger seat as Maria steered the car out of the nursery school parking lot. "I mean, I know he's okay, and totally safe at the school, but—"

"You're a mother," Maria said through a smile. "That's what mothers do."

"Is it always like this?"

Maria hesitated to answer, wondering if her daughter had ever *asked* for her wisdom before. "Yes, you'll always worry." Sancha nodded her acceptance, and Maria continued. "But this... Aaron is very different."

AARON WATCHED the last of the parading parents leave their young children in the care of strangers. The din dwindled to a low rumble punctuated with the sniffles of a few teary-eyed toddlers.

"All right, then," announced a tall, thin woman with dark hair in large waves, her smile as sure as a lighthouse's beam. "Who's ready for a truly *fun* day?"

The woman's excitement gleamed in contrast to the bewildered babbling of the children corralled at her feet. "*My* name," she spoke, with exaggerated enunciation and remarkable patience, "is... *Miss... Beth-a-ny*. Can *you* say 'Miss Beth-a-ny'?" The toddlers stared blankly, few in her direction.

Miss Bethany continued, her smile unwavering, her energy growing. "Now, I would love to get to know each—one—of—you," she said, teasing a pointed finger at various children.

Minutes felt like hours to Aaron as each child was prompted in turn and urged to make some semblance of legitimate syllables. His own complex thoughts resounded in his mind, seeming more foreign by the moment. By the time the round of questioning reached him, he was almost hypnotized by the agonizing process and the stifling environment.

"And who might *you* be?" Miss Bethany sat on her knees next to Aaron. Her face nearly touched his own, her wide eyes beckoning.

TRES, he answered to all in the voice only he could hear. *I do not belong.*

I am Tres, and I am neither here nor there.

"WHO... ARE... YOU?" the woman's voice knocked again at his consciousness, penetrating his thoughts in high-volume echo.

"*Aaron,*" he spoke against his own will—and aloud for the first time—announcing himself to his surroundings, pronouncing himself forever locked inside a foreign form.

Outwardly, his small shoulders sank, his posture folded. Inwardly, part of himself seemed to float farther away, just out of reach, fading into the dark abyss of his boundless awareness.

The woman's face smiled on him, approving, breaking his identity down yet further as his public denial of himself was officially accepted and rendered permanent record. She patted his head, and *Tres* felt like a true child. He sank into the crevices of his infant body, fitting it more comfortably, soaking into his own skin.

A FISSURE FORMED—UNSEEN, undetected. Electrons raced to mend the molecules in his mind. Thoughts and memories separated, shooting into far corners of his subconscious. Abandoned abruptly, they were left without meaning—and without the guiding energy that connected them all.

Tres fell away, leaving Aaron alone.

The distance wrenched between them was so great that *he*— his whole self, his truest self—remained only as a bystander, an observer of the vacated self. He succumbed, withdrawing into submission so naturally—as if it was meant to be all along.

PART III

RELINQUISHING

Etiam capillus unus habet umbram suam.

— Even a single hair casts its shadow.

1

_____

"WORK ISN'T SUPPOSED TO BE FUN," MARIA REMINDED SANCHA AS she focused on the road ahead, her foot heavier than usual on the accelerator as she followed the route from the factory to Aaron's nursery school.

"It's horrible," Sancha whispered between gritted teeth as she peeked beneath the medical tape wrapped around eight out of her ten fingertips.

"Remember why you're doing it."

"Is that what you do?"

"Of course it is."

"Didn't you ever want to do something different, something _better_?"

Maria winced before answering. "Yes."

"Then, why didn't you—"

"Because I didn't have a _choice_—not at the time. And then—"

"I came along."

Maria chose silence, hoping to extinguish the discussion that had no positive possible outcome.

"I hope Aaron's all right," Sancha said, volunteering to change the subject.

"Of course he is. And we'll see him in just a few minutes."

Maria found a parking space near the entryway of Little Sophie's Sprouts. Sancha swung the passenger side door open and leapt out before Maria pulled the key out of the ignition.

———

SANCHA RAN through the swarm of parents descending on the school and zoomed through the open doorway to Aaron's new classroom. She scanned the crowd of faces high and low for the child with the dark gold hair and bottomless oceans for eyes, the toddler with the impeccable posture and shining confidence beyond his years.

"Mom," Sancha muttered as Maria joined her. "I don't see him. I can't—" Too many golden-haired children ran in circles around the room. Too many meandering parents continually blocked her view.

"Let me look." Maria left Sancha's side with a reassuring pat of her hand on her shoulder. "Aaron..." Maria called from one corner of the classroom. "Aaron?"

"Where *is* he?" Sancha demanded, her throat tightening with growing desperation. "Aaron!"

No answer came; no small head turned in the direction of their frantic cries. And none of the parents raised an eyebrow.

"Can I help you?" a gentle voice rose behind Sancha.

Sancha spun around, greeted by a smile she didn't appreciate. "I can't find him!" she cried.

"This is my class," continued in a calm, teacherly tone. "I'm Miss Bethany. Are you looking for your little brother or sis—?"

"My *son*," Sancha spat.

"Oh—please forgive me—and his name is...?"

"Aaron. Please—I don't see him. I don't know where—"

"Oh, he's right over here, safe and sound. Come this way."

Miss Bethany made her way through the crowd dominating her classroom and sat on the circular rug in the far corner. "Aaron, your mommy's here. Look! There she is," she cooed.

Aaron followed her guiding finger until his eyes locked with Sancha's. "Ma-ma!" he cried out.

Sancha ran to him, pulling him off the floor until his feet dangled in the air. Maria joined them, resting her arm across Sancha's shoulders.

"Everything's just fine," Maria said, her own shoulders relaxing.

"Oh, I couldn't find you!" Sancha complained with her cheek tightly pressed to Aaron's. "I was so worried! Horrible, horrible, horrible."

"Sancha, it's all right now," Maria said. "He's fine. You can let him stand on his own."

Sancha let Aaron slide off her waist onto his own feet again. He wobbled as she let go of him, reaching for her legs to steady himself. Worry replaced his smile.

"We had a terrific day. Didn't we, Aaron?" Miss Bethany asked, prompting his excitement. "We played circle games, got to know the other children, made finger paint portraits, played outside..."

"Ou-side," Aaron chimed.

Miss Bethany continued, "We had a very good nap and... there was just one close call—*almost* an accident—but we did make it to the potty on time, didn't we?"

Aaron's smile disappeared as he pressed his lips together.

"To be expected in a brand-new place," Miss Bethany excused.

"But he doesn't—" Sancha started.

"I don't understand," Maria directed to Miss Bethany.

"Oh, no big deal. We just had to put on the spare under-pants. We're totally prepared for that." Miss Bethany's smile remained intact. "*Someone...*" she teased, pressing her face close to Aaron's, "just isn't quite ready to wear those big-boy pants." She looked up at Maria and Sancha. "But all in due time!"

SANCHA TRIED to match Aaron's tedious pace as they followed Maria through the parking lot. "Aaron, do you want to walk a little faster? Let's get home and play in the back yard before dinner time!"

Aaron studied the gravel underfoot, carefully plodding his way as he gripped his mother's hand. Maria reached the car and turned to wait—and watch.

"I wanna pain wid fingas!" Aaron yelled with surprising volume.

Sancha stopped. "Aaron, what's..." She watched him kick at the gravel beneath his feet, uninterested in her words. "Aaron, look at me."

Aaron pulled on her hand as he squatted and reached for a handful of pebbles.

"*Aaron.*"

"Leave him be," Maria interrupted. "It's been a long day."

Her eyes remained on her grandson as he required his mother's help to get onto the back seat and settle into the infant seat.

AT HOME, Sancha and Maria silently studied Aaron's behavior as he sat on the living room rug, occupying himself and showing no interest in either of them.

"Vroom, vroom," he mouthed as he ran a toy truck back and forth over the same path along the rug.

Sancha whispered to her mother, "Why's he acting like... a *baby*?"

"I don't—" Maria sought the right words to reassure her daughter with. "It is *normal*—for his age."

"Vroom!" Aaron roared.

"Aaron?" Maria called over his sound effects. "I have something for you: a present!"

Aaron's attention was theirs, the truck's movement frozen in his grasp. Maria revealed what she held behind her back. Aaron frowned.

"It's a book—a new one," Maria said, kneeling before him. "A *scientific* encyclopedia, filled with all kinds of interesting things. A very special present in honor of your first day of school." Maria's smile was broad and hopeful.

Aaron continued to frown as she laid the book on his lap. "Ow!"

"Open it," Maria urged. "There are so many pictures, maybe even things you've never heard of."

Aaron made a face at her; Maria's excitement melted.

He pushed his toy truck over the glossy, embossed cover of the book. "Rrrrr!" he sounded.

"No, no. Look. It's a *special* book," Maria said as she rescued the hardcover volume, smoothing her hand across the cover. "Not for playing, for *reading*."

She studied the book in her hands, then her grandson.

Maria pulled herself up and carried the encyclopedia to the bookcase, sliding it onto a high shelf.

"Come," she said to Sancha, leading the way to the kitchen. "Help me make dinner."

A new form of pain crept over the young mother's face.

THE TWO FOLLOWED their dinnertime routine: Sancha setting the table, Maria fussing over the stove. When Aaron joined them later, Maria and Sancha ate little while he played with his food.

"Aaron. Why aren't you using your silverware?" Maria said.

His focus stuck to the lines his fingers made across his plate. "Finga pains!"

Maria frowned, forfeiting further words. Sancha fought off tears. They both remained silent through dinner and after, finding no words capable of consoling.

That night, the nightmares began.

2

"Aaaaaahhhhhhh! Huh, huh, aaaaaaaahhhh!" The cries hurled through the house, jarring all awake.

Maria reached Aaron's room first. She wrapped her arms around him as he sat up in bed, tears streaming down his cheeks.

"Aaaaahhhh! Aaaahhhhh!"

"Shh," Maria consoled, rocking his small body gently. "It's all right, Aaron. You're safe and sound. Everything's all right."

Sancha arrived, her pajamas still twisted around her, as Aaron spoke more than he had all day, fighting to catch his breath.

"Mean guys! All oba me... an' big sords! An—"

"Shh..." Maria held his head to her chest.

"But he doesn't even watch TV," Sancha said.

Maria shook her head. "Maybe from the books? Or at the school today?"

"*Swords?* Is that what he said? They wouldn't... with kids so little?"

Maria shrugged. "I don't know. I just don't know."

Aaron continued, exclaiming between gasps. "Mean! Mean to me! A big horse. An' lions an—"

"Shh," Maria tried again. "All gone now—just your imagination, just pictures in your mind. Nothing to worry about."

"It's all right, Aaron." Sancha wrapped her arm around his shoulders. "Just a dream, just *pretend*."

"Wanna git me," Aaron whimpered, his breathing finally slowing.

"They're not real, Aaron. Now, let's tuck you back into bed and—"

"No! Don' go!"

Sancha and Maria found themselves sharing an expression of confusion yet again. "I'll stay with him," Sancha offered.

Maria nodded, unwrapped herself from Aaron, and pulled the bedcovers back. Sancha crawled in, and Maria tucked them both in.

"Goodnight," she said, leaving a quick kiss on both foreheads.

THE NIGHTMARES CONTINUED to plague the household nearly every night. Maria and Sancha tucked Aaron into bed, leaving him with encouraging words and new suggestions for keeping the bad dreams at bay—and always, with the bedside lamp left on. Within hours, they woke to the heart-wrenching resonance of a child's terror.

There were always new villains in Aaron's dreams, frightening adult scenarios, and elaborate themes he was incapable of communicating with his newly limited vocabulary. And they lingered even in the daytime.

Maria continued to study Aaron—watching, waiting,

wondering what afflicted such a young mind, worrying that the strength she once glimpsed in him would never reemerge.

She missed his laughter. She missed her daughter's.

4

"PERFECTLY NORMAL," DR. PHILLIPS ANNOUNCED WITH A SMILE, "which is the best report a doctor can give you." He beamed at both Maria and Sancha in turn, awaiting their shared exuberance.

"That's good," Maria answered. "There's just—"

"Yes?" Dr. Phillips turned to Maria like an eager puppy.

"He has trouble sleeping. Nightmares."

"Easy," he replied. "Video games. They start so young these days, and they're not quite mature enough to understand—"

"No, he doesn't play video games—or watch TV. He has... a vivid imagination."

The doctor searched the ceiling for his next diagnosis. "Well, it's perfectly natural."

"*Every* night."

The doctor's brow furrowed. "Hmm. Well, not to worry you, but it could be an early warning sign that we shouldn't ignore."

"For what?" Sancha asked.

"We'll cross that bridge when we come to it," he said.

"We want to know *now*," Maria insisted.

"Of course. I'm sure everything's fine." Dr. Phillips watched

Aaron happily suck on the lollipop he'd just been handed. "But sometimes, certain mental *conditions* reveal themselves quite early."

"Mental conditions!" Sancha's outburst spoke for her mother as well.

"No, I don't think that's it," Maria agreed.

"Well, sleep is very important, especially for a growing toddler—and for both of you." Dr. Phillips scribbled on a form. "Aaron's actually a bit young for nightmares, though I have seen them occur in two-year-olds before. Let's give him a boost of serotonin and—"

"We've tried that," Maria interrupted. "Well, no pills but lots of quiet time before bed, warm milk, a snack or—"

"Of course." Dr. Phillips handed the slip of paper to Maria. "That's all very good, but if the nightmares are continuing, we should try something a bit stronger."

Maria looked at the paper. "A prescription? For medication?"

He nodded. "A serotonin reuptake inhibitor, a mild antidepressant—for his anxiety."

"I don't think he—" Maria said.

"You'd be surprised how many children suffer from anxiety. We just don't know what goes on in their little minds." The doctor smiled. "Sometimes, they just need a little boost, some help with some things we assume are only adult problems. If the antidepressant doesn't work, we'll try an antipsychotic. But the effects of antidepressants can be really transformative. We could see results very quickly—in just the first week or two—and then, we'll know we're moving in the right direction." His smile seemed permanent, induced by the topic of pharmaceuticals.

Maria glared at the prescription.

"Well, if there's nothing else..." Dr. Phillips stood outside the examination room when Maria looked up again. "We're all done for today, and the nurse will help you schedule your next check-up." He disappeared down the hall.

"Is Aaron that sick?" Sancha asked her mother.

They looked to Aaron and his worry-free, cherubic face.

"I don't know, Sancha, but we'll do everything we can for him."

SANCHA PAUSED in the doorway to Aaron's bedroom. "Should we give him the medicine now?"

"Not yet," Maria said, peering into the room. She watched Sancha approach Aaron's bed and pull the covers over his shoulders, folding them comfortably under his chin. Sancha's kiss lingered on his cheek before she left the room again—bedside lamp on, door left ajar.

As Aaron fell asleep, Maria entered and knelt next to his bed, admiring his angelic features. She knew he'd sleep peacefully for a few hours before the nightmares announced themselves.

"Where do they all come from?" she whispered to herself and to the inner workings of her grandson's mind. She reached across the sleeping child and swept the silken strands of dark gold hair from his forehead.

Aaron's breath was calm and steady, almost whistling through his parted lips.

"And where have you gone?" Maria asked.

BEFORE RETIRING to her own room, Maria stood alone in the bathroom. The small, angled plastic bottle rested in the open medicine cabinet, conspicuous with its wordy labeling, innocuous in its virgin white and pastel colors.

With sudden motion triggered by firm decision, Maria snatched the bottle off the shelf and hurried downstairs to the kitchen trash bin, burying the Zoloft safely beneath a weeks' worth of trash.

She returned upstairs and slid into the comfort of her bed, her consciousness at ease and acquiescing. She slept soundly, for as long as her grandson's plague of nightmares allowed.

5

THE CLASSROOM AT LITTLE SOPHIE'S SPROUTS BUZZED WITH THE colorful and chaotic celebration of Aaron's birthday—all the pomp and circumstance a three-year-old could wish for or withstand. Sugar-high children crawled faster than usual underfoot, weaving around the legs of tables topped with trays of cupcakes.

Sancha and Maria stood among the activity, watching Aaron rummage through a pile of presents. They both questioned his enthusiasm as he unwrapped gifts of the standard, safe toys for toddlers they never collected for him. And, just as quickly, they brushed the observation aside in favor of focusing on his smile. Though not as sophisticated or potent as it once was, it still lit up the room as pure delight sparkled from his vivid blue eyes.

"Happy birthday!" Sancha called out when the last present had been thoroughly inspected and tossed aside with the others. She scooped up her son and swung him around, succeeding in squeezing out a symphony of giggles.

"Iz my buff-day!" Aaron squealed.

"And how many are you?" Sancha prompted.

Before he could configure his fingers, Maria interrupted.

"Sancha, say it correctly. Don't use that *child's language* with him."

"But that's how he... oh, *fine*." Sancha turned to Aaron again. "How many *years* old are you, Aaron?"

"Dis many!" he shouted, holding up three chubby fingers with pride.

"Wow. You're so *big* now!" Sancha cheered. "And that is..."

"Free!"

"Yes! And what super-cool things did you get today?"

"Um... b'loons!" Aaron pointed. "An' tory time. An' cah razing. An' games!"

"Perfect." Sancha started her search for Miss Bethany to initiate their quick retreat to the peace and quiet of home.

Maria watched the expressions and motions of her grandson, her mind prodding her with the fact that his birthday arrived without any sign of his former personality. She distracted herself with collecting his belongings from his assigned cubby, eager to escape the revelry—and the nagging sense of loss.

"SMALLER PIECES!" Maria snapped, finally revealing her inner stress as she leaned over the kitchen table.

"Okay, okay." Sancha sliced the slab of birthday cake in two, not allowing her mother's tone to ruin her own enjoyment of the occasion. "How's that?"

Maria frowned. "Who knows how many cupcakes he's already eaten today."

"It's his birthday," Sancha said. Her smile almost relieved Maria's uneasiness.

"Where is Aaron?" Maria scuttled between each entrance to the kitchen, leering into the adjacent rooms.

"He was just playing out back," Sancha answered, rolling her eyes, "next to the swing set."

Almost immediately, Maria stood at the living room window facing the back garden and pulled the floral print curtains to the side. "I don't see him."

"Well, he can't go anywhere. He still can't reach the latch on the gate." Sancha continued portioning the homemade two-tiered cake. "What's with you, Mom? You've been all... *not fun* since we got home."

"No, just the last five or so minutes..." Maria said as she stepped onto the back stoop. "Something doesn't feel right," she mumbled to herself.

SANCHA CARRIED the birthday-themed paper plates to the dining table, arranging them next to the matching paper napkins. She ripped open the plastic packaging of the party banner, humming the tune of "Happy Birthday."

MARIA RAN to the side gate, found it still securely latched, then bounded around the perimeter of the back yard. "Aaron... Aaron! Show Grandmom where you are!"

Behind the wide trunk of the maple tree at the side fence, Maria found her grandson crouched and cowering, his eyes wide, his eyebrows disappearing under his dark gold bangs.

"Aaron, why didn't you tell me where you were? I was worried!"

He remained silent and still, clinging to the bark of the tree, his small fingers white with the pressure of his grip. He stared at the wooden fence on the opposite side of the yard.

"Aaron, what is it? Did you see... an animal in the garden?

There's nothing dangerous here—just the friendly foxes, remember? Or the neighbor cat again?"

Aaron stared at the same spot on the fence. He didn't blink; he didn't seem to breathe. His mouth refused to release a single word.

"Aaron, honey, talk to Grandmom. What are you..."

His head began to turn to the side—toward Maria—his eyes still refusing to blink, their focus trained on the fence line and slowly following it around the full perimeter of the yard.

"Aaron." Maria's voice cracked; her hand reached for his shoulder.

His head continued its smooth, careful turn as his focused stare persisted, unwavering. His gaze reached the far corner of the yard, then progressed along the back perimeter, his head turning at the same slow and steady pace—his own fear tangible beneath his grandmother's hand.

Then, Aaron's focus intersected with Maria herself. Her body blocked his view of the far end of the side fence: a targeted spot only a few yards behind Maria, only a few yards away from where they stood in silence together.

Aaron's chin lifted as his neck stretched to recover his line of sight. Once he viewed the space behind his grand-mother, his eyes opened to almost perfect circles. His eyes were their darkest blue in the shade of the maple tree—almost black, as if his irises were consumed by the pinpoints of his pupils.

His heel inched backward, away from his grandmother. His shoulder tugged against the grip of her hand.

Maria's voice failed; then, she found a hoarse whisper. "Aaron, what are you looking at?"

Aaron's parted lips opened wider. The full weight of his body pulled against his grandmother's hold.

"Him," he said.

Aaron yanked himself free and ran across the yard and back into the house.

The seconds seemed to slow as Maria realized her grandson's escape and felt compelled to turn on her own heels. She distinctly felt *something*—something in motion, something *oppressive*. She glared at the scene her grandson ran from.

What she sensed—despite its overpowering grasp—remained just out of view, just at the corner of her perception, no matter which way she turned her head. Her own eyes were incapable of following the path of the overwhelming *sensation* as it moved in her presence—encircling her, *toying* with her.

Maria stared at the space behind the maple tree, the area of fence within her arm's reach. She stared at the emptiness that revealed nothing at all.

AFTER BIRTHDAY CAKE, ice cream, and a rendition of "Happy Birthday" sung out of tune, Aaron played with his new toys, making all the usual sound effects and mumbling childish chatter. He happily played alone, showing no concern for—nor recollection of—his experience just outside the back door and steps away from where he sat on the living room rug.

He lost all interest in playing in the back yard, as if it no longer existed—to his awareness—at all.

OVER TIME AND ONLY OCCASIONALLY, Aaron looked over his shoulder as if something suddenly caught his attention. Or he stared, for a few moments, into an empty corner of the room or a vacant space just out of his reach. Even less often, Maria caught him doing so.

She didn't fear for his safety; she feared for her grandson's sanity.

6

"WELL, EVERYTHING CHECKS OUT, AND THIS IS THE IMMUNIZATION record the school requires." Dr. Phillips handed the paper booklet to Maria. Turning to Aaron and adjusting his tone, he continued, "You're all ready for the first grade."

Aaron lowered his head to stare at the tile floor beneath his dangling feet.

"He's excited," Sancha said, offering her own enthusiasm for Aaron.

"He grew really fond of the staff at the nursery school over the past five years," Maria explained, looking at her grandson. "But I know he'll like his new teachers just as much. And there will be all kinds of new games and equipment, things to learn..."

Aaron swung his lower legs back and forth as he hummed an unrecognizable tune.

"And new friends—more friends!" Sancha chimed in.

Aaron fought off a quick smile, kicked faster.

Dr. Phillips said, "Oh—we'll just need to get a quick blood sample. I almost forgot! Not needed for school, but I just want to check on a few things."

"Is that part of the," Maria asked, her question tangled in a sudden cough. "Sorry, excuse me," she continued, "part of the checkup?"

"You mean, will your insurance cover it? Yes. No worries there. I'll write it in as part of the usual examination."

"Good."

"Do you want me to take a look at your throat quickly? That cough sounds—"

"No, no thank you. Just a tickle in my throat."

"You don't want to give a cough or cold to the little—"

"No—I'm fine. Just tired, that's all. I've been feeling kind of... no, it's no matter."

The doctor's concern spread to Sancha. "I haven't noticed you—" she started.

"Just sluggish," Maria intervened, "a pinched nerve now and then. Aaron can be," she said through a smile, "quite a handful."

Dr. Phillips nodded, responding as Maria hoped in hearing the standard excuse.

Sancha mumbled, "He's not a h—" before giving up her son's defense.

"I'll send the nurse in, and you'll be on your way." Dr. Phillips leaned over to Aaron on his way to the door. "And if you can be very still—and don't cry—she'll give you a lollipop after. Don't tell your dentist." The doctor left, chuckling to himself.

"But you're not afraid of needles," Sancha reminded her son.

He shook his head. "Nope! I'm not afraid of anything!" Maria and Sancha shared a smile.

Within moments, there was a quiet knock on the door, and a broad-chested older female nurse stepped into the room. Without ushering any greeting, she focused only on the cabinet above the counter and snatched the necessary supplies.

"All right. Which one of you is getting your blood drawn?" she asked.

Maria and Sancha looked at each other.

"It's a joke," the nurse said, unsmiling. "I know it's the little guy."

"I'm not little," Aaron corrected, still playfully swinging his feet.

"Well, then, you're not going to give me any trouble, are you?" The nurse's tone gave away her contrasting expectation.

Aaron shook his head with a six-year-old's enthusiasm. Maria grew uneasy, tempted to remark on the nurse pre-empting Aaron's discomfort.

"All right, then." The nurse turned to face her patient, rolled her chair next to the examination table, and affixed a rubber strap above his elbow. "I'll be done in a flash. You won't feel—"

"*No!*" Aaron shouted, yanking his arm out of her grasp. "No, no, no, no, no!" He continued shouting as he crawled to the far end of the table, crossing his arms and hiding them behind his drawn-up legs. "No, no, no!"

"Aaron!" Maria shouted. "What are you doing? Be *good*. This isn't any different from all the other times. Just sit still, and it won't hurt at all."

"Noooooo!" he screamed for as long as his breath lasted.

"I don't know what's the matter with him," Maria apologized. "He's never been like this. I just don't..."

Sancha watched, her expression reflecting more curiosity than fear.

"No, no! Not *her!*" Aaron shouted.

The nurse rolled closer to him. "Now, you're just going to hold your arm out for me, or I'm going to have to—"

"Nooooooo!"

"Aaron," Maria tried again, rubbing his back tenderly. "It's *okay*. What's so different this time?"

"He doesn't want *her* to do it," Sancha said matter-of-factly.

The nurse glared at Sancha; Sancha glared back.

Maria interrupted the joust. "That's just silly. I'm so sorry. He's never been like this. He's such a good—"

"Well, I don't have time for this. I'm going to inform Dr. Phillips. He can deal with this." The nurse walked out of the room.

Maria turned to Aaron. "What in the world?"

"She—her—she's gonna *hurt* me!"

"Nonsense."

"I believe him," Sancha said, staring at her son.

Maria glanced at her, then turned to study her grandson again. His body was still curled into a fetal position. "He can't know... that's just your imagination."

DR. PHILLIPS RETURNED to the examination room, impatient but carefully drawing Aaron's blood without incident. Aaron only sniffled, wiping away his remaining tears as he held his arm in place.

NEITHER MARIA nor Sancha read the local newspaper. Neither was aware of the short article printed six months later, buried among the ads. Nor did they catch the television broadcast about the nurse cited for stealing stimulants from the clinic's pharmaceutical supply to feed her addiction—or of the high number of patients she'd injured during routine examinations.

7

SANCHA RUMMAGED THROUGH AARON'S CHILD-SIZE BACKPACK. "You've got your new pencils and—Mom, where's his lunch box?"

"Right here," Maria answered, handing the bright plastic box to Aaron. "I made your favorite: creamy peanut butter and strawberry jam—with the crust left on."

Aaron smiled, taking the handle carefully from his grandmother. Maria winced, rubbing her hands together before smiling to reassure Aaron that he did nothing wrong.

Focused on her task, Sancha mumbled, "I don't think he has enough pencils."

"He'll get a big list today, remember? Then, we'll have to go buy all sorts of silly stuff, and—"

"Oh, yeah." Sancha released a fraction of her stress through her smile. "I almost forgot! Okay, then, I guess we're ready!"

"Mom..." Aaron whined, "do I have to go to Lay... Lank..."

"*Langston* Hughes," Maria carefully pronounced for him. "And yes, you *do*. It'll be—"

"But it's a *stupid* name for school!"

"Shh! Where are your manners?"

"Sorry, Grandmom."

Maria crouched before him. "Remember your first day at Little Sophie's Sprouts?"

Aaron nodded, then shook his head side to side.

"Well, you weren't nervous at all. All you could think about were the new things you'd get to see and do. And when your mother and I came to pick you up at the end of the day..." Maria's gaze drifted with her words.

Sancha forced a smile for Aaron. "You loved it there, didn't you?" He nodded. "Well, you're going to love first grade too. I just know it."

Aaron pursed his lips, then considered his lunch box. "Do I get a dessert?"

Maria pulled herself to her feet again. "*Yes*—just this once."

"Yay! Yay!" Aaron hopped up and down in rhythm with his outbursts—then stopped. "But... is it a *real* one?"

Sancha smirked. "What? You mean, one that's *not* good for you?"

Aaron nodded, shaking his smile up and down.

"I think Grandmom put something extra special in there for you," Sancha said.

"Kit Kat!" Aaron shouted.

"You'll see." Maria zipped up the backpack and handed it to Aaron. "All right, let's go check out your new school!"

"HAS everyone swapped quizzes with their buddies?" Ms. Cartwright stood at the blackboard at the head of the class, her bluish-silver hair glinting in the fluorescent lighting. "Yes? Okay, then. We'll start grading them."

She proceeded to read out the answers to the first "pop quiz" after promising there'd be a lot more of them—always a surprise!—throughout the school year. Aaron shot a worried glance at his own paper now gripped in the hands of a stranger. Based solely on sharing the same two-seat table and same first letter of their last names, Finlay Richter was Aaron's assigned "buddy" for the entire year ahead.

Since the moment Finlay assertively introduced himself, his every word and gesture declared enduring friendship. Yet, Aaron found being near his new partner undeniably unsettling. That was all; that was enough.

Aiming to look in Finlay's direction as little as possible, Aaron didn't catch the smile he flashed, but he did react to being gently elbowed next.

"Don't worry," Finlay whispered with confidence. "I'll mark all your answers right."

"No, she'll see!"

Finlay's smile swept into a smirk. "No, teachers don't really pay attention—especially, *old* ones. You'll see."

"How do you know?"

"My dad—my new dad—says so. He knows lots of things. He says you can get away with anything you want, most times, if you're smart enough."

With each answer Ms. Cartwright read aloud, Aaron cringed, expecting his desk buddy to ask him to cheat with the grading in turn. However, Finlay answered every question correctly while Aaron missed three out of the five.

"One-hundred percent!" Finlay declared by public announcement and verified with the digits scribbled at the top of Aaron's quiz paper.

Aaron lowered his shoulders and hung his head even lower.

"*She won't know,*" Finlay reminded him, sealing the promise with a commercial-quality smile. The quizzes were passed forward over the rows of tables, sweeping away Aaron's final chance to free himself of his guilt.

"Next time," Finlay offered with another jab of his elbow, "you can just copy my answers."

BY THE END of the first day of first grade, Aaron had an official best friend. Finlay Richter declared himself so. As far as Aaron knew, they were the only two first graders who had one.

"Wanna come over to my house after school? My mom won't care. We have a pool." Finlay hurried behind Aaron, his head of dark hair hovering well above Aaron's, his dark eyes glinting with excitement.

Aaron waited inside the school's main entrance and stood on his tiptoes to search the crowd for his mother and grandmother. Ignoring Finlay didn't produce the desired results.

"Hey." The corner of Finlay's textbook poked Aaron in the shoulder. "Did you hear me? Do you wanna come over? Rosa, our housekeeper, always makes snacks. Probably cupcakes or— hey, did you hear me?"

Aaron tried not to smile too much when he finally spotted Sancha in the hallway, peeking into each classroom doorway. "Bye!" he shouted, forcing the required etiquette before he bounded away.

"Hey! Is that your mom?" Finlay called after him. "Want me to ask her for you?" He suddenly stood right behind Aaron again, grabbing his shoulder.

"No. See you tomorrow," Aaron said, successfully slipping out of his new best friend's grip.

SANCHA OPENED HER ARMS WIDE, and scooped up Aaron's lanky

body to swing him off the ground before he slid out of her arms again. "How was it?"

"Okay," he answered.

"Just okay? Everyone around here looks pretty happy."

"Teacher gave out *homework*."

"Homework? On your first day of school? Want me to talk to her?"

Aaron's nod caught Sancha off guard.

"Well, that was supposed to be a joke." She laughed to prove it. "*Maybe* you'll survive it—your homework. I'll help you, okay?"

Aaron frowned at the floor as they waded through the ocean of parents and students. They found Maria waiting for them on the walkway in front of the entrance, resting on the stone half-wall and trying to avoid the narrow flower bed at her feet.

"How was the first day of school?" Caught up in the excitement, she coughed over Aaron's answer before quickly recovering and asking again.

"Okay," Aaron mumbled, taking the steps in front of the school two at a time.

"He's got his first homework," Sancha explained to her mother. "I promised to help him with it."

"I see..." Maria answered, remembering the baby nestled in his infant seat, listening to—learning from—his mother's every word.

8

Aaron adjusted to grade school, gradually giving up his attachment to the more coddling, carefree environment of nursery school. He followed directions, learned to live by instruction, and fit into first grade. He continued to conform—without ever making the conscious commitment.

The only disturbance to his smooth transition was Finlay's advances of friendship—especially because Aaron had no idea why Finlay made him feel uncomfortable. While every other student gravitated toward Finlay—his good looks, great jokes, and big smile—Aaron felt it was best to avoid him. The inclination was as natural as eating when he was hungry—or picking up his pencil when he felt the urge to draw.

He mindlessly scribbled in his notebook during class, urging the minute hand on the clock to twitch a little faster. Hundreds of thousands of short dashes, fluid lines, and smoothly shaded shadows poured over countless wide-ruled pages. He drew through Finlay's constant chatter and attempts to gain his attention; he doodled away his boredom.

Sancha and Maria sat before the teacher's desk, the classroom eerie in its emptiness. Ms. Cartwright's contemplative gaze ensured the two felt the full weight of the middle of the school term—and her authority.

She glanced at her watch. "Thank you for coming in. I don't get to see the two of you as much as I'd like."

Maria shuffled in her seat, pretending interest in a hand-made wooden pen holder.

Ms. Cartwright wriggled her impatience, proceeding in her teacherly tone. "Aaron *is* a good student—generally. You know his grades are... acceptable. He doesn't struggle with any of the lessons—no more than any of the other students—but..." Sancha and Maria leaned closer to her desk. "Aaron's not as *attentive* as he could be," she huffed.

"But you said he's a good student," Maria defended.

"Yes, it's just that he gets... distracted at times. Maybe you see this *outside* the classroom as well?"

Neither Maria nor Sancha answered, and Ms. Cartwright came alive at the opportunity to educate. "He's either cutting up in class—talking too much, a little chatter box—or just staring off into *space*."

Sancha and Maria replied only with expressions of bewilderment, inviting Ms. Cartwright to continue their lesson. "Aaron doesn't seem to get along with his buddy," she said.

"Buddy?" Sancha blurted.

"Yes, his—everyone has an assigned buddy. They work in pairs. It helps promote better performance, a bit of healthy competition, instill teamwork. And the students build relationships faster."

Sancha and Maria weren't convinced.

"Aaron is paired with a very bright student, Finlay Richter, but he—Aaron—doesn't seem to be very fond of him."

"I'm sorry," Maria said. "I'm not sure I understand what—"

"He's just *like* that—with some people," Sancha offered with a tinge of sarcasm only her mother detected.

Ms. Cartwright's thin lips curved downward. "Well, the two have a lot in common, actually. They're both missing their fathers and—"

"*Excuse me?*" Maria's voice was louder than she expected.

"Well," Ms. Cartwright quickly returned, "they *are* missing a father figure. Finlay's mother recently remarried, but even so, that requires an adjustment period for Finlay and—"

"Aaron doesn't *need* a—" Sancha started before she felt her mother's hand on her arm.

Maria said, "I'm sure Ms. Cartwright will explain what she means."

"Yes, well," Ms. Cartwright continued, "the school psychiatrist is actually more qualified to address those issues Aaron may be struggling with, but there is also the *drawing*."

"Drawing?" Maria repeated.

"The doodling. Aaron is constantly scribbling—*during* class time. Just this week, I caught him daydreaming during a key lesson—just scribbling away in his notebook, completely absentmindedly, and wearing his pencil *to the nub*."

"What is he drawing?" Maria asked.

"Nothing! Nothing at all. Just a jumbled-up mess of—"

"All right," Maria attempted to divert the negative direction of their discussion. "Well, drawing is probably a *good* habit, don't you think? At least, he's not passing notes to other students, distracting them, or causing any kind of—"

"What's going on *at home*?"

"I beg your pardon," Maria snapped.

Ms. Cartwright cleared her throat. "Ms. Rivera, under the circumstances—well, I think we *both* know that it sometimes indicates the child is reacting to a certain environment in the home. Children do pick up—"

"Ms. Cartwright," Maria interrupted. "With all due respect, there is nothing that—*nothing*—to trouble Aaron. It's just my daughter and I. Everything's just as it always has been, and Aaron's always been a very... content boy. Nothing has changed. He has nightmares, but we've discussed those with you before, and we've all adjusted as well as we can. Otherwise, we wouldn't know what you may be referring to or what would be causing Aaron to act any differently in class—differently than *you* expect of him."

"Well, I..." Ms. Cartwright paused as Maria stood, prompting Sancha to follow and ending the parent-teacher conference.

"Thank you for your time," Maria delivered quickly. "We'll talk to Aaron. I'm sure everything will be fine."

Ms. Cartwright was left to stare at their vacated seats.

ALONE IN THE hall with her mother, Sancha struggled for comprehension. "What just—"

"It'll be fine," Maria said. "She's just... I'm sure Ms. Cartwright has a certain way she expects every student to behave and *of course* Aaron is fine."

"But what if he's—"

"He's *fine*."

THAT EVENING, Aaron sat at Sancha's feet, playing with one of his favorite action figures while a television program held her full attention. Maria wandered upstairs unnoticed and slipped into her grandson's bedroom.

She glanced around the room without any specific intention. Aaron's room was reasonably tidy: the bed made, the floor dotted with only a few pairs of discarded socks. Next to the child-sized desk in the corner, the wastebasket was full of crumpled paper.

Maria picked up a random wad and carefully unfolded it. The crimped sheet of notebook paper was covered in pencil markings, almost black corner-to-corner. She started to crumple the paper again when the center of the page caught her attention. She lifted the sheet into focus and peered into an area filled with slashes and swirls.

Before her eyes, the entire page transformed into an elaborate scene of the finest detail, as if she'd decoded its language in that moment, instantly translating the rich imagery all at once.

The most sophisticated scene revealed itself in her hands: countless figures all deliberately drawn, so many distinct faces with intricate expressions. Goosebumps rose on Maria's skin as she peered into the absorbing details. The hand-drawn setting resembled a meticulously rendered historical painting filled with its endless events and interactions—the foreground just as elaborate as the background. In her hands, Maria held an entire saga.

Aaron's footsteps broke her concentration. "Hello," she greeted in her usual voice. "I was just—"

"That's trash," Aaron said with nonchalance.

"Is this what you've been drawing in class?" She was curious, not accusing.

Aaron kept silent, his body tensing.

"Oh, I think it's wonderful. And Ms. Cartwright was very impressed."

"She... she said so?"

Maria fought to avoid making her lie more official. "She didn't want the other students to feel... to be encouraged to draw in the middle of class." She smiled. "I'm sure none of the other students are as talented as *you*." Pride sparkled in her eyes.

Aaron's forehead wrinkled as he considered the new notion. "I dunno," he said with a shrug.

"Oh, I'm sure. Did you see these things on television? Or in one of your schoolbooks?"

Aaron shook his head.

Maria spoke more carefully, mustering an even more cheerful tone. "Are they... from your *dreams*?"

"Can't remember my dreams," he replied, serving up the usual answer.

"They're very good—every detail. I can see every face so clearly. You don't remember where you saw them before?"

He shook his head again. "I didn't see them anywhere. I just drew them."

Maria considered her grandson's casual reaction—his inability to recognize his own *ability* as anything unusual. And she was thankful for it.

"Okay," she said. "Well, they're very beautiful."

Aaron wrinkled his nose at her word choice, almost making Maria laugh.

"They're very *cool*," she corrected herself.

Aaron smiled.

"You can show them to me—if you want. You don't have to throw them all away, but maybe you could save the drawing for *after* school? So the other kids don't get jealous."

Aaron nodded, still sporting his big smile. He left his room, forgetting why he entered to begin with.

Maria held his drawing in view again. She found herself pulled into the depths of the imagery—mystified by it. She yearned to unravel the vital meaning she felt—without question —was held there: the untold story so plainly told just on the outskirts of her own comprehension.

9

As AUTUMN ARRIVED IN FULL, SOON TO BE OVERTHROWN BY A harsh winter, Sancha stared through the open doors of the nearest factory exit as her hands automatically fed material beneath the chomping needle. She turned to glance at the single sewing machine left quiet in the rising and falling rhythm of rows of machines purring all around.

Maria's station sat empty, her half-finished stack of precision-cut vinyl still resting on the tabletop as she'd set it aside when the factory bell sounded the beginning of lunch hour, four hours earlier.

As the final bell rang over the factory floor for first shift, Sancha double-stitched the end of her last seam, released the foot pedal, and snipped the thread. She packed up her belongings while scanning the aisles of women for her mother, then walked through the back entrance and sat at a concrete picnic table in the break area outside.

By the time she searched the parking lot for the tenth time, reconfirming the family car was nowhere to be seen, the second shift employees had already arrived and settled in to start their own workday. As Sancha considered going inside to use the phone, Maria drove into view. Sancha ran to the passenger-side door and swung it open.

"Mom, is everything all right? Where did you go?"

"I just went out for lunch. Come on. Let's go." Maria motioned for Sancha.

"But you're so late. You didn't even say anything about—"

"You were out here with your friend, the one with the frumpy hair. I didn't want to interrupt. Get in, or we'll be late to pick up Aaron."

Sancha settled into her seat, closing the door and snapping her seatbelt into place. "But, Mom, you don't usually just disappear like that."

"I just had to take care of some things, okay? It's nothing. Just the best time to fit it in."

"All right." Sancha stared straight ahead as they pulled out of the parking lot. When she couldn't stand the silence any longer, she blurted, "Will you just—please tell me what it was. It's not like you. You're scaring me."

"Oh, honey, I didn't mean to." Maria's exhaustion sounded in every syllable. "It's just... some things are better done on my own, you know?"

"No, I don't."

"It's nothing—just this cough I've had. It's been niggling at me for so long, and now, it's difficult at work. Sometimes, I'm just *worn out*. And I don't meet my quota."

"Oh. Well, that's not really a big deal."

"No. It's not." Maria smiled to reassure Sancha, as well as herself. "Just good to know what's going on."

"So, what's going on?" Sancha couldn't remember when her mother last visited the doctor for herself; Maria was the type who seemed impervious to illness, the would-be strongest survivor after an earthly apocalypse. "I noticed you don't eat as much."

Maria chuckled, then welcomed a full laugh.

"No," Sancha apologized. "I mean, I thought you were just trying to be healthier or something."

"Thanks!"

"Haven't you lost weight?"

"I guess, but no, I haven't been trying. Have you ever known me to diet?"

Sancha finally smiled. "So, is it just one of those colds that won't go away or something?"

Maria shrugged. "No. Dr. Phillips doesn't know. There's not really an explanation for it, just random symptoms. Maybe it's even just stress-related—*probably* stress-related—but he prescribed some antibiotics. And that should clear it all up."

"Good. I don't like it when you're sick."

Maria smiled. "Neither do I. I'm getting old, I guess. Mysterious things start to happen."

Sancha frowned. "Well, they better not happen anymore."

"Oh, nothing's going to happen to me. You're stuck with me for a *long* time." Maria almost giggled, a failed attempt to disguise her own anxiety.

"For as long as I'm alive?"

Maria drew her gaze away from the road ahead, long enough to smile in her daughter's direction. She knew such a wish could never be granted.

10

————

MARIA FINISHED SEWING THE VINYL WELT BETWEEN DIE-CUT PIECES of soft leather with an artist's care and a doctor's precision. Sancha leapt up from her own work station—the second most reliable signal of the beginning of the allotted lunch hour. She made a beeline for the break room vending machines as Maria caught her arm.

"Just real quick!" Maria reassured.

"I've got to get there before the line starts, or lunch'll be half over before I get my Snickers bar!"

Maria flinched at the resurfacing teenage whine. "You should eat better—but I just wanted to let you know that I'm going out for lunch. Would you like me to bring anything back for you?"

"Where are you going?"

"Well, I just—"

"Arby's? Then, I want some curly fries. Large ones!"

"Well, okay then—yes, I can stop there. Anything else?"

"Mmm, chocolate milkshake!"

"*With* your Snickers bar?"

"I *told* you, if I don't get at the head of the line, I *won't* even have time to eat it!"

"Okay, okay. I was just teasing. Go. Run!"

Sancha followed orders, leaping with youthful energy Maria was instantly jealous of.

MARIA RUSHED to make her appointment, praying the clinic wasn't behind in their patient schedule. After a ten-minute wait, she was led to an examination room. She felt instant relief when Dr. Phillips finally knocked on the door.

"Well, you look happy to see me!" he greeted when granted permission to enter. He quickly sat, pen poised in hand. "So, you mentioned to the nurse that you're experiencing new symptoms?"

"Yes. And the old ones are just as persistent." Her voice was rushed, her annoyance evident.

He frowned as he jotted notes in her file. "We're going to have to run more tests."

"More?"

"Yes. Still, nothing to worry over. But, as the combination of symptoms grows more... *complex*, I want to make sure we're not missing anything. *And* I want you feeling better rather than worse."

Maria nodded. "I'm just feeling... just *tired*, so weak. And there are always challenges, of course. Aaron's school schedule varies, and just picking him up and dropping him off—"

"Is he still having the nightmares?"

She nodded. "No, I'm not going to give him the..."

"Zoloft? That's fine. It *is* your choice, but he might continue to—"

"He's fine. We're fine. I'm just... the symptoms are really wearing me down."

"Are you all getting enough sleep?"

"Yes. I make sure of it. His nightmares... they run like clockwork."

Dr. Phillips nodded, glancing at his handwritten notes. "Is the general malaise the only new symptom?"

"No—and it's not a new one," Maria huffed. "I'm finding bumps on my skin."

"Like a rash?"

"No, just skin-colored, but they weren't there before." She ran her fingers over her forearm as she answered.

"Are you sure you haven't seen them before?"

"*Yes.* They're here—on my elbows."

Dr. Phillips rolled his stool closer, inspecting Maria's dry elbows with gloved hands. "Hmm. Do they hurt at all?"

She shook her head.

"Any other skin changes?"

"No, not that I've noticed."

"Mm-hmm. Anything else then?"

"My stomach's not quite right."

"Your stomach?"

Maria read the disbelief on the doctor's face with a mother's expertise. "Yes, and I've always had an iron stomach."

Dr. Phillips smiled. "A blessing. But how is it now?"

"Just uneasy. Nausea occasionally."

"After you eat or at any particular time that you've noticed?"

"No. I don't eat much."

"Oh. I do see your weight's gone down... ten pounds?"

Maria's eyebrows raised. "Hmm. That's something."

Dr. Phillips forced another smile. "Well, we prefer it if your weight's *not* fluctuating. Have you changed your diet or—"

"No. I might just be eating less?" She shrugged.

"Okay. Well, that's not really a concern, but if the occasional nausea continues, I want to hear about it. And try to determine if there's any consistency as to when, or possibly, why."

Maria nodded.

"How's the muscle pain?"

"Same."

"And joint pain?"

"Sometimes."

"I'm just going to check your lymph nodes, if that's all right?"

"Mm-hmm."

The doctor's gentle touch pressed in circular motion under her arms and jawbone. "Just a bit swollen perhaps. But again, nothing to concern us. Just the body's natural reaction to anything going on that it's unhappy about."

Dr. Phillips rolled back to the counter. "We'll run another cycle of blood tests. There are a few more things I can look for. And we'll check on those white blood cells, see if they're still abnormal."

Maria slowly nodded as yet another examination delivered no new information.

"Now," he continued in a softer voice, "how are *you* holding up? Still feeling positive?"

She blinked slowly and nodded her perseverance.

"Good. That's the very best medicine. We'll get to the bottom of this. Nothing at all to worry about." His professional smile lingered too long.

By now, Maria's own concern was the only constant; she was accustomed to the daily changes in her general wellbeing and new symptoms continuously arising. As long as she was capable of going through her daily routine without too much pain, the mysteries of her health were only a nagging nuisance.

"THERE'S something I'm not supposed to tell you," Maria told Sancha as she turned the steering wheel, pressed the accelerator lightly, and freed the both of them from their work for another day.

"What?" Sancha asked, searching her mother's face for clues.

"Maybe I shouldn't say."

"What? Is it something bad?"

"Oh, no! No, sweetie. It's good—*very* good."

"Then, what is it?"

"I was talking to Charlotte, in the office, and she said, they *might* be giving out a raise."

"Oh," Sancha stared out the window. "Is that all?"

"There's a very good chance, she says! Though, they're still deciding for sure, but we *are* overdue for one. And—"

"How much?"

"Well, at least another fifteen cents an—"

"*Fifteen cents?*"

"That's quite a lot. When you add it up, that's—"

"It's not worth it."

"What? You should be—"

"It's not—and I'm thinking of..."

"Yes?" Maria used the pause in conversation to calm herself.

"Quitting," Sancha answered timidly before rushing through an explanation ending with, "It's just not what I really want to do. I'm... I'm getting too old and—"

"I beg your pardon."

"Well, I'm just not supposed to be working there. It's for—"

"Sancha." Maria's tone was Sancha's most dreaded. "I've been working there almost since you were born, and don't you *dare* talk down about the—"

"That's not what I meant. It's just, well, everyone's been working there *all* their lives. Or because their mom did. Or since right after high school."

"Like you."

Sancha nodded, staring at her hands clasped in her lap: the Band-Aid on her forefinger, the calluses on her fingertips. "I don't want to be like *them*."

Maria's face twisted, restraining the response that raged within.

"I mean," Sancha continued, "I'll be stuck there—for the rest of my *life*—if I don't leave and—"

"You can't quit."

"But Aaron's in public school now, and we don't need the money any—"

"We *always* need the money. Sancha, do you not realize what it costs—how much I have to pay—for *every* expense for the three of us, everything we need?"

"But, I'll get another job. I just need to figure out—"

"And how long will that take? You can't guarantee you'll find something else that quickly. It's a bad time right now out there—people who can't find any work—and you want to—"

"It's not *that* big of a deal. I'll get another job fast enough. It can't be that—"

"With what skills? What resume? You said you don't want to work in fast food, and just where do you think you can go—"

"Mom!" Sancha's plea was for mercy rather than in complaint.

"I'm sorry. It's just that... it's not easy. I worked very hard to get you a position at the factory. There were a lot of women who would've loved to have that job, and—"

"I don't *want* to work there anymore."

"What are you going to do instead?"

"Well, Aaron's out of school—for the summer, soon—and I thought I could—"

"Stay home and *play*?"

Sancha's answer came in instant tears.

Maria reached for her daughter immediately. "Sancha, Sancha, listen to me. That really does sound wonderful; it really does. It's just that... you have responsibilities now—and not just to your son. We *all* do. We have to pull together."

"But, won't it be all right for... a little while? Maybe just the summer, and then—by then, I'll know—"

"Sancha." Maria stared straight ahead, returning her hand securely to the steering wheel as she turned at the final intersection before Aaron's school. "I know what you're thinking but... you're not thinking of *everything*."

"Well, can't we just *try* it? Then, I can just work again—right away—if I have to."

Maria shook her head and released a long-held breath as she pulled the car into the school parking lot. Once parked, she released her seatbelt and turned to face her daughter. "What if something *happens*? What if you have to take care of every—"

"What do you mean?"

Maria's lips squeezed together; she diverted her eyes. "What if something should happen to *me*? And if you have to take care of Aaron all by yourself and look after the house or—"

"No." Sancha started shaking her head.

"Sancha, you're not being practical. Anything can—"

"No! Don't *say* things like that!" Sancha's seatbelt was off, slapping against the door frame as she yanked at the door handle.

"Sancha! I just want you to—"

The passenger door slammed, leaving Maria alone in the car, forced to calm herself before her grandson would come running up to the door awaiting his hug.

She didn't venture to bring up the thought—her deepest fear —again. Instead, she prayed for its needlessness.

11

ONE NIGHT, JUST BEFORE THE LIGHT OF DAWN, SANCHA TOSSED IN her bed. All else was still. Only the occasional creak of the old house disturbed the quiet after the family settled in for the allotment of sleep granted after Aaron's ever-reliable nightmares were subdued.

Sancha opened her eyes and blinked at the ceiling above her. She traced the crack meandering from one wall to the next, its intricate pattern memorized since childhood. The blue-hued light of the waning moon seeped over the uneven ceiling, casting a comforting glow divoted with pockets of shadow.

A choking sound disrupted her concentration: someone or something gasping for breath within the walls of the house. Once, then again.

She sat up, the icy winter air soaking through her flannel gown as the bedcovers fell around her waist. She darted toward the door, leaving her slippers behind.

As she stood in the hallway, she turned her head in every direction, her ears awaiting the next clue. The next struggling rasp came from her mother's room.

SANCHA FOUND HER MOTHER SLEEPING, covered in her heavy, handmade quilt and without a single sign of distress. Sancha relaxed, suddenly feeling the cold. She stepped along the hardwood floor, back toward the doorway, before she rationalized Aaron must be the one in trouble.

Sancha ran out of one bedroom and into the next. She found Aaron sound asleep, his eyes dreamily darting beneath his eyelids, his breath slow and steady, not a single golden hair on his head out of place.

Then, she heard that terrible sound again.

She darted back to her mother's room and softly landed on Maria's bedside. She reached over her mother's chest, saw her lips parted, and caught the sight of her throat fighting for breath.

"Mom! *Mom!*" Sancha shook her with both hands, clenching her broad shoulders.

Maria blinked awake, yanking her arms free. "What... what is it?"

"Mom, you... you weren't breathing. I heard you..." Sancha's throat tightened as she spoke.

"What... what do you mean? Me?"

"Mom! You were *choking!*" Sancha couldn't hold back her tears.

"Sweetie, I'm okay. I'm fine. Look at me."

Sancha wiped at her cheeks, her sleep-deprived mind churning as she looked into her mother's eyes. "But you were. It was *horrible!* It sounded like you—"

"Shh... come here." Maria lifted the quilt, creating an inviting cave. Sancha crawled in and nestled up to her mother's warm body.

"Shh... don't cry, darling," Maria whispered. "I'm all right. I don't know what in the world you think—"

"I *heard* you." Sancha's voice was muffled under the covers. "It sounded like you couldn't breathe."

"Oh, you must've been dreaming. You poor thing." Maria brushed her daughter's hair from her face and kissed her forehead.

"I wasn't asleep. It sounded *awful.*"

"Okay. Okay. How do I sound now?"

"Fine," Sancha moaned, her voice low like a little girl's.

"Then, there's nothing to worry about, is there?"

"But... what if it happens again? What if you can't—"

"Shush now."

"But I heard—"

Maria chuckled softly. "How do you know I haven't always made strange sounds in my sleep?"

"But I never—*maybe.*" Sancha snuggled closer.

"Maybe I always make music in my sleep."

Sancha giggled.

"Now, how about if we try to go *back* to sleep?

"Mm-hmm." Sancha made no effort to move.

"Stay, and keep me warm. Just like you did when you were Aaron's age."

SANCHA FELL ASLEEP EVEN before her mother could move into a pleasant position. Maria was the one left awake, pondering the new, unnatural rhythm of her own heartbeat.

12

———

Ms. Cartwright stared down her students—seemingly one-by-one—as she caressed the smooth stack of paper still warm from the photocopy machine. All children tensed as she began to walk the first row of tables, counting out copies of the first test of the new calendar year: the "big test" she'd enjoyed warning them about for weeks.

Finlay smiled at Aaron. "It can't be hard," he whispered. "It's just first grade!" His smile made his dark eyes shine all the brighter.

Aaron's stomach knotted up, threatening to kill his appetite for his packed lunch. Finlay patted him on the back, and handed him the dreaded sheet of paper fresh from the hands of their classmate seated in front of them.

"Eyes forward!" Ms. Cartwright reminded all. "Everyone should be finished when the big hand is on the six."

Every pair of eyes turned toward the clock hung above the teacher's head.

"Begin," she ordered, settling into her chair and picking up a glossy magazine.

Finlay sucked in a huge breath, then slowly let it out. Aaron focused on the first question; a smile spread across his face as he discovered he knew the answer. Studying with his mother had paid off.

The minutes ticked by as the students drew circles in pencil to the sounds of Ms. Cartwright flipping one page of her magazine, then the next. Her sudden shout took every one of them by surprise.

"Excuse me!" She shot out of her chair, its legs screeching across the floor.

Every student faced her. No one had any idea what she referred to—except for Aaron. Despite her outburst, his attention remained in the opposite direction, his head turned away as he stared at the back of the classroom.

"Aaron Rivera!"

His head swung back to face her, his cheeks bright red.

"*Whose* paper were you looking at?" She marched between the rows of tables, stopping to stand over Aaron.

Finlay looked at him, then at the teacher, his mouth hanging open.

"I will not have *cheaters* in my class!" she screeched.

Aaron's voice was shy but sure. "I'm not a—"

"Do not *lie* to me!"

"But I..."

Finlay slowly raised his hand, causing Ms. Cartwright's frown to grow deeper.

"Not right *now*, Finlay," she seethed between clenched teeth.

Finlay's arm remained in the air. Aaron's hands balled into fists in his lap as his shoulders sank.

"Aaron." Her tone was frightfully gentle. "*Honesty* is the best policy. Aaron, tell the *truth*."

"I..." he finally spoke, "I was looking..."

The eyes of the two students seated behind Aaron grew wide. One shook his head, making an angry face.

Aaron continued, "There was—"

"Aaron Rivera, if you don't tell the truth *right now,* I will send you straight to the principal's office!" Ms. Cartwright's eyes bulged over the bridge of her nose.

Finlay spoke in a burst of withheld breath finally released. "He wasn't cheating, Ms. Cartwright."

Aaron shook his head in agreement.

"Nonsense!" Ms. Cartwright shouted, slamming her hand down on the tabletop. "Finlay, I will excuse you this time, but it is *not* okay to lie, not even for your buddy. Aaron, come with me—*now*."

NEAR THE END of the school day, Aaron sat in the small lobby of the principal's office, his ears still red with the injustice of his reprimand. Sancha walked in, her face pale with worry.

"Aaron!" She rushed to him, pulling him to her. "What happened? Ms. Cartwright said—"

"I didn't do it."

"Do what?"

"Cheat. I'm *not* a cheater."

"Of course, you're not. Is that what—"

"Ms. Rivera? You'll need to sign the warning." The principal's secretary slid a sheet of paper across her desk.

"What is this for? I don't understand." Sancha stared at the verbose memo.

"It's just a warning—this time. We need you to sign your acknowledgment. Here." The secretary stabbed at the bottom of the form with her pen.

"But he... my son says he didn't do it."

The secretary stared blankly.

"He didn't do it," Sancha repeated.

"You're only signing that you acknowledge that your son has received the warning. The rest... is between you and his teacher."

Sancha frowned as she signed. Without another word, she took Aaron's hand and walked him out of the office.

"Are we..." Aaron hurried to keep up with his mother's pace. "Do I have to go see Ms. Cartwright?"

"No. We're going home."

"I just can't believe—!" Sancha's temper flared in a show of fiery eyes and clenched fists as she paced the kitchen floor.

"It's just a piece of paper." Maria continued to try to force her daughter to share her perspective. "It means nothing."

"But it's in his *record* now." Sancha's youthful hatred of authority couldn't be swayed.

"It's just—oh, just don't *let* things like that bother you so much."

"He has to go back tomorrow, and the teacher already thinks he's—"

"It will be *fine*. Aaron doesn't seem bothered. Did you notice?"

"Only because *we* believe him."

"And that's all that matters. But..." Maria debated sharing her next thought.

"But what?"

"There's probably a bit of truth behind it. Did you ask Aaron what happened?"

"Well, no. I'm sure he—"

"You should ask him."

"*All right.*" Sancha punctuated her consent with a pout. "I just don't want to upset him."

"He's definitely old enough. And... he's tougher than you realize."

Sancha meandered up the stairs. Maria returned to washing the dinner dishes in the sink.

"Mom!" Sancha's voice carried flawlessly down the stairwell.

"Just a minute. I'm almost finished," Maria called in return.

Sancha's immediate, second scream startled Maria enough to grab the dishtowel in her suds-soaked hands and bound up the staircase with uncommon quickness.

As she reached the landing outside Aaron's bedroom, she met with Sancha's wide-eyed stare. Maria followed it to Aaron where he sat on the end of his bed.

"He... he won't answer me," Sancha said.

Maria studied them both. "Aaron?"

"What's he... staring at?" Sancha whispered to her mother, now at her side.

Maria felt a familiar chill take hold of her shoulders. "Aaron," she spoke with urgency. "Aaron, answer Grandmom."

He didn't move. He sat perfectly upright, his legs hanging off the end of the bed, his hands resting on either side of his lap. His torso was twisted toward the wall behind him, his unblinking stare locked on the corner of his bedroom where only his nightstand and small lamp stood.

"Aaron," Maria repeated. "I'm asking you to answer me—*now*."

His lips pressed together. The outside corners of his eyebrows dropped slightly.

"Then, *show* me," she said.

Almost instantly—to the surprise of both women—Aaron's right arm began to raise until it was outstretched horizontally, straight as a rod, finger pointing at the empty wall next to his nightstand.

"Is it... still there?" Maria asked, her voice steadfast while her irregular heartbeat pounded in her chest.

Sancha looked to her mother, her face so pale her freckles were almost in hiding.

And Aaron nodded—just once.

Maria spoke again, so slow and steady that her own anxiety was undetectable. "What is—"

"It's gone," Aaron said, turning around again and reaching for the action figure splayed on the bed beside him. His demeanor changed completely—instantaneously.

Both women studied Aaron's play for a few moments, then Sancha spoke, slanting her head toward her mother as she still faced her son. "What just... what did he..."

Maria opened her mouth with a quick intake of breath, then closed it again.

Sancha insisted. "Mom, I don't—"

"Sancha, I want you to go downstairs and make sure I turned the water off—at the sink."

"But, Mom, I—"

"It's all right. Everything's... all right. I just want to talk to Aaron."

Sancha left the room. Maria's ears followed the sound of her daughter's fading footsteps, and she closed the bedroom door.

Maria's face transformed, configuring a smile and a light in her eyes as she knelt before her grandson. "Aaron," she spoke, her mind searching for the right words, the most casual tone, before relenting to choose at random. "Was there... something there or... were you just playing?" Maria's pitch incidentally rose as she spoke, nearly playful with its last word.

Aaron shook his head, pursing his lips to confirm the negative response.

Maria rested her hand on Aaron's knee. "Did you *see* something or just feel—"

Aaron nodded immediately.

"Did..." Maria joined her grandson in admiring the toy figure in his hands. "Did he see it too?"

Aaron looked up at his grandmother, scrunching up his face and shaking his head. "It's just a toy," he said with a big smile.

"But *I* didn't see anything, Aaron."

He made a face again. "You didn't?"

Maria shook her head. "Neither did your mom."

Aaron cocked his head to the side, then started to manipulate the limbs of his action figure into a fighting pose.

"He was at school, too," Aaron said, attempting to make his toy stand on his lap.

Maria's voice caught on her only word. "*He*?"

Aaron nodded, continuing to fidget with the toy.

"What... what did he look like?"

Aaron shrugged before finding the words. "Dark," he said. "Just... black."

Maria's expression changed again, and she left her grandson alone in his bedroom. She was fully aware that she was the only one who was afraid.

And that was not enough to comfort her.

"It's an imaginary friend, isn't it?" Sancha asked, her voice cheerful but still unsure as she peeked out from beneath layers of bedcovers.

Maria relaxed as she sat on the edge of her daughter's bed. She marveled at how quickly her own head nodded in response.

"Aaron has an imaginary friend..." Sancha pondered, flashing her expression of curiosity at the ceiling above her. "I didn't think older kids do, but I guess he's not that old yet." She smiled.

Maria shrugged. She squeezed Sancha's hand and leaned over to leave a kiss on her forehead. "Sleep well," she said as she left the room, hiding the concern etched on her face.

"Lord," Maria whispered into the darkness, wrapped in the warm comfort of her own bedcovers, "I'm not ready to go. But... but if it is my time, please watch over them."

Her voice wavered beneath the threat of tears. "*Please* keep them safe."

13

As the school year at Langston Hughes Elementary School began to wrap up in a tidy bundle of progress reports, pop quizzes, and first-through-fourth-graders bursting with budding egos, Aaron had adjusted his habits and temperament along with all the other students. Neatly groomed for succeeding at the next grade level, he fulfilled the role of a perfectly normal, perfectly average student.

And he tried—with all his might—*not* to look over his shoulder.

Not even when he got that certain urge to. Not even when his skin prickled with the undeniable certainty that *someone* watched him—and *only* him.

14

WELL AWARE THAT HIS BIG SEVENTH BIRTHDAY WAS COMING UP soon enough to start counting down the days, Aaron assumed Ms. Cartwright actually wanted to share in the excitement when she rushed up to his desk one afternoon.

"Aaron," she whispered in his ear above the noise of the classroom buzzing with the energy of summer break looming. "You need to collect your things. Your mother's coming to pick you up."

"Now?" Aaron asked under Finlay's watchful eye.

"Yes, please. She'll be here soon."

Aaron didn't ask more questions. Finlay wanted to—his natural urge was to speak for his friend who always chose to remain quieter than their classmates—but he didn't.

Aaron zipped up his backpack and slung it over his shoulder. The other students stared, muttering their jealousy.

"See ya tomorrow," Finlay tossed at Aaron's back.

Aaron followed Ms. Cartwright to the door. She led him into the hall, then leaned over wearing an expression he didn't remember seeing on anyone before.

"It's your grandmother, dear." Her use of an affectionate

term jarred him before his mind could register the meaning of her words. "Something... happened—but she's all right. Your mother's coming to get you. You should all be together at a time like this."

Aaron couldn't interpret what his teacher tried to convey. He only construed he was supposed to be upset, without knowing what *kind* of upset.

"Just go straight to the principal's office," Ms. Cartwright directed. "Your mother will collect you there."

WHEN AARON REACHED for the handle to open the glass door to the principal's office, Sancha was already waiting for him. She ran to him, holding him longer than usual. Then, her tears poured, and Aaron learned what kind of emotion he was supposed to feel.

"Grandmom's in the hospital," she managed to say between sobs.

SANCHA RACED through the hospital's main entrance, Aaron's hand tightly clutched in hers. She appeared frail and trembling beneath the fluorescent lighting flooding the reception area.

"I... I need... my mother," she blurted at the receptionist. "I mean, she's here. She had a stroke—at work. They brought—"

"I just need her name." The receptionist's controlled voice was calming.

"Maria. Rivera."

"Let me just take a look... she's still in the ICU but stable." The receptionist pointed. "Next building over, third floor. They'll direct you when you get there."

Sancha clung to the image of the stranger's smile as she pulled Aaron through the exit doors, mumbling as she followed the woman's directions. The sense of urgency and confusion spread to Aaron.

———

AT THE NEXT nurse's desk, Sancha's voice was more hurried—on the verge of breaking. "My mother—Maria Rivera—she's..."

"Just one moment." Another stranger tapped at a computer keyboard. "Room 22B—just down that hall." No smile was granted this time.

Sancha and Aaron were met at the door to 22B by an exiting nurse. "Are you her daughter?" she asked.

Sancha nodded.

"Good. You can see her now, but she really needs her rest. She's not asleep at the moment, but the drugs will make her very sleepy. And she... might not be *herself*. Just try to be calm and help keep her relaxed." As an afterthought, she smiled and asked, "Okay?"

Sancha nodded, pushing past the woman and finally releasing her grip on Aaron's hand.

———

MARIA LAY in the single bed in the sparse, cold-white room with her eyes closed and the heart rate monitor beeping at her side.

Sancha stood in solemn silence and reached for Aaron to hold him at her side, wrapping her arm around his slight shoulders. They stared together in respect for the woman who was the heart and spirit of their small family.

The source of their strength lay prone, her face inanimate, her body large and heavy in the narrow metal bed—devoid of any sign of her usual exuberance and vibrancy. Sancha breathed audibly; she urged Aaron closer to her. He pressed his face against his mother's waist, wishing to close his eyes but unable to force them.

"Come on," Sancha whispered to him. "Let's let her know we're here."

Aaron took a step back before tentatively following his mother's path around to the side of the bed and the unmoving figure it held. Sancha studied her mother's still face, realizing she'd never seen it so barren of expression before, even while Maria napped in the comfort of her own bed.

Aaron's mind raced to uncover the meaning of the scene he witnessed; he found none. And he didn't dare ask. Whatever happened was uncomfortably different from anything else before. And that was completely unwelcome for every reason.

He watched Sancha inch closer to the resting body on the bed. She slid her hand over her mother's as it rested on her belly.

Maria opened her eyes, and she smiled, the life filling her face again. "Hello," she said, the greeting packed with genuine joy.

"Mom!" Sancha pressed herself to her mother's body, crying onto her chest, nestling inside Maria's arms as they wrapped around her.

"Shh, don't cry," Maria spoke cheerfully. "Really, there's no reason to. I'm fine. It's all over now."

Sancha raised her face to her mother's, then pulled herself upright again. "What... what do you mean?"

"I've had my stroke." Maria's smile remained, strong as ever. "It's all over now. I can go home soon, and everything will be back to normal."

"Really?"

Maria nodded. "I'm not going anywhere, anytime soon."

Sancha bent forward and squeezed her mother again. "Oh, God. I was so scared! I didn't know... I wasn't ready. I didn't know what to..." Her words transformed into tears, soaking her mother's hospital gown.

"Shh. It's all over now. We did it. We made it through—*again*. We always do. Don't we?"

Sancha nodded and peeled herself away, allowing her mother to breathe deeply again.

"You're," Aaron spoke softly, "you're okay?"

"Come here, my beautiful grandbaby." Maria raised both her arms, covering Aaron's head as he stepped in front of Sancha and lay against Maria's broad chest. "Yes, yes," she said. "Don't you worry. Grandmom's here to stay. I'm not going to leave you two. I feel as fit as a fiddle!"

15

TWO WEEKS LATER, MS. CARTWRIGHT COULD HARDLY CONTAIN THE explosive excitement of her students, regardless of any amount of control she presumed she gained over them through the school year. There was only one week of school left. Every student knew the graduation ceremony for the first-graders at the week's end would be the last time they'd be required to step foot on school grounds before the seemingly endless summer. Nothing but exciting, unknown possibilities were ahead.

"Are you going to the graduation?" Finlay asked Aaron during recess.

Aaron contemplated the curved steel slide before him and propelled himself down, disappearing out of Finlay's view.

"Are you going to the graduation?" Finlay tried again, yelling this time.

"We *have* to," Aaron snapped as he dusted off his bottom after landing in the sand.

"Yeah, but your... your grandma's still—"

"I know!" Aaron kicked at the sand.

Finlay slid down and stood next to his friend, despite all signals that he shouldn't. "When's she gonna get to go home?"

"I don't know." Aaron dug circles in the sand with the toe of his sneaker.

"What's the matter with her?"

"I don't know!" Aaron ran toward the school building to wait for the bell.

———

"WHAT DID you do in school today?" Maria asked, straining to smile at Aaron as he frowned in the chair in the far corner of the hospital room.

"Answer your Grandmom," Sancha pressed from her seat at her mother's bedside.

"Don't push him," Maria said, her constricting throat hampering her speech. The beeping of the heart rate monitor accelerated. "It's okay," Maria rasped to reassure her daughter.

"What's wrong with you?" Aaron asked, clinging to his anger, uncertainty frightening him most of all.

Sancha snapped at him, but Maria answered calmly.

"That's a very good question." She struggled to adjust her position in bed, the pain revealed on her face as she moved. "The truth is... nobody knows. The human body's such a mysterious thing."

Sancha rolled her eyes, shaking her head at the response she'd heard from her mother—and so many doctors—too many times before.

"But I'm fighting it," Maria continued. "It hasn't beaten me yet." Her hacking cough reverberated through the small room, right on cue.

"I just don't see *why* they can't—why don't they know?" Sancha's face matched Aaron's.

"Sometimes," Maria made a great effort to speak, "they just don't." Seeing the look on her daughter's face, she offered more.

"My lungs aren't working very well, and my heart's not—it just feels like every part of me is shouting out at once, trying to tell me something, but... but I don't know what. No one knows what."

"It just doesn't make sense! How can a cold turn into—"

"It might not have even been a cold—not with the stomach stuff too. And now, I can barely force myself to eat."

The last statement stirred the greatest reaction in Sancha, her display of anger displaced with worry.

"But I'm eating." Maria coughed again, no longer bothering to burden the aching muscles of an arm to cover her mouth. "I know I need to."

Aaron swung his legs from his chair as he stared at the floor, pretending he wasn't listening. Both Sancha and Maria worried, most of all, about the effect Maria's illness would ultimately have on the youngest member of the family. They clung to that focus—neither realizing their shared conviction—as they desperately fought to avoid all temptation to turn their attention to the worst possible scenario—and its very real probability.

"Please try not to worry," Maria said.

Sancha only glared at her.

"The doctors are doing their best. They'll figure it out."

Sancha's belief in a positive outcome was gone. She grew older by the minute: ready, preparing herself, even if only subconsciously.

"So," Maria spoke, beckoning her cheeriest voice possible at the moment, "I have an idea."

Aaron's eyebrows raised, but he refused to lift his head.

"Summer's almost here and *somebody* isn't going to have to go to school anymore."

"Yeah," Aaron answered sharply, without looking at his grandmother. "But you're making me go to daycare, and I'm too old now."

Sancha breathed in deeply, watching his movements, his mood.

"You wouldn't like being in that big, old house all by yourself all day, would you?" Maria asked. "And I think you're not quite old enough yet. Don't you think?"

Aaron swung his legs faster.

"I've got an idea that's even *more* fun. Daycare in the summertime *will* be lots of fun but... how about if we sign you up for *swim* lessons—huh? You love going to the swimming pool, and you can learn all kinds of cool new tricks. And you can show me when I—" This time, for the first time, Maria stopped herself, realizing her overabundance of forced optimism usually had the opposite effect on her daughter and grandson.

"Would you like that, Aaron?" Sancha asked, fully aware that Aaron was already registered.

His daycare would even provide the transportation, giving Sancha much needed time to recuperate, at least for a couple of hours a day, from being so strong—for him, for her mother, for all the questions her coworkers inundated her with every day at the factory. And both women knew every distraction would help keep the child they cared so much for in *childhood* for that much longer.

"Will they teach me to swim like a frog?" Aaron muttered under his breath, still staring at his feet.

"The frog stroke?" Maria asked, wishing her inclination to laugh wouldn't hurt so much. "I'm sure of it!"

Sancha smiled the moment Aaron did. "And we're going shopping for pool toys!" she announced.

Aaron's smile grew even larger, delivering a generous dose of much-needed contentment to both women.

"Well," Sancha said, standing up, "we might as well go right now."

Aaron jumped out of his seat and ran to his grandmother's

bedside, squeezing her harder than he had in several days. Sancha noticed her mother wince but also spotted the delight in her eyes. Aaron released his grandmother and ran to the door as Sancha leaned over to deliver her hug.

"What's that?" she asked, focusing on her mother's arm as she hovered over her.

Maria frowned as she twisted her arm and revealed the newest purple-hued lesion to appear on her skin. She shook her head. "The newest symptom," she mumbled, choosing not to face her daughter to see the expression she knew she'd find there.

Sancha drew in a long breath and hugged her mother. "I love you," she whispered in her ear with all remaining strength and conviction.

"Me too," Maria said, holding back the desire to cry, reserving her tears for the evenings—when she was alone.

16

THE GRADUATING FIRST-GRADE CLASSES OF LANGSTON HUGHES Elementary School congregated in the school cafeteria with relatives and friends-of-the-family galore, the ceremony about to begin. The students clamored for their assigned rows of chairs, sliding in next to their best friends of the school year. Finlay waved to Aaron, signaling to the reserved seat beside him.

Aaron pretended not to notice. Instead, he also ignored Ms. Cartwright's final instruction and insisted on sitting with his mother, among the other students' family members. No teacher fussed over his rebelliousness under the circumstances, their pity for Aaron's personal situation outweighing their own pride.

Sancha squeezed his hand, giddy with enough excitement for the both of them. "This is pretty cool," she said in the last minutes before the crowd would be hushed. "They didn't do things like this when I was a kid."

Sometimes, Aaron forgot his mother was so much older than himself. She always smiled more, laughed more, joked and played more, than any kid Aaron had ever met. She was the most *fun* person Aaron knew—until recently. Now, in Maria's absence, Sancha seemed older than even his schoolteachers. And he felt older too.

On the small stage at the front of the cafeteria, the teachers' and principal's statements were kept brief enough for the short attention spans, then each first-grader was called onto the stage by name. They proudly paraded through the rows of visiting families and pranced before the principal to receive a paper diploma—rolled and tied with a big, red bow—and a plastic medal hung over their shoulders. Aaron accepted his trophies with suitable solemnity and finally acknowledged Finlay's friendly wave.

After the ceremony, Aaron quickly approached his fill of cake and fruit punch. Sancha already had her fill of questions and meaningless, standard statements of sympathy. After just fifteen minutes of socializing with fellow parents and school staff members, Sancha didn't trust herself to not yell, "She's not dead yet!" at the very next stranger mentioning her mother's illness.

"Ready to go home?" Sancha asked Aaron, trying not to sway his decision.

He nipped the last bite of his third slice of cake off the end of the plastic fork in his hand, then nodded with protruding, cake-filled cheeks.

"All right. Which is the fastest way?"

Aaron pointed his fork, and Sancha led the way.

"Aaron!" a familiar voice called after them. Finlay stood with his hands in his pockets and a smearing of chocolate cake obvious on the lapel of his miniature fitted suit. "You can come over if you want. My parents are having a party—for me."

Aaron looked up at his mother, his request obvious.

Sancha smiled at Finlay, then offered, "We're on our way to the hospital."

Finlay nodded, fully accepting the excuse, then spoke to

Aaron again. "You can come over to my house—whenever you want—over the summer. My new dad is gonna take me to the water park—the really big one. You can come too, if you want." Finlay stepped closer to Aaron and leaned into his line of sight. "He said I could bring my friends if I wanted."

Aaron shrugged. "Maybe," he said, earning his mother's approving smile.

"That's very nice of you, Finlay. I hope we see you over the summer," she said.

Finlay flashed his biggest smile and raced across the cafeteria to join his mother and stepfather.

17

"LISTEN UP!" MR. MICHNER SHOUTED IN GREETING, SETTING THE tone for Aaron's summer.

The row of barefooted young boys in swimming trunks and t-shirts stared up at their swim instructor. Their fear and anticipation mingled with the chlorine fumes wafting from the Olympic-sized indoor swimming pool looming before them.

Mr. Michner paced back and forth, confidently following the edge of the pool as he locked eyes with his new enrollees. Aaron pondered the lone patch of gray hair nested in the man's close-cropped crew cut. "You're here to *learn* to swim, which means you don't know *how* to swim," he continued, releasing a slight smirk.

Aaron winced. He didn't like his swim instructor—not at all. He felt that familiar churning deep in his gut like getting sick but without the sickness ever coming.

"Safety first," bellowed from Mr. Michner. "You will not dip one single, crooked little toe into that water—" he pointed, and all heads turned toward the pool's rippling surface, "unless I give you permission to do so. And you *will* get in that water when I tell you to do so. I won't have any scared little boys crying for their mommy and holding back the entire class."

Even the most confident students let go of the last of their enthusiasm as they peered into the water—now a sea of infinite dangers. Mr. Michner lectured on, his hands clasped against the small of his back, his posture rod-straight, his stride precisely measured.

Nearly an hour later, his students had lost all hope of being granted access to the cool waters of the swimming pool before the first day's lesson was up. Finally, Mr. Michner issued his final directive for the day.

"And by the end of the six weeks we have together, you *will* jump off that diving board."

All heads turned toward the far end of the pool. Every boy studied the trio of diving boards of varying heights. One student timidly raised his hand. Mr. Michner raised his eyebrows in response.

"Um," the boy started, "which one of those diving boards over there?"

His classmates hunched lower, shrinking in size and courage as they realized the instructor may not be referring to a diving board but *the* diving board—the one prominently poised in the center of the three, the one with steps going as high as heaven itself, the one that surely meant instant death for anyone who dared to leap off of it before he was a professional swimmer for at least many, many years.

Mr. Michner smiled. "The big one."

18

"YOU DON'T HAVE TO VISIT EVERY DAY," MARIA WHISPERED TO Sancha as she grew more hoarse with each word. "The hospital's not—"

"Of course, I'm going to be here every day!"

"I just mean," Maria managed before struggling through a succession of coughs. "You don't have to. You should..."

Sancha waited with patience as her mother's coughing fit resumed, then finally calmed.

Maria continued, "Take some time off. You two should... go do something—together." The next slew of coughs bellowed from deep in her chest.

"Stop trying to get rid of me," Sancha teased. "I'm fine." Her tone softened. "I want to be with you."

Maria nodded, then winced as she tried to adjust her position in the hospital bed. "Aaron?"

"Having fun." Sancha smiled. "I guess the swim instructor is kind of serious or something, but Aaron loves showing me the new strokes he learns. He loves the frog stroke."

Maria strained to smile.

"He's not as good as the other students," Sancha continued,

"but he's having fun. I think the instructor makes it too technical for him—or something—I don't know. He's not very confident." She chuckled. "You should see him tread water. He doesn't quite get it. He looks like a fish outta water—but *in* the water."

Maria allowed herself to smile in full, swallowing to fight off her throat's urge to cough.

"He loves it," Sancha said. "And it keeps him... thinking of other stuff."

Maria nodded, then jolted—slightly but painfully—as Aaron burst through the door in his usual style. Maria forced a smile for her grandson.

"You found the Kit Kat bars," Sancha said, rolling her eyes.

"Yes!" Aaron shouted. "In the machine—that was broke—by the stairs downstairs."

Maria's face contorted, unnoticed, as she felt the familiar pinch of nerves in her leg before the entire limb succumbed to numbness. She comforted herself by gazing at her lovely daughter, then at her bright-eyed grandson.

Then, she felt a sharp cold prick at her ear—not a symptom, something else entirely. She turned her head away from her family with great effort. She looked toward the corner of the room nearest the door—she wondered what compelled her to. When she realized the sudden silence in the room, she looked toward Aaron.

He stared at the doorway as well.

"Is it—is he—there?" Maria asked, forgetting her daughter's presence.

Aaron faced his grandmother. "Not anymore," he said, proceeding to unwrap his chocolate bar.

Sancha opened her mouth, then dismissed her confusion. Maria reverted to her mental preparations—for the inevitable.

19

—————

AARON GIGGLED AT THE EXAGGERATED FACE THE BOY SITTING NEXT to him made, mimicking Mr. Michner's. They sat elbow-to-elbow with all the boys in class along the edge of the swimming pool, their bare feet and legs dangling in the water with new confidence.

"All right. Who's next?" Mr. Michner called out, his shining metal whistle hanging out of his mouth. "Rivera and Samuel —your turn."

Both boys happily dropped their weight into the shallow end of the pool, poised to push off the side and race their hearts out. Mr. Michner sounded his whistle, and the great show of splashing began.

"Keep your legs *under* the water!" he shouted as he walked the edge of the pool alongside the swimmers. "Aaron! Why are you *still* keeping your head above the water?"

Aaron kicked and splashed, never lagging too far behind his classmate. He finished last, as usual, with a smile on his face and to the amusement of the other boys watching.

Mr. Michner shook his head and turned his attention to the

next two in line. "Forester and Williams, you're up. And remember what I taught you!"

Aaron's feet left puddles on the tile floor as he returned to the bench on the sidelines. He glanced toward the small bleacher stand, empty now, where his mother and all the other parents would sit in a few days' time to cheer on the demonstration of their sons' achievements as the six-week course ended.

"Who's left?" Mr. Michner shouted. "Masterson and... Narrows. Show us what you've got."

The boys jumped in the water, one swimming off before the whistle sounded.

"Narrows—Billy—*where* are you going? Did you *hear* me blow the whistle? Back on your mark!"

The race began again, ending with results too close to call.

"All right," Mr. Michner addressed his students. "We've got about half an hour left. Who's ready to dive?"

To Aaron's surprise, at least half of his classmates raised their hands.

Mr. Michner gathered up neglected towels. "Well, *all* of you are going to. Line up, and we'll head down there."

***

MARIA'S BREATH—RASPING, catching on itself—began to slow as her immobile body settled further into the indent in the hospital bed mattress.

Her organs struggled in tandem, gradually succumbing to the relentless attack—to the battle waged against her that she did not have the capacity to win.

***

THE BOYS FOLLOWED Mr. Michner's lead toward The Deep End.

Only a few pairs of dripping feet attempted to slow the group's pace as their instructor's commanding tone added to the anxiety-filled atmosphere.

"It's just like we've done before—in the shallow end. And no fancy stuff! I don't want any of you breaking your necks. You can jump off if you want to or just walk off—your choice."

Aaron's steps carried him farther from the edge of the pool as he tried to follow the other boys in line until he wasn't in line at all. From a safe distance, all his senses honed in on the quivering surface of the water—its fluid, undulating movement almost hypnotizing.

SANCHA FELT the pressure of narrow fingertips digging into her shoulder. She lifted her foot off the sewing machine's pedal and turned to face the floor supervisor standing behind her.

"You've got a call."

Sancha remained in her seat. "What?"

"Call. For you. Now."

Sancha left the unfinished material fastened beneath the machine's needle and followed her supervisor to the break room. The woman pointed to the telephone on the wall.

"Hello?" Sancha spoke into the receiver as her supervisor glared.

"Miss Rivera? I'm calling from Memorial Medical. I'm afraid—"

"Oh, God. Oh—no..." Sancha fell against the cement wall, somehow managing to remain standing under the pressure of instant, profound heaviness.

"Miss Rivera? I'm afraid your mother... has taken a turn for the worse. The doctor suggested that you come—"

"She's... still alive?"

"Yes," the voice seemed to speak with hesitation. "But she's not well. The doctor thinks it's best if you—"

"I'm coming now."

Sancha slammed the phone back into position and ran through the aisles lined by roaring machines. She grabbed her purse from her station and raced to the exit.

All eyes on the factory floor followed her path; every coworker's expression poured with sympathy.

———

THE OLDEST BOY in class plunged feet-first into the seeming bottomless depth, his body disappearing for too many seconds before his head finally emerged, bobbing over the surface of the water. He swiped the water from his eyelids and smiled at his classmates. Every student clapped and called out—even the frightened ones—except for Aaron.

"Great job, Smith," Mr. Michner said without enthusiasm, making a checkmark on his clipboard. "Next!"

A chubby boy struggled to climb the steps up to the highest diving board but walked the board's length with ease and took a quick step off, immediately on cue. The next in line climbed just as easily but—once at the top—hesitated to place either bare foot onto the diving board itself.

"Chase! We don't have much time," Mr. Michner yelled up the length of the steps. "Just walk! It's only water."

Frightened into movement, the boy stepped onto the diving board, careful not to agitate it enough to prompt any vibration. When he reached the end of the board, Mr. Michner was out of patience.

"Just put one foot *forward*... and gravity will take care of the rest. Hey—Mathew! What are you doing? I specifically told you *not* to sit on it. That's asking for an injury! Do you want to crack your skull open on the way down? You will *walk* off the end of that board!"

The boy's eyes transfixed on the water below him as his instructor shouted again.

"Jump!" Mr. Michner demanded.

The boy's arms flailed and flapped as his body dropped through the air, curling into a protective fetal position before breaking the surface of the water.

"That's gonna hurt," Mr. Michner mumbled to his clipboard.

"But *why* can't I see her!" Sancha's fists waved at the nurse standing before her.

"I'm sorry. No visitors."

"But you *called* me—someone did. I want to see my mother!"

"Miss Rivera, that's just not possible right now. She's in *critical* condition. Just *wait here*." The nurse yanked Sancha's hand off her clothing. "Dr. Haversham will speak to you as soon as he's available."

Alone in the corridor outside the room her mother had occupied for so many months, Sancha didn't allow herself the comfort of crying.

She thought of her son, forced herself to focus on the consoling image of Aaron splashing in the swimming pool, his wet face smiling, his child's mind carefree and devoid of all concern.

"Rivera, you're up."

Aaron heard the words, but his feet didn't move.

"Up!" Mr. Michner yelled. "You're all taking way too long. Aaron—move it!"

One foot in front of the other, Aaron's body somehow walked on its own accord, like an obedient machine and against all inner commands. Internally, he screamed in protest.

The soles of his feet clung to the cement like suction cups, forcing him to exert extra effort to peel them off again—and again—as he made his way toward what he thought must be the tallest ladder he'd ever seen.

"Did you forget how to climb a *ladder,* Rivera?"

Aaron climbed. His eyes focused only on each rung in his grasp, refusing the view of the water itself.

<hr/>

"Miss Rivera? Thank you for coming." The unfamiliar doctor extended his hand in introduction, then retracted it at the sight of Sancha's cold stare. "I'm Dr. Haversham." He dared divert his gaze as he delivered, "Your mother—she's in critical condition."

"I know, I know! Just tell me what's going on! Is she all right?"

"At this point, we can't predict—"

Sancha buried her head in her hands, then pulled at her hair as she lifted her head again, her eyes delivering silent threats.

The doctor continued in monotone. "It's her organs. They're giving out on her. Everything we've tried has—"

"But you haven't *tried* everything, have you?" Sancha's grating whine blended with pure, damning hatred. "If you tried *everything,* my mother would be *fine* right now—back at home where she belongs!"

"Miss Rivera, we're doing all that we can. I want you to—" Suddenly aware of the emotion legible on his own face, the doctor transformed himself. He stood straight, returning to his beyond-human composure. "You should prepare for *every* outcome."

Obedient only to his professional training, he waited for Sancha's response. She had none.

"We'll see what the latest tests reveal—if anything. I'll return as soon as anything changes." He turned to leave.

"When can I see her?" Sancha asked, plying him with a show of calm while refusing to honor the man with eye contact.

"I'll let you know."

AARON CLUNG to the end of the handrail. The cold steel beneath his palms was a dreaded reminder of the danger yet to be faced.

He stood, hunched and cowering, at the base of the diving board. The height soared several feet beyond the towering height of the old maple tree he'd climbed in the safety of his own back yard.

"Walk!" yelled Mr. Michner to the accompaniment of glaring, giggling boys.

It was surprisingly easy for Aaron to command his small hands to let go of the rail—not so easy to walk the length of the diving board against all sense of self-preservation. His own weight jeopardized his balance with each step. His feet slid like slugs, sticking along the path laid out for him—the only path.

Mr. Michner guarded the only exit—a sentinel at the bottom of the steps discouraging retreat.

Aaron's rapid, short breaths starved his lungs as he stood, teetering, at the very end of the diving board. The echoing screeches of children and adults at play bounced around him. All the splashing activity seemed so distant from where he stood.

The sounds began twisting together, rising in volume, battering at his eardrums. His vision grew gray, cloudy. Passing seconds stretched to narrow strings about to snap.

"I'm going to count you down," was Mr. Michner's final warning.

Aaron, the smallest boy in the class, began to quiver in his stance. His body swayed, along with the ability to command his own muscles.

"Ten."

Aaron's toes stretched forward, his body unmoving.

"Nine... eight..."

Aaron felt the balls of his feet reach the definitive edge of the board, toes dangling in the thick, humid air rising from the depths below.

"Seven... six..."

Aaron closed his eyes—his last defense, his final, ineffective retaliation against overwhelming fear.

"Five."

I can't... breathe...

"Four."

A slight patch of dampness—a single, slick spot—shifted under Aaron's heel, offsetting his precarious balance. It caused his leg to twist, his body to tip.

Horizontal—and face-down—he plummeted.

"No! *Miss Rivera!*"

Two nurses held Sancha back as she stood only a few feet from her mother—only a door standing between her and the embodiment of all her strength.

"Aaaahhh!" Sancha screeched—more animal than human—

before she stopped, pressing against the pair of women and freeing herself to pace the empty corridor.

"*Calm down,*" the older nurse warned without sympathy. "The doctor will—"

"Oh, the doctor, the *doctor*! None of them know what they're *doing*!" wailed Sancha, her eyes ablaze before tightly closing. "No one's *helping*. No one's doing *anything*!" She allowed herself to breathe. "She's all alone in there..."

She opened her eyes and found herself abandoned.

"*She's* not giving up! My mother doesn't *give up*!" she screamed at no one—and at the entire world.

THE DAMP AIR enveloped Aaron's body, like moist tentacles reaching for him. He slipped, weightless—for an eternity.

He heard nothing, saw nothing, *felt* nothing—until the approaching wall of water slammed against his body, stinging the surface of his skin, bruising his limbs, bending his back, swallowing him, filling his mouth, his nose.

The water permeated, penetrated, dragged his damaged child's body down, down—into the abyss.

"I'M LEAVING!" Sancha declared, glaring at anyone who would acknowledge her existence.

"That's not a good idea. The situation is very tentative right now," yet another uniformed doctor declared. "You should remain here at the hospital—in case—"

"No. No, I'm not going to listen to you—*any* of you—*anymore*!"

Sancha's outpour of emotion attracted the attention of a full waiting room. An infant nestled in its mother's arms burst into tears.

Sancha continued her tirade. "Not if you won't even let me *see* her! What does it *matter*... if I'm here or not, if she... *if she...*" Sancha fell silent, looked to the ceiling, blinding herself by the fluorescent bulbs. She wiped at her dripping nose, her wet cheeks.

Her tone declared undeniable determination. "I'm going to get my son. We—*all of us*—need to be *together*." Sancha ran to the elevator.

THE WATER'S grasp held Aaron's beaten body still, like a million hands—gentle but strong—holding him down with no intention of release.

His sinking slowed; he continued to inch deeper down, farther from the air all others breathed and he could not.

Dark obscurity surrounded him. His eyes clamped shut, rigid against his reality. His lungs ached beneath the pressure of the water, tensed, braced themselves for the action of intake they would force upon his declining consciousness.

So much.

Too late.

No... more.

SANCHA RACED the car down one street, then the next, sliding beneath yellow lights, tires screeching on the hot pavement. She needed her son; she needed family.

She felt it all seeping between her fingers like loose sand, fading away like a distant memory—an illegitimate dream.

In her anger, among the traffic of clueless strangers, Sancha was unashamedly, fiercely, ready to say *goodbye*—but only to one.

HIS LIPS PARTED, his mouth opened.

Aaron swallowed the water pressing at the back of this throat. His physical body still refused to unlock his airway, contending alone with the barrage of perilous fluid.

His mind held no concern at all.

He was ready—as ready as consciousness can ever be. He braced to release childhood—and life—altogether.

So alone.

He sunk.

He let go.

Aaron acquiesced.

And the bitter, burning water was finally welcomed and invited within.

SHE KNEW IT; she *felt* it happen. The wave of sensation was sudden, entire, like a knock at the door of her mind delivering the clearest message.

The tears came—in instant recognition, in solemn tribute.

Sancha pulled the car to the side of the road and rolled into a random parking lot in her daze. Her forehead fell to the steering wheel—her hands sealed to their positions, gripping with all remaining strength.

She cried like a child consumed with helplessness, bereft of any capacity for hope.

She cried like a woman, her body aching, wrenching with

mourning, weighted with the pain no one could have felt as completely before.

Mommy... her heart called, heard by none.

BAREFOOT BOYS in wet swim trunks chattered like bickering birds. Only a few amused themselves by watching the swirl of white water hovering over The Deep End where their classmate had plunged abruptly, awkwardly—humorously.

Mr. Michner glanced up from his clipboard. His whistle fell from his lips.

Before any witness had any rational reason to be alarmed, one small boy had already drowned.

PART IV

AWAKENING

Dum spiro, spero.

— WHILE I BREATHE, I HOPE.

1

SANCHA STARED THROUGH THE FILM OF HER OWN TEARS. WITH AN intake of breath, she blinked away the residual emotion and pushed the previous outpour out of her thoughts.

She restarted the car, yanked at the gear shift, and pulled back onto the busy street with devout fearlessness, refusing to first look in either direction for oncoming traffic, refusing to look in any direction—from that point forward—but *ahead*.

SWIM...

STILLNESS. Silence.
 Sedation.

SWIM, the voice urged again, strong and sure: a singular prompt surfacing from within, resounding head to toe and all at once.

Swim, came the whole-bodied message—rebellious, defiant, provoking every cell to action.

You know how, coaxed the identity locked in the child's mind. *Swim,* the voice commanded, offering no other option.

FINGERTIPS FLINCHED. An ankle jerked. The weight of the water lessened, allowed.

Body unfolded, straightened, then relaxed as it reinvigorated.

Limbs positioned themselves with purpose—solid, steady, muscles soft and sinewy.

Eyes flashed open with renewed brilliance, alert and unaffected by the sodden environment.

The voice moved into the muscles, fueling cells, energizing form, encompassing identity. As body conformed, the voice configured. As physical form flowed, the voice consumed the whole.

Other became I—once again.

AND AARON SWAM—UPWARD, toward the now-visible light—with the elegance of effortlessness, the grace of experience, the smooth strokes of serenity.

SANCHA PARKED THE FAMILY CAR, her hands still clenching the steering wheel as she breathed in the stillness. She closed her eyes to the world around her, to the dark shadows and the blazing shards of undesired sunlight.

She moved like a machine—one joint, then the next, in automatic rhythm—until she'd crossed the parking lot outside the community center where her son attended swim lessons.

As she reached the entrance, she was oblivious of others, taking no notice of a stranger holding the door for her. Numb to all, she strode across the floor, down hallways, past people she would never know.

And she walked into—unknowing, incapable of comprehending—the scene of her child's transformation.

POISED at the edge of the pool, Mr. Michner leaned over the languid depth. His own fear reached every child in his care. Their whispers changed to worries, suggestions of the darkest possibilities. They watched him toss aside his clipboard and pull his t-shirt over his head in one deft movement, his arms forming a church spire before him, his knees bending to deliver instant propulsion.

Aaron broke through the surface of the water, his face pointing toward the glass ceiling high above the pool. Water poured over the top of his brighter, almost-white hair. His arms rested along the sides of his linear figure as his masterful kicks propelled him upward.

He soared high above the surface of the pool, nearly completely free of the depths that previously held him captive and complacent.

His body fell again, fluidly. He buoyed as if born of the water, at home within it, floating free of fear. He flipped in form and swam—with uncanny ease and sure speed—the full length of the pool.

SANCHA ENTERED THE POOL ENCLOSURE, continuing her slow, steady steps. Before she forced herself to raise her head and search for the face of her son, a flash of light flowing over the pool's surface caught her attention.

She followed the sight of the small body with the almost-white hair as it glided through the water and to the near end of the pool. She stopped.

Sancha recognized the gleaming, wet face of her own child. She surprised herself by smiling beneath her bloodshot eyes. His skill—and serene spirit—dominated the environment.

Aaron wiped his eyes of water and opened them to his mother.

She stepped back, then forward again; she stumbled at the sight. As those eyes flashed open, she was struck—by their astonishing, crystalline irises, with their utter *otherworldliness.*

"Hello," Aaron said through a brilliant, bold smile.

It was the sound of *that* voice that trapped Sancha's own words. The tone was familiar, from far within her memories. The greeting rattled with impact, as if shared for the very first time—or for the first time in a long, long while.

MR. MICHNER RUSHED to the edge of the pool to hover over Sancha and Aaron. He opened his mouth, then snapped it closed again. He glared, wide-eyed—first at his student, then at the woman who held him.

The other children huddled together at the far end of the pool, their young minds struggling to comprehend the spectacular sight they witnessed.

Without a word spoken, Sancha lifted Aaron from the pool and guided him toward the stack of towels near the exit. She wrapped one around her son and led him through the doorway.

SANCHA FASTENED her seatbelt and started the car. Beside her, Aaron stared straight ahead, his demeanor completely relaxed. The new brilliance of his eyes shone even more vibrant in the late afternoon sunlight as they glazed over with the softness of daydreaming.

Sancha gained strength in the presence of her son. She focused ahead, on the route they took together every day: the same dismal path leading from the community center to the hospital where Maria's form lay.

Sancha's intuition declared—screamed—that this would be the final day.

As THE CAR rolled through the final intersections before reaching the hospital, Aaron disturbed the silence.

"Where is Maria?" he asked.

Sancha caught her foot before she leaned too heavily on the brake pedal. "You know where. She's still... but she's—"

"Where is she?" Aaron repeated, his voice soft and gentle.

"She's... your grandmom's..." Sancha's throat tightened around the words. "At the hospital."

She lost control of her tears, of the emotions bottled behind her detached expression. "Do you mean..." she blurted, her voice wavering under the threat of replenishing tears. "Do you feel... can you tell that your grandmom—that she's *gone*?"

"Has something happened to her?"

The gravity of the moment—of the entire afternoon—overwhelmed Sancha, her sudden confusion so close to transforming into heartbreak.

When they reached the hospital, she felt a moment of relief

as she pulled into a parking space and turned off the ignition. The relief only lasted for an instant.

She realized the full implication of her son's richer, more sophisticated speech. She finally heard, through the haze of her mourning, every nuance of Aaron's demeanor—its essence unveiled.

"Take me to her," was her son's request—his command.

WHEN SANCHA REACHED the nurse's station in the ICU, she was beyond any ability to hold back her tears.

She clung to the tangible elation of regaining a long-lost friend; more than a friend, he was her son. Aaron stood at her side—whole and complete. His calmness helped subdue her growing sense of loss.

"I don't know where else to go. I just want to see her," Sancha whimpered at the desk nurse, beneath the onslaught of tears, between gasps for air.

"I'm sorry?" the nurse asked without emotion. Then, she caught the sight of Aaron's *luminance*. Her complacency fell away; her attention honed.

"My mother," Sancha gasped. "She was here, but I know she's..."

"I'm sorry, you're going to have to be a bit more clear. I don't have the time to—which patient are you looking for?"

"Maria Rivera," Aaron spoke with arresting clarity.

The nurse stood on her tiptoes, leaning over the counter for a full view of the owner of the small, yet startlingly substantial, voice. Rolling back on her heels again, she tapped on the computer keyboard. "Same room," she said, "22B."

"Oh. I thought they would've taken her somewhere else."

Sancha sought Aaron's reaction. "Thank you," she muttered to the nurse before turning away.

The nurse continued to stare after the pair as they solemnly walked down the corridor, hand in hand.

SANCHA STARED at the small placard reading "22B." She didn't trust herself to look at the latch on the door itself. She peered down the corridor, expecting a nurse's consolatory gaze or a doctor's reprimand.

All sound faded away, retreating into the distance before vanishing in complete silence. The air felt hot, humid; it stuck to Sancha's skin, holding her back.

Aaron pulled on her hand and reached for the door handle.

Maria's body lay as it always had: conformed to the narrow bed, barred by the cold metal rails preventing her from returning to her home as her former vibrant self. Now, her form was straighter, more artificial, suspiciously poised. And her face was perversely pale, her skin like limestone permanently set around her closed eyes.

Sancha supported herself against the door frame. Only Aaron continued to approach his grandmother's place of rest.

At her bedside, he reached for Maria's hand lying at her side. He placed his smaller hand over hers—his smooth, flawless skin in stark contrast: the vibrancy of life confronting life's absence.

Aaron's expression shifted; he looked to his mother. Sancha's feet compelled her forward to stand next to her son and cover both hands with her own.

Maria's lips moved. A whimper escaped.

Sancha jumped backward, both her hands covering her mouth. Aaron remained in place, his expression unchanged.

Dr. Haversham entered; a momentary flash of emotion

revealed his surprise at discovering the visitors. "She's stable now," he said. "But not responsive. May I talk to you outside, Miss Rivera?"

Sancha's voice failed her. The sound of the heart rate monitor flooded her ears, jarring her senses—prompted by the doctor's sudden appearance. She cried invisible tears.

"Miss Rivera, there is something you should be made aware of—if we can speak in private?"

Sancha looked at Aaron; he seemed to listen intently to his grandmother's beleaguered breathing. "Aaron, I'll just be a moment."

Aaron shook his head—as a directive.

Sancha awaited the meaning of his negative response. He beckoned her to his side, gesturing with his free hand while still gripping his grandmother's.

"Miss Rivera," Dr. Haversham interrupted, adding extra volume for authority. "We should really discuss—you're going to have to face—"

Ignoring him, Sancha returned to Aaron and joined him in peering down at the woman they both felt more love and admiration for—now—than ever before.

WHAT HAPPENED? inwardly asked the man inside the child's body, only recently returned himself. *Where have you gone?*

My Maria...

Aaron sensed her presence: weak but near, fading but lingering. He leaned closer to her ear, not knowing—but feeling—his message would be received.

"*Omnia vincit amor,*" he whispered for her only. "*Aut viam inveniam aut faciam.*" From a place deep within—a place of absolute knowing—he repeated his promise: "Love conquers *all.* I will either find a way... or make one."

He stood tall again and shut his eyes, closing himself off to all surrounding him. For the first time—since years past, years detached from, years departed—Aaron let go.

He opened—to all within him. In a relentless, unforgiving assault of images and experiences, he saw, felt—was savaged by —*all* that he had ever known or lived before.

"AARON!"

Sancha caught him as he collapsed beside her, his soft body crumpling over her extended arms.

"Aaron... Aaron!"

His fragile frame shook—gently, precisely—as if experiencing the wildest adventure deep in sleep. His eyes rolled side to side beneath his closed lids.

"What... what's happening!" Sancha demanded. Dr. Haversham responded, shouting into the corridor for assistance before running to Aaron's aid. "Just hold him as well as you can," he instructed calmly.

As soon as the words sounded, Aaron's eyes opened again. Only seconds had passed.

His body was still, unharmed. He looked to the doctor, then Sancha, and wrestled himself free of their arms. His attention returned to Maria; the doctor's and Sancha's attention followed. All three observed the single teardrop emerge from Maria's closed eye and glide down her sullen cheek.

Aaron tugged on Sancha's pant leg. She leaned down to him, following his direction. He whispered to her as Dr. Haversham attempted to explain to the arriving nurses what he'd just witnessed.

"I..." Sancha spoke quietly in reply to Aaron. "All kinds of things. Do you really..."

Aaron's unblinking gaze answered her question.

"Stomach stuff," Sancha whispered first. "She even lost her appetite. And, well, it was like the flu—or a cold—and then... coughing."

Sancha stood straight gazed, gazed toward a blank wall, and focused on her memories as she tried to block out the conversation between the nurses and doctor. "Weird breathing," she whispered to Aaron, his expression unchanging as her own reflected the return of her fears. "I thought she was *choking* one night—I swear it sounded like that—and then... she had a stroke. She's been in the hospital ever since. The doctor says her lungs are terrible. She's got those spots on her skin and—"

Aaron motioned for his mother to bend toward him again. He whispered in her ear.

Sancha stood again, hesitated, then spoke over the in-room chatter. "Doctor," Sancha interrupted, "Um... can we—can I—see the..." She straightened her posture and finished her request. "I want to look at the lab results."

Dr. Haversham flinched, then scowled. "I don't see—"

One of the nurses elbowed him. "Give her the file."

"It's not *classified,*" the second nurse chimed in, rolling her eyes.

Both nurses smiled, enjoying the doctor's frustration.

"Here." He dropped the overfilled folder from under his arm and shoved it in Sancha's hands.

Sancha sat in the chair at Maria's bedside and flipped through the pages while Aaron peered over her lap. He nudged her gently; she turned the pages faster. He leaned to whisper to her.

This time, Sancha looked to her mother's pallid face and then, to the watching medical staff. "There's—in the file—ee-oh-sin-o..."

"Eosinophilia," Dr. Haversham pronounced for her through his smirk.

"Extravascular," one of the nurses added, waiting for Sancha's next comment and welcoming the diversion from their regular duties.

Aaron whispered to his mother.

"Neuro..." Sancha started.

"Neuropathy," the second nurse assumed. "Yes, *polyneuropathy.*"

"I'm sorry." Dr. Haversham stepped forward, gesturing for the return of the file. "I don't have time for this. Miss Rivera, if you have any... *questions*—or concerns—the nurses will be happy to—"

"Let her talk," the first nurse said, then turned her attention to Sancha again. "What else?"

Sancha leaned her ear toward Aaron, then relayed, "The pulmonary..."

"Yes, pulmonary infiltrates," the nurse finished for Sancha.

Sancha passed on her son's words once more. "Abnormal... her sinuses?"

"Abnormality of the paranasal sinuses!" the second nurse blurted with enthusiasm, smiling like a newly declared prize winner.

The doctor threw his hands at his hips. The nurses focused on Sancha, enjoying the game. Sancha looked to Aaron for his next question but found him focused on the nurses.

"Is that it?" the second nurse asked playfully.

"No," the first nurse spoke with sudden sobriety. "That's four out of the six."

The second nurse struggled for comprehension.

Dr. Haversham reached the limit of his patience. "All right, you've had your fun. I'm afraid I'm needed—"

Blocking his exit, the first nurse glared at him and repeated, "*Four* out of the *six*."

The second nurse's eyes widened with revelation.

"Extravascular eosinophilia," the first nurse listed. "Non-fixed pulmonary infiltrates. Polyneuropathy. *Abnormality of the paranasal sinuses.*" Pausing for the doctor's response and receiving none, she continued, "Four out of the six conditions for identifying—"

"Churg-Strauss syndrome!" the second nurse shouted, propelling herself onto the tips of her toes.

Sancha squeezed Aaron's arm as her focus darted between the staff members. She waited, as did the nurses, for the doctor's response.

Dr. Haversham gathered himself, projecting disinterest bordering on hostility. "*Most* cases of Churg-Strauss follow a history of asthma." He almost smiled as he continued. "And there's no record of the patient ever being diagnosed. In fact, the family practitioner has no record of it either."

He pushed past the nurses and stood before Sancha. He held out his hand for Maria's file.

"My mother," Sancha spoke with maturity, "*had* asthma—when she was a little girl. She told me—once, when I was little, and they thought I might have it. She *used* to have asthma."

Only the bustle outside in the corridor resonated through the room. The doctor spoke, flipping through the file Sancha released to him. He blinked the evidence of his own embar-rassment.

"I'll order a biopsy," he managed before forced to clear his throat. "Of the pulmonary tissue," he directed at the nurses.

"Yes, you will," the first nurse spoke at the doctor's back as he left the room. "Don't you worry," she said to Sancha, leaning to place a hand on her shoulder. "Your mother's going to be all right."

Sancha, mouth agape, looked to Maria—to the body so devoid of life. Her own lips began to quiver. She reached for Aaron and buried her tears on his shoulder.

2

HOME AGAIN, AT LAST. AARON STOOD ALONE IN THE CENTER OF THE living room—feeling, breathing in the space, noting the emptiness of Maria's absence.

Now and again, Sancha paused in her blur of enthusiastic busyness to glance at him. Her questions remained unasked. Curiosity could not compel her to risk upsetting the feeling of relief she enjoyed for the moment.

AFTER THE DINNER Sancha almost forgot to prepare, she and Aaron remained at the kitchen table, both casting a sideways glance at Maria's empty chair.

"She could be home soon," Sancha said, convincing herself as she spooned her macaroni and cheese in a neat mound on her plate.

Aaron smiled with his nod.

"I can't believe—" Sancha said before yielding to embarrassment.

Though she couldn't name it, what she felt—now while at

home alone with Aaron—was intimidation. She'd aged through the ordeal of her mother's failing health, but she felt younger than her own son.

She glanced at Aaron again, noticed the precision with which he lifted the fork to his mouth, his athlete's posture—*that* hair, *those* eyes.

"Sancha," he said, startling her from her impromptu trance.

"Mm-hmm."

"You may ask me... anything you like."

She stared at him as he continued to eat. "I don't really have..." she tried.

"It's all right." His voice was an adult's—more *aged* than Sancha had ever heard spoken, by anyone.

She smoothed her paper napkin over her lap. "You were... *gone*—weren't you?"

He carefully laid his fork across his empty plate. "Yes."

"Did you... did you *want* to go—away from us?"

"No," he answered immediately.

"Well, then, why—"

"I don't know." He met her gaze as she finally raised her head. "I don't know. I don't know what happened."

He focused on the specks of blue dotting the Formica tabletop while Sancha watched with patience.

"Perhaps," he continued, "it was a means of—for my own protection or... because I could not..." He had no answers.

Sancha nodded, despite her lack of understanding. "Did you come back for Maria?" Her own formality surprised her. "Your grandmom?" she corrected.

"I did not know... what happened to—" He struggled for the right words, for any way to define even one aspect of his experience. "*Part* of myself... was not even aware... of the part that was left behind."

A flood of new questions circled Sancha's mind like a

whirlpool feeding from a bottomless body of water. She felt she was supposed to ask more questions, probe deeper—that Aaron even wanted her to—but she didn't dare.

She couldn't bring herself to face more alone. She needed her mother—in strength and presence.

THE SUMMER EVENING's chorus of chirping crickets extended the day's dream-like quality. Sweet, humid air enveloped the house, pouring through the open windows, wrapping itself around Sancha and Aaron as they sat together on the couch, nested in its sinking cushions.

Sancha urged her heavy eyelids open in protest to the inner call to sleep. She welcomed the distraction of the television, keeping her worries—her questions—at bay. Even Aaron seemed contented by the flashing images onscreen.

When he leaned his head against her shoulder, she didn't move. She began to feel securely herself again, to feel like a mother again. When he curled his small body against hers, resting his head on her lap, she wrapped her arms around him —the same arms around the same child she felt so connected to so many years ago.

WHEN THE DAY's onslaught of adrenaline finally subsided, Sancha nudged her sleeping son and led him up the stairs to his room. She treasured tucking the bedcovers around him, the way her mother did for her. She savored the smile he gave her beneath his clear blue eyes as she wished him goodnight.

As she left his bedroom, leaving the door ajar, Aaron called to her, his eyelids still closed.

"Would you turn the light off, please?"

Sancha hesitated, tempted to reconfirm his wishes. She walked across the room again and pulled the cord beneath the lamp on his nightstand. He whispered a thank-you as he drifted to sleep.

Aaron slept through the night—never waking, never disturbed by attacking images or vivid scenes waging battle in his mind.

3

"I HAVEN'T SLEPT LIKE THAT IN... NEVER!" SANCHA MOANED through a long stretch and a series of yawns when she found Aaron sitting alone in the living room. "And you," she continued, "no bad dreams?"

She was flashed an expression of wide-eyed ignorance.

"You mean," she said as she plopped herself beside him on the couch, "you didn't wake up in the night?"

Aaron shook his head.

Sancha rolled her lower lip between her teeth. "Do you remember them?"

"I'm sorry, I don't know..."

"All the *nightmares*."

His forehead wrinkled. "Did I have nightmares?"

"Every night."

He considered the information, then looked across the room and through the window to the back yard. "May we go to Maria?"

"Of course! As soon as I get dressed... and we get some breakfast. I already told them I'm not working today."

She hopped up with a smile, scooting in her slippers to the kitchen.

"Oh," she mumbled aloud to herself. "There's some messages on the machine." She pressed the play button on the answering machine.

"Miss Rivera," a familiar female voice sounded from the recording, "we called your work number but were told you wouldn't be there today. We want to confirm that you'll be coming to the hospital this morning. Your mother... please let us know if you'll be coming in." The nurse finished her message with a rushed, "Thank you."

Sancha ran to the living room. Aaron still stared across the room and out the window.

"We're going *now*," she said.

THE ATMOSPHERE in the ICU felt different to Sancha: clearer, more room to breathe. It was the odd behavior of the nursing staff that left her on edge.

"She's not here," one nurse said in a flat tone.

Sancha held Aaron's hand, her nonexhaustive anxiety returning. "I don't understand."

"She's been moved," another nurse added, offering a smile. "I'll walk with you."

"What... is it?" Sancha called out as she and Aaron tried to match the nurse's pace down the corridor.

"You'll see," the nurse replied, staring blankly at the doors opening for the arriving elevator.

THE ROOM WAS awash with morning sunlight; the air smelled

clean, alive. Maria rested beneath crisp bed sheets, her eyes closed. Sancha skirted around the nurse and rushed to her mother's side. Aaron stayed at the foot of the bed.

"Go ahead," spoke the nurse, remaining near the closed door. "You can speak to her. She's awake—just resting."

"Mom. Mother..." Sancha called gently. She looked to Aaron, then at the nurse. The nurse gestured for her to try again. "Mom?" She placed her hand on her mother's arm.

A deep, unhampered breath signaled Maria's waking. Sancha's eyes grew wide; her mouth dropped open. Tears formed in her eyes for the thousandth time in several months.

She watched her mother's eyelids flutter open, revealing the welcome sight of her warm, brown eyes. They glimmered with renewed life. And they smiled at Sancha.

"My dearest," Maria said.

Sancha released her tears, folded herself over her mother's bed, and pressed her face against her chest.

"Shh... there, there," Maria comforted. "It's okay."

"We were right," the nurse spoke. "Your mother has been diagnosed: Churg-Strauss syndrome. We began treatment overnight. She's going to recover quickly. Her body's already responding to the prednisone."

Sancha reluctantly released her mother. She stared at the nurse, waiting for more reassurance.

"I don't know how you..." the nurse pondered. "She's going to be *okay*."

Maria cast a sidelong glance at her daughter. Sancha slowly shook her head, then nodded toward Aaron. Maria set her eyes on her grandson for the first time in several weeks.

"Oh, my..." she said, against her usual ability to restrain spontaneous emotion. "You—it must be my eyes—you look so *different*."

Aaron's blue eyes seemed to shimmer a brighter hue despite his face remaining expressionless.

"Come here," Maria said, stretching her smile larger as she patted the bedcovers at her side.

The nurse moved to open the door. "I'll leave you three alone. Take it easy on her," she directed to Sancha before leaving.

"My beautiful grandson," Maria said, taking his hand in both of hers. "Your eyes, they're so..."

He blinked, curling his fingers inside his grandmother's folded hands.

"I dreamed of you," she said to him. "I dreamed that you told me everything would be all right." She turned to Sancha. "Is it true?" she asked. "That you had something to do with—"

Sancha shook her head. "It was Aaron. He... all I did was ask his questions for him. And the doctor, the nurses—well, they... it was like they could finally see what was going on, what was wrong with you."

Maria studied her daughter and grandson, perplexed by their unrevealing faces—and by the subtle impression of a subtle glow surrounding Aaron and his near-white hair.

"I will not leave you again," he spoke, causing both women to quickly turn to him. "Not in that manner."

Maria began to cry. The tears fell uncontrollably, as if it was her grandson who'd been in danger and slipping out of their grasp all those years.

4

———

"Careful now, Mom. Just watch your step." Sancha attempted to support Maria's full weight as they approached the cement steps leading to the front porch, arm in arm.

Aaron held the front door open, standing taller than his grandmother remembered him being just months before.

"I'm perfectly fine!" Maria attempted to convince her daughter. "I can walk—or they wouldn't have let me go."

"Well, just... well, *fine.*" Sancha stepped aside, still eyeing her mother's every step.

Maria's stride was slow and tentative, but sturdy. She was almost a vision of her former self. Aaron smiled at her as she walked past.

She stepped inside the walls of her own home, savoring every detail—dust and dirt and memories alike. Her voice wavered as she spoke, "I almost can't believe... I'm *home.*" She opened her arms to her grandson and daughter. "Oh, I love you both so much. Thank you. Thank you for *everything.*"

Sancha eventually pulled herself from her mother's arms. "You're going to have to stop saying that—at some point."

"Never," Maria promised. "Now, what should we do first?"

"Shouldn't you rest?" Sancha asked, almost insisting.

"*No.*" Maria chuckled. "That's all I've done for... way too long."

She left her grandson's hug and walked through to the living room, the others following. She peered through the screen door to the garden that sprung to life in her absence. It resembled a jungle—flowers and bushes untamed and wild—but still a rewarding sight for her return.

She opened the screen door and breathed deeply, closing her eyes to the direct sun lighting her face. "Mmm... let's have a picnic!"

A wide, childlike smile spread across Sancha's face, memories of favorite childhood moments dancing in her head. Aaron stumbled backward, his sudden movement catching her attention.

"Aaron," Sancha said, directing her words to Maria, "doesn't like it out there—anymore. Remember?"

Maria turned around, letting the screen door snap shut with a loud metal clap. "I forgot."

His apology appeared on his face, preserved by his silence. Maria lowered herself into the upholstered armchair near him.

"Come here," she called softly, patting the arm of her chair. Her voice was gentle, nurturing. "I think... it's time for *you*," she continued, patting his chest, "to teach *us*."

Aaron's gaze locked with his grandmother's. He waited for the questions he'd known would come one day—questions he expected but could never be fully prepared for.

SANCHA FOLDED her legs beneath her, fitting her slender frame into the corner of the couch across the room from Maria and

Aaron. She watched them as a child watching adults, trying to uncover the perpetual mystery of their minds and intentions.

Aaron sat on the arm of Maria's chair, his shorts-bared legs resting over her lap at her encouragement. She studied his face as she tried to determine her next words.

Then, she spoke in her special tone developed just for him: a motherly resonance with an added aspect of high respect.

"You..." she said—slowly, purposefully, "are—" She broke eye contact, glanced at her lap, then looked up at her grandson once again. "*You* must be here for some very special reason."

Aaron studied his grandmother's face, inspecting her thoughts.

She continued, "I don't expect you to know what that reason is. You *are*... just a child—our child—but... you're *more*." She took his hand in hers. "Aren't you?"

Sancha's stare was unbreakable, locked onto the moment as her own mind emptied, waiting to be refilled with things she was sure she couldn't possibly understand.

Aaron nodded. Maria waited for more.

"You weren't with us—for a while—were you?" she asked. As he shook his head, she continued. "Do you know why?"

He shook his head again.

"Did we... do something to make—"

Aaron shook his head vigorously. "I—part of me..." His small forehead wrinkled. "I am *here*," he said—with finality. "This... is *me*—now."

The statement discomforted Maria in a way she couldn't name. She nodded at her grandson, accepting his words. "Stay with us," she said. "I think... we need you."

Aaron waited, the silence only interrupted by the occasional chatter of songbirds flitting among the trees outside. Maria wiped her mind of emotion again, composing herself with full breaths.

"Where do your words come from?" she asked.

Aaron looked deep into the dark eyes staring back at him. He found them clear, compassionate, vulnerable.

"You speak," Maria prompted him, "*beautifully*, but... you don't just recite the words you've read, do you? You *know* them —somehow—from...?"

Aaron didn't answer, but he spotted the tears welling in her eyes.

"Your words saved me," she said. "Where did they come from?"

Even Sancha recognized her mother's question as one demanding an answer. Aaron's pupils grew as he reflected inward.

"From before," he said. "When I learned them—*before*."

His explanation—on the surface—was devoid of meaning. Yet, Maria was shocked by her whole-body response, by her own sense of self—her views, the limits of her imagination—being inexplicably combated by a *child's* simple words.

Aaron observed the inner struggle raging within his grandmother's eyes. He wanted to help her, to reach for her in some way, to pull her out of it. Instead, he knew—without doubt— that the woman sitting before him, buried in her own beliefs, had to navigate her own way.

She glanced around the room, searching for her own feelings, desperate for some iota of understanding. She wriggled uncomfortably in her seat.

"The pictures," she said suddenly, staring at the coffee table in the center of the room. "Your drawings. Where do *they* come from?"

He followed her gaze. Sancha picked up one of the pieces of paper torn from a notebook and offered it to him, then returned to the security of the couch.

Aaron held the page in his hands and surveyed the fine

details of the scene: the tiny figures and events, the story fully bared in simple lines, curves, and penciled shades—the scene undeniably historical, *centuries* old.

"They are... my memories," he answered, still peering at the paper.

Maria's brow tightened; her eyes squinted at the boy sitting across her lap who spoke impossible things.

"Who *are* you?" she demanded, her body shrinking away from him.

AARON'S HEART BEAT FASTER, crying out against his circumstances, threatening to bore a hole right through his child's chest. His skin burned with the same anger, endangering the connection between himself and those he loved.

He *heard* Maria's feelings, the full force of her targeted accusations—no matter how vague within her own consciousness.

For every answer he had to give, he had his own questions that remained unanswerable.

I am myself, resonated his thoughts. *I am Tres. I am here.*

With those declarations—those absolute truths—he knew nothing more. No whys, no hows. He only *was*.

And he was left wanting.

Forced to conform—to mold himself around how the world approached and behaved toward him—he most desired acceptance. If *they* accepted him, he could begin to accept himself: he, the immeasurable whorl of eons of earthly existence. He could proceed. He could finally focus forward. *Forward* held discovery—now unfathomable but unquestionably inevitable.

Outwardly, Aaron stared into the eyes of the woman who could not help but fear him as she reactively recoiled from the anomalous boy before her. Inwardly, he addressed his deepest desire, his deepest pain.

I am myself, echoed from the recesses of his mind, growing louder, more insistent.

Know me, he pleaded with Maria and with his mother—*this* mother—and with the world.

AARON SLID from the arm of the chair, separating himself. He stood before Maria and Sancha, presenting himself to this grandmother and this mother, his hands folded before him.

As naturally as a diplomat, he silently conveyed his mutual respect and assured alliance. He granted the highest emissarial offering.

"I am... *Tres.*"

Never before spoken, the name bubbled inside the flesh, filling it out, connecting body with self, sealing form to essence —his immense age reflecting in his eyes.

And he relaxed, slipping into himself, fitting all the creases and folds—for the first time in *this* lifetime.

SANCHA'S VOICE came as a surprise. "Do you want us to call you that?" she asked, smoothly extending a gift.

He turned to her and smiled; Maria remained tightly closed, unaware of her strained grip on the arms of her chair.

"I like it," Sancha said, her smile replying to his. "I knew you had a name."

Maria's lips parted as she heard the exchange and considered the meaning revealed. She recognized the reemergence of the bond her daughter and grandson shared. And she felt, with calming certainty, that it was true and inviolable.

"*Tres,*" escaped her, demanding their full attention.

She met her grandson's gaze. "It," caught in her throat before emerging more clearly, "sounds right... somehow."

She thrust her arms in front of her. "Come here," she exclaimed, just as she'd called from her hospital bed upon waking to the sight of her glittering-eyed savior.

He ran into her arms.

"You're my *grandson*," she whispered into his ear above her strong embrace. "That's all that will ever really matter."

He melded with the security wrapped around him. He felt his mother's arms enfold him as well. The family of three confirmed their pact—the unspoken promise made long before.

5

_____

"Maybe we should take him out of school," Maria considered aloud one evening during dinner preparations.

Sancha hovered over the kitchen table, silverware in hand. "What do you mean? What'll he do instead?"

"We'd have to homeschool him. But who knows what that involves for a child that knows—for _Aaron_."

"I don't know... it's just, well, everything's so _confusing_."

Maria smiled. "So is raising any child."

"I will continue to go to school," Aaron answered for them as he stepped into the kitchen.

Maria spun around. "I'm sorry. I... I forget sometimes—that you're not a child."

"I am _meant_ to be," he said, smiling.

Maria distracted herself, speaking over her own thoughts before her mind could indulge in its newest habit of poring through dozens of extended meanings for her grandson's words.

"You have to be a part of..." she thought aloud, nodding to herself. "_This_ is your life."

Aaron nodded.

"I'm glad," Sancha said, returning to her task and dropping

the silverware on the table unceremoniously. "I can't imagine any of this... being any other way. Not now."

She continued to work her way around the table, setting knives and spoons over folded paper napkins. Maria prodded at the browning ground beef, pushing it around the iron skillet on the stovetop.

Aaron watched them carry out the activities of daily life, his mind drifting to the possibilities for continuing discovery tucked into everyday, ordinary events—of *his* life, the life he was selected for—or which had selected him.

6

─────

As the summer days continued to shorten, Aaron reveled in the trappings of childhood, teaching himself to balance his impatience for adulthood with the necessity of being young —again.

He trained himself to honor the carefree aspect—the freedom—of youth, alongside the expanded truth of all that he knew himself to be.

Aaron played ambassador to himself, bridging the different needs and directions of his life with those of his *lives*.

─────

On an afternoon particularly golden-hued with sunlight, Aaron sat under the shade of the front porch with a lengthy novel. He was lost in the story, caught up in the retelling of an ancient adventure tale, when a neon-pink bicycle zoomed past, racing along the sidewalk.

Aaron ignored it, never looking up from his book—until the fifth time the bike swept by. He raised his head and followed the pink haze moving across his line of sight. The bicycle stopped; a plump, short, ruddy-haired boy slid off the bicycle—without subtlety.

"Hey!" he yelled at Aaron.

Aaron only stared as the boy made his way up the front steps and right onto the porch.

"It's a girl's bike," the boy said, brushing his too-long bangs out of his eyes. "My sister's. I'm too big for mine. My dad said I'll get a new one for my birthday."

Aaron continued his silent study of the stranger, and the boy continued to talk without any prompting or encouragement.

"I'm looking for friends," the boy continued. "I just moved in." He held out his hand to shake Aaron's. "I'm seven. You look like you might be seven too."

Aaron took the boy's hand in his and nodded.

"I just moved in," the boy said. "Down there—where that man's washing the car. That's my dad. What are you reading?" He moved to tiptoes and peered into Aaron's lap.

Aaron closed the book, holding his place with his hand tucked between the pages. "The Odyssey," he said.

"That's... a *college* book, isn't it? Or maybe a high school one. It's on the shelf at home. I haven't read it. Dad said it would be boring to me. Is it?"

Aaron shook his head, and shook loose a smile.

"You don't seem only seven," the boy said.

"Nor do you," were Aaron's first words to him.

"That's because my dad's an engineer. And my mom's a nurse." The answer seemed well-practiced, prepared ahead. "They're really smart. They never talked to me and my sister like babies." He looked to the clouds for his next thought. "My name's Bennett."

Aaron offered his own name in return—the name for *this* life, now comfortable and secure like a warm blanket.

"Okay," Bennett said with a curt nod—then, "Is your hair *white*?"

Aaron shrugged.

"That's cool," Bennett said.

Aaron realized he liked Bennett—a great deal—even before Bennett asked, "You wanna be friends?"

"If Bennett's talking your ear off, son, you just ask him to please slow down that little computer in his head to a regular, *human* mode of operation. That's what his mother and I do." Bennett's father chuckled loudly, tugging his checkered shirt collar straight with a subconscious flick of his thumb and forefinger. His hand returned to the steering wheel, and he swiftly turned the car to the left as Bennett and Aaron swayed right in unison in the back seat.

Bennett's enthusiasm converted to a full-face pout. He pretended to find something interesting outside the window next to Aaron. Aaron flashed a forgiving smile at his new friend.

"And you, Aaron..." Bennett's father raised his voice to ensure it reached his captive backseat audience. "You don't like to talk much, do you, son?"

As expected, Aaron answered with silence.

"That's the sign of a high-caliber intellect," Bennett's father continued, raising his chin to smile widely at the rearview mirror. "You two are going to be the best of friends—I know it," he said, winking at the mirror.

A smile spread across Bennett's face as his father added, "And I'm absolutely elated to have the company of *two* exceptional young men to see the new movie with—not Bennett's mother's cup of tea *at all*."

"Thank you for inviting me... sir," Aaron said.

"Please call me Jim," Bennett's father returned with gusto. "We're *all* friends now! All we need is a team name..."

"Dad! That's dorky," Bennett whined.

"No such thing!" Jim declared, tweaking his shirt collar again.

7

———

"ALL READY?" A FROWN TUGGED ON THE CORNERS OF SANCHA'S mouth as she wriggled beneath her own anxiety.

Aaron nodded, calm as ever.

"Mom!" Sancha yelled at the doorway. "Are you ready?"

"Don't shout," Maria answered as she joined them in the kitchen. She directed a smile at Aaron. "Here we go," she said, clasping her hands together to punctuate the occasion.

Sancha—already at the front door, her hand poised to reach for the knob—jumped back when the doorbell rang. She looked to Maria and Aaron before opening the door to find Bennett waiting with noble patience—and a little red bowtie beneath his round chin.

"I came to ask if Aaron wanted to ride to school with me— and my dad. He's the one driving. My dad, I mean."

Sancha's usual smile appeared, wedging itself between her pink cheeks as she turned to Aaron. He stepped around her and leaned to whisper in Bennett's ear.

"Oh, I understand," Bennett answered, then looked up at Sancha. "I hope you have a nice drive as a family."

Aaron smiled his approval, matched Bennett's wave, and

headed for the family car in the drive. Maria and Sancha followed close behind.

"He sure is weird," Sancha mumbled once Bennett was out of sight.

"He has a good heart," Aaron said.

Maria nodded her agreement.

STUDENTS and extraneous family members inundated Langston Hughes Elementary on the first day of the new school year. As planned, Aaron found Bennett waiting at the school entrance.

"My old school was bigger than this one," Bennett said, observing the crowd huddled into family units.

"Aaron," Maria said as she walked up with Sancha. "Do you want us to go in with you?"

"No," he answered. "Thank you."

"You're good parents," Bennett interrupted. "I mean... mom and grandma. My dad would say so—and he doesn't like many people. I mean, *approve* of them." He almost tripped over the word—despite his best efforts—but his expression didn't admit to it.

"Okay, then," Sancha said, giggling.

"Thank you, Bennett," Maria said. "That's very kind of you."

"Well, it's true. My dad says you should always pay a compliment when a compliment is due," said Bennett, still studying the swathe of strangers surrounding him.

"Well, we better go," Sancha declared. She planted a kiss on the top of Aaron's bright head, and Maria did the same. Aaron watched them wade through the crowd and find the way back to the school parking lot.

"I'm glad we're in the same class," Bennett said. He pulled on the straps of his backpack and kicked at the tile floor with the toes of his shoes.

Aaron patted Bennett's shoulder and led the way into the entrance hall. Bennett followed, down corridor after corridor and into their assigned classroom.

"Aaron!" came a shout from somewhere within the rows of desks.

Aaron searched the room until he was flagged by a waving arm. Finlay—grown yet taller and more handsome over summer break—signaled to an empty desk beside him. "I saved you a seat!"

Aaron navigated his way down the aisle. "I'm sitting with Bennett today."

Finlay looked at the short boy in the collared shirt and snap-on bowtie. "Who's Bennett?"

"Bennett is my friend," Aaron answered.

"And what happened to your hair!" Finlay stared at Aaron's head, then realized his silence. "Cat got your tongue?" He chuckled to himself before his smile disappeared. "You seem... different."

"So do you," Aaron said—an observation he hadn't intended to make aloud.

Finlay opened his mouth to speak before confusion buried his thoughts. He watched Aaron continue his path down the aisle with Bennett trailing behind.

As they settled into their new desks on the opposite side of the classroom, Bennett launched his questions. "Who's that?"

"Finlay."

"He seems friendly."

"He is, but he's—" Aaron glanced across the rows of desks; Finlay turned away. "He's changing."

"What do you mean?"

"It's difficult to explain."

"Well, you can sit with him if you want. I don't mind."

"No, I'll stay here." Aaron lined up his pencils on his desktop and turned his attention to Finlay again, observing his every movement.

AARON ABSORBED every activity around him, filing away the teacher's words and connotations, every habit and interest of his fellow classmates. Even as he enjoyed the education he'd been so eager for, the bustling environment affected him as never before. Every incident was intense, unavoidable stimulation forcing Aaron to push back every rising memory of *former* childhoods, former teachers, former challenges.

As classroom activity grew more innocuous, Aaron's memory wandered. His daydreams drifted to all former *dreams*. The relentless rhythm of inundating voices, gestures—the subtlest nuances—triggered waves of overpowering memory rising and falling, leaving Aaron gasping for air.

He struggled, as inconspicuously as possible, every minute of the slowly progressing morning. He fought for sound mind, for a single *self* to cling to.

"AARON," Bennett whispered across the aisle during the teacher's speech about her expectations for the school year. "Are you okay?"

"Headache," Aaron answered as he massaged his temples with his fingertips.

"What are you doing?"

"Trying to make it go away."

"Does that work?"

"Sometimes."

"You know all kinds of stuff, don't you?"

"Bennett!" yelled the teacher. "Quiet, please," she suggested calmly once she'd secured his attention.

When she announced recess and directed the students outside, Bennett gently tugged at Aaron. "Come on. Get some fresh air," he said.

Aaron relented and followed Bennett to the playground.

"You should go to the nurse," Bennett suggested when they reached the largest swing set.

"She can't help me."

"Sure she can. She'll have aspirin. Or something." Bennett sat in the swing next to Aaron and started to swing his legs. "Maybe it's a *him*. I guess it could be a male nurse. Is it?"

"I don't know."

"Hey!" Finlay's shout rattled Aaron's headache. "Hey, Aaron!" He closed the distance between them and stood in front of Aaron's swing.

"Why didn't you want to sit with me?"

"Bennett wanted to sit with me."

"But... I'm your friend, too."

Aaron didn't respond. Bennett slowed his swinging.

Finlay squinted at them both, then leaned toward Aaron. "Do you still want to be my friend?"

"He just," Bennett intervened, "has a headache."

Finlay's focus remained on Aaron.

"I'm sorry," Aaron offered, despite the pain of his compounding headache. "I don't feel well."

Finlay's face broke out in patches of pink; his hands formed fists at his sides. "You're not being very nice. What happened to you? Your hair's *white*, and I *know* your eyes are different. And you sound *strange*—not smart, if you're trying to. So, stop pretending!"

Bennett looked on, tempted to get off his swing to intervene but waiting for a signal from Aaron.

"I am very *sorry*," Aaron said, his honesty obvious to all.

"*I'm* your best friend!" Finlay stamped his complaint into the ground with his foot, then stomped toward a group of children collected by the jungle gym.

Bennett and Aaron sat in silence, watching their classmate disappear into the crowd at the other end of the playground.

"You were right," Bennett said. "I don't think he's very friendly anymore."

As AARON WORKED to focus only on the teacher's words in the afternoon, he was also Finlay's sole focus.

"He's looking at you again," Bennett whispered, leaning across the aisle.

Aaron continued to massage his temples, to press away the burning sensation just beneath the skin. Pressure ratcheted inside his skull; vibrant images burst in his mind from every direction. He closed his eyes in defense, blocking none of it.

Every child's whisper around him raced circles around the teacher's droning voice. The intensity of Finlay's stare cavorted with the faces of enemies past, fading in and out, in and out—pressing, pressing, pounding.

Aaron's inner voice cried out as he winced at the onslaught of imagery. His heart raced, pumping with adrenaline, rising in his chest, tangling his breath.

I... can... not. "I can't!"

"Can't *what,* Aaron? You can't what?" The teacher's demand was sudden, reaching into Aaron's consciousness and yanking him back to the surface of his awareness. He opened his eyes—and found all eyes in the classroom were set on him.

"Just calm down," the teacher continued, her own tone more tender than he first realized. "Try to catch your breath. Just *slow* down."

Bennett wriggled in his seat and in his helplessness, confused by all the differences in his friend's demeanor appearing in just one day.

And Finlay smiled as he watched.

"Breathe in," the gray-haired school nurse pleaded, holding a respirator to Aaron's mouth. "Just breathe *in*!"

He closed his eyes against his surroundings, tried to focus on his breathing, tried to slow himself—*all of his selves.*

"That's good, that's good," she approved. "Now, I want you to do it yourself. Open your eyes, honey. Just press this button— see? Open your eyes, honey. Press here, and then, just breathe in. Okay?"

Aaron opened his mouth to speak, but his short breath failed to fuel his words. He refused to open his eyes, even as they began to water.

"*Breathe.* Please, honey. You'll be all better then. You just need to catch your breath."

Aaron gasped for air.

"Breathe!" the nurse begged.

"I called his mother," a younger female voice called, following the sound of a door opening behind them. "She's on her way."

"Good, good," the nurse replied. "She can tell us what's going on," the nurse replied.

"It's not in his record," said the younger voice.

"I know, I know. These parents—someone needs to make sure they fill out the medical forms in *full*." Her momentary anger was immediately replaced with a motherly tone again. "*Breathe,* honey. That's it. Good."

WHEN SANCHA ARRIVED at the school nurse's office, she ran to Aaron before the assistant could point in his direction.

"Aaron! What happened? How are you? How are you feeling?" She knelt before him, smoothing his near-white hair, holding up his small chin to draw his line of sight to hers. She waited for him to take a few deep breaths.

"I am..." he breathed, "It's all right now."

"Well, what *happened*?" Sancha nearly yelled.

Aaron looked toward the nurse watching them from the corner of the room. "I'll be at my desk," she said, walking away promptly.

Sancha repeated her question.

"It's..." Aaron tried. "All the..."

"Tell me! Oh, baby." She wrapped her arms around him and nearly squeezed the breath out of his small chest again. "I was so worried! You've always been fine," she said with a heavy smile. "You're supposed to be the one that's always fine."

He shook his head. "Everything just... it was too much—for me. I don't..."

"What is it? The teacher? The other students? Didn't you get to be with Bennett all day?"

Aaron nodded. "Everything just... came in."

"What? Like... the nightmares?"

He shrugged, then nodded. "Everything inside." He pointed at his head. "All at once."

"Aaron, baby, look at me. Look at Mom." She held his face between her hands. "Whatever's in there—in your mind—it's not *here*. It's just in *there*. You have to just... control it somehow."

"I can't. I've tried. I've *always* tried."

"Look at me." Sancha's voice grew louder. "You're... you're something *special*—so different. I've seen you do all *kinds* of things a kid shouldn't be able to, and... and you're *not* a kid. I mean, Aaron, I *know* you can control all that stuff inside when you need to."

"I don't know how."

"You have to find a way. There must be one. And I know you can figure it out." She spoke softly, pleading with rare self-assurance. "You can't live with... all of that. It's too much—for anyone. You have to focus on what's happening *right now*. Aaron, look at me."

He lifted his eyes to meet his mother's. He looked deep into her eyes, wishing he could crawl into them, escape, feel their clarity.

His breathing slowed yet more. The brightest-blue irises of his eyes reflected specks of her emerald green. He saw the eyes that greeted him as a newborn: the first eyes that his met in this new life, the eyes that promised safety and security, the eyes that shouted *meaning*.

"Everything will be all right," Sancha said, plucking the words from Aaron's own thoughts. "See? You're feeling better already, aren't you?"

He nodded, breaking the connection but still left with its reassurance.

"Now, let's go home."

"WHAT DO you mean he couldn't—*asthma*? She thinks he has asthma?" Maria unpacked her large purse she'd plopped on the kitchen table and continued to dig for the empty Tupperware container from her packed lunch. "He doesn't have asthma," she said once she'd found it. "We would've realized it before."

"Well, he doesn't go out—not really," Sancha said, never lifting her chin from its perch on her arm stretched over the table. "He could be... allergic or something—*to* something."

"Nonsense. He's always been a healthy child."

"I know, but the nurse said he was hyper..."

"Ventilating?"

Sancha nodded. "He couldn't *breathe,* Mom!"

"All right. We'll take him to see Dr. Phillips. He's overdue for his checkup anyway."

The worry lines already sprawled across Sancha's forehead raised in astonishment.

"Oh, don't worry." Maria huffed. "I've been—I don't know how I missed the last appointment, but he's fine. He's always been fine. You..." Maria crossed her arms. "You coddle him too much."

"*What*?" Sancha jerked upright, yanking her arm off the table. "What do you—you've never said anything like that before." Sancha studied her mother, tried to pinpoint the source of the uncommon affront.

"I just think maybe we've been indulging him too much."

"What do you mean?"

"It might not be right for him—for *us*—to entertain his silly—"

"What—his silly *what,* Mom? Aaron is *different. You* know that! He *saved your life!* Did you forget that already?"

"Sancha—calm down. He'll *hear* you. It's easy to get carried away, to think that certain things are possible when they can't really—"

"*You weren't there*. You were, but you weren't." Sancha's head fell into the palms of her hands, her face buried behind her cascading hair.

"I know. I'm sorry. I'm just... trying to do what's right for us—all of us. I don't know what happened at the hospital that day, but what if... what if I wasn't supposed to—"

"To *live*? You think he wasn't supposed to *save* your life?" Sancha's chair shot out from under her as she stood in one quick movement, glaring at her mother. "What's gotten into you?"

"Sancha!" Maria glared at her, rage sparking in her eyes.

"It's not like you," Sancha spoke carefully. "*This* isn't like you. You *believe* in things. You *knew* Aaron was... something *more* —even before I did."

Maria nodded. She wanted to reach for her daughter, hold her tight, reassure her, but she couldn't order herself to move. "I don't know what I believe," she said quietly.

Sancha stomped out of the kitchen, mumbling about not being hungry for dinner. As Maria's opportunity to impress her own suggestions upon her daughter left, so did her own rising desire to *cause* her daughter heartbreak.

AARON STOOD JUST outside the dining entrance to the kitchen, unseen by his mother or grandmother—exactly where he'd been stopped by an overwhelming sense of fear, as if stepping into a dark fog heavy with foreboding.

He observed the entire conversation, including the striking contradictions in his grandmother's behavior. Her words, posture—her overpowering, uprising emotions—did not stem from love. They were rooted in hostility.

WHEN THE DOORBELL rang a second time, Maria jogged out of the kitchen. "Sancha, honey," she called up the staircase, "could you please get it? My hands are covered in dough."

A door slammed upstairs, and Sancha's stomping followed. "Fine!" she yelled as she passed the doorway to the kitchen and yanked open the front door.

"Hi, Bennett!" she sang, springing back to cheerfulness.

"Hi, Miss Rivera," Bennett greeted. "I just—"

"Sancha—please. You make me sound *old*." Sancha scrunched her face to prove her point.

"Oh, sorry. My dad says a young man should always... never mind. Thanks. Um, I just wanted to see if Aaron is all right?"

"He is, and that's very nice of you. Want to go up and see him? He's in his room."

"Okay. Thanks." Bennett stepped just inside the door and promptly removed his sneakers. After aligning them at the edge of the rug, he padded up the stairs.

"HELLO THERE," Bennett said, standing in the doorway to Aaron's room.

"Hello," Aaron answered from his seat at the foot of his bed. "You may come in," he added when he realized it was necessary.

"Thanks." Bennett tiptoed across the room. "Were you doing something?"

"No."

"It looked like you were... staring at something."

"No. Just thinking."

"Oh." Bennett looked around the room. "I just wondered how you are—after everything."

Aaron smiled. "I'm fine. Thank you."

"Did the nurse know why you got the big headache?"

Aaron shook his head, then stopped, looking deep into his friend's eyes. "I do."

"You do? Why?" When Aaron didn't answer, he asked, "But you're okay now, right?"

Aaron's eyes darkened as he slowly nodded.

"No, you're not."

Aaron blinked, breaking his stare.

"You always tell the truth," Bennett said with a rise of his shoulders. "I can tell when you don't."

"You can?"

Bennett smiled. "Yep."

"What if... I can't tell you *some things*?"

"Why can't you?"

"It's... too much."

"I'm no dummy."

Aaron couldn't contain his own smile.

Bennett sat down next to him—without asking permission first. "What's on your mind?"

Aaron's smile dropped with his gaze. He took a deep breath as he stared at his feet dangling off the bed. "I don't know how to describe it."

"Something at school?"

Aaron shook his head. "Here. At home. Downstairs."

"Your mom or—"

Aaron shook his head again. "By myself. It was... I couldn't *breathe*."

"Like at school today?"

"No—more. I couldn't breathe *at all*, as if... I was suffocating —*suffocated*."

"What..." Bennett shivered and wrapped his arms around himself. "What do you mean?"

"It was *bad*, something very bad—in this house, in the kitchen—with Sancha and Maria."

"Who was it?"

"No, not someone—some *thing*. A feeling... I guess. A very

bad feeling. I didn't see anything. I didn't go in—into the kitchen —I couldn't. I didn't want to." Aaron started shaking his head. "I didn't want to."

Bennett's eyes lit up. "Like a... a ghost or something?"

"No. Just... *wrongness*. Something very, very bad—directed at *me*."

"At you?"

Aaron nodded.

"Well, did it go away?" Bennett asked. "You didn't see anything? What do you think it—"

"It happened before."

WHEN MARIA HEARD the screen door at the back of the house snap closed, she nearly jumped out of her house slippers. She didn't first notice the creak of the heavy wooden door—or the footsteps of the two boys.

She froze in place, listening. When she heard Bennett's voice, she reached for the rolling pin and continued coaxing the pizza dough into a smooth, elastic circle over the countertop.

"SHOW ME," Bennett urged, his hands hiding in his shorts pockets.

"I don't *go* out there." Aaron stared into the expanse of the back yard, its boundaries stretching farther than he remembered.

"You're here now." Bennett kicked at the lawn beneath their feet.

"I haven't been—since... the *one* time."

"Where did you see it? You can just point, if you want." Bennett shielded his eyes from the sun, scouting the back yard.

Aaron raised his arm and pointed to the left side of the yard, where only the tangled branches of a blackberry bush grew.

"There? Next to the fence?"

Aaron nodded. "Only Maria knows."

"Did she see it?"

"She... didn't say. It was a man—*male*. I remember sensing that."

Bennett wriggled against the sensation of goose bumps rising over his upper body. "I thought... you said you didn't know what it was."

"That time, I did know."

"Is it—is he—there now?"

Aaron shook his head. "No." Then, he added, "I think—I feel —I *would* know, if he was."

Bennett nodded. "What do you think *he* was?"

Aaron stared into the darkest corners of the garden, then slowly shook his head. "Nothing I have ever encountered before —so long as I have lived."

Bennett turned to face his friend, his child's intuition and his trust in Aaron confirming the truth—and depth—of the answer offered.

8

———

"LEAVE HIM ALONE!" BENNETT'S SHOUT RANG OUT TO EVERY student standing in the hallway as the school day ended.

Finlay's new, wicked smile beamed like a bad omen. "Too bad you can't play with the rest of us anymore. I would've beaten you at *any* sport—at all!"

The words rocketed toward Aaron. He fumbled with his prescription respirator, pressing the container with both hands as he tried to breathe in but only gasped in short, embarrassing bursts.

"Just ignore him!" Bennett urged Aaron. "Do you need anything? Water or something?"

Aaron shook his head frantically as Bennett took his arm and guided him toward the boys' restroom across the hall.

"Yeah, just *hide* in the bathroom!" Finlay screamed as they left his view. "Suck on your *baby* medicine!"

As the door closed behind them, Aaron threw his respirator across the floor toward the urinals.

"Why'd you do that?" Bennett chased after it and returned to Aaron's side, respirator in hand. "It's kind of dirty now," he said, wiping it off with his t-shirt. "I don't think this thing works anyway." He abandoned his attempts to make the respirator hygienic. "Hey," he tried instead, putting his hands on Aaron's shoulders. "You got to... to *calm down*. Finlay's just *stupid*. I don't know why he doesn't like you. You're..."

Aaron gasped for air as Bennett's voice faded behind the curtain of gray now clouding his vision. He stared up at the ceiling, searching for stillness, for answers.

BREATHE, Aaron begged of himself. *Breathe!*

The moments passed in slow motion. Aaron's oxygen-deprived brain communicated consolation to itself, imagining satiating, long breaths. And it recalled *memories* of breaths, of having too little—or too much. Memories co-mingled with now-moments, consorting together, conspiring against him.

Too much. Too many. I cannot...

"AARON... AARON!" boomed the voice of *this* boyhood friend—barely audible, filtering through from the existence Aaron hadn't yet mastered, *may never master.*

A GIGGLE CREPT into his thoughts—his own—bouncing inside his head wall to wall. No—a *cackle.*

Never before—not this.

Agony. Can't control... my own... thoughts.

Can't contain...

Selves.

They threw themselves at him, berated him, teased and taunted. The memories terrorized—with the heft of their characteristics, with the richness of their detail, with their meaning.

And they had no place—not in this life—and no purpose, none that Aaron, in all his wisdom, could decipher.

"AARON, *BREATHE*. PLEASE!" Bennett's voice, muffled by lapsing awareness, slipped into his consciousness.

AARON CLOSED his eyes *within* his eyes.

The images still wafted across the black screen of his mind like full-color ghosts—of him and him, and her, and them and they... then, *those:* the eyes of his mother, *this* mother, the mother representing all the urgency, the latest battle, the current fight for survival. They shone brilliantly green, intense and piercing, maintaining their front-of-mind position, locking in his full attention.

Look at me, they spoke to him in her voice. *Breathe, Aaron. You can. You can block it all... out.*

Hhhhhhhhuuuuuuuhhhhhhhhhhhh, he breathed—long and slow and sweet.

And *they* were gone—all of them, all others. Only he was left —clear, open, free.

"I MUST FIGHT," Aaron spoke aloud, in his own strong and steady voice fueled by adequate air.

"What?" Bennett stared at him, still resting his hands on his shoulders, afraid to let go. "*Fight?*"

"To *be* here. I can't allow it... to do... whatever it is—"

"Who? Aaron, what are you talking about?"

"*Him*—the wrong one."

"What does that—"

"I have to go." Aaron pulled from Bennett's reach. "I have to *be* there!"

"Aaron!" Bennett called after him. "Where?"

AARON RAN past Sancha's waiting arms and into the school parking lot, searching for the family car.

"Aaron! What are you..." As Sancha caught up to him, she grabbed his shoulders, turning him to face her. "Aaron, what in the world's got—"

"We have to go home."

"Well, where do you think we're going?" she laughed.

"*Now*."

Sancha's smile fell away. "Aaron, what is it? Were you... did you get sick again? Did you remember your respirator?"

"Yes. No. It's not that." He jerked a meaningless gesture. "She *needs* me."

"Who? Your grandmom?"

Aaron's bright hair flashed in the sunlight as he nodded rapidly.

"She's in the car," Sancha said. "She's fine. She just wanted to close her eyes for a bit."

He spotted the family car—and his grandmother's face wistfully looking through the windshield at them. His whole body loosened. He caught his breath and warmed to Sancha's touch. She gave him the hug he'd run past moments before.

"Do you want to tell me what's going on?" she asked.

Aaron shook his head and walked to the car at a quick pace, only able to relax completely once he verified his grandmother seemed very much like *herself*.

WHEN THE FAMILY arrived home together, Aaron sensed no danger. Nothing was out of place; he sensed no unwanted visitors present.

Still, the clarity and truth of his sudden sense of danger remained, undiminished.

9

Bennett tagged along behind Aaron on their way to class, eager to catch up after missing a week for a family vacation. "Have you... seen it? Did it ever—"

"No," Aaron answered.

"Good." Bennett withheld his own doubts, changing the subject. "Was the test hard?"

Aaron paused outside the classroom door, the slightest glimpse of a smile on his face as he shook his head.

"Of course not," Bennett said. "Everything's easy for you."

Aaron chose not to argue the assumption and proceeded to lead the way to their desks.

"Maybe she'll make up a different one just for me," Bennett worried aloud. "Maybe it'll be harder." His frown slowly faded as he unpacked his backpack and slid into his seat. "What about Finlay? Anything happen while I was gone?"

Aaron proceeded to doodle in his notebook without looking up. "He has a new friend."

"Is it that kid he's talking to right now?"

Aaron answered without diverting his attention from his drawing. "Mm-hmm."

"Good. He probably won't bother *you* anymore then."

―――――――――

At recess, Bennett and Aaron claimed their usual spots on the swings at the perimeter of the playground. Bennett watched the game of tee-ball that their classmates started up nearby.

"You should join them," Aaron said.

"Nah." Bennett started to swing his legs. "I like hanging out with you."

They both glanced over in time to watch a girl repeatedly miss the hollow ball atop the waist-high tee, swinging the plastic bat as if shooing away a large insect headed for her face. Her turn at bat ended, earning ridicule from Finlay and his new friend even though they stood on the same team.

"Do you think," Bennett said, seeking distraction from the bullying antics, "you'll be allowed to play sports again soon?"

Aaron shrugged.

"My mom says asthma—"

"I don't have asthma."

"What?" Bennett slowed his swinging.

"They just assume that I do."

"Who? The doctor?"

"All of them."

"Well, how do you know?"

Aaron looked up at him.

Bennett nodded, "Yeah, you know a lot of stuff." He kicked at the sand beneath the swing set. "Why do you have to use the respirator?"

"They think it helps. Sometimes, it does."

"But you can't breathe—sometimes—so, if you don't have asthma—"

Bennett and Aaron noticed the group of boys walking

toward them as the tee-ball game ended, their other classmates trailing off to make the best use of the remaining time left for recess. As the group grew closer, they realized Finlay led the pack.

"Hey, *Aaron*..." he whined as he approached. "I have a *new* best friend."

The group of five boys stopped as Finlay did, all eyes on Aaron and Bennett. Aaron scanned the group, his expression unchanged—until his gaze met that of the older-looking boy to Finlay's left.

"He's *nine*," Finlay bragged.

"Well, if he's in our grade, then that just means—" Bennett blurted before Aaron shot him a warning look.

"And he doesn't like you *either*," Finlay added.

The new boy said nothing, nor did he flinch to confirm or disconfirm Finlay's claim—but Aaron slowly slid off his swing, encouraging Bennett to follow.

"You look weird," the boy said from a toothy smile.

Bennett looked to Aaron, then back at the new boy. Finlay remained in place, but his new friend took the slightest step forward.

The boy's arm appeared from behind his back. He started to playfully swing the tee-ball bat uncomfortably close to Aaron and Bennett.

"Hey, you shouldn't—" Bennett stuttered, stepping back.

"What?" the boy accused, his voice shockingly deep. "What are *you* gonna do about it?"

"What is it that you *want*?" Aaron asked Finlay.

Finlay shrugged. His friend lifted the bat, pretending to take aim at Bennett.

BLOOD POURED over Aaron's vision—invisible to all others.

Manic scenes—red-stained scenes—strobed in his mind. Each one inflicted profuse pain, the exact pain he'd felt—internal or external—when he *lived* them.

Screams. A lover's cry. Flashes of feeling: menace, helplessness, danger.

And Aaron began to drown—in them, among them, falling into them.

Can't breathe.

"Oh, no," came Bennett's voice, muffled as if transferred through water. "Aaron," it sounded again. "What do we do?"

Not now! Aaron cried out to himself as the sense of impending threat fell onto him like a great weight, crushing his breath all the more.

I... am... here. This time.

Sancha's face—her love-filled eyes—appeared to him, within him—instantly soothing, calming the very cells of his struggling lungs.

This *time,* he repeated.

This... time.

And his lungs filled with air once again.

Aaron opened his eyes to the enormous sense of calm. Then, he felt Bennett's hand squeeze his arm, began to feel the pain of the desperate grip.

Aaron didn't turn to his friend; he faced his enemy. Standing taller, he extended an invite. "Would you like to race?"

The older boy started to laugh, his arm naturally relaxing and lowering the bat. The rest of their gang laughed with him.

"Who? Me?" the boy asked, amused. "Aren't you *sick*—or something?"

"Not you," Aaron answered him, his eyes unblinking, his stare as steady and self-assured as any adult's. "You," he said, looking into Finlay's eyes.

"Me? You wanna race *me*? I've never seen you run in your life!"

"I will win," Aaron said, every muscle in his body perfectly controlled.

The entire group laughed at him—Finlay most of all. "You have asthma! You're not even *allowed* to run," he said.

"He'll probably fall over *dead*," the older boy said, causing Bennett new concern.

"Do you want to race? Or *not*?" Aaron asked—demanding an answer.

"Fine," Finlay answered, "but if something happens to you, it's not *my* fault."

IN THE LAST minutes remaining of recess, most of the children gathered to watch the race sure to be the most entertaining spectacle of the school year: the small, sickly boy matched against the tall, thin, popular boy.

When Finlay knelt down in a racing stance, a lump formed in Bennett's throat, conflicting with the confidence he had in Aaron's cleverness and general good sense of self-preservation. And his worry grew even more as the older boy started counting down to the start, and Aaron's body posture gave no hint of the slightest ability to run.

"Two..." the boy continued. "One... go!"

Finlay jettisoned from his footing, kicking up a divot of grass in his wake, while Aaron began to jog with the smoothest stride any child had ever had. The two began their single lap around the large perimeter of the playground—Finlay leaps and bounds ahead of Aaron.

Then, Aaron leaned into the air around him—cutting through it, joining with it—and he steadily gained on his opponent.

"He cheated!" the older boy yelled to the audience crowded around.

"No, he *didn't,*" claimed a short girl in glasses, bravely. "Finlay started first."

The students watched as the one they largely ignored—the small, quiet boy—seemed to float over the ground, gliding around the playground equipment in effortless sweeps until he was even with his competitor.

None of the students noticed Finlay's leg stretch to the side ever-so-slightly—the quick maneuver well out of others' view—but every student witnessed Aaron's dramatic fall.

Aaron swooned onto the hard ground like a legless body, chest first. Then, his arms stretched over the ground around him and lifted his body up to standing again. Aaron's small form shot forward, flying over the grass-covered field once more.

Aaron pushed away the force of thought. He focused on *feeling* only.

He felt the ground beneath him connect with the soles of his feet, his shoes and socks rendered superfluous. He joined with the earth, coupled with the air; every muscle in his body was fluidly controlled and perfectly synchronized with every other.

He remembered—through sensation alone. His memories became application; all nonessential information fell away. Memory served necessity—immediate, active, inexhaustible, all-flowing.

Aaron raced, as he had millions of times before, for thousands of varied reasons. He raced for singular purpose and infinite purpose. He raced to become himself; he raced into himself.

In that moment, anyone looking on could view the flashes of all of himself, all of the one they called Aaron, fully bared and wholly revealed—but only if they were perceptive enough, *receptive* enough—capable of believing such possibility.

Aaron's second overtake of Finlay was observed by all. And so was his wide circle around the last turn as he reached the crowd—and the finish line.

Finlay also watched his former friend fly around him with ease, leaving no room for foul play and no way to recover his loss.

Aaron swooped into the crowd of students, his near-white halo of hair swirling around him, his small legs pulsing with energy, the muscles feeding on the opportunity to utilize all their capability.

Leaps behind, Finlay finally reached the finish line himself. Not a single student acknowledged his arrival.

All awe focused on Aaron, the one who quietly walked away with his friend following.

Finlay's exhausted body dripped with sweat and disbelief. When he left the scene at the sound of the bell, he was followed by the first jeers his classmates specifically created to target *him*.

"Your teacher was very concerned," Maria scolded.

"But look at him!" Sancha yelled, half in excitement. "He's perfectly fine!"

Maria glared at her grandson. "Well, at least we have a backup respirator here, maybe two. And I want you to *use* it. Do you understand?" Bending over him, she peered into his eyes and squeezed his shoulders. Focused only on instilling her wishes, she wasn't prepared for his answer.

"I'm not going to get sick like you did."

Delivered calmly and matter-of-factly, the statement stung both women, yanking at painful memories. Yet, the claim rang true to Maria, inexplicably.

"Did you really run all around the playground today?" she asked.

"You know that I can run," Aaron answered.

And Maria remembered. She remembered the toddler who once ran freely—fluidly—over and around the back garden.

"But you..." she wanted to argue, even as she was already aware of the resistance building in her grandson. "The doctor said... you have to be *careful*."

"I do not have asthma."

"You... don't have asthma?" Maria repeated.

Aaron shook his head, and his grandmother believed him.

"We didn't ask *him*," Sancha said, unaware of the maturity of her own deduction. "And he's the smart one." She flashed her characteristic, brilliant smile.

Maria's face remained tight with worry. "But when you have trouble breathing—"

"Not anymore," Aaron answered.

Both women reacted physically, their expressions twisting with their conflicting thoughts.

"Are you sure?" Sancha asked.

Aaron nodded—and gently slid a little bit more into himself.

10

"Everyone in school knows," Bennett whispered to Aaron across the aisle, "that Finlay Richter actually *lost* at something. He doesn't even look at you now. Did you notice?"

"He looks," Aaron answered, doodling away at his desk while the teacher cleared her throat to greet her students before roll call.

Bennett turned around quickly and caught Finlay looking away. "Well, he doesn't look so mean anymore—more like... he's afraid of you."

Aaron looked up from his drawing and toward Finlay's desk. Finlay chatted to a classmate, oblivious to having the full attention of the one who held his own the most.

As Aaron opened his mouth to speak to Bennett, a shiver snaked its way down his spine.

The cringe was instantaneous, enveloping his entire body: a sensory presence residing all around him, all at once. His breath halted. He waited—for information, for explanation.

All perception homed in on the sudden arrival of *another*.

The class—every student—was left undisturbed. Only Bennett detected the change in Aaron.

"What is it?" he asked, studying Aaron's odd expression and posture, as if he was stuck in a peculiar moment, unable to free himself. "Hey. Aaron..."

Aaron's ears registered no external sound, his total awareness dedicated to the *other,* to the arrival.

He felt a distinctly foreign presence looming—close and consistent, radiating. It resonated; it *urged*. It made itself known with delicately increasing temperature and subtle electric energy.

It emanated a warning. It thrust forth an outright attack of intimidation.

"It's *here,*" Aaron whispered in a strange voice.

Their classmates remained oblivious, but Bennett's heart raced as his mind translated his friend's words.

"Behind me," Aaron said, refusing to face it himself.

Bennett turned left, then right, peering into the empty space around them. "I don't..." he said, his voice shaking. "There's nothing there." He faced Aaron again. "What are you gonna do?"

There was nothing Aaron *could* do—as he felt the presence growing nearer, its expansive existence making Aaron feel vulnerable, breakable, in his child's body. The presence weighed on him, over him—threatening him, *taunting* him.

As Aaron sat at his desk, he willed his own neck to subtly twist, his head to turn, his eyes to see.

It stood there.

At the back of the classroom, invisible to all others, it presented himself. It wore the face of dominating ill will—a face fashioned from a multitude of masculine faces, all borrowed from Aaron's own memories.

The intent was clear, while the manifestation's own identity remained disguised.

And then, it was gone.

"All right, everyone," the teacher called out. "Quiet please."

Aaron's gaze fell to his desk, to his drawing. He finally released the breath he held.

"Is it gone?" Bennett asked.

Aaron nodded—in answer to Bennett's question and his own. Bennett realized he hovered above his own seat, holding himself over it, prepared for escape. He sat down again, his eyes still fixed on Aaron.

IT DOES NOT COME *for them,* Aaron realized, pronouncing the fact to himself.

It seeks me.

And now, it's found me.

"I DON'T KNOW ANYTHING!" Aaron screamed at Bennett in the privacy of his bedroom.

Bennett stumbled away from the outburst.

"So many *questions.*" Aaron seethed through clenched teeth and hands hiding his face.

"I'm sorry," Bennett said in his smallest voice.

"Not you—*everything.*"

"Maybe... maybe you should tell your mom—or your grandmother."

Aaron's hands dropped, revealing the expression of a weary adult. "No, I can't."

"But they're *adults.* They might be able to... or maybe they know—"

Aaron shook his head; a sarcastic grin appeared. "Not this, Bennett—I know."

"*You* know what it is?"

"No, I don't *know! They* don't know!"

"All right. Okay. But... what are *you* gonna do?"

"Wait for him. He'll return. I know it."

11

SOONER THAN EXPECTED—AND SO SUBTLE THAT IT WAS ALMOST missed completely—a sensation distracted Aaron as he read alone in his room one evening. He detected the nearness of something—something *other*.

It was suddenly with him.

It resided at the perimeter of his vision—without being an actual *sight*. It—someone—watched. And it felt masculine—just as before. And yet, no memory—no previous experience nor facet of ageless knowledge—offered Aaron the ability to label *this* occurrence.

One fact struck Aaron with such force and immediacy that it was a slap across his consciousness. *This* one meant him no harm. This visitation—just beyond his view, occupying an indeterminate space behind him—wasn't of the same. It was not the one he waited for.

In that moment, Aaron experienced the same sensation: of presence. He did not feel the same sense of *intention*.

Aaron shivered. His back and shoulders curved into a hunch; his body curled itself away. His mind switched from all focus on *one* to recognizing a *newer one*. The possibility panicked him.

He cowered, as if he could hide behind his current life, wishing he'd never been seen.

There are more.

And this one was *familiar*. This one was *frequent*—from as far back as *this* birth.

Locked in memories of this life, tidily tucked outside of Aaron's everyday awareness and consideration, were the recorded moments of when he had been watched—many, many times, *continuously*.

He remembered all the times he'd sensed its presence, all the times he turned his head to face it, to find it, to know it.

Aaron wanted to turn now. He wasn't afraid. *Why,* resonated within him, thrumming from his core.

Why?

The question swelled in his mind, pushing at the inner surface of his skull. It *demanded,* almost with impetus of its own.

And *questioning* was returned.

It was not echoed in words; there was no sound, not even a feeling. There was only an impression, a vibration.

In reply to Aaron's internal question, *questioning* resounded back at him—from *outside* him.

His body relaxed—only slightly—as rising curiosity dominated his trepidation. He tested the exchange again.

Why? Aaron pushed outward, screaming in silence.

Questioning returned again—instantly. And, again, it wasn't his own.

Aaron lifted his chest and shoulders and straightened his posture, offering strength and support to his body as well as his mentality. Then, he turned.

A familiar face met his—one from this life, never in lives before. It was expressionless, translucent—a figure, tall and still. It emitted neutrality, remained non-reactive.

It—*he*—didn't disappear. He didn't offer any indication that he resided within another's perception, no suggestion that *he* was aware that he was *seen.*

He only watched.

Why? Aaron asked once more, still within the confines of his own consciousness.

The figure remained still—inhumanly inert. And *questioning* hit Aaron's awareness with even more precision—as if his own perception naturally tuned into another mode of communication, detecting and homing in on its precise frequency.

Aaron perceived no emotion, no motivation. He detected no sign of intellect.

Sitting on his bed, facing the presence before him, Aaron felt no fear, no hesitancy.

What are you? he asked in the same silent, focused manner, expecting no response.

OnLooker, the visitor answered.

PART V

UNFOLDING

Abyssus abyssum invocat.

— DEEP CALLS TO DEEP.

1

FEI'S FORM DISPERSED, SLIPPING FROM TEMPORAL *CORPOREALITY* and re-establishing himself wholly within the greater *Apart*. He withdrew from his task as smoothly as he'd transported himself into it.

His articulation had been routine by any account—until he made the grave error of communicating with his ObServed.

The ObServed hears!

Fei was still alight with his excitement. A momentous alteration of the conditions of his chosen role had spontaneously occurred. His very relationship with his ObServed was inexorably altered.

He refocused his attention on absorbing the calming solitude of his created sensory environment. He concentrated on his perception of the phasing, pulsing, white-intentioned boundaries surrounding his form; they wavered under the translation of his inner sight. He allowed himself to sense the serenity that his choice—of their radiating color and perceived texture —provided him.

His next duty reigned obvious. He must inform the Consultation.

Connecting with the Consultation required no process or hierarchy. Merely his intention was necessary to bring any information or request to the attention of the deliberating committee of the Apart. And this intention, Fei found himself withholding.

His necessary action determined, he need only select the appropriate moment. On *this* choice, Fei hesitated. For this choice, he did not feel prepared.

As OnLooker, Fei had defied the simplest—and most sacred —of the guiding principles of The Natural Order of Things. He'd *intervened* in his ObServed's corporeal life—albeit unintentionally.

Fei desired, least of all, to *upset* The Natural Order of Things. Most of all, he bemoaned being the *first* to do so.

IN HIS OWN self-created environment within the Apart, *another* awaited his moment. His entire form filled with desire, seethed with enthusiasm, and teemed with tremendous impatience. His time had come—would come—*soon*.

His one goal—his crowning achievement—would be his and his alone. Rising on his just dues, withstanding all as he must, he was ready—beyond ready. His plans were well at hand.

He allowed self-righteousness to consume him, to permeate his every atom. His form glowed bright in a red-orange hue of vibrancy best suiting the ruling sensation he was most enamored with in the moment.

Soon—so very soon, he permeated with all his energy.

FEI TRAVELED down the passageway lined with entrances to individual, idea-encased environments created by others within the

Apart. His path led him down corridors and past entryways manifested with various degrees of experience and design: all alluring results of others' experiments and creative play.

Fei thoroughly enjoyed the examples on display and accepted them as inspiration for his own ventures in the manipulation of and creation of matter. And he permitted himself the distraction—the procrastination.

He withheld *the* moment: the moment of necessary notification to the Consultation of his own adventitious communication with his ObServed.

In Fei's perception—within the reality of the Apart—there was no delay, hardly any hesitation. One moment simply became the next: each, in turn, presiding as *this* moment, the only moment to actually exist.

For Fei's ObServed, nine years passed within his corporeality's concept of *time*.

2

"Ooh, what's that?" Sancha asked, leering over her son's broad shoulders as soon as she walked into his bedroom.

Sixteen-year-old Aaron stared at the shape shaded in heavy layers of charcoal on a sheet ripped from his drawing pad. "Nothing," he said, before remembering his mother wouldn't accept such an unsatisfying answer. "Just... an apparition."

"Ooh, like a ghost!" she squealed, standing on her toes in her flip-flops. "They creep me out."

"I know." A wide smile broke across Aaron's face.

"Is that for art class?" Sancha peered over him and into the depths of the drawing again. "Isn't that like... the others—the things you draw most of the time?"

"Yeah. Pretty much."

"Why's your head so filled with *ghosts* then?" she teased, ruffling the unruly length of his striking hair that remained white-blonde well past his childhood. "You won't even watch a scary movie on TV!"

"They're silly. And Grandmom doesn't really like them."

"True... well, *you and me,* we should watch one together sometime anyway—before we don't even have the chance."

"Mom..." he whined in his perfectly adapted teenage twang, "I'm not going anywhere."

"You could be. It's your choice; you're practically an adult."

The look Aaron returned was Sancha's favorite: the treasured reminder of all that resided within her unique son, even if he'd adapted to his biological age so expertly.

"I told you," he said. "I'm sticking to community college."

"Well, you've still got all of senior year to change your mind."

"I've already made up my mind—*and* you're kind of nagging."

"Oh, I am not!" Sancha hid her pout from view. Then, shaking off the mood, she declared, "We could make a night of it! Spooky Movie Night! You could invite..."

"Jen?"

"Yes! I didn't forget her name."

"Well, you can."

"Aaron! That's not very nice! *Why*? What's the matter? Don't you like her?"

"She's all right."

"Aaron." Sancha plopped herself onto the bed beside him, her frown only mocking her attempt to scold him.

"What?" he asked. "It's nothing." Before his mother had the chance to prompt him for an explanation, he managed, "She's nice, but—"

"That's a *good* thing!"

"I know."

"I can't believe you haven't had a *real* girlfriend yet—and I *know* you like girls!"

"Mom!"

"It's *okay* to have a girlfriend. They don't even have to last for long." She wasn't hushed by the disapproving expression on Aaron's face. "Just... try it out."

"It's just—she's nice and all but..." Aaron's next words came

quickly. "It's not *her* really. They just—all of them—seem so...
young."

In the quiet that followed, Aaron marveled at how he'd
spontaneously happened upon one of the rare statements that
succeeded in making his cheerful, chatty mother fall silent.

"Yeah. I know what you mean," Sancha finally said as she
stared at nothing in particular. Then, she nodded, acquiescing.

As she walked to the doorway, she added, "Just wait it out
then—if you can, if you want—*whatever* you want." With that,
she left—understanding but not understanding, believing but
not believing.

Aaron never asked more of her.

3

Aaron looked toward the bleachers, waving when he caught Bennett's eye. He also noticed Jen made her way up the stands, then stepped down the row where Bennett sat—as close as possible to his girlfriend Melissa. Aaron turned his attention to the track beneath his feet.

"Aaron," his track coach called out, "remember to pace yourself." Louder, he called to all, "On your marks!"

Aaron backed into the pedals of the starting block, folded his body into position, and awaited the most beautiful words of all.

"Get ready..."

Aaron eyed the track ahead, following the lines of his lane as it curved to the left. His track teammates lined up on either side of him. Finlay's glare targeted him from two lanes over.

"Set..."

Aaron cleared his mind completely, *remembered* how it felt to run.

"Go!"

The wall of teenage boys broke free, separating, following Aaron's own path as he raced with all he had. Aaron convened with the air around him, felt its natural flow, and joined with it as it carried him over the ground.

Finlay caught up to him, off to Aaron's right, veering onto the edge of his lane and teasing closer to Aaron's. Finlay's own lean and muscular legs pushed him forward, his enduring hatred propelling him all the more.

The finish line visible and just within his awareness, Aaron released. He detached, grasping for the sensation of complete freedom, of weightlessness. He shot forward, gaining centimeters—then, meters—on every other teammate.

Finlay was defeated by his oldest rival, yet again.

"THAT WAS AWESOME," Bennett said with full belief. "But aren't you supposed to save all your big moves for the meets?"

"What moves?" Aaron asked, using the bleachers to continue his cool-down stretches.

"Right. You have none. You're just... awesome in your own right."

"Yeah," Aaron smiled at him.

"Well, Mr. Awesome, the girls and I would like to request your company. This Friday: you, me, them. Have some fun. You have no choice."

"Girls?"

"Yeah. Melissa... and Jen. We thought—"

"I've gotta rest. The next meet's on Saturday."

"No. There's always a meet. *And* it's almost summer break. Even athletes need time off. You don't have to be in perfect condition. You'll win the race anyway. You *always* do. Just come out. Please!"

"Yeah, I'll think about it."

"Hey, Aaron," Jen appeared beside them, holding up a hand

to shield her eyes from the late afternoon sun. "I just wanted to say... you were really amazing out there."

"Thanks," Aaron mumbled under his breath, picking up his towel and swinging it around his neck before walking away.

"Hey!" she called after him. When he paused and turned to face her again, she rushed her plea. "It would be fun—if you'd just come out with us—all four of us together. I promise." Her nose turned up as she flashed her broad smile.

"I'll think about it," he granted before walking on.

AARON ONLY SLOWED his pace when Bennett caught up to him, following him into the school gymnasium.

"You don't have to try so hard to avoid her," Bennett said. She knows you don't really like her—for some crazy reason—but she's a *nice* girl."

"You and I have been over this a million times."

"*I know*. I know *all* your secrets—but are you really going to *avoid* all the fun stuff in life?"

Aaron answered with a tilt of his head.

"You can't!" Bennett exclaimed.

"I'm not."

"I know you're... that you think about everything differently —*feel* things—but, that's got to be a good thing, right? Something cool? Something that *means* something?"

Aaron shook his head and walked into the men's locker room.

"Hey," Bennett called through the doorway. "Did anything happen? Any new—"

"No," Aaron answered. "Just the usual."

"And it didn't..." Bennett looked around to ensure they were alone. "It still won't *say* anything to you?"

Aaron returned to Bennett's side. "He never does."

"But that one time—"

"I talked to *him*—thought to him."

"Then, why don't you do that again?"

"I *have*. Nothing comes back."

"He just *watches* you?"

Aaron nodded.

"Well, maybe that happens to *all* of us," Bennett considered aloud, chuckling to make light of the subject more for his own sake than Aaron's. "And *you're* the only one who's realized it."

4

—————

AARON STRETCHED OUT ON THE SOFT GRASS WITH HIS HANDS folded beneath his head as a pillow, his eyes focused on the sky above. Despite the temptation of the shade of the maple tree spilling out over the back yard, his lazy body defied movement and continued to roast in the summer sun.

"Hello," Bennett called as he neared him, his voice quiet to honor his friend's relaxed state.

Aaron smiled up at him, thankful for the cooling shadow he cast over his face.

"And I thought you didn't do anything but perfect your sprint when I wasn't around," Bennett said.

"Mmm... later," Aaron bothered himself to say.

Bennett sat on the grass beside him, glancing up to locate whatever interesting sight Aaron's focus might be set on. "Well, I'm supposed to ask you if you want anything special for your birthday."

"Yeah? Which one put you up to that?"

"Your mom—this time."

"Kit Kat ice cream."

"What?"

"Kit Kat ice cream. She invented it."

"That sounds amazing. I'm *definitely* going to make sure she's on that."

Aaron smiled at Bennett and the sun.

"Nothing else though? You could always ask for a car, see if you actually get one."

Aaron laughed. "That's not going to happen."

"You never know. Parents can get a little crazy sometimes, do the unexpected. Especially for a kid who's the school track star —probably the state's—*and* you always ace every exam, whether you pay attention in class or not."

"I don't ace them. I miss a question here and there."

"On purpose!"

"Well, you know what happened in third grade. I wasn't going to go through that again."

"Yeah, when Mr. Jackson swore you were cheating."

"His personal vendetta to prove it."

"Ah, those were the days." Bennett leaned back, closing his eyes to the warm sunlight as he straightened his legs to full stretch. "Can you believe we're going to be seniors soon? Then, college, careers, wives, *kids*."

Aaron chuckled between his words. "Don't be in such a hurry."

"Me?" The sun struck Bennett's eyes as he turned to face Aaron. "You're the one in a hurry."

"Not for that stuff, for—"

"I know," Bennett said, turning away and closing his eyes to the sun again. "For answers."

5

"Surprise!" cried the crowd of familiar faces at Maria's signal. Bennett's voice trailed behind as he turned to Aaron, anticipating his reaction.

Aaron absorbed the sight of the small kitchen inflated with friends and family, then turned to Bennett and squinted his disapproval. Bennett only offered a bemused shrug.

Sancha launched herself from the front of the gathering to wrap her arms around Aaron. "Are you surprised?"

"Yes," he answered with perfect, believable timing.

"Good!" she exclaimed, finally releasing him.

Aaron scanned the faces all around to thank each with a smile. Bennett's father stood on tiptoe to wave above the crowd before his wife pulled his arm down again. Melissa stood at the back, almost forced into the next room due to the lack of space. And Jen stood beside her, her mouth curving in a careful smile when Aaron spotted her.

"I invited Jen," Sancha whispered in his ear. "Just in case."

"In case what?"

"You decide you like her."

A<small>ARON UNWRAPPED EVERY UNEXPECTED GIFT</small>—EVEN a few surprisingly thoughtful ones—and spoke with every guest by the time the gathering started to dissipate later in the afternoon.

"There's still time to do something else—if you want," Bennett said, spooning more Kit Kat ice cream into his mouth. "I've got my sister's car."

"I thought you refused to drive it," Aaron said, his focus on Jen's location across the room.

"Why? It's a car!"

"It's a pink Mini."

"I like to think of it as an exotic sports car in disguise." Bennett lifted another heaping spoonful to his mouth before he realized Aaron didn't laugh. "What is it?" he asked as he noticed Aaron's stare no longer had a target. "Is it..."

Aaron nodded.

"The *good* one?" Bennett asked.

When Aaron nodded again, Bennett's shoulders relaxed. He swallowed the mouthful of ice cream, his eyes still focused on Aaron.

Aaron spun on his heels and faced the bare wall behind him. Across the room, Jen stood on her toes to see through the crowd.

Aaron continued to glare as Bennett watched him, occasionally glancing at the blank wall himself. "Aaron," he whispered, "someone might *see* you."

I<small>F</small> A<small>ARON'S</small> focus took physical form, it was a calculated funnel, blocking all external, unnecessary sensory data while homing in on the focal point of his attention.

Who are you! he demanded within his thoughts. *I know that you hear me!*

The presence remained as vague as ever, subtly wavering in brightness and form. It returned nothing.

Then, why?

No answer.

Aaron's stare pushed forward—sharp and steady, unforgiving.

OnLooker... Aaron verbalized in the privacy of his own mind —as a plea and an accusation.

OnLooker.

The ObServed's conveyance of the term—the concept the ObServed *should not know*—vibrated in Fei's awareness, infused with implication—and demanding action.

Fei returned the effect of a stare, responding to his ObServed's.

The two connected, atoms co-mingling, electromagnetic fields integrating: a most natural phenomenon of verging psyches. And Fei felt the urgency in the steady gazes of all other corporeals as they noticed the ObServed's conspicuous behavior.

The corporeals were not capable of realizing Fei's presence in their individual aspects. They did not detect him—nor should Fei's ObServed be capable.

Yet, he was—he *did*.

Fei's visits *affected* his ObServed, against all guidelines and all necessary conditions—against the very sanctity of the ObServed-OnLooker relationship.

Upon the spontaneous awareness, Fei dissipated from his ObServed's aspect and returned wholly to the Apart and the perceived boundaries of his personalized environment once more.

And he initiated contact with the Consultation.

"Aaron!" The quiet shout pierced his attention. "Aaron!" it demanded again.

Aaron finally blinked—and straightened his stance from one of crouching attack. He looked at Bennett, then to the others around them.

Bennett whispered, "You're being watched—by them, I mean."

His heart still racing, his eyes wide with old fury, Aaron attempted an apology to the guests. "Sorry. I must've—"

"Too much excitement—and ice cream—for the birthday boy," Bennett exclaimed on his behalf with a wink at Sancha. He added a hearty pat on Aaron's back.

Aaron nodded his gratitude and managed an awkward smile as conversation filled the room again. Jen filed through the crowd, gaining Aaron's attention by grazing his forearm as she stepped near him.

"I didn't know," she said, a strand of mousy blonde hair clinging to her cheek, "if you'd want me to come. But your mother, she—"

"It's all right," Aaron answered. The immediate adjustment to his tone surprised even himself. "Did you have fun?"

Jen smiled; her entire expression warmed to his attention. "The ice cream's amazing!" she said. "Where did you—"

"My mom makes it."

"Oh, wow. That's really amazing." Her voice faded as she set her paper cup down and started rifling through her handbag. "I got you something..."

"Oh, that's okay. You don't have to."

"No, I already did." Jen revealed a large manila envelope. "I don't really know what you like, but it's a birthday party, so..."

"Really, you weren't supposed to bring anything."

"Open it."

Bennett agreed with his elbow, and Aaron relented, tearing open the envelope.

Jen said, "You're always drawing stuff—in class—so, I thought..."

"Drawing paper. That's really cool, thanks."

Jen beamed, leaning forward as her shoulders lifted. Bennett's eyebrows lifted as well as he watched the awkward drama unfold.

Aaron didn't move. "Well, thanks," he repeated.

Jen's smile disappeared as she wriggled under her own nervousness. "Oh, okay. Well, I was just gonna go..." She gestured to the door. "I'll just go say 'goodbye' to Melissa first."

Bennett and Aaron watched her disappear into the crowd.

"You really don't like girls, do you?" Bennett accused, getting an elbow from Aaron before his sentence completed.

They both continued to watch the party guests as impartial spectators. When Bennett finished scraping the melted ice cream from his paper plate, he asked, "Is it... still here?"

Aaron nodded, struggling against the pressure of his own exhaustion.

6

Fei articulated himself within the awareness of the three comprising the esteemed Consultation. They presented themselves as hovering figures of ambiguous white light fading into the blue-hued expanse they chose as the backdrop to reflect their calming inclinations.

One member of the Consultation consolidated his form with a golden sheen as he welcomed Fei. *The Consultation's guidance is wholly available... as serves aself's intention.*

Fei imparted to each personality of the Consultation, *I desire... to offer awareness to the Consultation.* His form shifted, hovering higher, then sinking into a darker shade. *I... intervene.*

Intervene? one member questioned.

As OnLooker? another assumed.

Within the ObServed's corporeal life?

Fei's form dispersed, then recollected itself with renewed determination. *Indeed,* he confirmed. *I... as OnLooker... communicate with my ObServed.*

Collectively, the aselves of the Consultation brightened before returning to their individually chosen, subdued hues.

Without intention, Fei clarified.

All... is of intention, one member immediately reminded.

Indeed, another agreed.

Fei expressed his explanation in waves of light. *I conveyed in answer... to my ObServed's question. My ObServed... is aware of... myself, as OnLooker.*

The ObServed, questioned one member, *is aware... while in corporeality?*

The shimmer passing over Fei's form answered his audience.

Unusual indeed, imparted another member.

Never before, imparted the third.

Perceives... OnLooker's articulation within the ObServed's aspect? the first inquired.

Indeed, Fei imparted, *upon most every obServance... if not all. My ObServed has indeed sensed my presence as OnLooker.*

The ObServed is aware...

Of aself's articulation... within the ObServed's aspect.

Upon each occasion?

Perhaps... Fei imparted to the three, *since my ObServed was... of new.*

The ObServed... responds.

To OnLooker's articulation.

Since the ObServed's corporeal birth?

Fei awaited further questioning of the Consultation as the members collectively—soundlessly—continued to construe among themselves.

Does the ObServed... remember?

Of course, another member of the Consultation answered.

Of course?

All conditions arise together.

The ObServed has... awakened?

My ObServed... is unaware, Fei interjected as the three deliberated among themselves.

It would be—as all is...

Of The Natural Order of Things.

Indeed.

Yet... an ObServed has awakened... while within a corporeality?

While corporeal?

Never before.

Thus, there is... a second.

Within Fei's perception, the three joined in form, compounding their mutual agreement, then separated as three individual masses of light once again.

It is a first, the Consultation imparted in unison. *There are two... awakened... of the same moment.*

The consensus conveyed was of affirmation. The Consultation confirmed the possibility—the new reality—as well as the due procedure.

The ObServed's training commences.

Indeed.

It is The Natural Order of Things.

There are two.

As selected by The Natural Order of Things.

Aself must articulate in the ObServed's aspect, one member imparted to Fei directly.

At once, another agreed.

And invoke the ObServed to the Apart, the third concluded.

The ObServed's instruction begins, the Consultation imparted in a mutual flash of green light.

Indeed, Fei imparted as he transferred his attention elsewhere, removing his articulation from the presence of the Consultation.

———

ANOTHER HUMORED HIMSELF, electrifying the particles around him, coercing them into action, and creating imagery for his entertainment within his self-manifested environment. A memory of music configured within him, conjuring the connected memory of the sense of *missing* it as he lamented the foregone sensation and physicality of the corporeal ability to *hear* such music.

He would not experience corporeality again—not as one singled out for a purpose *beyond*.

The spontaneous receipt of communication ended his ponderings abruptly. The conveyance was a request for information. He dutifully transmitted all required, exchanging details about his ObServed's progress and current status.

Then, he proceeded to amuse himself with the joyful frivolity of creation.

And, he waited—to know more, to learn more, to grow in strength and skill. He practiced, and he anticipated—eager for his next approach, thoroughly enjoying being *the one selected*.

7

Aaron redirected the air vent, blasting his face with warm, humid air pumping from the hard plastic dashboard. He swiped at the sweat gathering on his forehead and pulled at his damp t-shirt to separate it from his skin.

"It's about time!" he shouted out of the driver-side window.

"*Shannon* wanted to talk to me after class," Bennett chided as he walked around the front of the car and slung his backpack through the open passenger-side window.

"Isn't it against the rules to date a TA?"

"We're not dating." Bennett hopped into the passenger seat and fastened his seatbelt. "And... I don't think it is."

"Well, it should be."

"Thanks for your support."

Aaron started the engine, and the Impala rumbled to life, rattling Bennett to the bone as he shouted above the engine's whine, "At least you *have* a car."

"Because I have a *job*."

"Hey, I would *love* a job, but I actually have to *study* to pass Chemistry 101."

"I offered to teach you a few tricks. You'd know all of it in no time."

"I want to earn it."

Aaron shot Bennett an overused look. Once they left the campus parking lot, Aaron asked, "How's your dad today?"

"Not so good."

"And your mom?"

"Oh, you know, being the best nurse in the world. She's tired though. I can tell."

Aaron nodded, focusing on the turn ahead.

"They're still smiling though," Bennett said. "Joking and stuff."

"That's good. Really good," Aaron said with a doctor's confidence. "And you know they appreciate you being here in town."

"Yeah, I know. And... I wouldn't've ever done anything else, you know?"

Aaron nodded.

"But," Bennett said, "*you* didn't need to stick around."

"I like being around you."

Bennett chuckled. "But *community* college?"

"What about *you*? You could've gone anywhere you wanted."

"Yeah, but... my dad. I can always transfer when—" Bennett cleared his throat and sat higher in his seat. "But you... you're meant for *bigger* things."

"I like being around my family too, you know. I just want to be here for them."

BOTH AARON and Bennett gave Maria a prolonged hug when they walked into the kitchen. She rocked back on her heels, blushing, before laying a plate full of freshly baked cookies in Bennett's hands.

"Ah, Maria! You know the way to a man's heart!" he said, laying the plate on the table and snatching two cookies for himself.

"Stop it!" she answered, turning her back to him quickly.

Sancha walked in, her eyes on her fingertips as she picked at their scabs. "Hello, Bennett. How's your dad?"

"He's... good."

"Good, good. I don't know what I'd do if—"

"Sancha," Maria blurted, "would you hand me that bowl of chopped onion?"

Sancha followed the request, adequately distracted.

"Thanks... all of you," Bennett said as he dropped down into a chair at the table, studying the cookie in either hand. "You've always been there—for everything."

"All right," Aaron said, pulling up a chair beside him. "Sugar always makes you sappy."

"I haven't taken a bite yet!" Bennett whined. "No—you know what I mean. I hope you're all around... forever."

"Well, I do hope to die of old age..." Maria said, "but we don't get to choose, do we?"

"Grandmom! Don't talk about dying," Aaron said.

Sancha leaned over Aaron to grab a cookie. "I wanna be old too. And gray. And a granny!"

"Mom!" Aaron pleaded.

"But you were so cute when you were a baby," Sancha teased.

Bennett laughed, spewing chewed cookie over the table-cloth. Aaron patted his back playfully.

Maria turned away from her task, facing the debauchery in her kitchen. "All right" she said, stopping mid-sentence to stare at Aaron.

Bennett followed her gaze to the stiff expression on Aaron's face. Bennett looked away again and proceeded to pick the table-cloth clean, carrying a handful of chewed cookie to the trash bin.

"There—all cleaned up," he announced louder than necessary. "I'm sorry, Maria, I—" His volume failed to distract the women from their awareness of Aaron's sudden stillness.

"I'm just going to..." Aaron said as he left the kitchen table. He ran up the stairs, closing his bedroom door behind him.

"Don't worry about him," Bennett said, blocking Sancha's path as she started toward the stairs. "He wanted to study or something."

Sancha accepted the explanation and grabbed another cookie off the pile in the center of the table. Bennett sat down again, drumming his fingers on the tabletop as he awaited Aaron's return.

AARON STOOD JUST inside his room, the closed door at his back. He stared at the corner near the head of his bed; he fixated on the space above the nightstand.

Aaron stood his ground, claiming the space for his own —*controlled* by him alone. His arms hung at his sides, hands cupped in a natural curve, his head and chest forward. He was battle-ready.

The image hovered within Aaron's perception like a faint cloud, white in color but hinting at other hues within. It emanated neutrality—even goodwill.

Aaron's intention did not waver. "I need *answers*," he spoke aloud.

The apparition wriggled, undulating like waves of smoke. It offered no communication, no intelligible notion or nuance.

What do you want? Aaron tried again with his internal voice.

The response came immediately.

Aself... does not... want.

Aaron stumbled backward, clinging to the door for support. He hesitated—in thought and movement—privately considering whether he truly desired a *second* acknowledgment or response.

Aaron focused his concentration, bundling emotion with anticipation and insistence. And he hurled his question at the one who had always watched—since the day he was born, to *this* life.

Who, Aaron demanded, *am I?*

FEI—SUDDENLY swarmed with infinite ideas—consciously combated the whirlwind of all answers, all with vast and immeasurable meaning. His perception swatted at them as he attempted to regain clarity and control.

He flickered visibly within the ObServed's aspect. He wilted with the unexpected energy influx—overwhelmed by the newest challenges assumed by his role.

Fei infused with fulfillment. The articulation of his form adapted a visible glow: a brightening, a surge of will. He convened within the ObServed's consciousness and translated his own intention flawlessly.

Awareness... reveals all, Fei promised before he dissipated from the ObServed's aspect and faded to the Apart once more.

AARON STOOD ALONE in his bedroom, surrounded by the constant and familiar, which suddenly seemed *questionably real*. The objects and symbols of *this* childhood, this family, this life, offered little comfort. They only prompted more questions.

The newest experience incorporated into his memory—the one with no equivalent, no reference within *all* his memories—

replayed in his mind relentlessly, consuming his attention completely.

He paced, his hands twitching as they hung at his sides. His mind rehashed the same questions—and the same lack of answers.

WHEN A KNOCK later came at Aaron's door, then others, he dismissed them all with casual, calming replies. *This* experience he couldn't share. This, he could not put into words, of any language. This was his alone to bear.

Eventually, he succumbed to his mental and physical exhaustion. He crawled into bed and allowed the stillness of darkness to envelop him. He concentrated on the calm silence filling the house, let its reassurance carry him to sleep.

And he dreamed—remembering, reliving—still seeking, always *waiting*.

AT FIRST FAINT—AT-ONCE familiar—the vision appeared within the dreamscape stretching across Aaron's consciousness.

All was darkness, except for the one appearing before his mind's eye: the image of so many sightings and a lifetime of conditioning.

The vision gathered itself into fine and focused formation, taking a new shape, postulating a *personality*. A face appeared, one capable of expression but expressionless, identifiable but never before so clearly *seen*: a dark-haired man, eyes opaque but gleaming, a gentle demeanor, calm and still.

Tres... the masculine figure communicated, its manifested mouth unmoving. It reached, within and around. It conveyed the name that challenged, stirred, called the absolute attention of the dreamer, even as he continued to sleep.

Come, the figure suggested, wafted.

And *Tres* followed—without walking, without the burden of a physical body. He flowed, transitioned, melded with his surroundings.

He answered to his true name never acknowledged in his dreams before—those of this life or any others.

Farther, the figure urged. *Separate. Refuse... thoughts. Release... all known. Become aware... to all that surrounds... to nothing, to everything.*

Tres continued to follow, encouraging his mind to slip to deeper sleep, to release, to open, to expand—to receive the answers he'd waited his entire life for, the answers withheld from him through all lifetimes.

Light arose from nothing, converging in the darkness, revealing the teeming activity within what Tres assumed to be the inconsequential void surrounding him. There, all things hovered, awaited—expecting, buzzing, encouraging creation— nothing and everything at once, opposite and same alike.

The light commanded his attention. Tres followed the figure, his guide and new companion, toward the light's source—into the unfamiliar but not *unknown.*

Sense the boundaries that surround, the figure prompted. *'See'... if mind prefers.*

Tres did see. As he let go, refusing his mind's desire to re-imagine his actual surroundings—to distort and reconfigure— Tres detected the *intended*: smooth, white walls, soft and supple, warm and welcoming. The room was small, comfortable, perfect in suitability. A seat appeared; the figure gestured in its direction.

If preferred, the figure conveyed.

Tres's body—the *image* of it—formed as the *consideration* of it formed as well. He thought of sitting; he sat. And he relaxed into the comforting reassurance of the recognizable.

The masculine figure's mouth subtly moved but did not speak. Yet, Tres received its intended message with precise clarity.

Tres... is aself... 'a-self' of the Apart.

The name—his own name, the name he'd *felt*—resonated in Tres's thoughts, ringing with truth and joy and acceptance as it was acknowledged by another. Tres did not question the figure's knowledge or how it came to be—how it *could* be. Instead, Tres reminded himself that he was merely *dreaming.*

All... welcomes... Tres, the figure conveyed, abruptly and without its usual calm decorum, as if stating the greeting as an afterthought.

All? Tres's question formed and floated, without the backing of his complete attention.

Indeed, the figure answered.

And... you? Tres asked, immediately condemning himself for his own insistence.

I... am the one called Fei, the figure granted in answer.

Fei... Tres repeated in thought alone.

The figure continued his introduction, conveying in unheard message, *I serve as your OnLooker. I look upon... your corporeal life. You... are my ObServed.*

I am... dreaming, Tres's own prominent, pushing mind repeated before forcing it to explain all perception away.

Indeed, the one called Fei imparted. *Connection in the transient state of your dream is... necessary. To beckon you to the Apart wholly —before you choose—invites great... resistance... from your corporeal consciousness.*

But I am dreaming... but I see you, Tres argued to himself, unknowingly offering open access to his own internal consideration.

Indeed, Fei imparted, *yet, still within mind, still with connection to body—still encapsulating all within thought, within the perceived safety of dream state.* The bombardment of concepts awaited Tres's mental perception. *You also... feel...*

Tres's attention turned to the seat his body weighed upon. *Yes, I can feel it,* Tres answered with pride.

No, Fei imparted.

No?

The feeling... is a necessity of your mind's attachment to your corporeal body. There is nothing... beneath your perceived body.

Tres felt the heaviness of his body fall to the floor.

As there is no... 'floor,' Fei conveyed casually, before his articulated form quickly reached for Tres's hand—effectively holding Tres's perception of himself in place.

Tres's mind battled, pitting sense and perception against truth. The form of Fei gradually released its grasp on Tres perception, leaving Tres to the sensation of hovering once more: limbless, bodiless.

You are not, Fei imparted, *joined with your body. Your body is not... you. It is merely a manufacture, an agreed upon mental representation, of your corporeality. Tres is... 'a-self'... with or without... body. You—all that is of you—is present with me, the one called Fei.*

I'm... 'a-self,' Tres considered.

Indeed, Fei answered. *You... are more than corporeal form.*

Where is... my body?

In corporeality. Fei allowed his answer to settle around Tres's consciousness before clarifying, *Where you... left it.*

Tres's mind wandered—of its own accord, without direction or instruction. It focused his attention on various levels of thought and awareness, between the perception of body and no-body.

That is enough... for now, Fei conveyed before fading into the dark distance.

TRES ALSO FELL AWAY, slipping from the Apart and reforming himself, his identity, within his own aspect of his corporeality—naturally, effortlessly, and without a thought.

8

"I had the craziest dream," Aaron shared with Bennett, rushing the words as they formed in his thoughts.

"Yeah? Was she hot?" Bennett settled into the passenger-side seat next to Aaron.

"No, a really cool dream—far out."

"Far out? Like aliens or just groovy?"

"Stop! I'm serious."

"Oh, *that* kind of dream."

"Well, it was just... I can't really explain it." Aaron accurately assumed the face Bennett made at him. "Well, it was like an explanation—like my brain made it up or something—for... for the thing, for *him*, who's shown up over and over again."

"Cool. That's a first. So, is it a good thing or scary or...?"

"Well, nothing, really. But I did wake up just... *feeling* better."

"Then, that's a good thing."

"Yeah. Yeah, I guess."

"So, it was one of those dreams that feels really *real*."

Aaron nodded. "And *surreal*."

"Crazy how our minds can conjure up stuff like that."

Tres... echoed through Aaron's mind as his body fell into deep sleep at the end of another day.

Tres, imparted the familiar vision now infused with personality and the promise of adventure.

Tres's transition—his transportation—flowed more quickly this time, seamless and self-assured. Again, he found himself facing the one called Fei, as they stood-floated-flowed together within four walls, a floor, and a ceiling that all seemed to vary in size upon every glance.

Again, Tres fashioned in his thoughts.

Indeed, emanated from Fei with the impression of a hint of humor.

The environment, though dark-tinted and subtly aglow, felt safe to Tres—steady, wholly welcoming.

This is my selected environment, Fei conveyed without sound, *of my own creation.*

You... built this?

No, resonated like an actual chuckle from the form of Fei. *I... created it—for aesthetics, to please myself. It is... comforting.*

Yes, Tres thought.

Yet, Fei continued, *it is not necessary. Aself requires no... 'dwelling,' no... surrounding imagery—only as it pleases aself.*

A... self?

One-self... 'I'... another... all. And... 'you,' Tres.

Tres settled himself—his perception of himself—into the seat awaiting him.

Me, Tres considered. *Why... am I here? Again?*

Your instruction... commences.

My instruction? What do you mean?

It is of your awareness... as you... welcome awareness.

You mean, I know the answer? How can I... be aware?

A self opens... to awareness. It is a choice—one of many.

But... how do I choose?

Do not 'think' with mind. Allow... awareness.

The headache manifested, throbbing in Tres's temples, the temples almost slipping from his touch even as he reached for them with his envisioned fingertips.

You... perceive pain? Fei asked without words.

Yes, I... have a headache.

Become aware. You... have no 'ache.' It is of your... creation. You may create anew—if you desire.

The headache grew, in point and pressure.

Create anew, Fei urged. *Allow awareness of the creation—of your own choice—and its association solely with corporeal form.*

Tres immediately turned his attention downward, looking for his body again. He was distracted quickly by its tendency—his actual sense of it—to appear and reappear unpredictably. And his headache was gone.

Very well. Your awareness expands... 'quickly'—as you define 'time,' Fei congratulated, not without confusing his student.

Define time? Tres questioned.

Your agreed upon concept... of 'time.' Fei further explained, *There is... no 'time.' All is now. All... 'is.'*

Is what? Agreed with who?

There is only... this moment. You alternately choose... to perceive 'time'... as it is conceived of, acted upon, and created—jointly, simultaneously—by all within your corporeality.

Tres felt the headache reforming. This time, it developed in pieces, phases, prodding at his awareness, leaving itself flexible to his direction.

Very well, Fei encouraged. *You exercise your creative abilities.*

Tres inwardly smiled as he applied Fei's instruction and found the threat of a renewed headache easily manipulated.

Fei continued. *'Time'... suits your corporeality, for the most part.*

Yet, it is not. Here, now—of the Apart—all is now. All occurs at once. You... abide here... just as you are born within your aspect... just as you also ascend from the same... just as you perceive your other lives and perceive them to be of... before.

My... other lives... Tres felt the pressure of beckoning tears: sorrows and sympathies intertwining within himself as memories swirled in his consciousness.

Indeed.

How do you... know?

All aselves... transition among various aspects—perceiving to and from the Apart, to and from corporeality—again and again. And simultaneously.

All... Tres attempted to comprehend, to believe. *I'm not the only one?*

It is... The Natural Order of Things.

IN HIS BED, as he slept in the darkness, Aaron's arm flung to his side—a reflex, as the remainder of his body remained stiff with sleep. Aaron reactively flinched at the dynamic information fed to him, to the *essence* of him—to Tres.

9

IN THE SAFETY—AT THE *INVITATION*—OF HIS DREAMS, AARON tested new talents, toyed with new ideas, played at what it means to *be*. His guide was always patient, always jovial, and endlessly enlightening—night after night.

His dream-nights, as Tres, grew longer. His days, as Aaron, grew shorter, each one feeling more mundane, more inconsequential, more redundant than the last.

And still, his consciousness insisted every visitation, every meeting with his new companion, was merely a dream.

YOU MUST LIVE FULLY in your corporeality, Fei imparted as his form emanated in gold and green patterns within Tres's perception.

You mean, in real life? Tres's thoughts returned to the figure in his dream while he sensed his surroundings altering, seemingly randomly—at every perspective.

There is no life more 'real'—only what is, only be-ing. You must not reject the lessons to be learned in your chosen corporeality. All are yours to collect, to adapt within your awareness.

But I've lived... so many times.

As have I... and all. Each corporeal life is selected for what it specifically offers.

By who?

By aself.

I... chose... this life?

Indeed.

Why?

That is of your own awareness.

Tres shifted, moving, unaware that his own form altered slightly. *But... I don't know.*

All aselves—you—are aware. Fei brightened his own form, sharpened his projected image, and lured Tres's deeper concentration. *Aself follows aself's own path—aself's selected path—seeking and exploring, aself-developing, enlivening aself's... mien. It is The Natural Order of Things—in its most basic essence.*

The vision of Fei flickered, developing a reflective quality that Tres had learned to connect with the process of considering, at least as he knew it. Fei continued, volunteering the explanation Tres waited to ask.

Aself's mien... is the motivation for creation itself, the 'call,' the connection, the magnetism that draws all energy together... to other, to itself. Aself—and every choice—serves aself's mien. That is all. That is everything.

Like a goal, Tres's limited comprehension shaped.

No, Fei imparted. *Not 'goal,' not even 'purpose' as extolled in your corporeality. Mien is free-flowing: subtle but strong, adapting but steady. Mien is akin to what is termed 'theme' in your corporeality— as a 'string' aself follows, a preference, a tendency—aself's... joy.*

In this life? Tres presumed.

With and through... all lives—and without.

Tres permitted his memories to flow, allowing them to pour gently, seeping around and within, trickling tens, then hundreds, at a time. He searched them for a common theme, for meaning, for one driving force to connect them all.

The controlled pour turned controlling. The memories began to flood, completely filling—overwhelming. Races... battles... relationships... crusades... births... deaths... faces... words... wounds... expressions... goals. All intertwined, knotting together, simultaneously melding and ripping. And then, the striving—fierce and continuous—with hope... loss... condemnation... rage... exhilaration... motivation... spirit... possession... redemption... searching... discovery... avoidance.

To be free, Tres grasped. *Free from all—unhampered, unlimited, unrestricted. To be free to... know.*

Fei delivered no response.

10

Aaron's attention drifted in the afternoon sun as Bennett's voice faded from detection. Aaron peered at the cloudless sky as he lay along the bench opposite the metal picnic table he shared with Bennett in the common area on campus.

"So, *anomie* means—oh, no one uses that word!" Bennett complained, slamming his textbook closed. "Hello? You're not even listening to me."

"To you complain? Yes, I am—unfortunately."

"Well, you're supposed to be helping me study for the sociology exam, not daydreaming. I know it's not a big deal to you, but you don't have to make it so *obvious*."

Aaron couldn't contain his laugh.

"Oh, great. My misery entertains you."

"An absence of social norms, lacking a sense of purpose."

"What?"

"Anomie."

Bennett grumbled, then squinted to force the definition into his memory. He continued to read sample questions aloud, answering some of them, prodding at Aaron for others.

Aaron's thoughts slipped away, drifting into dream-flashes—

all flowing more freely, fluidly, than ever experienced before. Images and experiences with Bennett passed among Aaron's thoughts as he organized his friend's characteristics, compared his traits, and assessed their shared experiences together.

"My companion..." he pondered aloud without realizing.

"What?" Bennett asked.

"Nothing."

Bennett moaned and threw his attention at his textbook again.

YOU GROW IN AWARENESS... *of mien,* Fei imparted, appealing to Tres's ever-accepting dreaming mind—and to his truest self.

Tres smiled inwardly, his form aglow with pride, as well as excitement.

It serves as a guide, Fei further offered. *One of many.*

Like you.

Indeed—such as myself, flowed from Fei with the warmth of amusement.

Tres enjoyed the sensation emanating from his translucent acquaintance, before his own consciousness turned to darker thoughts.

It has... always been you? Watching me? Tres asked, unaware that his form reflected his anxiety.

Indeed. I look on. As you... are my ObServed.

It has always been... you, reverberated within Tres's thoughts, agitating his perceived nerves. *There are no... others? Not... another?*

Aself—while in corporeal life—is served by a single OnLooker. OnLooker serves but a single ObServed. Every corporeal life is... looked upon.

Tres shuddered within, rumbled without.

It is a role, a choice—as with all others, Fei added, incorrectly presuming the heart of Tres's discomfort. *Aself chooses many corporeal lives. Most aselves choose the role of OnLooker when... between. OnLooker serves as guide... yet does not... intervene. OnLooker serves as watchful presence... offering only a point of reference, a reminder.*

A reminder of what?

Aself's mien.

Tres permitted himself the sensation of lapsing time, of a pause for processing, and Fei joined in the imaginings for the benefit of his pupil.

You have always watched? Tres questioned again, reacting to his corporeal mind's agitation.

Indeed, Fei answered, even as he sensed the need for embellishment. *Always of the moment. Yet, not all activity within your concept of 'time' is obServed. Your creation of 'time'—you are aware—is not of reality. It is merely agreed upon... by all within your corporeality. Here, of the Apart, all aselves are aware—and all experience—that all is simultaneous, all is now. In your limited awareness, you perceive the passage of 'time.'*

We have... limited awareness?

As you choose.

That's why I... was the only one who saw you—all those times.

You are the only to 'see'... among the aselves of all corporealities. You... are the first.

I am... the first?

Indeed. The first to 'see'... within a corporeality—the first to sense... aself's OnLooker. And the only.

I'm... the only one?

Indeed.

But why?

You... need only invite... the awareness.

ANOTHER PRACTICED AND STUDIED—EMBELLISHING every lesson, building upon his own knowledge—fueled by his limitless desire.

He relished reconstructing and deconstructing his form, experimenting with ideas, concepts, and manipulations of energy. He formulated and configured, growing into his powerful role.

His heightened impatience was balanced with concentration on the expansion of his abilities, giving him great joy, pride, and impetus. And his strength surged with the inevitability of the satiation of all his desires.

11

"THANKS FOR THE RIDE. IT'S GOOD TO SEE YOU." BENNETT fidgeted in the seat next to Aaron, training himself to avert his eyes. "You're... a difficult one to get ahold of these days."

"Hmm?" Aaron replied, focused on steering his car through a busy intersection. "How's your dad?"

"Same."

"That's good."

"No. No, not really."

Aaron glanced away from the road ahead. "Really? What happened?"

"It's..." Bennett began, reluctantly warming to Aaron's attention. "It's not good that nothing is changing—that he's not improving. So, maybe we all just have to face—"

"No," Aaron insisted, his eyes gleaming with affection. "No, don't think that way."

"I don't have a choice. That's what the doctors are telling us."

"Doctors don't know anything."

"Well, I think they know more than you do."

Aaron's jaw tensed against his desire to speak. He continued driving in silence, then was the first to break it.

"Hey, isn't that..." Aaron pointed as he turned the steering wheel.

Bennett's eyes followed to the figure walking down the sidewalk. "Finlay," he confirmed.

"He doesn't look so good," Aaron said, glancing into the rearview mirror for a final look.

"What do you mean? He's still good-looking, *and* he knows it."

"No. His posture's different. Something's... weighing him down." Aaron glanced at Bennett. "Do you know what he's up to these days?"

"Aside from excelling on that big scholarship? I don't know. If he's back in town—well, I don't think it'd be any school holiday we don't get or something."

"I wonder how his family's doing."

"Fine, I think. My mom saw his at the mall last weekend. She was on some big shopping spree, carrying lots of bags—she was wearing some really expensive sunglasses." Bennett mumbled, "My mom's words, not mine."

"Hmm," was all Aaron offered before Bennett changed the subject—and relished his success in eventually making his best friend laugh again.

AARON PULLED into the drive at home and pulled the key out of the ignition. He grabbed his backpack and launched himself through the front door, nearly running into Sancha as she descended the stairs.

"Hi, Aaron!" she called after him as he swung around her, maintaining his trajectory. "How was class today?"

"Fine," he yelled from the top of the stairs.

"That's it? Do you have to study now or something?"

"No!" reached her ears, then a door slam.

"Of course not. You never do," Sancha mumbled to herself as she walked into the kitchen. "Nice to see you..."

Maria glanced up from wiping the counters to offer her daughter a warm smile. Sancha shook her head, staring at the floor as she walked through.

Aaron tossed his backpack across his bedroom, flinching as it landed hard on his desk. He fell onto his bed, folded his hands behind his head, and sighed deeply as he stared at the ceiling. He slowed his breathing, willed his body and mind to relax, and waited for sleep to come.

What's left... *for me to learn?* Tres's impatience hovered around his form, surrounding him as he greeted his returning companion as his corporeal body slept through the night.

All... that you resist awareness of, Fei imparted.

But I'm not resisting. Tres's rebuttal hung in the air, unanswered. *Why are you teaching me all of this?*

It is... The Natural Order of Things.

That doesn't... mean anything to me. I want to know... why me?

It is The Natural Order of Things.

Tres detected the flicker in his own vision of himself as his restlessness grew. He noticed the empty seat, just as faint but still perceptible in the corner of the room with the moving walls. He considered his new preference to ignore the crutches—the remnants—of what his dreamed companion referred to as corporeality.

Tres wondered if he was capable of transforming himself—here—into a mere wisp, to zip to and fro while in conversation with Fei. *Of course, I can. This is only a dream,* he answered himself, the communication available to all.

Only the dream of your temporal mind, Fei corrected. *Aself always abides in the Apart.*

Is that... where you lead me each night—here?

The Apart is all—all there is.

Tres unwittingly transmitted his image more solidly with better-defined boundaries, congruent with his mind's defense.

Fei imparted, *Aself's awareness of the Apart... and aself's playing at creation... are always available to aself.*

Tres felt the sensation of being studied.

Fei imparted, *You must accept... reality.*

Real life... when I'm awake, Tres mind insisted for its self-preservation.

Reality is... here, now, Fei imparted.

But I'm dreaming.

Aself is aware... of reality... for all of aself's corporeal life.

And before? I never knew about this—of the Apart, of anything else—before.

Within all of aself's corporeal lives, aself is aware of only aself's own aspect. As is The Natural Order of Things.

I was only aware... of that life—each life at a time, Tres imparted.

Indeed.

Then, what changed? Why have you appeared now, in this life?

I have not.

The color of Tres infused with bright yellows and reds before subduing again into somber gray.

Fei continued his student's instruction in wafting, blue rays of light. *OnLooker does not 'appear.' OnLooker merely obServes. OnLooker articulates in the ObServed's aspect—of a moment—as OnLooker abides within the Apart.*

You haven't answered my question.

I have indeed. You have only... to accept it. Fei's form softened as he offered, *OnLooker does not—may not—'appear.' You... have been aware of the OnLooker's presence.*

You do not appear... but I know you're there.

Indeed.

Why now? Why have I noticed you, my OnLooker, in this life alone?

It is The Natural—

Why... now?

The Natural Order of Things... selects... Tres.

12

"Do you wanna come over later on? I won't ask you to help me study—I'm sick of studying. We could kick around the ball or something?"

Aaron finished swiping mayonnaise on a slice of bread before mashing it on top of another stacked high with sliced ham, cheese, and barbecue-flavored potato chips; the phone receiver was wedged between his ear and shoulder, its cord stretched taut over the kitchen table. "We've never kicked around a ball," he said through a smile headed for his sandwich.

"We used to," Bennett said, in a voice similar to the one he had as a child.

"When we were kids."

"Okay, I'll let you race me."

"You don't like losing."

"You can let me win."

Aaron laughed, almost losing a precious bite of sandwich. After a short bout of coughing, he continued, "I think I'll just... do some reading or something."

"Reading—on a day like this? Come on! Let's get out and go do something." In response to the resounding silence, Bennett confessed, "Okay then. I miss hanging out with you. And... I'm worried about you."

"Me? Why?"

"How come you don't run anymore? Even with Coach Sandford begging you to join the team?"

"I run—when I need to."

"You know what I mean." Bennett's shorter breaths revealed his impatience as he listened to Aaron chew through another bite.

"I don't know," Aaron finally answered. "I don't need to, I guess."

"Did you need to before?"

"Yeah, sort of."

Bennett let out a long sigh. "Just come over for a bit—Mom's making a chocolate mousse pie—or I can just come over there."

"No, not tonight. Sorry."

"What do you *have* to do?"

"I just need to... think about stuff."

"And you don't want to tell *me* about it?"

"It's complicated."

"Are you still having those weird dreams?"

"I've gotta go. Sorry, Bennett."

"Fine." Bennett shuffled his phone in his hand before bringing it to his mouth again. "I'm beginning to think you have a new best friend."

"Not a chance. That'll never happen."

"Well... good."

Aaron finished his bite and delivered a quippy closing comment before realizing Bennett had already hung up on him.

13

WHILE HIS BODY LAY SLEEPING IN WHAT SEEMED LIKE A DIFFERENT life altogether, Tres's consciousness concentrated on his perception of Fei, the steady, light-infused figure appearing in his continuing dream.

Aself selects corporeal life—the environment of a specific aspect—for the purpose of attainment, Fei imparted. *Aself is inclined to seek experiences—situations, challenges, relationships—serving aself's mien. It is... The Natural Order of Things.*

I chose... my life—this life? The people in it... everything that happens to me?

Indeed—of a sense and to an extent—and for all of them, for each of aself's corporeal lives.

Fei continued Tres's education with the usual careful and gentle approach, judging Tres's acceptance and understanding at each point and with each new concept. Fei seemed playful this moment, vanishing from Tres's perspective entirely before reappearing at a different angle.

Why don't I, Tres relayed in his thoughts, *know—about my choice—all my choices?*

Aself... is aware. And aself's neglect of awareness... is the agreed upon condition of corporeal life.

We—everyone—agrees to forget, to ignore all that we know... while we live—in any life?

It is... the experience of corporeality itself: to focus, of a manner, on the corporeal experience alone. It is the method by which aself is offered the most intensive attainment. Allowing Tres's awareness the energy exchange necessary to adjust to the information, Fei continued. *Aself is aware of aself's true and whole self upon denying corporeality.*

Denying it?

Returning to the Apart, in whole, in all awareness.

You mean... the end of life? When we die?

Aself does not 'die.' There is no 'death.'

Tres floundered in form as if suddenly washed away, his energy dispersed. His imagery returned, hazy and subdued, awaiting more of his tutor's communication but without the desire or courage to ask questions.

You—your true self, Fei imparted, *is not with corporeal body of this moment. Yet, you... are.*

Are?

You exist. You are 'a-self.'

Tres moved his visible limbs—the form he felt—before fading again. His consciousness considered the detachment from his actual body he sensed in that moment.

There is no death? he questioned.

There is no 'death,' just as there is... no 'life.'

But... corporeality...

A choice. An awareness. An aself-selected perspective. Fei continued happily, wholeheartedly. *Aself is all. Aself is... of The Natural Order of Things. Aself is always of the Apart. The Apart is all.*

Aself, Tres imparted, his corporeal consciousness wondering at his own use of the foreign term, *chooses... many lives?*

Indeed, responded Fei, subtly glowing with playful energy.

Forever?

There is no 'time,' only the infinite now.

Yes, yes, but every one of us, each of us, lives over and over again?

Aself experiences as many varied corporealities as desired.

And... you?

Indeed.

But you're not in a life—not now. You're here, with me.

I choose the role of OnLooker, to obServe another—as many do, between corporeal lives. Or... do not.

And I chose you?

Aself chooses aself's corporeality and aself's individual aspect. OnLooker... chooses... the ObServed—the ObServed offering corresponding aself-development.

14

"I CAN FEEL YOUR EYES ON ME!" SANCHA GIGGLED EVEN AS SHE accused.

Aaron's stare didn't waver; he continued to study his mother as she wandered through the back garden, picking the flowers that suited her mood at the moment.

"You're just going to keep staring at me?" she teased as she strolled past him.

"Sorry. Just... lost in thought."

Sancha's voice grew quieter as she leaned over a rose bush for a single bud primed to bloom. "Happens a lot these days..."

Aaron walked over to the swing set, and dropped himself onto the sun-warmed wooden seat. His attention flicked toward the opposite corner of the yard, where one of his strongest memories was born. He glanced away, pushing off the ground and swinging into the air.

"Be careful. That thing's old and rusted. Don't know if it'll really hold. Especially now that you're *so old*!"

Sancha frowned when Aaron didn't respond. She walked over to him, a rainbow bouquet of flowers in her gloved hand. She set them on the ground at one end of the swing set and sat in the swing next to him. "You probably already know it, but... I'm glad you stayed here—for school."

Aaron's smile brought her instant contentment.

"Sure you don't want to do anything specific for your birthday?" she asked as she swung past him, her glittering hair swirling around her.

"I barely realized it's almost my birthday," he answered, looking toward the sky.

"That's just sad. And you're going to be the big two-oh."

"That doesn't mean anything."

"Well, Mister Sour Puss, I just meant that you can do something else for your birthday—with Bennett or whatever—if you want. I don't mind."

"And Grandmom?"

"Oh, she'll probably mind—a lot."

Their laughter came easily as they continued to swing through the hot summer air.

"No, we can just celebrate here, at home—like always," Aaron confirmed.

"Are you sure?"

"Yep."

"So, we'll have Bennett over and... anyone else? New school friends or a girl..."

"Nope."

Sancha sighed as she swung past Aaron. "All right, then."

"Don't act so surprised!" Aaron shouted into the phone. "Are you going to keep harassing me or let me tell you what I was calling for?"

Bennett changed his tone. "All right, all right. It's just—good to hear from you, Aaron."

"My birthday... turns out, it's soon. Are you coming over?"

"I'm invited?"

"Of course, you are! You always are!"

"I just thought you might have other plans this time or something."

"Nope—the usual. Mom and Grandmom are planning it all already. More food than two-hundred people can eat, you know, and I just wanted to make sure you're gonna be here."

"Yeah. Of course. It'll be really fun to hang out again."

"Cool."

Bennett waited for Aaron to continue, but received only silence.

"Is that all? I mean, while I've got you here, is there... anything else you want to talk about?"

Aaron chuckled. "No. I won't bore you."

"It's just that... these days... it's like you're on some other *planet*—or something."

15

FEI ENFOLDED OVER HIMSELF, PROJECTING NEW RHYTHMS AND patterns for Tres to attempt to replicate. His form twisted, warped, as did their simple surroundings.

Why, Tres asked internally, *do you always bring me here—to your... to this room?*

It is of my creation, indeed. It is also created... for your comfort.

But there aren't even any chairs anymore.

Fei didn't detect the joke. *Aself may create as aself desires.*

No, I mean, why... is there nothing else?

There is all.

But it always looks the same—well, different, but the same: the same tiny room. Is this... all there is? Where—aren't there... others?

Indeed.

So, where are they?

Every-where. An aself is all. All is aself.

I don't understand.

You have only... to open to awareness... to expand your perception.

Tres's attempt at harsh, commanded concentration amused Fei.

No, Fei imparted, *it is aself's mind that limits perception, aself's thoughts that control and contain aself's awareness.*

Tres's form undulated, affected by his confusion.

Awareness... requires no mind, Fei imparted. *Detach from the boundaries of corporeality. Expand. Open.*

Tres detected nothing new in his surroundings—nothing within, nothing without.

Close... your perceived 'eyes,' Fei suggested.

But they're not really here, Tres considered. *I'm not here. My body...*

Indeed, your body is not. Body is only of your corporeal creation. Detach from the corporeal, from the temporal.

I can't...

You do. You are of the Apart. And you are aware... that no aself is alone. Other aselves... abound all around.

Where...

You sense them. Yet, your mind clings to the corporeal, the temporal... even now. You must... deny mind.

Tres's struggle continued.

As you create and play with form—of the Apart and within corporeality—so too, you may free yourself from corporeal body. Perceive the form before you, the form of your OnLooker, Fei directed. *Sense its fluidity, its transparency, its lack of temporal matter.*

Tres watched, *imagined* with the eyes his mind could not deny, and sensed the vision of Fei's figure expand and contract, dispersing and reforming, revealing its elasticity, its undeniable impermanence.

Sense your own form nearing my form, Fei continued, *and... move... through.*

At once, under his tutor's instruction, Tres sensed as though he was instantly near Fei, closer than he had ever perceived himself before and—almost as quickly—*within*... and without.

Very well. Your awareness is... anew.

AND AN ENTIRE WORLD opened up to Tres—instantly, all around, everywhere. He pointed his perception upward, downward, at every angle. He sensed movement, flow, energy converging and diverging, light and sound pulsing—and other forms, *smiling* at him.

The figures surrounded, changing in shape, characteristics, and concepts constantly—with and without recognizable faces —all imparting goodwill, acceptance, curiosity, and *welcome.*

They're... Tres's thoughts flickered with his form, *all around —everywhere.*

The Apart, Fei conveyed.

It's... so many. And they're... all looking.

Aselves are interested, curious—naturally.

In me?

In all.

But... have they always been watching—looking at us—while I'm here, with you?

Indeed.

But how... I didn't see—

You choose... limited awareness.

Who are they?

No one. All.

Others?

If you prefer.

Like me?

Yes... and no.

Like you?

Yes... and no.

OnLookers?

Of some.

And... the rest?

Of their own creation.

And they...

Fei formed himself, conveying the vision of himself surrounding Tres, gathering him, reconforming him, helping him converge into a more familiar form again.

They, Tres continued, mentally battling his own exhaustion, *they've lived... many lives?*

As aselves desire, as serves aself's mien, as expands individual aself-development.

ANOTHER LINGERED—ONE not as gracious as the others.

He warmed as the others cooled, energizing as the others dissipated. Concealing himself by outward expansion, he remained undetected by any—as he desired, as he commonly preferred. He was inclined to look on while others looked away. It was as he was trained.

The diabolically contrary act he intended to commit, *was not.*

THE FACES—THEIR forms—faded, retreating into darkness. The sense of their extended welcome lingered in Tres's awareness.

They're... they're gone, he imparted to Fei.

Only aside... from your awareness—to allow you the recuperation your corporeal mind yet requires.

Your... the little room—it's gone.

You no longer require the perception.

PART VI

SEEKING

Dum inter homines sumus, colamus humanitatem.

— AS LONG AS WE ARE AMONG HUMANS,
LET US BE HUMANE.

1

IS THIS... ALL THERE IS? TRES'S QUESTION HOVERED: A SEPARATE, identifiable cluster of energy in itself.

All is... everything, Fei's answer formed and floated.

When we die... this is where we go?

There is no 'death.' Aself remains—as always—within the Apart. Aself only chooses to affix aself's awareness anew. Aself... ascends from corporeality.

This... is what it really looks like—everything?

Aself relies not upon corporeal senses for the truth of awareness. Aself's perception is of aself's choice, of aself's preference.

The darkness?

It is of your choice.

I... choose darkness?

If darkness is as you perceive.

What do you see?

I am aware... of vibrancy. Aliveness. Alertness. Rhythms of energy. Fluidity. All.

What does it... look like? I mean, how does it... seem...

Open. Become aself-aware.

Without further instruction, Tres focused his attention on

his companion, on the form of Fei himself: the hovering ball of moving light pulsing nearby. Tres moved toward it, concentrating on its movements, on the smaller points of light making up the larger. He followed the patterns, the randomness, the contraction and expansion. He sensed *between*.

Landscapes unfolded before his awareness: divergent worlds, flowing, swarming, undulating—every color imaginable, every shape imaginable. Tres opened his awareness—simply, naturally—to the Apart.

Its infinite reaches, without and within, were obvious, undeniable, and all around—as were the infinite aselves.

They're here! Tres energized with wonder.

Indeed.

So many. And they're all... so different.

As aselves desire.

Some of them... are looking toward me.

The aselves... attend Tres.

Attend me?

To convey aselves'... attention.

They're... focusing on me?

Indeed—with meaning.

Meaning?

Message.

The term triggered Tres's consciousness, dialing into a new focus, delivering enriched awareness. The sense of sound streamed into him, flowing as visible rivers, smooth and dense.

Hello... came a strange voice, not heard or seen but felt. *Welcome...* communicated another. And both held additional information—notions, layers of perception—Tres could not decipher.

They're... kind, Tres imparted to Fei and, unwittingly, with all.

A concept similar to a chuckle emanated from Fei, traveling visibly, wafting from the center of his light.

Can... can they hear me? Tres asked.

Your communication is effective... yet rudimentary. And, of some moments, quite 'loud.'

Sorry, Tres thought-shouted to all. He watched, straining to interpret. He noticed the flow of movement—of light and sound —as the core of him, the sense behind his mind, translated them. And he recognized the dance occurring all around—the dance of aliveness itself.

Very well, Fei encouraged. *You grow more aware... of connection... of the interconnectedness of all.*

The balls of energy, they're... people?

The corporeal term holds no meaning.

Beings? Souls?

Aselves.

They... come together, then separate like they... merge—like... combinations of energy or... like they're the same... or made of the same...

All is.

What... is it?

Creation. It is alive... as energy is alive—not of the corporeal sense. Creativity is free of limitation. Boundless. Infinitely fueled, infinitely supported. Always evolving.

Energy...

Of 'is.' Of 'now.' Of 'am.'

As Tres's awareness expanded to include rather than exclude, so did his form. He rose, toward what felt like *above*; he hovered higher, to be caught in the gentle flow of connectedness. As he was swept—over, through, around—Fei followed, ever-present, ever-guiding.

It's... Tres attempted to determine, *it feels... like happiness.*

Creation is joy. Aliveness is energetic. Fei continued to direct Tres's discovery. *Allow yourself to be aware of the attraction among, the natural inclination of all to seek and merge, to become aware... to attend, to join.*

To join?

To be near, to connect, to communicate... to gain from each other.

I don't understand, Tres imparted, along with his awareness of the evidence for the concept.

Aself is attracted to others... as aself seeks support of aself's mien—aware or not, actively pursuing or not. It is The Natural Order of Things.

As energy... in the Apart?

Of the Apart, as in corporeality.

People too?

Indeed—corporeals as well. Aself is naturally drawn to supporting energy—as aself chooses a particular aspect within corporeal life. Detecting the delay in Tres's realization, Fei transmitted, *As OnLooker, I obServe the same in yours corporeal life.*

In my life?

The gathered, supporting energies... of Estre... Leal... Rien... Liet... Veoir.

Fei's form fluttered as he added, *And Tela... the connection is most strong.*

2

THE WIND COOLED AARON AS HIS STRIDE STRETCHED OVER concrete, leapt across pavement, and glided over the hills marking the city limits. He raced, taxing his muscles and challenging his body as he further mastered his own movements.

He ran—again, and with passion, with purpose. He ran—not for freedom but because he felt *free*.

SEPARATE FROM ALL, connected to everything, *another* sweltered with his own intention. He watched—aware of all—intensely desiring to *affect* all.

His impatience burned within, permeating his form and function—growing, feeding itself, multiplying. His desire—full of potential, limitless in its creative ability—conjured, arranged, devised—with life of its own.

"I'M SORRY, Bennett, he's not here right now," Sancha spoke into the phone in the kitchen while wrapping the cord around her finger.

"He really oughtta get a cell phone," Bennett replied.

Sancha giggled with the lightness of eternal youth.

"Actually..." Bennett said, "I could get him one for his birthday!"

"No, no. That's too much. Besides, he's weird about them—or he'd have one by now."

"The weirdness never ends."

Sancha's smile sounded over the phone. "Well, he's Aaron."

"The coolest guy on the planet—and the weirdest."

"I'll tell him you called when he gets in. Or... maybe he's headed your way anyway?"

"Doubt it. Yeah, just tell him."

"Okay, Bennett, and... give your mom—and dad—my love."

"Will do. And... thanks."

3

ASELF IS INTERCONNECTED... WITH ALL, FEI IMPARTED, PERMEATING Tres's awareness, *with aself and with other.*

Other? Tres's consciousness inquired.

All. All is interconnected. All is alive... with vibrancy, awareness—impetus. Not all... chooses to identify as aself.

You mean... like animals?

'Animal,' as conveyed in your corporeality, is aself.

Like us? Like humans?

Of the Apart, there is no 'us'—only all.

Then, animals... they live... continuously as well?

Indeed.

Insects?

Of course.

Tres portrayed his form for Fei's benefit as a bright blue hue, jovially rising and falling in its perception. *Plants?*

All, as aself chooses. The infinite cycle of articulation and recreation are apparent even in corporeality. Aself—of any articulation—seeks interconnectedness, nurturing, and to serve aself's mien.

But not everything is... aself?

Indeed. Much is created by aself—manipulated, articulated—all with the possibility of creating aself anew.

Tres's form bobbed, rotated, as his realizations merged to intensify understanding.

All merges and re-emerges, Fei imparted. *All is interconnected. Creation begets creation.*

It is, Tres chided, *The Natural Order.*

Of Things—indeed.

4

Aaron rested, catching his breath as he leaned over, hands on knees. He looked out over the city below, smiling at no one and everything. He gazed over the miniature-looking buildings and homes with affection, feeling more a part of all—even as he grew more distant in mind and body.

Stretching his body, he felt loose, malleable, fluid. He felt lighter than ever before—carefree even. He scouted his return route home and began his descent along the winding, well-worn footpath down the first hill.

There was no sound but the warm breeze through the surrounding trees, no scent but of the heady musk of late summer.

An altogether different sense alerted him—to the one just to the right and above him, at the top of the hill, where the rolling fields of the hilltops fell away to a harsh rock face overlooking his path.

Aaron's head jerked in the direction of his expectation. Nothing out of place was visible. Still, he sensed danger—a feeling of ill ease—in his surroundings. He turned around to walk up the path again for a clearer view.

There, Finlay stood—calm and still at the edge of the drop-off—taking in the same view Aaron had moments before.

Without hesitation, Aaron called out to the one he hadn't spoken to in many years.

"FINLAY..." Aaron's voice carried between the trees that separated him from the figure standing at the top of the hill.

"Finlay?" he called again as he approached after a short jog.

Finlay turned toward him, the etchings in his face the antithesis of youth. "Aaron?" He stepped back, farther from the hill's edge, maintaining his distance from Aaron.

"Hi," Aaron prompted, studying Finlay's face.

"What..." Finlay's face tightened into the most familiar expression. "What do *you* want?"

"Nothing. I just saw you and—"

"And what?" The harshness of Finlay's tone contrasted with the beauty of their natural surroundings.

Aaron's awareness continued to heighten—without conscious direction—homing in on the atmosphere surrounding Finlay, collecting all information.

"What... are you... *staring* at," Finlay seethed, his posture leaning forward slightly, his own gaze just as piercing.

Aaron looked into Finlay's dark, near-black eyes and shivered in reaction to the cold emptiness he found there. "You," he insisted. "What *is* it? What's the matter?"

"I asked *you* that."

"No... something's *wrong*. You need something. Just tell me what it is."

Finlay's eyes widened to spheres; his feet shuffled backwards. "I... I don't know what you're talking about."

"Just tell me."

"Why should I?" he shouted.

Aaron had no answer, only a great desire to assist, in any way he could. "Because I can help," he said.

Finlay's head turned slightly, gesturing against Aaron's statement. His shallow breaths quickened. He stepped farther from Aaron—closer to the edge of the embankment.

"Finlay..." Aaron started, just as he acutely felt another presence—not too near but close enough.

He turned to see the expected vision of Fei. Instead, there was nothing, only the park-like setting awash in sunlight.

Still, something was there—without a doubt.

It hovered like a dark cloud—invisible but foreboding. It seeped into the environment, hiding within the sunlight, spreading, surrounding, leaving Aaron confused and his apprehension growing.

The sound of slipping gravel forced his attention toward Finlay again.

"Finlay, *trust* me," he pleaded with a cluster of emotions.

"Why *should* I?" Finlay's screech soared up to the clouds. He scurried backward yet more.

"Because you always have!" Aaron shouted as he reached toward his former classmate, grabbing his hand and yanking with all his strength.

Finlay fell toward him, one foot just brushing off the edge of the hilltop, sending loose stones tumbling into the ravine below. Finlay's hands clenched Aaron's shoulders—with desperation and restraint.

"How... did you know..." Finlay breathed, his voice soft with apology, "that I was going to... I came up here to..."

Aaron's gaze chased after the dark presence as he felt it dissipate. "I don't know," he answered.

Fᴇɪ ᴀʀᴛɪᴄᴜʟᴀᴛᴇᴅ ʜɪᴍsᴇʟF ᴀs ᴄᴏɴᴛᴇɴᴛ ɢʀᴇᴇɴ ᴀɴᴅ ɢᴏʟᴅ ᴀs ʜᴇ convened with the Consultation.

The ObServed flourishes, one member imparted.

The ObServed's awareness expands, another conveyed.

With fluidity.

My ObServed's early awakening, Fei offered, *proliferates his separation from corporeal life.*

Indeed.

It is unique.

It is... The Natural Order of Things.

Training... of the two...

Progresses expeditiously.

Preparation for the ConCentration is proficient.

As engenders... The Natural Order of Things.

Fei conveyed his leave of the Consultation, joyous in his affiliation with the imminent ConCentration.

Tʀᴇs Fʟɪᴄᴋᴇʀᴇᴅ, receiving Fei's conveyances while toying with tuning into—and out of—his awareness of the others—the *aselves*—always around them.

You dream. Yet, you dream not, Fei imparted to his student.

I am dreaming now, Tres replied.

Indeed. Your corporeal body and mind are in dream state. Yet—of the Apart—you are very much awake.

But I'm dreaming.

You are not.

I don't understand.

You still cling to your corporeal mind, its temporal functions and limiting manner. Your mind conjectures... that you only dream.

How do I know I am not?

Aself is aware... of truth.

I don't understand, Tres imparted, his inner struggle affecting his hue. *All of this,* he conveyed as his articulated form swished through his perceived environment, *is just a dream—from my mind—conjured.*

Aself's corporeal mind—flesh and blood—is, too, of aself's own creation. Its function is to assist with relating to corporeality. Yet— just as of corporeality—the mind does not exist. The mind is merely perception.

How do I know that... this exists? That... you do?

You are aware. Truth is all-apparent. Fei articulated his own form in a manner designed to draw more of Tres's attention. *Your attachment to corporeality only impedes your instruction.*

6

"DON'T PUT IT ON TOO SOON. IT'LL RUN RIGHT DOWN THE—"

"I know! You warn me *every* birthday!" Sancha lashed back at Maria as she laid the butter knife back on the kitchen table, far from the bowl of still-warm, homemade frosting.

"Not on *your* birthday," Maria said. "I do the frosting."

At the sound of his voice, they both turned to greet Bennett with smiles as he entered the kitchen. "Anything I can do to help?" he asked.

"No, no, sit down," Maria urged, a tinge of anxiety in her voice. "Sancha, did you get all the presents out of the closet?"

"Yes."

"This is a *ton* of food," Bennett said, sitting at the table. "You really don't have to go to so much—"

All three turned to look toward the front hall as the doorbell sounded. Maria glanced toward Sancha who only returned a shrug of her shoulders.

"I'll get it!" Aaron called down as he ran down the staircase. "Hey. Come in," he said as he temporarily disappeared from view and pulled the front door open.

Maria and Bennett faced the kitchen doorway while

Sancha's mouth hung open, her eyes alight with anticipation. Aaron entered, followed by a face neither Sancha nor Maria recognized—while Bennett's stare revealed volumes.

"We've got one more for dinner," Aaron announced, "to help us eat all this food. This is Finlay. We used to go to school together—remember?"

Bennett studied the two standing side by side, his anxious smile flattening to a straight line.

THE FIVE SAT around the dining room table, sinking further into their chairs under the weight of bellies filled with second helpings of dinner and dessert. Sancha and Maria gazed through the back windows overlooking the flowering garden as Finlay ventured to speak.

"Thanks—thank you—for having me." He looked to the women of the household for acknowledgment.

Sancha flashed a giant smile while Maria complimented him on his politeness and extended the open invitation to return. Aaron smiled his approval.

"How's... everything?" Bennett forced himself to ask.

"It's... uh, school's—"

"You're going to the university?" Sancha asked.

Finlay nodded.

Sancha's green eyes glowed. "Wow. That must cost—"

"Sancha," Maria blurted. "That's not—"

"His parents are loaded," Bennett interrupted.

Maria's frown stooped lower, but Finlay nodded. "My mom —*not* my stepdad," he clarified.

Aaron studied Finlay's expression.

"And thanks to him, probably not for long," Finlay said, staring at his empty dinner plate. "Nothing you can do about it."

"YOU REALLY DON'T HAVE TO," Sancha said, accepting the clean and dripping dinner plate from Bennett's hands. She dabbed at it with a dishtowel as she pondered the meaning of Bennett's expression.

He continued to scrub through the pile of dirty dishes in silence, his head tilted toward the view of the bottom of the staircase through the kitchen entrance.

"Why don't you go up and join them?" Sancha offered. "You've already done too much."

"No, that's all right. I wanna help," Bennett insisted, his ears straining to detect any audible fragments of the conversation upstairs.

AARON PEERED through his bedroom window and over the back garden. "Sorry about that."

"They were just trying to make conversation," Finlay mumbled as he pretended to admire Aaron's book collection.

"I'm glad you came."

"Well, I didn't have anything better to do," Finlay answered too quickly. "And Mom... eh, you don't care." He turned his attention to the row of books at eye level.

"Sure I do."

Finlay glared, his eyes cold, black disks.

"I'm sorry," Aaron said, "that we... didn't get along—when we were younger."

"We don't get along now."

"That's not true. We just haven't talked... in a while."

"Why'd you invite me?"

"'Because... it's my birthday—more fun to share with other people."

Finlay smirked, his gaze wandering, searching for anything else to focus on. "Why were you on the hill the other day?"

"I run up there."

"On top of the hill?"

"No, up the hill."

Finlay's wry smile complimented the shake of his head. He picked up a marble wedged at the end of a shelf in the bookcase. "Well, you don't have to—make an effort. I can take a hint."

"What do you mean?"

"That you don't want to be friends. I tried... *whatever*."

"It's not about that. I just want... to help."

Finlay's hushed voice grew louder. "I don't need your *help*."

"Fine. But... I'm here—if you need. That's all. It just feels—"

"What?" Finlay delivered as an accusation.

"Maybe I could do something."

"Well, you can't. And you don't even know what the freakin' problem is." Finlay's stare intensified, his entire face squinting. His body leaned toward the bedroom door. "And I don't *have* a problem—anyway."

Aaron nodded; Finlay didn't break his stare.

"Why'd you do it?" Finlay asked.

"Do what?"

"Refuse to be my friend." Finlay's face softened. "We were just *kids*. I was *nice* to you! What was the big deal?"

Aaron drew a deep breath and glanced down at the rug beneath his feet. "I just felt..."

"Felt *what*?"

"That you didn't really like me."

"I did—*then*."

"I felt, later on, you wouldn't."

"So, WHAT'D I MISS?" Aaron asked too loudly as he stepped into the kitchen, commanding the immediate attention of Maria, Sancha, and Bennett all at once.

"Why'd your friend leave so fast?" Sancha asked.

"Finlay? Don't know. I guess... I don't know. Something's bothering him. I don't know what."

"Here? Did we do—"

"No, no. Nothing like that. He had a great time."

Bennett scrubbed the last dirty dish and let it sink beneath the sink full of soapy water. "Why don't we go outside? On a day like this, we shouldn't just sit indoors."

"Sure," Aaron answered with a shrug.

"So," Bennett said as he followed Aaron's slow stride around the perimeter of the back yard, "what's the deal?"

Aaron glanced at him, offering no words.

"Finlay!" Bennett erupted. "What the hell? You guys have been lifelong *enemies!*"

"Not really, not officially."

"Official enough!"

"That was a long time ago."

"It's been the *same* ever since I've known you."

"Yeah, I know."

"So, what's going on?"

Aaron continued his path, staring at the ground before him. "Remember that time we saw him, just looking all... lost or whatever?"

Bennett nodded.

"I saw him again," Aaron continued. "He didn't look too good. I think he was about to... I just felt bad for him."

"He was really shit to you—last I saw."

"I remember."

"Well," Bennett finally smiled as he squeezed Aaron's shoulder. "That's what I'm here for."

"I don't know..." Aaron looked to the sky. "Whatever's going on—with him—just seems really serious."

Bennett's sigh was loud—and long. "Okay, but what can *you* do about it?"

"I don't know—help in some way."

Bennett searched Aaron's face for the clues he knew he'd never find there.

"It just *feels* right," was all that Aaron offered.

7

Why, Tres asked his translucent companion, doesn't everyone see their OnLooker—the one who watches—if everyone has one?

It is not... The Natural Order of Things, Fei answered.

But I saw you. I see you now.

It is possible... at the periphery... of aself's awareness—while in corporeality. Many may sense... accompaniment, presence, in aself's corporeal aspect... as a 'glimpse from the corner of the eye.' Or aself may wake from dream state... with residual awareness of OnLooker's guidance.

Like how you communicate with me?

Yes. And no.

And why... wouldn't you speak to me—if you could hear me— when I saw you all those times and when I spoke to you?

OnLooker does not intervene in corporeal life. OnLooker merely obServes.

But you did. You... did... intervene. You spoke to me and then—

It is The Natural Order of Things.

Tres's form fluttered, phasing in and out as he projected himself. *But... if people did see—did know—that they have an*

OnLooker, someone watching out for them, they might... live differently. They might... find it comforting.

The awareness would conflict with corporeal life... with the aself-development it offers, the aself-development aself chooses. Fei glowed golden with the truth of his message. *Aself chooses... limited awareness—the chosen experience of corporeality. OnLooker merely obServes.*

THE GENTLE KNOCK on his bedroom door rapped at the sense of peace and tranquility Aaron enjoyed while he dreamed. The sound jarred him from all imaginings, yanking his mind alert again.

"Yes," he groaned, untwisting himself from his bedcovers.

The door opened, revealing his grandmother. "You're still asleep?"

"What time is it?"

"Late!"

Aaron rubbed his eyes with one hand as he sat up.

"Good dream?" she asked as she sat beside him on the bed.

Aaron nodded. "It felt so real."

Maria smiled. "You're sleeping in later these days. It's a good thing you don't have morning classes."

Aaron yawned, then rested against the headboard. "Is there something wrong?"

"No, no. Just wanted to chat. We don't get to do that very much these days."

Aaron smiled his agreement.

"Did you have a good birthday?"

"Yeah. Always."

"Good, good. And Bennett? He had a good time?"

"Yeah, I think so."

"He seemed a bit quiet."

"Maybe."

"He wasn't upset, was he?"

"I... don't think so."

"Did he know... about your spending time with Finlay again?"

"Oh, that. I guess I should've told Bennett I invited him."

"Yes, maybe. You two are the closest I've ever seen anyone—a bond that's worth protecting."

"Yeah—yes. He's still my best friend."

"Good. You two aren't spending nearly as much time together these days."

"Yeah, it's just... hard."

"Why?"

Aaron shook his head and pulled himself to sit up straight. "I don't know. I guess... I'm just not in the mood."

"*None* of us see much of you these days."

"I'm here most of the time."

"Yes... in your room—alone."

Aaron made a face his grandmother couldn't interpret.

"Anything you want to talk to your grandmom about?" she asked.

"No. There's... not anything really. I can't really explain it. I just feel..."

"Distant."

"Yeah—like I don't know... what I'm supposed to be *doing*, you know?"

Maria nodded. "Well, it is a tough time. You're *twenty* now. The world expects you to have a plan, know what you want to do—"

"And I don't. Everyone else does—or thinks they do—but I don't. Not... this time."

"Aaron," Maria twisted to face Aaron fully. "I know Sancha

and I have had a hard time understanding, but... *you've* always had a way of understanding—of knowing things—that she and I just... can't."

She continued, "So, trust yourself. All the answers are in there." Maria gently prodded Aaron's chest. "And that doesn't mean you have to know them all now, but when it matters, you'll know just what to do."

Her smile was broad and warm. She pulled herself off his bed, her knees creaking. "You *always* have."

Aaron watched his grandmother leave, closing the door behind her. The content of his dreams hung vividly in mind, even as he felt himself gently, lovingly, pulled from them, beckoned by his family and the life he still lived.

8

Expand—open to... your awareness, Fei instructed his student within dream state. *Guide attention... through all—even as you are with all.*

Blackness surrounded Tres, weighing on his senses as warm emptiness.

Perceive... the Apart. Envision... all energy... and between.

Tres let his imagination roam unrestricted, his quickest connection to escaping the bounds of his mental thoughts and matching his perception to the descriptions his tutor provided. Images of light—fine points—began to appear to him, all around, in abundance, merging and separating, moving, alive.

All energy... and between, Fei repeated. *Focus on... between.*

Tres watched the dance around him, noticed the patterns and the randomness, observed the seeming darkness *between* that slowly revealed itself to also be light.

Attend to the movement... the fluidity... the simultaneously occurring acts of creation.

Tres's perception uncovered more intricate flows—waves and pulses—akin to looking at the atmosphere through a microscope, all particles visible—the particles within particles within particles. He discovered the gaps between, as it unfolded, brimming with light—all endless, infinite, connected.

Perceive the whole... the all... the Apart. Aself joined with aself... all relating, all combining.

Tres encouraged his attention to focus outward, to distance itself, to witness the greater patterns of movement and light. He sensed the personalities within personalities forming greater personalities—some with the semblance of faces, most merely visions of moving light.

Expand, Fei imparted. *Become aware... of the whole. Open.*

Tres let go—of his own identity, of the always-present mental pull to hang onto himself. He released all—trusting his tutor, reassuring his consciousness that all was just a dream, that there can be no true danger in mere *dreams.*

What transformed—morphing before Tres's perception—encompassed *all,* even himself. He sensed the presence of all—all within view, all communicating with him simultaneously, with a single voice.

And he sensed Fei's form—his personality—fading, growing more distant, then falling out of perception entirely.

WELCOME, a new voice imparted within Tres's awareness, announcing itself, conveying personality with message as it instilled the sensation of expansive, inexhaustible capability.

I am the one called Saig, it conveyed.

———

THE BLUE TINT of morning light barely peeked above his closed bedroom curtains when the blaring ringtone sounded from his new mobile phone—giving Aaron the worst awakening of his life. He felt blindly for the wriggling phone as it spun in vibratory circles over his bedside table, and he jabbed at it to accept the incoming call.

"You've *got* to tell me how to change the ringtone!" he shouted at the bottom of the phone.

"All right," Bennett said. "Sorry, I—"

"And the thing vibrates all over the place—like it's alive! I was asleep."

"All right, all right. I'm sorry, I'll... look, it's my dad. They just raced him to the hospital. Can you... would you... *I need you there.*"

"Yeah—of course. Want me to pick you up?"

"Please. Hurry. I don't know what to—"

"Don't worry—okay? I'm on my way."

ENTERING THE HOSPITAL UNNERVED AARON, prompting flashbacks to memories so current, they seemed to hang in the air around him like Polaroid snapshots dangling from the ceiling. And yet, that part of this life *felt* like eons ago.

"How do I find... I don't know where... Mom said..." Bennett muttered, turning in one direction in the reception area, then another.

"Don't worry. I got it," Aaron said, reaching for Bennett and trying to contain him in one place. "Just sit—if you can. I'll find out where he is."

Bennett stared blankly as Aaron talked to the nurse at the reception desk. Aaron returned with a smile and took Bennett's arm. "This way."

Aaron sat in a chair outside the room holding Bennett's father hostage. Only the muffled speech of Bennett and his mother sounded over the chaotic din of the intensive care unit.

Aaron's mind wandered, searching for suitable words of condolence, of wisdom offering reassurance. *If this is his time, he'll have another,* was the thought most prominent—and the one he would not say aloud.

Instead, he silently shouted it at the clinical surroundings and the sense of urgency, stress, and potency of emotion they contained. The intensity—the poignancy—of life and death seemed to shout back from the hospital walls.

How fast and fleeting it all is, Aaron thought. *But there are others...*

A nurse rushed past, headed to a different room, a different patient. A phone blared; a nasal voice shouted into it. The intercom beckoned yet more cause for urgency and concern.

Surrounded by all those living out the *only* life they believed they were gifted, Aaron felt more foreign, more out of place—and *time*—than ever before.

In the same moment, a sense of peace washed over him, the sense of time slowing. He felt connected to the embodied emotions all around him but also a detachment from all. He felt the need to free himself—and the deep desire to *free all of them.*

As Aaron gazed with glazed eyes—looking at nothing but absorbing all—one figure stood out from the rest, among all the faces in the bright light of the corridor. Aaron stood—feeling his body reaffix itself to the physical world—and walked down the hall toward the face he felt drawn to.

"Finlay," he spoke softly.

Finlay jumped at the sound of his name and the touch of a hand on his arm. "What," he managed, before deciding to wait for Aaron to explain his own presence.

"Bennett's dad, he has cancer. Did you know? It's getting the best of him—they say."

Sympathy poured over Finlay's face before his own discomfort returned. "I... I was just—"

"Why are *you* here?"

Finlay locked his gaze with Aaron's and shuffled on his feet. His hands fidgeted in and out of his pockets. He scrutinized the tile floor as he spoke. "My mom."

"Is she all right? Is she sick?"

Finlay shook his head, still staring at the floor. "She fell—down the basement steps." Then, his head lifted, revealing his wide, dark eyes. The truth—in full detail—was visible to Aaron before Finlay felt compelled to hint at it. "That's what she told the doctors anyway."

Aaron continued to search Finlay's eyes. "*Tell me,*" he urged with his truest voice.

Finlay glanced around them. His jaw clenched; he wet his lips. "My stepdad," he whispered. "I don't even live with them anymore. I think that's part of the problem. It's my—"

"Your stepdad," Aaron restated, prompting Finlay to confirm the information he already knew.

Finlay nodded and looked over his shoulder again.

"What are you going to do about it?" Aaron asked.

Finlay shrugged. "What *can* I do? Mom, she won't talk to the police. She's scared to death of him. And I can't be there every minute..."

"You need to *stop* him."

Finlay's pale face erupted in swatches of red; his eyes grew smaller, more piercing. "I *can't,*" he seethed.

"I don't believe that."

Finlay delivered his words slowly, harshly. "*You...* don't know... *anything.*" He turned and paced down the corridor.

"Is he here?" Aaron shouted after him. He ran up to Finlay and caught his shoulder. "Is he *here*?"

"Always!" Finlay shouted back, yanking his shoulder out of Aaron's grasp and hurrying down the hall.

Aaron matched every step.

AARON APPROACHED the window looking into the hospital room Finlay entered. He peered to see through the partially opened blinds inside, finding Finlay standing next to an even taller man with heavy presence.

The man's large hand squeezed Finlay's shoulder as he spoke in low tones into his ear. Only Finlay focused on the woman lying in the bed before them, her face so swollen and deformed that it was utterly unrecognizable, even while she attempted to move her lips to speak.

Aaron allowed his mind a single statement of warning. He honored it with acknowledgment, then disregarded it. He chose to enter the room unannounced and uninvited.

The man he'd never met immediately responded by standing straighter, taller, eyeing Aaron with suspicion, saying nothing but communicating the precise message he intended.

"What are you..." Finlay started to ask in a weak tone Aaron had never heard from him.

"I heard... of your mom's... accident," Aaron answered. "I wanted to—"

"My *wife* doesn't want any *guests,*" Finlay's stepfather spoke, lathering his voice with aggression as he stepped toward Aaron.

Aaron stood his ground and maintained his neutral tone. "I just felt I could—"

"I *said* you are *not*—"

"You should *go*," Finlay intervened, his eyes emphasizing his plea.

Aaron remained still, allowing Finlay's stepfather to complete his approach.

He towered over Aaron, his chest wide and pushed forward, his eyes squinting. "I don't know *who* you are, but you're gonna leave right *now*," he spat from between clenched teeth.

Aaron stood, calm and still. He peered into the open, accessible eyes hovering over him, glaring at him—their truth laid bare. The essence of the man unfolded—his every desire, need, and dream revealed.

"I'm only gonna tell you *one* more—"

"You don't need to," Aaron said with unbreakable calm.

"*Good*. So, turn around and—"

"I'm not leaving," Aaron stated, unblinking.

Finlay's stepfather cocked his head. His eyes closed to tight slits. The tendons in his neck bulged. His hands squeezed into fists.

Finlay's foot slid forward, then back again. A moan rose from his mother, the battered woman lying in bed.

"*You...*" Aaron spoke with the assurance of wisdom.

Finlay's stepfather inched forward, leaning yet further over Aaron in final warning.

Aaron maintained his unblinking stare of neutrality and unwavering attention. "You *promised her* you wouldn't do it again."

The stepfather's chin lifted slightly. A whimper lifted from the bed behind him. He smiled, his lips stretching to the sides of his face, his large teeth bared. "*No*—I didn't."

"Not her," Aaron corrected. "Your *mother*." The words clung to the air, hanging there, their meaning resonating throughout the room.

The stepfather's expression twitched. His thick, tight-knit

eyebrows slowly rose. His smile fell open, forming the questioning face of a confronted child inflicted with parental humiliation.

"*Remember that,*" were Aaron's last words.

He stepped away. Finlay's stepfather curled slightly—his shoulders hunching as he folded in on himself like an embarrassed child.

Aaron looked to Finlay for permission, then approached the woman he remembered to be so much younger and so beautiful.

He smiled at her—with his gleaming blue eyes alone—communicating all of his feelings, intentions, and promises with ease and eloquence. A tear rolled down her cheek, and she reached for his hand. Her own message was also clear.

Aaron turned, nodded to Finlay, and quietly left.

As AARON TURNED down the corridor leading to Bennett's father's room, he found it filled with familiar faces. Sancha and Maria talked with friends of Bennett's parents and a few neighbors. One young woman sat alone at the edge of the group of visitors.

Jen's face appeared older, still plain but with delicate, natural beauty. Aaron walked up to her, his mind racing to find the right words.

"Hey... you're here," was all that he managed.

Jen's smile was instant and bright, fully finishing her face with artful curves. "Hi, I... didn't know you were here."

"I came with Bennett. I was just... I went for a walk."

She nodded, glancing away before facing Aaron again. "It's... been a long time."

Aaron smiled. "Yeah. You're going to..."

"State. Not the best school, but not too far from home either. Their liberal arts program is pretty good."

Aaron nodded. "Cool. It's nice of you to come by. I'm sure they appreciate—"

"I talked to Bennett already. He seems... like he's handling it all right."

"I guess so. But it's not going to get easier."

Jen nodded as Aaron slipped into the chair beside her. The awkward silence dissipated when Bennett appeared.

He nodded at Jen, then turned to Aaron. "Where *were* you?"

"I just—"

"I *need* you here. It's... this is all just..." He paused to breathe.

Aaron jumped to Bennett's side. "Hey, I'm here now. It's going to be *okay*."

Bennett's glare sliced through Aaron's casually delivered reassurance. "He asked for you," he said.

"He did?"

Bennett nodded without breaking his cold stare.

"Should I—"

Bennett answered him by turning the handle to open the door to his father's room.

AARON SHUDDERED at the sight of Bennett's father's gaunt face and the emaciated body lying beneath the bedcovers. Aaron was grateful Bennett's mother was absent for the moment, leaving his reaction was unseen.

"Still recognize me?" The dry-throated voice still carried a jovial tone, instantly comforting Aaron, just as intended.

Aaron smiled as he approached the bedside and studied the face of the man who'd made him laugh so often throughout his childhood. "Of course, Jim—as long as you've got your check-ered pajamas on."

Jim laughed, and the moisture appearing in his eyes thanked Aaron for the gift. "You're such a smart one," he managed to say after wetting his throat with a sip of water.

"Bennett said you asked for me?"

Jim shrugged his skinny shoulders. "Gives me something to do," he said through a smile, "and makes them feel better—if I'm doing all the things they think a dying man ought to be."

The smile growing on Aaron's face disappeared. "Don't say that."

"Hey," he said with sudden strength, grabbing Aaron's arm. "I can say anything..." He raised his head to survey the room, then whispered, "anything I *darn well* please—I've earned it. And that's just about... the only thing I get out of all this."

Aaron nodded. "Do you need anything? Want me to get you some more water or—"

"Nope." His answer came quick and with all his character-istic cheeriness. He smiled up at Aaron, staring at him intently. "You know, I think I actually feel *better* with you in the room." He continued to stare, searching Aaron's eyes for something. "Like I have a comrade-in-arms, someone who views all this the way that I do: like an engineer."

Aaron shook his head.

"No, you do," Jim said, his enjoyment of the subject evident on his face. "It's just another of life's mysteries, just like all the rest of 'em. Another challenge—and I do love a challenge." He turned away, his eyes focused on the room's emptiness. "But this one... this is a problem I can't solve, no matter how clever I am."

Aaron covered Jim's hand with his own. "I... I wish I could help you—do something—somehow. But I can't think... I don't have any memory of—"

"No." Jim's attention returned, targeting Aaron with full

intensity. "No, that's not it, you see? That's my *point*. The *mysteries*, Aaron—the ones you *can't* solve—those are the best ones. They're the ones that make life so... fantastic!"

Aaron watched his best friend's father, his own friend, shed a smattering of tears—tears of contentment, of reflection upon a life well lived. And he couldn't help but feel the same joy in return—even, seemingly, at the oddest time of all.

TRES... THE NEW, MORE RESONATING VOICE CALLED FROM HIS dreams.

The black of the void surrounding Tres's presence edged toward gray haze, then to blue hues infusing light all around. The *all* gathered into *one*—features forming, drawing themselves—directed at Tres's awareness. The gradually appearing lines and curves of facial countenance resonated with naturalness, humility, informality, and an ever-expansive tranquility.

While Fei's chosen representation had been vague, wafting, more a hovering haze of flickering light, this personage manifested itself as more characteristically human: a translucent body complete with limbs, even the concept of clothing.

Welcome... again, the new identity mused, transferring concept in the same wordless manner.

Tres did not consciously acknowledge his own question before it was answered.

I... am the one called Saig. The accompanying smile—not seen but sensed—rippled with gentility, formulated of joy itself. *You are most welcome,* Saig replied with uncanny quickness again. *I took great joy in concocting this form just for you. I am glad it pleases you. I have done well.*

Tres reflected back in ambiguous form, expressing his acceptance of the environment of the Apart.

You are free to be... as you prefer, Saig imparted in response, again with amusement and glee. *You have adapted well to your instruction thus far... as the Consultation conveys.*

Saig again delivered his answer—*simultaneously* with Tres's asking of the question itself, and even before Tres's mind finished processing the most recent communication.

The Consultation... Saig delivered as his form flickered. He continued with an apology. *I will allow you to complete your thought. I recognize you are uncomfortable with the efficiency of my communication.*

What is... the Consultation? Tres's mind finalized, weary with effort.

Very well. You do indeed adapt well, Saig praised. *Allow me to offer the first of my instruction to you.* The vision of the calm, content older man carried itself forward and back, as if pacing through the blue-tinted surroundings. *As you have learned, in articulating with the one called Fei, your thoughts are conveyed to all... unless you do withhold their... amplitude, their breadth. As such, your thoughts are known to me—as they are to all aselves of the Apart. But you do not yet grasp the... simultaneous... occurrence of the activity, of the... transmission.* Saig's purple-tinted emanation fluttered. *You will, in time.*

But... there is no time—You are correct, Tres's thoughts blended with Saig's reply.

My apologies, Saig imparted. *I again—'miscalculate' is your corporeality's term?* Saig vibrated his pleasure in the discourse. *I am... 'out of practice'... with the agreed upon habits of your corporeality... and the 'time' your corporeal mind requires.*

Tres detected the sense of a giggle reverberating from Saig's form as he continued to convey the lesson.

I will attempt to offer you... more 'time'... as you continue to require it within our exchange. And you will learn to recognize the intention... before... the thought, the inward message... before the outward message conveyed to all. As you become aware of the separation, you will no longer feel the... unpleasant... sensation of aself... invading your mind and 'snatching your thoughts.'

The intended humor danced in the vision of the atmospheric; particles of light drifted with aliveness and vibrancy before subdued once more.

I have a lot to learn, Tres imparted openly in a successfully controlled manner. His personal pride was supported—congratulated—by the perceived environment.

Less than you assume, Saig replied. *As to your previous question, the Consultation gathers and informs. It is merely a convening of aselves—as they have individually chosen—which aids in overSeeing the general activities and design of The Natural Order of Things. Collectively, the aselves of the Consultation serve as a guiding energy— merely. They are available to aself—any aself—seeking such guidance.*

Are they... in charge of the Apart? Tres asked.

Saig's laughter rippled in visible waves without sound. *Forgive... my amusement. I do enjoy... the aself-development offered even as I instruct. In answer to your question, Tres, no aself or gathering of aselves is 'in charge.' Of the Apart, there are no 'masters,' no 'followers'... no 'government.' Such... are concepts of your corporeality —and some others—only.*

No... no one's in charge? At all?

Does aself require... a ruler? Saig challenged before ignoring his own hypothetical question. *All aselves... choose for themselves. All... is choice.*

But... there must be... organization, Tres's mind argued.

All... is most naturally... organized. It is The Natural Order of Things.

So, The Natural Order of Things controls—

Your attachment to the agreed upon concepts of your corporeality is still strong. You are capable... of opening much greater awareness.

There is nothing, Tres tried again, projected his notion in brilliant light, *in control?*

There is only creation... which all aselves are capable of —created of.

Everyone is equal?

Indeed—if you prefer the term.

We all—when we're in the Apart—just do our own thing?

What else... would you have aself... do?

Tres's confusion—his mind's inner tantrum—rebelled with rising red hues. *Then, wouldn't everyone... be the same? Why are there different roles: OnLookers and the ObServed, corporeal life and the Apart, the Consultation?*

For aself-development, to serve aself's mien. All are naturally... aware. Awareness is not subject to your corporeal concepts of 'quantity' or 'rank' or 'hierarchy.'

All are aware, Tres pondered.

As aselves desire.

The Consultation... only offers guidance.

Indeed. As any aself is capable.

They are just... aselves, like the rest of us.

Indeed. And they are three.

Three aselves?

Indeed.

Why?

It is... The Natural Order of Things.

And they—the Consultation—know me? They're watching me? Tres imparted.

Humor visually careened all around as Tres began to detect the patterns of Saig's consistent playfulness and delight.

Only aself's OnLooker looks on, was the reply received. *You are the ObServed of Fei.*

What does the Consultation—

The Consultation merely addresses... your existence.

My existence? Why?

As dictated by The Natural Order of Things.

Why me?

Your training commences.

For what? I don't have any idea—

You will. Saig's form wavered. *You do now... as you free your awareness, allow its expansion.*

I don't—

That is all for now. I wish not to 'overwhelm' you, Saig mused. *And... you do have a 'life' to live.*

AARON LAY IN BED, his lower legs entangled in a wad of bedcovers, his eyes wide-open to the ceiling. His ears filled with the sounds of the waking house: Maria bustling in the kitchen, Sancha stirring in the hallway bathroom.

His lazy eyelids blinked open. His wistful breaths flowed in and out of his chest. His thoughts swayed—from the environment surrounding his physical body to the ideas permeating from his dreams.

What is real... what really matters?

He felt *nowhere*—as if his feet dangled without firm ground to stand on, as if he had no foundation for his mind to form concrete decision from.

Why does it matter if I even get out of bed? What am I getting up for?

He turned his head to the side, one eye buried in pillow. The other stared at his mobile phone lying on the bedside table. He reached for it, fumbled through the icons and menus to find his contacts.

He selected the phone number most recently added and dialed it.

"Hello?" Jen's voice was soft and soothing.

10

You only need remove the limits you have placed on awareness, Saig imparted to Tres's awareness, *to become aware of the entirety of reality.* He continued, *Corporeal dreams are merely... translation, language demanded of manifestation in your corporeality... to convey messages of the true self... to your corporeal form.*

This is just a dream. It has to be. The statements seemed separate from himself, even as Tres's mind declared them, insisted on them. *You told me I have a life to live. Why is that important if... if this is real?*

All serves aself's mien. All serves aself's aself-development. Saig rearticulated his form to draw his student's increased attention. *You remain attached to corporeal concepts, to the concept—the belief—that dream is merely corporeal.*

If dreaming—the body sleeping—is not corporeal, what is it?

It is... between. And of the Apart, as all is. Dream state offers the most accessible 'channel' for your return to the Apart, your always-present connection to the Apart, Saig conveyed.

My dreams are... not real?

They are not... corporeal. Dream... is indeed reality. All... is reality... in a way, and as funneled by your awareness.

If this is really real—being with you here, now—why do I have to go back to... to my life?

Corporeal life is to be lived. And it is as you chose, Tres.

Then, why am I pulled here, every night, in my dreams—away from my life? Why... are you now here—with me?

For your instruction, of course.

To be an OnLooker? Is that why—?

Of a sort. Saig's undulating, visual giggle came as a surprise to Tres's perception.

Will I learn... everything you know of—are aware of?

Some, not all... for I have also lived many corporeal lives... choices, paths, experiences... imparting knowledge serving my own mien... as your lives have served for you. Your instruction... serves other purposes.

What purposes?

Those selected by The Natural Order of Things.

Tres's image rose with his frustration. *What really is... the 'natural order' that every—?*

It is all. It is creation, the perfect, self-fulfilling, self-supporting flow of the Apart.

I didn't choose this. I didn't ask to be instructed.

But you are 'this.' And all is choice... even if you reject the awareness.

No, I'm just... it doesn't make sense—none of it.

Your lingering attachment to your corporeal mind limits your... pleasure. You... are the organization of all, its creation. Awareness is your choice.

I'm trying...

Your awareness is expanding. You only have to allow awareness. It is your choice. All is your choice—and your choice alone. It is The Natural Order of Things.

But I didn't choose... to be here.

You have—or you would not... be.

Tres flickered with impatience as his mind battled conflicting thoughts.

You have only to become aware... to feel at peace, Tres. In awareness—in knowing—is acceptance, Saig imparted.

Acceptance of what?

Reality.

Which one?

All.

As light hues promenaded with dark, the surrounding expanse pulsed with energy—bulging, moving, sometimes revealing personalities coming and going. Saig's conveyance flowed freely into Tres's consciousness.

You are aware of the reality of the Apart. You are aware that it is not 'felt' in temporal terms—it is purely, truly, only... awareness.

As Tres experimented with the idea—changing his form, playing in his surroundings—Saig continued, *And the Apart is similarly known... within any corporeality. All you have to do is free your awareness. Allow me to invite you... to play with your awareness, Tres. It is yours to manipulate, just as reality is yours... to create.*

Saig's presence paced the open expanse, emanating patience and gregariousness. Tres willfully let his consciousness become absorbed by the image and its personality, recording the details, guessing at their implication.

11

"I DIDN'T THINK YOU'D EVER ACTUALLY CALL," JEN SPOKE THROUGH a warm smile. "But, I'm really glad you did."

She walked along the sidewalk bordering the city park, every step closing more of the distance between herself and Aaron.

Aaron formed a smile for her benefit, while his sight focused straight ahead, catching some of the details of people passing by, ignoring others.

"So..." Jen spoke, "how's Bennett's dad now? Is he still..."

"He's hanging in there," Aaron said, squinting at the sun, his walk slow and meandering. "Last I heard."

Jen nodded at the sidewalk below their feet, then followed Aaron's lead into the park.

"How are you doing?" she asked.

"I'm good. It's..." His sentence faded with his attention.

"You seem," Jen said, forced to squint as she looked up at Aaron, "different now—more... dreamy."

Aaron snickered. "Dreamy?"

"No, I didn't mean... not like that," she said between blushing cheeks. "Just distant. You used to be—"

"More fun," Aaron answered for her.

"No—I mean, I wouldn't know—but... yeah—I thought. When we were in high school, you were all... full of energy—big track star and all. You don't look like you've even been—"

Aaron smiled. "You know, I finally went for a run again the other week."

"Yeah? That's good."

"I guess—it felt good—I guess I just don't feel like I *need* to anymore."

"Hmm," Jen pondered aloud as she glanced at the playground just in view.

"You wanna go take a spin on the merry-go-round?"

"We'll have to kick those other kids off."

"Let's do it."

Jen beamed and mimicked Aaron's jog toward the playground equipment. As they neared it, two women gathered their children, directing them toward the jungle gym instead.

"I guess we scared them," Aaron said, stepping onto the merry-go-round.

Jen giggled, exaggerated the effort required to start Aaron spinning, then jumped on herself. When she glanced up again, Aaron stared into the distance, seeing past the kids at play and their parents huddled in conversation nearby—maybe past the city entirely.

"So," she said, "What have you been... thinking about lately?"

"Me? Oh, lots of random stuff."

"Know what you're gonna do when you graduate?"

"No idea."

"You always seemed to know exactly what you wanted to do."

"I did?"

"Mm-hmm. Or... you didn't seem worried about it anyway—like each day was a thing in itself."

"I guess." Aaron reached for the ground with the toe of his shoe, slowing their spin as he stared off into the distance again.

The light afternoon breeze flowed around him, gently pushing against his bare arms, allowing him to pass through it. His vision blurred, images growing fuzzy and faded; he stumbled off the merry-go-round. He sensed his surroundings falling away, the view altering, becoming fragmented—a view of parts, of *particles*.

"Aaron?" Jen whispered as she stopped the merry-go-round after it spun her around and next to him once more.

"Hmm?" he answered, turning to face her, startled to find he saw *through* her.

He knew she peered at him—silent and waiting, her face just inches from his. He scrutinized his view; his eyes grew smaller, searching for a different perspective. Jen's face remained fragmented, pieced apart, blending with the particles of its surroundings.

A wave of dizziness passed over Aaron. He swayed backward, his grip tightening on the bar of the merry-go-round to steady himself.

"Aaron?" Jen called again, her voice tinged with concern.

Still seeing through her, Aaron leaned forward, falling through the gaps between forms hovering in his vision. His lips pressed against Jen's—suddenly, sharply, but gently.

She kissed him back—re-establishing the distinct existence of his physical surroundings.

I CAN'T DO IT, Tres's form imparted as he was beckoned to the Apart yet again. *I can't... be in both realities.*

You do. You are, Saig conveyed. *And there is only one.*

It's too hard.

387

You are capable—more... than merely capable. Only your corporeal mind struggles... and it... is not... you.

I don't see why... I'm not ready.

Your training prepares you. You have only to absorb it, allow it into your awareness.

But what am I training for? Tres's form rose and fell with his consuming mood.

You... are aware, Saig's form imparted in reply. *You are... selected.*

But everything is a choice—my choice.

Yes.

It's all so... Tres compiled the perception he radiated, condensing, then expanding. *Every OnLooker has gone through the same training?*

Yes. And no.

And you?

Indeed.

How did you adjust... to living and learning all this at the same time?

I did not.

I don't understand—but you've had the same training...

You... are the first.

I'm... the first?

You are... the only. And your training continues.

12

"YOU'VE ALWAYS SEEMED *DIFFERENT* IN SOME WAY," JEN SAID, HER head resting on her folded hands as she laid on her side to face Aaron. "That's why I couldn't... stop thinking about you. I guess." Her gaze lingered, taking in the features of his face as they lay side by side on his bed.

Aaron's smile was genuine but brief; his eyes remained directed at the ceiling. Jen allowed a short sigh to slip from her breath, its message, the invite, not unnoticed by Aaron.

"Do you ever wonder," he asked, "if there's more?"

"Like, as we grow older? Of course, there is."

"Yeah, but... out there?" Aaron glanced at the window.

"Outer space? Like... aliens?"

"No," Aaron said, smiling at his own ambiguity. "Afterwards... I guess."

"After we die?"

Only after hearing Jen name his thought, Aaron remembered he already held the answer—had already been *given* the answer. "Never mind," he sighed, turning on his side to face her directly.

Jen's eyes brightened in response to his nearness. Her lips

squeezed together. Aaron leaned to answer the signal, their lips touching—but only briefly. Jen's smile disappeared.

"You're a daydreamer," she said to the face that was already turned toward the ceiling again.

"You think so?"

"Mm-hmm. You're not always... *here*—like you wish you were somewhere else."

"Not true," Aaron said, granting Jen his full attention as he rolled over to face her again. "I like it here."

He kissed her—lingering this time, savoring the sensation—and reached his arm around her.

As their lips parted, Jen asked, "How many girlfriends have you had?"

"How many?" Aaron repeated, mid-laugh.

"All this time, I thought you just avoided girls—you were so serious about track or something—but, you kiss like you've done it a million times before."

"Am I that bad?"

"No... you're that good," she said, leaning in for another. "But... I thought I was your first." Her moistened lips pressed into a pout.

"Well, you are," Aaron said with complete conviction.

"No. No, I'm not. What did you... have a hot babysitter or something?"

"No! I've never even had a babysitter." The last word caught in Aaron's throat as he realized the truth—in one life, one reality —to be a lie in others. "Unless you count nursery school or something and that was a *long* time ago."

Jen turning away, then asked, "How far?"

"What do you mean?"

"How far have you *gone* with a girl before?"

IT WAS INSTANT, unstoppable: a torrent of piquing emotion. Intense flashes and strobing visions faded, then reappeared with blinding brightness—striking Tres with blunt, brutal force.

"Not now," he groaned aloud, unaware. He felt heartache with happiness, joy with emptiness, intimacy with rejection—all at once and *unrelenting*.

His eyes watered as he rubbed at them, trying to blink away the uninvited memories. Instantly extracted, he was neither here nor there, now nor then.

"Aaron..." a distant voice called. "Aaron!" drew him back to one finite moment again.

"WHAT!" Aaron yelled.

"I just... are you all right?" Jen asked.

"Yeah." He sat up, holding his head in his hands, hiding the water welling in his eyes.

"No... what's wrong?" Jen reached for his shoulder.

"Nothing."

"I'm sorry. I didn't mean... I didn't think it was *that* personal."

"It's not—I don't care. Look, they'll be home soon."

"I didn't think that mattered." Jen stared at him, searching for a reason for his refusing to face her. "Fine." She climbed off the bed and stood over him. "You seem kind of moody anyway."

"I'm not *moody*. I've got a lot on my mind, okay?" Aaron lifted his head again, talking over Jen's response. "I don't get much sleep. My dreams are... never mind."

"Okay. Well, that's all right. You probably just ate too much sugar or—"

"No, it's nothing like that. I can't explain it!"

"All right! Whatever. But you can *tell* me about it. That's what girlfriends are—"

"You're my girlfriend now?"

"Well, no, I guess not! I guess I'm just wasting my time."

"It's not that." Aaron shook his head. "I just... I wasn't thinking about it. I just assumed you wanted to hang out." He pulled himself off the bed to stand beside her. "I don't have... *time*—for a girlfriend."

Jen threw up her arms and let them fall again. "And I thought you have nothing *but* time! Just what *do* you do all day? You're not with Bennett—at the hospital. I thought you needed me, liked talking to me or whatever."

"I do. I just..." Aaron searched his room for his words. "I can't make any commitments."

"Commitments! You think *I* want to? I thought we were just having fun, liked each other's company." Jen opened her mouth to continue, then focused on the bedroom door. "You *are* really strange. You know that? No wonder you haven't had any girl-friends or—"

"You were sure I had millions of them."

"Whatever. I'm leaving now."

Aaron didn't follow. When the front door slammed, he dropped onto the bed again, took a deep breath, and closed his eyes.

AWAKENED FROM SLEEP, Aaron breathed at his mobile phone, "What happened? Is he..."

"No. No, he's still... here." Bennett's voice was loud through the phone, amplified by the dark of Aaron's bedroom. "It's bad, Aaron—seriously bad. They don't think he's gonna make it through the—*please*. Be here with me."

"Yeah, of course. On my way."

THE HOSPITAL CORRIDORS were oddly quiet. Even the nurses seemed somber and lethargic. As Aaron approached Bennett's father's room, Bennett slipped through the door, closing it behind him, and joined Aaron in the hallway.

"Thank you—really. Everyone's so... I just can't take all the—"

Aaron laid a hand on Bennett's shoulder. "It's all right."

Bennett, devoid of tears, rocked beneath Aaron's hand. He teemed with anxious energy. "You don't know what it's like not even knowing and—"

"I do. When I was little—"

"Your grandmother—right. I forget. You guys were lucky."

Aaron opened his mouth to speak, then nodded compliance. "Hey, why don't you have a seat? Or we could go for a walk. Over to the cafeteria?"

Bennett glanced at the door to his father's room, clenching his bottom lip between his teeth, then nodded. "Yeah, okay."

PATIENTS, visitors, and staff were sprinkled around the large cafeteria, all politely quiet for the evening hours, none daring to wear a smile. Aaron and Bennett sat at a table in the far corner.

"You're so calm," Bennett spoke first. "How do you do it?" His eyes were wide, glistening, his nervous energy manifesting in the bouncing of his knee under the table, his shoe tapping the sticky floor.

"Take it as it comes, I guess."

Bennett shook his head. "But the world can throw so much shit at you—and you have no idea when to even expect it."

Aaron attempted to smile, unsure of the right expression to offer sympathy while his own concerns were so distant. "Maybe it's just all part of... I don't know."

"Part of what?"

"A plan? Or, not a plan—our *choice* even."

"You're saying *my dad chose* to be sick?" Bennett's body straightened, tightening in defense.

"No, of course not—not really. But, I mean, what are we *here* for?"

Bennett wriggled in his chair. "That's not what I need to hear right now."

"We just go about our lives, making choices. There's gotta be some line we follow, right? Some... common ground. Or theme?"

"I have *no* idea what you're talking about." Bennett stood. "I think I'm gonna go back to the room. Dad needs—"

"No, *you* need a break. You're a mess. You've been going through this... for a long time now. Just sit down."

"I appreciate what you're trying to do, but I should probably be over there—with them."

"Your dad, he might be... near the end of his life—he's on his own path. But you, your mom, your sister... you're not supposed to be dying with him."

"What in the hell are you talking about? Look, my father is *dying*." The syllables stretched, gaining heft as they shot from Bennett's mouth. "I don't want him to, but he *is*. I'm not going to leave him alone—or not be there for my mom and sis." Bennett's hands left his pockets to gesture in the air. "*You* haven't even been around—*at all*—and this is the most I've ever needed you in my life!"

"Hey, calm down—please. I'm here. All right? I'm just trying to help. You're the one—and your sister, your mom—that're gonna be here even after... even *if* something happens to your dad. You should be looking after yourself—*and* your mother and sister. I think—I *feel*—that's what we're supposed to do."

"Don't get all philosophical on me now."

Aaron couldn't prevent the half-smile that crept across his

face in response to the accuracy of Bennett's accusation. The result was the surprise of encouraging Bennett to smile too.

"Yeah, all right," Bennett relented. "That's exactly what the situation calls for, but you know I don't believe in God or—"

"That's not what I mean—just that there's got to be some *point*. There *has* to be. And I don't feel it's... misery."

Bennett sat down—this time, in the chair farthest from Aaron—and listened as he watched the strangers sitting at other tables.

"Your dad," Aaron said, "how do we know he doesn't have something better waiting for him? *No*..." Aaron raised his voice to prevent Bennett's interruption. "Not like *heaven* or anything else like that. I just mean, whatever's *next*."

"Like... we don't even die," Bennett mocked.

"Yeah. Maybe?"

"Where do we go?"

Aaron shrugged. "Maybe we're already there. And we just can't *see* it."

A frown etched its way across Bennett's pale face. "*Now*, who's the crazy one?" Bennett stood up again, smacking the tabletop with his palm. "I'm gonna go back over. Are you coming?"

"If you want me to."

"I'm not going to beg you."

Bennett huffed at Aaron's silence and changed his tone. "Sorry. It's just... I guess I just need you around, but I'm not ready for any... theories. I guess I'm just not ready to be optimistic. But I appreciate it—you—and I appreciate what you went through—when you were a kid, with your grandmother. But you guys were the lucky ones. Not everyone gets to be."

13

———

YOUR 'FRIEND,' SAIG IMPARTED, *IS COMFORTED BY YOU—BY YOUR presence.*

Bennett? You know him?

I am aware... of his corporeal life. I do obServe.

How do you know... what he feels?

I only need be aware. The information—its perception—is available to all... all present in your aspect.

Tres's form rose, hovering above Saig's own personable manifestation. Tres morphed in color and tone, consistent with his changing consciousness.

That's good, Tres imparted. *I care about him.*

Indeed. All share connection—some more than others.

Does he know, Tres asked, his visual form dispersing, glowing red-brown, *that I care?*

Yes, Saig answered. *The true self... is always fully aware.*

I'm not... a very good friend these days.

Your intentions do communicate—even without enacting corporeal activity. What is 'unseen' by your corporeal body, but perceived, is more substantial... than what is 'seen.'

You mean, life—corporeal life—is meaningless compared to... this.

All existence holds meaning. Corporeality holds many of the most prolific lessons to be learned.

Like what?

Those you have yet to learn, those that cannot be perceived... until they are.

You talk in riddles. The visible particles of Tres's form danced with humor.

Saig's joined in the revelry. *Your remaining attachment to your corporeal mind prefers to perceive 'riddles.' Your sense of play serves you well, Tres. Joy, play... are the motivation, the 'fuel,' of all creativity.*

Is that, Tres imparted, his form growing dense and subdued, *our... purpose?*

There is no 'purpose.' It is another term developed—and agreed upon—within your corporeality.

Is it our reason for existing?

You exist... as you choose.

Then, do we choose to... not exist? To end our life?

Of course. You invite the final moments—of a corporeal life—as you perceive all that you intended to learn, all that you intended to create... as you desire—as you reach aself-fulfillment.

We decide? When to die?

Of course, just as you... have—one corporeal life to the next.

I don't remember choosing—

You do... as you will your awareness. All of reality is available... as you choose to be aware.

And we... never—fully—die?

'Death,' as defined in your corporeality, is relative—a concept of only one chosen perception.

Life goes on... forever, then?

Aself continues to... pulse, to... energize, from one form to the next —as is most natural.

Living different lives, one after the other?

If aself chooses. Many choose to obServe.

As OnLookers?

Yes.

Or...

Or not. Many remain only in the Apart, as suits individual aware-ness, choice, mien.

And they can go back... to life and choosing a new life—if they want?

All aselves—but one.

14

"Wow, I don't know what to say," Jen said.

Aaron held her gaze as they sat on the blanket he'd sprawled out over the ground. "I wanted to make it up to you," he said.

"I can see that, but what exactly are you making up for?"

"Being so far away."

"But you've *always* been like that," she followed with a giggle.

"Well, I didn't mean to be." Aaron opened the picnic basket he'd carried up the hill. "Sandwich?"

"Sure."

"Ham and cheese or... ham and cheese?"

Jen giggled again, urging another effortless smile from Aaron.

"I like being with you," he said.

"Good. And feel free to tell me why—if there's a compliment in it."

"Well, you make me feel... like I'm *here*—right here, right now."

Jen squinted at his answer as she slowly chewed a bite of sandwich. "Sounds like something you don't need me for."

"No. I do, because you require *all* of me."

"I do? That makes me sound high-maintenance."

Aaron flashed a cheeky smile, then laid his sandwich in its plastic wrapper and leaned toward Jen as she nibbled at hers. "You... like me."

"I do?" she teased.

"Mm-hmm. I can see it in your eyes."

Jen took another bite. "And because I'm the one that calls *you*."

Aaron nodded, the smile still broad on his face. "You kind of... absorb me, draw me in, make me pay attention—to everything that's around."

Jen gently bit at her bottom lip as she contemplated Aaron's words. "That sounds... like a good thing?"

Aaron nodded, and pressed his lips to hers. Jen pulled away, smiling.

"So," she spoke softly. "You're here—right now—with me?"

Aaron nodded, leaning farther for her.

"Not somewhere else? Not daydreaming about anything else?"

Aaron shook his head.

"So," she continued, laying her sandwich down beside Aaron's, "what are you gonna do about it?"

"That depends," Aaron said, punctuating the words with another kiss.

"On..." Jen kissed back.

"On what *you* want."

Jen responded to the pressure of his kiss, her body gently falling back on the blanket. Her long hair splayed around her, framing her smile. Aaron's hands moved to either side of her body, supporting his weight as he leaned over her, only their lips touching. Jen's arms lifted to him, sliding around Aaron's waist and pulling him to her.

HERE. *Now.*

With her.

Aaron repeated the words to himself as he kissed her, feeling his own energy merging with hers in their embrace.

Be here now, he directed himself. *This is real. This is life,* he commanded himself to believe.

With every connection, every touch sensation, he felt the solidity of the tangible—confirming the perception of his conscious mind.

This is my life.

And still, every temporal touch gave way to the intangible: fingers fumbling between particles, the pressure of his body falling through contact with hers.

No. Stop. You're imagining it. This is real!

He calmed himself, consoling himself even as his effort focused on comforting the body beneath his.

No, I want this—as I have millions of times before. It's real. It's been so long... it's me—here, now—in this body. It's only sex.

Aaron grasped—feeling nothing—desperately seeking answers, confirmation, retribution. His hands ran over Jen's chest, down to her hips, feeling the softness of her clothing, then her skin—then emptiness.

Stay here. Stay here, he urged himself, his intention burning with unacknowledged anger.

She's just a girl. She likes you.

She wants you. Enjoy it.

His body weighed on hers—and he felt nothing. Aaron sought in desperation to feel something—anything—to know where his own self began and ended, where his own self existed.

Be with her. This is you. Again, again. Always again.

"Stop it!" He heard the shout to himself, loud with anger.

"Wait... what?" Jen looked up at Aaron as she pushed against his shoulders. "Did you just say—"

Aaron shook his head as he lowered his face again, his mouth reaching for hers.

"No, wait." She pressed him back again. "You've got that look in your eyes, like you're somewhere else. What's the *matter* with you!"

"I... I thought you wanted—"

"But you're not even *here*!" She pulled herself up, fixing her shirt over her chest again. "What—*who*—are you thinking of?"

"What? No one! You!"

Jen sat up on the blanket beside him, her eyebrows scrunched together, her eyes small and scrutinizing while her arms wrapped around her chest. "You kiss me... like you *mean it,* but your fingers..." She shook her head, looking at Aaron's hands. "It's like you don't really *feel* me. It's creepy!"

"What? I don't know what you're talking about! I—"

"No. No, it's never been right. You're... there's something *wrong* with you. You're just—"

"Jen, what are you saying? I don't even under—"

She grabbed her bag, brushed the grass off her legs. "*No.* No, I can't do this. It's just too... weird. All of it: you, the things you say, that spacey look in your eyes. I thought it was cool, that you're just different—in a good way—but you're... you're a freak!"

"What? Whoa, wait a minute." Aaron pulled himself up and reached for her shoulders as she clutched her bag against her chest. "You don't mean that," he said. "We have a good thing going."

She shook her head. "No. I know what guys are supposed to

be like—what they *are* like—and that's not *you*. You're not all there—here—whatever. I can tell."

He drew her closer, softening his voice, "Calm down. *What* can you tell exactly?"

Her gaze lowered to his chest. "You want me. But you *don't* want me." The threat of tears sounded in her voice.

"Jen, I'm sorry. I wanted—"

"No!" She shook herself out of his grasp. "You're not going to get it—*me*. You don't fit *here,* don't you see? You're somewhere else. You don't *belong* here!"

Jen walked off, rushing her steps as her tears came. She almost slid down the hill in her hurry.

"Jen!" he called after her. "You're going to hurt yourself! Come back! I didn't mean it! I don't..." His voice trailed after her, falling away as she disappeared from view.

You don't belong here, his own inner voice repeated.

———

AND *ANOTHER* LOOKED ON, leering into Aaron's corporeal aspect, perceiving every energized node of emotive tension—anguish— emitted for detection by all those aware.

Exercising tense restraint, he continued to watch, studying, still waiting—preparing for action.

If action was required, he would be aware—and he would not hesitate.

———

THE FRONT DOOR'S slam shook the framed photos on the wall of the foyer. Aaron stomped up the staircase, barricading himself in his bedroom.

You don't belong, the recording of Jen's voice replayed in his mind. *You don't want me. You're not here.*

The sentiments resonated, throbbing in his head, pressing at his own questions and continuing uncertainties.

"What am I doing here?" he asked aloud.

As Sancha arrived home after her shift, Aaron left his room, meeting her in the kitchen.

"You caught me!" she said, speaking through a smile dribbling with crumbs. Her hand holding the cookie disappeared behind her as if she awaited Maria's scolding.

Aaron's blank expression didn't change. He glared at his mother's perpetual youthfulness and the smile that never lost its original brilliance under any circumstances.

"There are things I never asked you," he said.

Sancha's eyebrows raised as she kept her lips tightly sealed around the oversized mouthful of cookie. She finished chewing and swallowed before Aaron continued.

"And you never told me yourself," he said.

"What is it?" She brushed her hands together over the kitchen sink.

He peered through the doorways leading back into the hall and living room. "Where's—"

"Knitting group night," Sancha answered. "I dropped her off on the way home. She really loves it. I think she's making new friends." Sancha walked up to Aaron, looking up at him with wide-open eyes. "Maybe she's finally realized we don't need her to look after us twenty-four-seven—anymore."

Aaron nodded away the subject. "It's been a really long time since we talked," he said in a cold tone.

"I love talking to you."

"Have some time now?"

"Of course!" Sancha brushed the last of the crumbs from her palms and headed into the living room. "Let's go sit on the swings!" She bounded out the back door and bounced toward the swing set nestled in the wide patch of shade beneath the maple tree.

"I've missed you," Sancha said as Aaron caught up with her. "You're all grown up—you always have been—but now, you're always... in your own little world." She plopped herself onto her favorite swing. "You don't *need* me anymore!" she whined. "I guess I've always needed *you* more."

She kicked her legs out in front of her, then back and forward again, sending herself soaring up into the air before letting the swing settle again as Aaron nestled into the seat next to hers. She didn't appear to have aged at all in his entire lifetime.

"Is it a *girl*?" she asked, hope gleaming in her eyes.

He hesitated before shaking his head. He stared at his feet as he gently swung side to side. "The years went by so fast," he sighed.

"Only twenty of them! Are you feeling *old* all of a sudden?" Sancha's giggling resonated around them.

He shook his head. "I just don't know where all of them went."

"You've been busy—always up to something, studying something, being the best son anyone could ever wish for."

Aaron's smile forced its way to the surface, thin with tension. "I'm just... me."

"And *that*, people tell me, is like the most problem-free child ever."

"Not problem-free."

"You mean, all the interesting stuff you put us through? No, it's been an adventure—the best adventure ever." Sancha stopped swinging and looked into his eyes. "But, why all this gloominess? You're not going anywhere," she said, followed by "Are you?" delivered almost as an accusation.

"I don't know. Maybe it's just that time in life—you know—when you start wondering what you're supposed to do or be or—"

"Nonsense. You're too young," she chuckled. "Look at me: I'm still working at the factory with my *mom*! I—"

"What *did* you want to do? You know, before you had me?"

"Before I had you..." Sancha stared up at the clouds overhead. "I was in high school. I hadn't even thought about it yet. Maybe I just wanted to do something big, you know, like every kid does."

Aaron nodded. "And then, what happened?"

Sancha's eyebrows rose; her nose twitched. "You mean..."

"You never told me—I didn't want to ask you. I mean, it's none of my business. I didn't know if... all that stuff *hurt* you or—and Grandmom never said. I didn't know if I was allowed to ask or not, I guess. But... maybe it matters, you know? It's part of the story—my story. And yours."

Sancha nodded, staring at her feet. "It's not a bad story," she said. "I mean, nothing worth telling really, not very interesting. I just... oh, you know how it is. Things just happen." She smiled. "And then, there was you! And everything happened so fast. You were a big learning curve for me *and* your grandmom, and our lives totally changed."

"And you never got around to... doing whatever it was you would've done, if I hadn't come along."

Sancha's smile fell away as she looked to the ground again. "It's not really a big deal," she defended. "I just—"

"Why not?"

"Why not what?"

"Don't you ever miss... don't you ever wish you were *doing* something?"

"You mean, other than raising you?" Sancha pushed hard against the ground, swinging herself higher, sending a breeze swirling around Aaron. As she let the swing slow again, she asked, "Do you wish I had?"

He shrugged. "If *you* do."

She stared across the garden, contemplating the question— perhaps, for the first time.

"Do you ever feel... lost?" he asked her.

"Aaron..." Her voice was small, like a child's, almost pleading.

"Like," he continued, "without any direction?" He faced her —and found tears waiting in her eyes. "I'm sorry. I just... always wondered."

"*Always?*"

Aaron took a deep breath, directing his eyes forward again.

"I thought we always talked," Sancha said, "about everything."

"I didn't want to hurt you."

"Well, it doesn't feel good *now*." A smile subtly wrapped around her quiet voice. "Do you feel like I didn't... do enough?"

Aaron turned to his mother. "No, not with me. You were perfect with me—all you could be. I just always believed... that maybe, you were waiting on me—to have permission to do whatever else it was you really wanted."

"I really wanted *you*," she said. "From the moment you arrived—when I looked at you. I didn't know it before then, but it was the only thing I was ever really sure about."

"I know. I could see it in your eyes."

Sancha smiled her relief and began to slowly swing again. "I just... didn't think about anything else—really. Maybe I should now."

"So, will you tell me... now?"

"Anything," she answered as she swung past.

"About... my father."

Sancha dug her heels in the dirt, coming to a full stop. "Of course." Her chest filled with a great gulp of air. "I don't really remember much—honestly. Didn't really... dwell on it." She smiled again. "I just lived in the moment, I guess."

"So, who was he?"

She glanced at the ground, then toward the sky. "I don't know."

Aaron waited for the explanation he thought would follow.

"I remember," she offered, "he was really good-looking." She started to swing again, her mood playful, casual, like a young girl describing her favorite flavor of ice cream. "I really can't remember—*except* his really blue eyes. I always thought blue eyes were the coolest—like yours." Sancha smiled at Aaron, then turned her attention to the blue sky again. "He was kind of mysterious—I don't even remember what made me think that then."

Sancha glanced back at Aaron for his response; he had none.

"He... it's so hard to remember," she whined.

"How... did...?"

"Your grandmom didn't even meet him," Sancha blurted. "I think that upset her most of all—worried her—but I don't even remember having the opportunity—if that makes any sense. It all happened so *fast*."

"Did he hurt you?"

"No! Nothing like that. I..." Sancha blushed. "Well, now, you're getting personal."

Aaron didn't blink, nor did his expression soften.

"There's nothing to know—really," Sancha offered. "I hardly remember it. It just *happened*."

"How can that—"

"It just *did,* okay? I..." Sancha's swing slowed as she stopped pushing herself, her gaze lost in the clouds. Then, the words rushed from her. "I didn't have any explanation for your grandmom. And I don't have—" She softened her tone as she faced Aaron. "I don't have much for you either. I'm sorry. I'm not hiding anything. It was just... so long ago. Nothing bad happened. It was all... *love,* I guess—if it's love when you're that young."

"How long did you know him?"

"I... I don't remember. I didn't even... know his name."

Aaron's forehead knotted; he started shaking his head.

"I felt like I'd known him for *ages,* you know?" Sancha continued. "It all felt... natural. I wanted—I didn't not *want* it! It was... well, especially now, it all feels like... a dream." Her attention turned to the clouds again. "Like I just fell asleep one night and woke up the next morning... and *everything* was different."

Aaron left his swing; he walked a few steps away while Sancha's eyes followed him. Then, he continued to walk back to the house.

"Aaron?" Sancha called to him. "Aaron, that's all I know!"

The screen door slammed shut behind him, its hinges screeching.

Sancha's swing gently rocked as she stared wide-eyed, blankly, then spoke in a childlike voice.

"I'm sorry. That's... all I have *to give you.*"

A DARK MOOD spilled over Aaron—a black veil masking his own existence, enmeshing his own sense of self. The never-ending questions pressed at the boundaries of his consciousness—expanding, coiling, replicating exponentially.

He waited for the breaking point—*his* breaking point—when all would shatter, transforming into what lay beyond.

He sat still and upright on his bed, hugging his curled body, watching his bedroom drown in a visible, gray haze. Through tainted view, he prepared to face his inner demons—should they choose to reveal themselves.

He knew they wouldn't. He knew there were none.

I just want to leave. I'm ready now.

YOU WILL NOT, drummed a separate voice—a voice as clear as Aaron's own inner speech.

It is not yours to choose, it threatened.

SANCHA KNOCKED SOFTLY on Aaron's bedroom door as Maria reached the top of the stairs, laying a gentle hand on her shoulder.

"Let him be," Maria said.

"But he's never been like this," Sancha argued, her eyes red and weary. "I don't understand why—"

"It's perfectly normal."

"But he's always—"

"Let him be normal."

As Maria continued down the hall to her own bedroom, Sancha rested against Aaron's door.

"Good night," she whispered.

15

Tres... PENETRATED RESTLESS SLEEP AS NIGHT FELL, CALLING IN the familiar voice of Saig.

Tres... he attempted—urged—to no avail.

Aaron's mind latched onto the taste of his anger, refusing to part with it. His full awareness subtly resisted before falling away, choosing deeper sleep, choosing denial of all it recognized as true.

There is much for you to learn, Saig imparted. *There is peace...* he added, *in total awareness. And... your continuing instruction awaits.*

As Aaron's consciousness visualized a wall—an impenetrable barrier—Saig's articulation sensed the same. Saig retreated, fading from Aaron's awareness.

MARIA WRESTLED WITH HER BEDCOVERS, twisting and turning, fighting fitful sleep.

IN HER OWN BEDROOM, Sancha's eyes finally closed, her mind overwhelmed with fears and worries. She succumbed to them. Her consciousness drifted, carrying her concerns away with it.

———

TRES TRANSCENDED, relenting, as he was drawn to the Apart by *another*—something stronger, compellingly mysterious in its allure.

Emerging in his deepest awareness, the unidentifiable presence felt powerful, determined, energized with great motivation —and somehow, *familiar.*

In contrast to the light and jovial playfulness usually represented by Fei—and Saig—this projection remained on the edge of detection, shrouded in dark recesses. It communicated clearly while guarding itself—and its intentions.

Shades of black formed a translucent, obscure shape, delivering its warning in scent and sound as well as cryptic language.

RETURN.

The message floated across Tres's awareness—strong in impact, seductively effective in its simplicity. *You... have no place... here.*

Without conscious consideration, Tres answered the command with light, open, inviting awareness. He replied with the revealing description of the newly aware—while retaining the resolute conviction of an ancient entity.

The choice is mine—as all choices are, Tres imparted. *I belong. I am of the Apart.*

The conflicting force—real and alive within Tres's awareness —rumbled in shape and sound, growing in energy, vile in its vigilance.

Then, it was gone.

SANCHA SHIFTED IN HER SLEEP, her pink cheek brushing against her pillow as she snuggled the blanket wadded within her arms.

She dreamed of open fields, of flying, of family gatherings filled with smiles and laughter. Her thoughts nestled in the comfort of memories of the past as they played with fantasies of the future. The recognizable and the invented frolicked together: a swirling vision of promise and hope.

A familiar presence slid between her thoughts—nestling itself—seductive and secure. Sancha's mind welcomed the arrival, maintaining focus on the pleasant dreamscape playing out before her mind's eye.

Aware of the one watching, Sancha ignored the figure standing in the distance of her dream—as she had most times before. Her previous attempts to interact were often ignored, even when she was just a child.

As she felt the translucent figure reach toward her, holding out a beckoning hand, she remembered the single time it had before. Only glimpses rose from her memory: still visions, disparate sensations.

And like the time before, Sancha's awareness accepted the gesture, following its direction. She allowed herself to be led by what she sensed could always be trusted.

In her dream, Sancha stepped behind the one sensed but not seen. She trusted—*transcending*, adhering to one simple instruction, then the next. She let her imagination carry her away—her dreaming mind innocent, compelled by curiosity.

She glided—through visions in still frame, through motions dictated by the one who guided her—wherever they may lead.

AND SHE CONTINUED TO SLEEP—PEACEFULLY, contentedly—even

as her physical body reversed the family car in the driveway, then drove forward through the gate at the side of the house and into the wide trunk of the maple tree.

She slept—even as her corporeal mind began to crumble, its physical manifestation destroyed. Her corporeal form succumbed, slipping from its final sleep.

THE SOUND of steel screaming its unwillingness to change shape woke Maria in the night. The blare of the car horn—ceaseless, penetrating—pushed her aging body out of bed and to the window.

She found the back yard awash in blinding light. A vehicle headlight pointed upward in an impossible direction. Mangled machinery cast a grotesque shadow across the lawn.

A SALIENT, stabbing pain, thrust at his chest, woke Aaron. And he knew—whole-bodily—that a gaping, empty cavity had been wrenched inside him.

Simultaneously, his new awareness alerted him of the reason.

Glaring light burst into his bedroom when he threw open the window curtains, the tracks of his fresh tears gleaming.

As AARON's bare feet touched the dew-covered grass blanketing the back yard, Maria's silhouette stood in his path, backlit by the still-shining headlight beaming as it dangled from its housing.

Her hands covered her ears against the gut-wrenching blare of the car horn.

Aaron approached his grandmother, carrying an air of otherworldly, calm acceptance. He reached for her shoulders to announce his presence.

"Be careful!" she screamed, shuddering at his touch. "The car... it might not be safe... but..."

Aaron's unwillingness to witness—to record the memory of —his mother's lifeless body was the only thought in his mind— until he realized his grandmother believed her daughter was still alive. And she expected her grandson to rescue her.

"She's not there," Aaron shouted over the unbearable noise, radiating as much compassion as he could muster.

"Yes! Her leg... or... her ankle—it's there!" Maria's arm swung into the air. "It's twisted... the door—"

"No, Grandmom. She's *gone*."

"No!" Maria's body twisted in Aaron's arms. Her tear-drenched face tipped toward his as she shook his unmoving body with all her might. "She's *not*! You have to... *get her out!*"

For the sanity of his grandmother—to fulfill the most urgent request she'd ever make—Aaron approached the almost-unrecognizable vehicle. When his view filled with the sight of his delicate, forever-young mother slumped over the steering wheel, hair painted with blood dulling its natural flame-colored sheen, his heart punched at his own chest—as if it would leap from his throat, leaving him heartless as well as motherless.

For Maria, he reached into the scene of Sancha's death, stretched his arms beneath her limp body, and carried her toward the house to lay her on the grass at the foot of the steps below the back door.

Aaron felt nothing but emptiness as he knelt on the lawn next to his mother. Maria stood over them, stalwart against issuing her goodbye. Then, she screamed in notes that made the sound of the blaring car horn fade far into the background.

"Save her! Save my little girl!"

Aaron's fingers were already on the pulse point on Sancha's neck. "I can't. She's already—"

"You *have* to! You have to!" Maria gripped her grandson's shoulders.

"Grandmom, I *can't*! There's nothing I can do!"

She yanked at the neckline of her nightgown. "No... no... no! You saved me. It should be *her*!"

Aaron shook his head—against the torrent of his grandmother's tears, against the gut-wrenching tone of her pleas. "She's not sick! She's *gone*!" His sight never left Sancha's pale face, her cheeks blushing with the rouge of her own blood. His voice fell quieter. "I can't do *anything*."

Maria's howl cried out without words, raging against the night—against life, against loving when loss is inevitable. Aaron reached to wipe a wet strand from his mother's forehead and close the lids over her vacant eyes.

AN AMBULANCE SIREN sounded in the distance as a neighbor climbed his way over the remainder of the wooden gate at the side of the house and ran toward the two huddling in the back yard. When the man spoke in a shock-induced stutter, Aaron couldn't answer.

The pressure pushed its way outward from inside his chest —forcing itself against his ribs, squeezing at his heart—growing heavier, larger, in mourning as well as warning.

The weight spread outside his body, darkening the already-black sky, relentlessly pushing against him, slowly suffocating.

They were not alone at the scene of Sancha's death. *Another* loomed over them, all around them, squeezing them in its grasp.

Only Aaron was aware. Only Aaron turned his face toward the night sky in search, finding nothing.

He squinted into the shadows residing past the headlight beams. He thought of the figure of his dreams—of Fei—hoping to find the extension of reassurance. None was there.

Only dread reigned—and the will to stifle life.

The voice emanating from within Aaron's mind—and without—rumbled the environment itself, rippling through this corporeality.

I AM THE ONLY, it proclaimed with absolute conviction. *I AM... THE OVERSEER!*

THE SIMULTANEOUS PULSE—INVISIBLE, irreconcilable—propelled itself against Aaron, forcing him to the ground.

SLEEP WAS IMPOSSIBLE. All eyes stared, wide-open, wet with tears or unable to still produce them—in the house marked by a wounded maple tree pierced by metal wreckage.

Sancha's body had been carried away by strangers in bright uniform. The neighbors reluctantly returned to their own homes, leaving Aaron to usher his grandmother to bed. He left her, sitting atop the bed, wrapped in her well-worn robe, staring in disbelief.

DOWNSTAIRS IN THE LIVING ROOM, without permitting a single

lamp to light the callous emptiness, Aaron allowed the sensation of the growing bruise on his chest to expand, seep into all his senses, draw his mind away from the woman—the mere girl—who was taken away.

He didn't wish for a friend's sympathy or support. He didn't long for Maria's own strength and words of wisdom. Aaron bore the burden of the disruption of life—the fresh wound cut into the heart of their small family—alone.

He felt more than helpless. He felt useless.

He felt lost, caught off guard—still a stranger in an alarmingly cruel world. And he felt actionless—directionless, hopeless.

His fingers curled to form fists. His muscles tightened, contracting. He glared at the opposite wall until he saw *through* it, until the facade of all that existed around him broke apart, disappearing altogether—until there was nothing.

Nothing but dark—and his tears.

PART VII

RENOUNCING

Fata volentem ducunt, nolentem trahunt.

— Destiny carries the willing man,
and drags the unwilling.

1

USE THE STRENGTH OF YOUR EMOTIONS, SAIG'S VOICE CALLED TO Tres. *Feel your always-present connection with the Apart.*

I don't want—You do, Saig's reply overlapped Tres's thought.

Your emotions are the communications—the messages—of your corporeal body, Saig continued, clear in sound, still invisible from view. *They are gifts—the teachings of corporeality, the tools you yourself choose to adapt.*

I don't care about any of that! Tres imparted, coupled with his vibrant, flaming appearance of form before Saig.

Saig also appeared, cool blue and calm, more solid and succinct than ever before. *Wasted communication is wasted energy,* he imparted, *subtracting from your own creativity and all possibility —a dishonor to The Natural Order of Things... and to all. And espe-cially... to me.*

Tres's articulated form rose and fell, a trail of gray mist following. *I don't want to be here,* his form pulsated.

More waste, Saig communicated with cold clarity. *Your truths reign apparent even as you work to manifest every untruth. You bind your own creativity, limit your own ability.*

Tres's consciousness strained to maintain the comforting

cover of rage in spite of the confronting calmness and obvious truth of Saig's every conveyance. *Why am I here?* he relented.

Saig's form warmed to yellow and orange, and Tres felt the gentle release of his attachment to his suffering corporeal body.

The current, formulated face of Saig smiled, flashing streams of white light. *You have access to all energy—all support and ability —you may ever need. All of the Apart is a part of you... even as you are a part of it.* Saig flickered a pastel palette. *You are here... now... because you desire to be.*

Am I sleeping?

You never truly 'sleep'—only your corporeal consciousness... subsides.

But did I fall asleep... this time?

No. Your body rests—awake—as you've consciously transcended to the Apart.

I... did it... on my own? I went to the Apart... awake?

Yes, indeed—and very well. Transcendence has always been available to you.

Is it... for everyone?

In different ways... and manners. All is the Apart. All are of the Apart. Yet, some... are different than others.

"AARON... AARON, ARE YOU OKAY?" Bennett's voice rushed in.

Aaron sunk further into the sagging couch, dressed in yesterday's clothes. He blinked, shutting his wide-open eyes momentarily against the blazing sunlight filling the living room.

"Where *were* you?" Bennett knelt down, studying Aaron's face.

"Here."

Bennett shook his head, then refocused on the most pressing concern of the moment. "I... I just don't know what to say. We've known each other for so long and... I *don't know* what I should say." His line of sight drifted toward the back yard. He didn't want to look, but he couldn't prevent himself. "*How...?*"

Aaron straightened himself and continued to stare out the window. The sounds of clacking pots and pans, a skillet sliding over the stove burner, registered in his awareness. "What time is it?" he asked.

Bennett looked at his watch. "Seven-thirty. I came over as soon as Maria called me. I think she's..." He lifted his hand toward Aaron, then dropped it to his side again. "Are you..." he tried, his voice trembling with his body. "Are you all right? Can I get anything or—"

Aaron shook his head. A shiver traveled down his spine.

"What is it?" Bennett asked in the tone reserved for the moments when his friend seemed out of reach, tuned into something beyond Bennett's own capability.

"*I can still feel her,*" Aaron stated.

"Wh—" Bennett followed Aaron's line of sight. "Your... *mother?*"

Aaron inhaled, then exhaled, "She's..." His throat caught on his own realization.

Bennett's expression knotted with mixed emotion.

"She's still... *hurting,*" Aaron said through a fresh supply of tears.

Bennett stared in silence as Aaron carefully stood, walked from the room and out the front door.

***

THE AIR WAS STILL and morning-musty, thick and dissuading. Aaron's increasing stride sliced through it, forcing it to break against the swift movements of his body and rush around him, through him. He ran until he felt the atmosphere give against him.

And still, his mother's own emotions streamed through him: vibrant, pungent, *living*.

Sancha traveled through him as a sensation only—without personality, without voice, only as an awareness.

Her heartache was broadcast to and through *all*.

I am ready. The desire of *another* permeated the Apart, unequivocally, unchallenged, accepted. Its bearer transmitted his form —and message—with strength, contentment, and unabashed conceit as he presented himself before the Consultation.

Aself's belief is acknowledged, the first reply pulsated.

Aself is recognized.

Aself's reason... for convening the Consultation? questioned one member.

The proud one accumulated his articulation of form, converging his appearance and his communication before his audience. *I am prepared to assume my role. My ObServed has ascended. My responsibility is realized.*

The Consultation is aware.

Aself's formal notice to the Consultation...

Is unnecessary.

All is determined.

By The Natural Order of Things.

My role has ended! The challenge raged before the Consultation, aglow in red tones. *I no longer ObServe as OnLooker.*

Be assured, returned as calm blue hues.

The Consultation is aware.

The truth is all-known.

All occurs.

As coincides...

With The Natural Order of Things.

The one appealing to the Consultation burst into separate particles, filling the environment with a clouded haze. *My ObServed has ascended! My obligations are fulfilled! I WILL BE... OVERSEER!*

The Consultation aggregated, building in brightness and focus. *All is as The Natural Order of Things determines,* rained over and through in singular message.

I AM THE CHOSEN! barraged in reply. *I AM AWAKENED! I AM SELECTED BY THE NATURAL ORDER OF THINGS!*

Molecules condensed and expanded. Particles formed and feathered, gathering and then, dissipating all around. The Consultation remained steadily present, strong in establishment, ever-patient and fully attentive.

And there is... one other, the Consultation collectively reminded.

Aaron raced, his muscles aching against the charge of his will, his legs reaching for new ground. He climbed forward, higher, until he reached the peak of the highest hill—and the greatest distance from the scene of tragedy.

He dropped to the ground and succumbed to exhaustion. He relented to the physical pain inflicted on his body, relishing the thought that his own over-taxed heart might break free from his chest and end his agony.

Still, *she* was with him. The sense of struggle—*her* strife—resided inside him, potent as ever.

Aaron latched onto his grief, gripping her distress.

He transcended—at will—to the Apart, denying corporeality, refuting the earthly lessons his dreams claimed he'd chosen for himself.

WHERE IS SHE! demanded Tres, beckoning all surrounding.

The environment came alive, revealing itself. Multitudes appeared, acknowledging the immense energy of the plea. The Apart opened itself to Tres but offered no answers.

The invisible tide of compassion, support, and love washed over him. All he could detect—and those he could not—made their connection to him known, ushered their condolences as well as their impenetrable joy. The lightness of their personalities conjoined, washing through him, cleansing and refreshing him—even as his own corporeal consciousness denied the joy and neutrality spreading through him.

The familiar articulation of Saig appeared, joining the others before they dissipated, their arranged visions of themselves fading into the perceived background until Tres could no longer detect their presence.

Irreverently calm—even cheerful—Saig imparted, *There is nothing to 'fear.'* The simple message vibrated with truth. *All perfectly suits The Natural Order of Things.*

Is she here? Is my mother... here—somewhere?

'Here' is defined only by your corporeality. All are of the Apart. You are here... as I am here... as she is... always.

Then, let me see her! Tres rose in a particulate cloud of dark red swirling in purple.

She is with you—as all are. You need only allow your awareness.

I feel her...

Yes, you do.

She's... hurting—struggling.

Awareness can be... 'confusing' as one ascends from corporeal life.

Concepts collide; beliefs must balance.

But I can help her.

She is supported... as all are supported by The Natural Order of Things.

But she needs... me!

Only the corporeal conscience she clings to calls for you—and for who that lingering portion of her... believes you to be. She need only release corporeality to remember her true self... her whole self.

But she's... calling for me. I can hear her...

It is only the message conveyed—energized—by her corporeal form... which no longer exists.

No. I know she's in pain!

I assure you... she feels no 'pain.'

I can feel it!

Saig brightened, glimmered. *Can you?*

Of course, I... Tres calmed, his consciousness imagining breathing in. He concentrated his mind upon all sensation, then focused his *mindless* awareness.

There is no 'pain,' Saig concurrently imparted.

How...

Do you... 'see'... any method—or manner—of its manifestation around you?

Tres looked—his lingering mind *assumed* vision. *There is nothing,* he imparted.

There is all, Saig reminded. *There is only... the truth.*

Saig continued, articulating himself nearer to Tres's self-concept. *'Pain' is a construct—a mental 'device'—of your corporeality. Suffering... grief... agony... fear... are all concepts limited to your corporeality... constructed long ago... passed on from generation to generation... conjointly conceived, confirmed by, shared among communities, cultures, countries, continents. They are defined only by corporeal life. They offer a choice, a single lesson—among all others— offered by your chosen corporeal life. The lesson only need be learned...*

once. Saig's manifestation of himself giggled. *You—those of your corporeality—often choose... to repeat it.*

Tres darkened in color, expanding, pulsing. *Can I... communicate with her?*

You can... as you are able to convey to all—to any. Yet... she will not... be aware... of you.

What do you mean?

One does not recall corporeal life—not one, nor another. Corporeal life—as chosen—is an opportunity offering instruction, advancement in aself-development. The experience is acquired—from one life to the next. It is not... remembered.

That can't—

It is The Natural Order of Things.

No! No, I remember!

You... are not... the same.

I don't... Tres's form fluttered, fading.

She cannot.

But... later... maybe...

She... 'will' not.

But everything is a choice. The concept manifested suddenly within Tres, emanating without. *Fei said—you... have said—*

The choice is... yours, Tres—once it is offered. Once aself is... selected.

I don't understand. I do... remember.

As you are... selected—by The Natural Order of Things. Saig's form rippled, glowing brighter. *There is only one.*

Only one?

There is only one... who obServes... all.

ObServes... as an OnLooker obServes?

Each corporeal life is obServed by an OnLooker. Many choose the role... to experience the responsibility, to guide... and to learn. But only one obServes... all. The one... obServes OnLooker, corporealities, and all aselves alike.

And The Natural Order of Things, Tres considered.

The Natural Order of Things is not... obServed. It is merely... over-Seen—with all-encompassing awareness, as no other aself possesses.

The Natural Order of Things is... a... self?

The Natural Order of Things... is.

The Natural Order... of Things, Tres conjectured—its aliveness, its entirety, its entity, emanating in his awareness as never before. *Like... you... and me? Like Fei?*

Yes—and yes. And no.

Tres hovered—heralded—in and among his contradicting assumptions, tangling in his attachment to corporeal theorizing.

The one, Tres imparted, encircling himself in a haze of soft blue, *who obServes all... has lived successive lives?*

Yes—many corporeal lives. It is postulated that the one who obServes all—the one who overSees—experiences more corporeal lives than all other aselves.

More lives... more lifetimes?

Indeed. But it is only a presumption, only... sensed.

Why isn't it actually known?

Only one is selected.

There has only ever been one?

Only one... of a moment. There have been others. There 'will be' others—those who... awaken.

What is... to awaken?

To remember.

Remember what?

To remember all. To remember... everything.

MEMORY BURST upon the screen within Aaron's mind, blazing with vibrancy against the backdrop of eyelids tightly shut against the unforgiving afternoon sun. Countless voices pummeled his consciousness, each delivered with weighty emotion.

On the bed of newly mowed grass stretching over the hilltop, Aaron's body lay, twitching against the onslaught. Disparate awareness—contrasting realities—collided. Both battled for his full attention and acknowledgment.

"No!" he cried to the cloudless sky above.

His eyes opened, blinking against the confrontation of blinding light. The view of the city spread before him, opening up to him, busy with the lives it contained and fostered.

Tres, an encroaching sensation called.

Aaron looked right, then left. He peered above, squinted at beyond.

Forget, the heavy tone imparted from within—but not of himself, of *another*—pressing against the underside of the bruise embedded in his chest.

Forget your instruction, it beckoned, *and you will hurt no longer.*

BENNETT FOCUSED full attention on Finlay, studying his pale, slender frame leaning against the wall of the foyer.

"I should go," Finlay mumbled, reaching for the front door.

"No." Bennett rose from his seat at the kitchen table. "I think... having people around makes her feel better."

IN THE LIVING ROOM, neighbors and friends surrounded Maria, showering her with sympathies while uniformed policemen trampled the back lawn.

She excused herself and walked into the kitchen. Her expression relaxed as she spotted the boys. "Do you... can I get you two... anything?"

"No, of course not," Bennett said. "We should be taking care of *you*." He motioned for Maria to take his chair at the table. "How about a hot cup of tea? Or something else?"

Maria glanced between Bennett and Finlay with swollen eyes. "I... I'm sorry he's not here. I don't know where—"

"I'm sure he just needs some space," Bennett offered. "He'll be back soon."

Finlay nodded, stepping into the kitchen to join them. "Is there anything I can..." The question hung in the air, unfinished, unanswered.

"I... I just can't believe... she's..." Maria muttered. "*My little girl*..." She covered her face with her hands, hiding a new wave of tears.

———

AARON SAT ALONE, high above the city, twisting his t-shirt in his fists as he braced against the sensation of Sancha's torment. Maria's heartache wrenched at him as well, tugging at him from all directions.

His thoughts contorted with the intensifying physical sensations. The landscape itself seemed to swirl within his view. It stretched, expanded, altered itself to the rhythm of various voices pleading with him from the reaches of his awareness.

A child's voice—one of his own—called to him, begging him to crawl inward, to escape inside and leave one reality for the deeper—where all was safe and pain-free.

Aaron felt himself slipping, traveling farther, distancing himself, until the voices and memories finally hushed—leaving only one.

Tres, open to awareness, wafted Saig's genial tone. *Do not resist. You only resist your true self. Release... accept... embrace awareness. And you will be set free. You will 'hurt' no longer.*

The words penetrated Aaron's core, pulling at one prominent memory—blaring before his mind's eye in acute warning.

Who are you? Aaron demanded, closing his eyes, transcending instantly.

SAIG'S FORM undulated with distinction within Tres's awareness. *I am the one called Saig, as you are aware. And you... must accept... who you are.*

I know who I am, burned from Tres's residing consciousness.

You deny truth. You grow in awareness, yet deny the knowledge it offers.

I'm... I'm the one who remembers.

You are—and more.

What... more?

Awareness is yours. As it has always been.

The memories...

Your awakening.

What am I... supposed...

Fading in from black, pinpoints of light grew to flickering orbs, expanding into tall, narrow forms of individual personality —three of them.

The Consultation convenes... in your honor, imparted Saig.

Welcome, conveyed a flicker of light.

Most welcome, imparted another.

The third presence embodied warmth and acceptance, communicating no message.

The one called Saig... verifies aself progresses swiftly, imparted one member.

And very well, imparted another.

Aself... enjoys aself's instruction?

Tres's inquisitive green tone vibrated. Saig motioned encouragement.

I... was all Tres communicated to his eager audience.

The sensation of smiling abounded; humor rang out between each personality.

Aself's reservation... one aself of the Consultation imparted.

Serves aself well, another finished.

In tandem with aself's instruction, the third added.

Is my instruction complete? Tres imparted, careful not to incidentally interrupt another's communication.

Laughter streamed through the environment in refreshing waves.

No, Saig's own smile communicated.

Awareness... is boundless, undulated from the Consultation's trio.

Learning is infinite.

Aself-development is the most natural...

Aspiration...

Of all.

It is... The Natural Order of Things.

And, Saig added, *I do have much left to teach you.*

Tres focused on his surroundings. *I... don't understand...*

Aself does, he was answered by one member before him.

Aself needs merely...

To open to all awareness.

And apply instruction.

Allow aself's... true self... to be.

But I... Tres questioned, *what am I supposed to—?*

Acknowledge your selection, replied Saig.

By The Natural Order of Things.

Selection is...

The most prolific honor.

And the most prolific responsibility.

What is... what honor? Tres requested by articulation alone.

To be... the one who overSees, answered Saig.

The one aware of... all.

The OverSeer.

OverSeer... Tres repeated, through form and motion, manipulation and concentration—remembering how it drummed through—and at—his mind *before.* No... his corporeality-bound consciousness argued, *there is... one already. There is one now. He...*

Indeed, Saig's form confirmed in a flash of white.

THE SHOCK of new awareness still gripped Aaron as he struggled to wrench his cell phone from his pocket, clearing his throat as he spoke at it. "Yeah?" he answered the rude awakening.

"Aaron, you gotta come home," Bennett's voice demanded. "Your grandmother really needs you. Everyone's here, at your house, and I think... it's too much for her."

THE RETURN PATH to and through town was even easier, faster, as Aaron ran against the rising afternoon wind—away from the drama unfolding only in his mind.

THE SIGHT of Maria's unending tears, coupled with the sound of her sobbing, only added to Aaron's own pain and frustration. Bennett's disappointment, obvious in his scowl, also added to the weight on Aaron's shoulders.

"I'm so sorry," muttered a rarely-seen acquaintance, his wrinkled hand clenching Aaron's shoulder.

"It must've been her time," dared a neighbor, his own

personal certainty—practically a promise—inscribed on his face.

Bennett and Finlay witnessed Aaron escape into the living room, pulling himself from Maria's arms. "All right—everyone—it's time to go. Thank you..." he forced himself to add. "But we need to be left alone."

The visitors hesitated, glancing at one another, questioning the capability of the grieving to interpret their own needs. One neighbor finally took the first steps toward the front door, setting down his paper plate. Soon, nearly all uninvited were gone.

"You too," Aaron said, returning to the kitchen and his attention to Bennett and Finlay. "Both of you."

Bennett's mouth opened before he dropped his head and faced the floor as he walked toward the front door, Finlay following.

"Hey," Aaron called in their direction just as the door opened, "don't worry about us." He pointed his attention at Bennett. "You have your dad to care for. I don't think he likes being left alone at the hospital as much as he says he does."

Bennett nodded and walked through the doorway with Finlay.

Finally, Maria allowed the true flood of tears to come. To Aaron, her wail reverberated through all matter. He silently watched the aura of all their surroundings reflect the emotional force storming around them. He wrapped his arms around his grandmother.

"I'm not going to leave you—ever," he spoke near her ear with his truest voice—the unguarded personality of his whole self, all selves combined.

"*Et si omnes ego non,*" he whispered with heavy breath, startling himself with the most natural release of his self-trained disguise. "Even if all others, not I," he translated for his grandmother, repeating the promise with yet more vindication.

2

The family home felt too empty as Aaron and Maria trudged through each successive day. Every creak of tired timber rang of Sancha's sweet voice. Every nook seemed to pocket her personality; every object memorialized her life.

Maria and Aaron spoke little to each other—avoiding others entirely. They coexisted in respectful silence, shrouding their shared pain. When they did speak, the subject was small, meaningless, a necessary distraction when the agony of being *without* was just too much—until Maria disrupted the comfort of their complacency one morning.

"I want to talk about it," she announced to Aaron, her voice breaking under the weight of her words.

They sat together on the couch in the living room, keeping to their mutual habit of averting their eyes from the view into the back garden.

Maria twisted her body to face Aaron, her knees brushing his as she lifted her eyes. "You can feel her, can't you?"

The statement hung in the air between them. Aaron nodded, and Maria began to cry.

"She's there—here—with me," Aaron admitted. "*Every moment.* She's—" He stopped himself, renewing his life-learned habit of self-censoring.

"No," Maria said, shaking her head. "I *want* to know—everything. Please."

Aaron winced, and Maria detected the breadth of what she'd never be permitted to know, nor ever be capable of comprehending.

"Tell me... how she is," Maria clarified, relieving a small portion of Aaron's inner struggle. Her stare demanded his honesty.

"She's... adjusting," he attempted to translate from his inner perceptions. "It wasn't... good—for a long time."

Maria's hands covered her mouth. "Is she hurting?"

"Not as much now."

"Oh, God."

"Not like that," he added. "She's fine—really—just... I feel... I think it took her by surprise."

"Oh, *my baby*," Maria sobbed, hiding her eyes behind her fingers.

"She's better, Grandmom—she really is. She's... learning. I don't—"

"What do you mean?"

"I can't... hear her—as much as I used to."

"You *hear* her?"

Aaron's expression reflected his struggle: the necessity to choose his words carefully. "She's adjusting to—"

"Is she... in heaven?" Maria asked, all hope tied to a single answer.

"Yes," Aaron granted—with truth and without hesitation—in answer to the *heart* of his grandmother's question.

Maria exhaled, her hands returning to her lap, folding together, self-soothing. "Of course, she is," she said. "Of course, she is." Maria looked up again. "Does she... *speak* to you?"

Aaron shook his head. "It's more like—I don't think she knows... that she can." Maria stared as she leaned forward, eager for more information. "I can hear her—her own thoughts, her feelings—but... she's not really talking *to* anyone."

Maria nodded at her own version of the insight playing visually in her mind.

"She's fading though," Aaron added, prompting the display of worry on Maria's face once more. "I can't feel her as often— like she's farther away—but I feel she's... more calm now."

Maria nodded again as her breathing slowed, steadying itself. "She's finding her peace," she said.

Aaron nodded genuine agreement—and caught a glimpse of his grandmother's smile—the first to appear within their home in Sancha's absence.

3

Tres... Saig's conveyance echoed, gently knocking at the new mental boundaries his student erected. *Your instruction awaits,* he coaxed.

Tres succeeded in blocking the vibrations of his own thoughts as his corporeal body slept.

You will... find peace, Saig insisted.

There is no peace, Tres imparted, breaking through his own boundary.

There is, Saig answered. *It is all there is.* Each conveyance, each truth, drew Tres nearer. *And it is yours now,* Saig imparted, *as it is for all... as you accept it.*

Tres erupted, his articulation bursting with color as he manifested in the Apart, nearly nose-to-nose with Saig's self-reflected vision. *None of that applies—here—in life! None of it matters!*

All 'matters.' All is integral. You, Tres... 'matter.'

Tres's form flickered, reflecting his receipt of the answer to his deepest, uncommunicated question. *Where is she?* he imparted in muted tones.

The truth cannot be translated in terms of your corporeality. She is a part of all... as all is.

Tres's form lifted, wafted, condensed in response. *She is... part of me.*

As all are. As is... The Natural Order of Things.

And, so is... Tres imparted, *my selection... to overSee all of it—all of them.*

It is... of your choice.

But there is already... an OverSeer. The reference—ambiguous in name but heavy with memory and meaning—alighted as a vision with form unto its own.

Indeed.

That one—the OverSeer—is... all-powerful?

'Power' holds meaning only within your corporeality. In the Apart, ability—creativity—is not measured. It is only learned, practiced—enjoyed.

But the OverSeer... he... sees... all?

Awareness—of all—is available... as necessary, as desired.

And he can... affect all?

Yes... and no.

He can't?

He... can. He does not.

He doesn't? He won't—

OverSeer merely... overSees all—providing singular guidance—as required, as requested. The OverSeer does not... interfere.

But what if he wanted—?

He would not.

But what if he... did—?

He has not.

In... corporeality... in... someone's life?

Saig's form flickered, wavered, questioned. *The OverSeer... does not articulate in corporeality. It is not... The Natural Order of Things.*

Can the OverSeer... affect—manipulate—in corporeality?

He is capable—he does not. OverSeer does not return to corporeal life.

But he's lived—like I have—many lives?

Indeed.

And then... no more?

The OverSeer... is awakened.

As I am, as I have?

Yes.

And then, he lives... no more lives?

As OverSeer, he does not—according to your corporeal concept of 'time.'

But... if he can't return to corporeal life... if he can't live more lives... and no one—nothing—ever dies, what happens to the OverSeer? You said there have been others.

The ConCentration occurs. The OverSeer conCenters. It is The Natural Order of Things.

What... happens?

Form conCenters. The OverSeer... conCenters.

Changes?

Indeed, in most creative splendor.

Into what?

Into another.

Another...?

Corporeality.

Life? Corporeal life?

More than corporeal life... and beyond. The OverSeer conCenters... forming corporeality anew.

I don't... Tres's projection of himself faltered, lapsed, then renewed in form. *Everything... changes?*

One corporeality is not altered... when a new corporeality is created.

But why would anyone—a self—choose to change that way?

To continue the creative process, aself's development, to provide guidance anew.

And I'm... how would I... I'm supposed to...

The choice is yours.

What if I don't want... if I can't—?

There is another.

Another...?

Awakened.

There's... someone else? Selected?

Indeed.

But I thought... The Natural Order of Things only selects one.

Until now.

Until... now?

Until... your awakening.

I don't understand.

One is selected. And... another.

And that one... where is—?

He... is instructed—prepared—as you are.

But there are... two of us. How will... who—?

As is The Natural Order of Things.

The OverSeer... the other one in training... is it—is he—you?

Yes. And no.

———

THE ROLE... *is mine,* the self-defined form of *another* imparted, vibrant and stalwart, converging with the Consultation.

The choice... is aself's, was returned by one member.

Upon the ConCentration, added another.

As offered by The Natural Order of Things.

To the selected.

To both.

There are two.

The one plying the Consultation undulated, then propelled his conveyance at his attentive audience. *I am the first!*

Aself's instruction continues.

As does... another's.

Instruction is finalized... upon the ConCentration.

Sparks of light, sound, sensation spun in a whirlpool of matter as the consulting presence conveyed, *I... AM... READY... NOW!* His projected form flitted, exploded, then reconvened. *I know all. I ascend from all corporeality. I am aware... of all.*

It is the awakening, communicated the first response, calm and uncolored.

The selection.

An honor.

Bestowed by The Natural Order of Things.

A choice.

The proliferation of aself-development.

And there is always...

Greater awareness.

More... to be adapted.

Integrated.

Learned.

I WILL... TEACH... ALL OF YOU! erupted the final message of the one who summoned the convening of the Consultation as he retracted his own focus from his audience.

DISTINCTLY AND EXPERTLY—AND aside from the Consultation's awareness—events, creations, and occurrences formulated. They *began*, their manifestation construed—all in line with great, vehement desire.

4

CLEARLY, SUCCINCTLY, TRES ARTICULATED WITHIN THE APART, NO longer requiring dream state or the guiding enticement conveyed by Saig. Tres's focus sought out his tutor, reaching him instantaneously.

You study intently, Saig complimented, *and practice with full awareness and focus... despite your corporeal consciousness's remaining rejection of all that is taught, all that is true.*

Tres's form shuddered, with strength and evident playfulness. *It feels natural,* he imparted toward the smiling face articulated by Saig.

Indeed. What is natural... is truth.

But I don't want it, Tres imparted without hesitation, with conviction confirmed by the solidity of his chosen hue. *It's not for me.*

What is it... that you do not desire? Saig inquired with delight.

You know. I'm not hiding my thoughts.

Indeed. Your... announcement... is professed to all.

Tres's conscious mind sought to look around—among—his surroundings, to see evidence of the others he knew must be present and tuned in. He found none.

We... are never alone, Saig imparted.

I can feel... I am aware—of them—but I can't see...

'Sight' is limited to your corporeality, to your corporeal form. Awareness... transcends all. As the awakened—

I don't want to be. Tres's desire forced itself upon his surroundings.

As you concurrently announce to all, Saig reminded, assured.

I can't be—I don't want to be... OverSeer.

Only truth... need be conveyed, Tres. Conveying mere corporeal emotion, temporal limitations, conscious 'fear'... is waste.

I don't want it! It's my choice and... it's not for me. Tres's form reshaped itself, projecting the image of his most prevalent, conscious emotions. *There is no need for further instruction,* he imparted. *I need... to live this life—without burdens, without... distraction.*

Awareness... accepting truth... of who you are—is not 'distraction.' It is truth. It is... 'life.'

Then, let me live it!

Corporeal life... is yours to live. It is not denied. No choice... is denied—but you must choose, Tres. And this life, as all others of yours, is... but one. The conveyance expanded as it was delivered, encompassing its surroundings, expressing the breadth of its meaning—of its reminder—in thriving form of its own. *All experiences... evolve, adapt, transform,* Saig reconfirmed for his student. *All choice... reaches fulfillment.*

Tres's confusion—his denial—resided around his form as rippling, contrasting energies.

Saig imparted, *All things... must come to their 'end.'*

But it is... my choice!

Indeed, the choice is yours.

And I choose... my life. I have to live it to the fullest—to the end, as I decide.

As is most natural. As is The Natural Order of Things.

And I can't... I can't be here... and there. It's... too much.

There is no 'too much.' There is only... opportunity, the choice of continuing aself-development. And the opportunity... is only offered to you, Tres.

But I'm not the only one. There is another. And there have been others: the OverSeer now, those before...

There are others, yet... you... are the first. There is no other occurrence of aself awakened... in corporeal life.

But that's what happens—awakening—to all selected.

The selected awaken in the Apart... upon completing the final corporeal life chosen. You... are the first to awaken... while in corporeality.

I... Tres shifted, faded. *I'm the only one—to remember—while... living?*

Yes, you are.

What does that mean?

'Meaning' is merely the goal of your corporeal mind. All that occurs... is The Natural Order of Things.

Tres absorbed Saig's conveyance, the truths imparted, and infused with them, considering them and then, extracting his attention from them.

Will my instruction end... now?

The choice is yours—the denial... your choice.

Tres's form undulated, particles hesitating before rejoining. *You ask me to deny... life.*

You, Tres... ask it of yourself.

As Saig's projected image weighed on the atmosphere— energized with its truth and consistency—Tres's form disassociated, parted, fell away in reflection of its incongruity.

Will I ever see you again? Tres imparted.

Saig's form pulsed, giggled. *You do not... 'see'... me now.*

Will I... be with you—again?

You... are of the Apart. You are... always with... all.

Tres trembled with this frustration.

You are aware, Saig imparted, *as you choose.*

And Fei?

Fei is your OnLooker. He continues to look on for the extent of your corporeal life.

And... I choose the extent.

The choice is yours—as your original choice of experiences and aself-development... is fulfilled.

5

THE SCENT OF SIZZLING BACON FAT PENETRATED AARON'S bedroom. The inviting smell of yeast followed—proof that Maria's breakfast specialty, homemade cinnamon rolls, awaited downstairs.

Aaron padded down the stairs to greet Maria with a warm hug. Her smile was wide, despite the redness around her eyes indicating prior tears.

"Is it my birthday?" Aaron joked.

"If you want it to be."

Aaron sat in the chair nearest to Maria's position at the stove. "No, I'm in no hurry to get older. I want life to pass by as slowly as possible."

Maria smiled, caught in contemplation of her own wishes.

"When will they be ready? They smell ready!" Aaron forced more enthusiasm than he felt.

"Soon, soon! But I'll need your help with the icing."

"My favorite bit!"

For a moment, the months survived through Sancha's absence seemed less heavy in their minds.

"Speaking of birthdays," Maria said, interrupting Aaron's

meditation on the delicious fragrance wafting around him, "Have anything in mind for yours?"

"My birthday? No. Not really."

"You should do something special."

"You always want to do something special, Grandmom."

"I think it would be nice."

Without her saying more, Aaron understood his grandmother's truest desire and all the reasons why a distraction—any distraction at all—was invaluable.

Then, he looked up at the clock hanging on the wall and shouted, "Oh, shit! I've got to run!"

"Language!" Maria shouted before changing her tone to ask, "What do you mean?"

"I'm booked. I almost forgot. I'm supposed to be there at nine-a.m. sharp, or I miss—"

"What in the world are you doing? You didn't mention any—"

"Can I tell you about it afterwards?" He paused at the kitchen doorway, wearing a cheeky grin. His smile grew wider when Maria's most youthful expression appeared on her face: the one that only shined through when she was caught completely clueless.

"What in the world..." she pondered out loud.

"I didn't want to worry you," Aaron said, resting his hands on her shoulders. "Just... meeting up with some other folks."

"Oh, well, that's good—very good." Maria relaxed. "Would you like to take some cinnamon rolls for them?"

"I don't believe that's such a good idea before—I don't have time anyway. I really gotta go." Maria's visible disappointment changed his mind. "Sure," he said. "If you can pack them up quickly. I'm sure they'll go down well after... after we hang out."

"Oh, all right. I'll do that. You go get changed. And brush those morning teeth!"

Aaron ran up the stairs, two at a time, and searched his dresser for clothing fitted and comfortable enough to wear under a jumpsuit.

AARON SAVORED THE FRESHNESS—THE injected fear—in the rare experience of an actual *first* experience. Life-threatening situations and risk-taking were not new to him; being forcibly cramped into fetal position while subjected to the mind-numbing roar of the Cessna 182 engine *was*.

He focused on relieving the pressure in his ears as the plane gained altitude at an agonizingly slow pace. The jump instructor knelt just behind the pilot's seat, grinning like a wild man—still selling the expensive experience as he addressed his four initiates. Six hours previous, the four volunteers swimming in their borrowed, bright-red, full-body suits were strangers. Now, they were practically family—connected by shared trauma and impending tragedy.

The fashionably bearded initiate sitting opposite Aaron—the one with a sarcastic comment for every line their instructor said throughout the morning's instruction—wore a ghostly white face. The tattoos revealed above his suit collar were all the more vibrant in contrast.

"All right..." their instructor shouted above the engine while his voice echoed from the headsets they all wore. "We're almost at altitude. Once we reach 4,000 feet, the drop zone comes up fast—so be ready." He scanned the faces before him as he radiated his own confidence, mocking the non-existence of theirs. "Any questions before go time?" No one managed to formulate a question out of their fears in the time allotted.

"Good," the instructor continued. "We don't have time for them anyway." His joke dangled in the air, unappreciated.

"Door's opening!" His shout reached their ears *after* the sudden change in air pressure and the flash of bright sunlight.

The initiates latched onto the small handles on the interior walls of the plane—or each other—as the circulating force of air entered the tiny aircraft, coaxing them toward the door.

"Jack... you're first."

The slender teenager—just old enough to sign the required waiver without parental consent—hoisted himself off the floor with the helping hand of their instructor. Following hurried gestures, he dragged his feet closer to the open doorway and the waiting expanse of open sky.

Aaron looked away, staring at his sneakers as he ran through his own mental checklist. When he looked toward the doorway again, the teenager was gone, and the instructor tugged at the bearded initiate still stuck to the wall of the plane like a suction cup.

"Chavez—Big Guy—you're up!"

Aaron felt the Cessna rock side to side under the transferred weight as the man rose. His feet never lifted from the floor of the plane as he slid toward the instructor.

"You gotta hurry it up!" the instructor shouted. "We're already circling back over the drop zone for the second time for you."

Chavez nodded, his eyes glassy behind his dented plastic goggles.

"Can you hear me okay?" the instructor asked, holding his mouthpiece to his lips. "All right. I need you to step out. Just like we did on the ground."

Instead, the man braced his arms against the doorframe, holding his body in place within the safety of the plane.

"Chavez, are you going to do this? We can't waste any more time." Without a response offered, the instructor's annoyance grew. "Chavez... bro... I need you to put that first foot out the door—*now*."

He finally stepped forward—his long, wiry beard splayed across the bottom half of his face in the sweeping wind. Aaron looked away again, choosing—this time—to leave the fellow thrill-seeker to experience the moment alone.

Soon, the instructor's voice called Aaron's name from his headset. Aaron looked up to find him smiling and waving his arm. Aaron pulled himself off the floor, steadied himself as he reached for each side wall, and stepped toward the instructor.

"I know you're not going to hesitate, are you?" the instructor prodded.

Aaron shook his head, disbelieving his own answer.

"Good. Now, feet out on the step when I give the signal."

Aaron clung to the handle near the doorframe, resisting the pulling strength of air encircling him. He peered, leaning carefully forward, to see the door's entry step hovering over 4,000 feet of transparent atmosphere.

"The drop zone is just there," the instructor said as he pointed. "I'll talk you down if you drift off course. You'll see the red flags marking a spot on that field there." Aaron allowed himself to breathe.

"And we're *go!*" the instructor shouted. "One more behind you, then I'll follow and see you down there. Feet on the step, then hands on the strut—when I signal."

Aaron held tight to the doorframe, encouraged by the instructor's nod. He placed one foot on the platform only wide enough for a pair of shoes, then the other.

"All right. Hands on the strut."

Aaron's body seized up, stiff against the swirling air. The two painted outlines on the strut of the wing, shaped like a pair of hands, seemed too far to reach. And below them, there was nothing at all.

"Hands on the strut!"

The words shuddered through Aaron, prompting flashes of memory and foregone fears. His head began to shake side to side at the scenes playing in his mind and the instructor. He shook his head at his own decision to skydive, at the emptiness beneath his own feet.

"Last chance, or we've got to circle around again," the instructor warned with unexpected patience. "Take my word for it. It's even harder on the second go-around."

Aaron nodded, suddenly aware of a *presence* near. A familiar form of Fei's revealed itself, looking on, wisping with the wind itself.

Aaron reached toward Fei, his hands slipping through the vision, fingers wrapping themselves around the edge of the strut. Both hands in place, Aaron heard the instructor's voice ring in his helmet once more.

"Feet in the air. Just hang on—*feel the breeze*—and I'll count you down."

Aaron obeyed, his eyes steady on his imagining of the gaze of his OnLooker. His legs lifted, stretched out—floating on air, waving in the force of the wind like a banner behind him.

"Three..." sounded in Aaron's ear. "Two..." His hands strained to hold his grip on the strut. "One... Airborne!"

Aaron let go, daring all—any—to extract him from this life and disprove the choice he'd been promised: the gift of choosing the moment of his own death.

———

ASELF HAS RENOUNCED THE CHOICE, *as selected?* the brightest shining form of the Consultation emanated.

He has, Saig confirmed before them all, *of this moment.*

Such a refusal...

Has not occurred.

Until now.

I am... Fei's conveyance rained over the proceedings, *my role... as OnLooker...*

Is as necessary as always, he was answered.

As Tres articulates in his corporeality, Saig imparted with warm reassurance, *the OnLooker's presence is as significant.*

Crucial, verified one member of the Consultation.

Essential.

Considerable.

And of your own choosing, Saig reminded Fei with delight. *A most incredible, creative experience of your own.*

The brilliant blue of joy radiated from Fei's chosen form, replacing his questions, reforming his hesitancy.

Unique, one aself of the Consultation imparted.

Of great worth.

And aself-development.

Of course, Fei imparted with whole-self gratitude, his form vibrating with renewed enthusiasm.

And the other? inquired one aself of the Consultation.

There are—indeed—two.

Of the awakened.... in preparation for the ConCentration.

The choice—for each—remains, as selected by The Natural Order of Things, Saig imparted with patience and calm awareness.

Aself proclaims his readiness.

Aself is impatient.

And so, his instruction is not complete, Saig answered all.

The choice remains with one.

The choice remains with the two, Saig corrected, his formulated self deepening in hue.

Indeed, the most aself-developed of the Consultation confirmed.

The ConCentration brings all apparent.

It is... The Natural Order of Things.
The moment unknown.

The one called Tres, Saig offered in a flash of yellow, *continues his chosen lessons of corporeality. He may experience many 'years' of the corporeality's construct of 'time'... many new manifestations of his corporeal consciousness, many new... choices.*

Indeed.

Fei's agreement transferred to all present in waves of iridescent violet.

It is The Natural Order of Things.

FREE FALL RESEMBLED the very act of dying—as Aaron remembered it.

As he held his breath—dropping toward the earth at the mercy of nature and man's physical laws—he welcomed the loss of control, the emptiness, the sensation of the suspension of life itself.

He invited death, felt its force against his body as it simultaneously coaxed his constant acceleration—his *slipping*—through space and cloudless sky.

Consciously, his mind released—his body already arrested by gravitational pull. He closed his eyes to the sight of the earth's surface rushing at him and surrendered—to the powers that be, *whatever* they may be.

Without warning, the static line still connecting his free-falling body to the perpendicular flight of the Cessna yanked at the parachute on his back, then released him completely. The force jolted his body upright, then tossed it into a swinging motion as his parachute opened perfectly, impeding his momentum.

There—suspended in the atmosphere, surrounded by

uncanny silence—time stilled. Aaron floated above the world he'd called home for eons, dangling over the landscapes that nourished him for countless lives.

Can it really be a dream, a projection, a manifestation... of the mind—of all our minds?

In that moment, he felt, it could be. He was separate, above, beyond. And Earth was just one point among many, one vision among infinite.

"You're doing fine," the instructor spoke into Aaron's ear. "You should be able to see the drop zone clearly now. Keep it in sight. Take note of the wind direction. Use your toggles, and... take your time. Enjoy the flight."

Aaron reached for the handles at the steering lines, gently tugged on one, and grinned as his body glided left at his command. Pure joy washed through him as he reveled in the experience created by his own *intention*, felt his energy mingling with the minute particles all around.

He'd rarely felt more alive—or felt less *inside* his own physical body. Embracing all sensory input, he remembered—relished—the unique offerings of corporeality—even as he tasted the truth of his constant, undeniable connection to the Apart.

"Did they like them?" Maria asked as Aaron skipped through the front door, throwing it open to smack against the near wall. His memory flashed with the image of the container of cinnamon rolls still sitting—untouched, forgotten—in the back seat of his car.

"Yes..." he answered, prompting his grandmother's smile.

"Good, good. Did you have a nice time?"

"Mm-hmm." Aaron tossed his jacket over a chair at the kitchen table. "Better than I expected."

Maria turned from her task to hold her buzzing grandson still for a moment. She looked into his eyes, squinting as she studied them.

"You look—something's different about you," she said. Only Aaron's eyebrows reacted to the accuracy of her deduction. "But something usually is," she muttered through her smile, letting go of his arms and turning away from him again.

"I went skydiving!" he blurted.

Maria spun around with uncanny efficiency. "You did *what*?"

"But don't worry—I'm still alive!"

"Oh, you!" Maria punched a questionably-playful fist at his chest before her amusement faded and her worry lines returned. "You're not going to do it again, are you?"

"I don't know. I—"

"*No,* you're not—please," she answered for him. "I don't want to go through..." Her newest expression passed over her face: the one devoted to sudden, full focus on the one they'd lost.

"No, I'm not, Grandmom," Aaron quickly promised. "I just wanted to try it—don't need to do it again."

Maria's stature relaxed into comfortable curves. "Good," she said, nodding. "*Thank you.*"

AARON LAY still on his bed, adrenaline still coursing through him, his blue eyes alight with life. He buzzed with the exhilaration of survival—of being born again by defying death.

Yet, he felt consumed by emptiness—devoid of a singular element central to his existence, to his current-life self-identity.

Sancha was *gone*—completely, absolutely.

The sensation of her he held within for so long—her *self*—

had left him. His mother was with him no more—no longer reaching, aching, or searching. His emotions were his alone—again—no longer mingled with hers, his pain no longer justified by hers.

Never before had he felt the loss of a loved one in the same way and so abruptly. Never before did a loved one linger, long, and then, leave—so wholly, so thoroughly—as Sancha had.

6

"You've *never* climbed before?" The thirty-year-old professional climber shook his head as he wiped the chalk from his hands onto his climbing shorts and unpacked a sandwich from his backpack. "That shit's dangerous." He smiled at Aaron, contradicting his words with genuine admiration.

Aaron silently ate his own packed lunch, seated comfortably far from the edge of the sheer rock face he'd just climbed.

"How do you feel now?" the pro climber asked between bites.

"Free," Aaron answered, staring out over the canyon below them that stretched as far as their eyes could see. "Empty."

The climber nodded as he chewed. "Yeah. All the usual shit disappears. It's just you... and whatever else is out there."

Aaron nodded, staring through the view.

"I'm trying to be *nice*," Aaron whined into his phone.

"Hey," Bennett's voice returned, raised in defense, "I don't *need* you to be nice to me. I'm trying to be there for you. If you need a friend—you remember what friends are for, right?—I'm still here."

"I just... I want to be alone."

"I can understand that—I did—but it's been six or seven months since..."

The silence blared from both ends of the phone connection.

"Thanks for reminding me," Aaron spoke first.

"I'm *truly* sorry. I'm just... I'm worried about you."

"Well, maybe I'm tired of everyone being worried about me. And I'm tired of worrying about everyone else. I can deal with it. I *have* dealt—I gotta go."

"You always have to go! And, in case you were wondering—"

"Bye, Bennett," Aaron said, ending the call and immediately regretting his behavior.

"...MY DAD IS HOME AGAIN," Bennett finished aloud, alone, and staring at his phone's screen. *I don't know why I bother anymore.*

"I NEED MY FREEDOM," Aaron confirmed to himself, feeling his connection to former teachings and realizations all the more deeply.

7

Aaron woke abruptly, feeling an invisible weight on his chest—not a burden, not fear—the weight of implication. In two hours, his life would be in the hands of an elastic cord—and the calculation of mass versus force constant.

More than emotion, he felt an awareness: confirmed, overt knowledge of portent, of impact. The sensation drew him, beckoning like an invisible hand clutching at his body, reeling him toward the inevitable—unknown but definite.

As he fully awakened, so did his corporeal fears—so did hesitancy, questioning, obsessive guessing. By the time he finished dressing and went downstairs, the worry was etched in his face.

"Aaron," Maria carefully prodded as she handed him the box of bran flakes. "You're not... *doing* it again—are you?"

Aaron poured the cereal into his bowl. "Doing what?"

"The... jumping out of an airplane."

"No."

"Because... you promised me. Remember?"

"Mm-hmm." He poured from the carton of milk handed to

him and looked up at his grandmother. "I'm not going to jump out of a plane again."

Maria's body relaxed. She pulled a spoon from the drawer and handed it to Aaron.

His breath halted. The pressure against his chest grew, demanding his full attention.

BREATHE, Aaron pleaded with himself. *Get ahold of yourself. This isn't any different than the other times. You choose your own death. You... chose against it. You chose life.*

"All right, all you daredevils. Who's first?" The staff member connected himself to a safety line, then scrutinized the lineup of pale-faced newbies cowering from the edge of the rooftop. Every male tugged at the straps of their harnesses crossed at their crotches. "Anyone jumped before?"

Heads shook; eyes veered away. The sudden gust of wind took them all by surprise. No one dared to peer at the awe-inspiring view outstretched around them.

Aaron's own trepidation forced him to dictate every intake of breath as the lack of sufficient oxygen darkened his peripheral vision.

You are already... free, was the message he internally received. *It is of aself's choice—as is all.*

"We'll have to do this the old-fashioned way, then." The same, overly extroverted man in the staff t-shirt continued. "The conditions are great. So, we're not gonna delay." He pointed, leaving his grin behind. "You—you're at the front of the line, so you're gonna show everyone else how it's done." The grin returned, thin and devilish.

Aaron glanced behind him, then at the staff member again. He stepped forward.

"Walk the plank," the man coaxed.

All eyes homed in on the narrow, steel beam extending far from the edge of the high-rise and hovering thirty stories over the crowded downtown streets. All eyes turned back to Aaron at the head of the queue.

Aself need not seek, merely to open, to allow... awareness.

Aaron received the guidance. His consciousness remained focused on a single notion that drove him forward, further.

My mien, he thought to himself. *To be free... the reason for it all.*

Fei looked on, refraining from interfering—and never *correcting.*

Aaron could not feel the cord attached at his feet, only the binding at his ankles as he walked the narrow path of metal jutting out into sky. Sheer wind pricked his exposed face and hands as he stood nearly five-hundred feet above ground level.

Only *this* life's memories filled his thoughts, welcoming the new, recording every sensation. The end of the inflexible, steel support beneath his feet seemed to give, urging his fears. His eyes glazed over. The cityscape below melted, dripped, and became fluid to his view until it was an ocean of unfathomable depth, of guaranteed suffocation.

Aaron knew he would jump. He knew he'd be pulled. He knew he would defer to whatever came next.

"On the count of three," the staff member shouted from his own position of safety.

Three came quickly. Aaron held his breath.

A voice behind him yelled, "You'll be fine!" It was strong but soft—warm and feminine—but too late to console.

Aaron stepped forward and allowed his body to fall. His form sliced through empty air, dropping, seemingly, for longer than any previous experience. Then, the bungee cord yanked at the dead weight of his limp body.

The earth swirled below his head, beckoning Aaron downward into the whirlpool of sweeping images of lives hurriedly lived. He closed his eyes, then opened them again to find the feet of surrounding buildings at eye level, their rooftops prodding at the clouds high above his own feet.

The elastic cord began to tighten, sweeping him toward the sky again. Then, it relaxed, leaving him to fall once more.

Over and again, Aaron bounced, defenseless. He screamed at the people passing below his head—and at the air that swallowed him, then spat him out again, relinquishing him.

Her voice resonated in his awareness. *You'll be fine,* it promised again, repeating from memory, ringing with truth.

PART VIII

SURRENDERING

Serva me, servabo te.

— Save me, and I will save you.

1

Relishing the feel of the ground beneath his feet again, Aaron sat in the small cafe inside the bungee company's lobby. His doughnut tasted divine, dosing him with the sugar needed to replace his blood glucose depleted by the adrenaline surge just minutes before. He relaxed on a stool at the counter—both hands coated with sugar crystals—as fellow first-time jumpers wandered in.

A feminine figure, topped with a dark ponytail, lifted herself onto the stool next to Aaron and proceeded to scrutinize the pastries in the glass cabinet beneath the counter. "I don't know which is the biggest thrill: jumping off a building or being told you *have* to refuel on sugar."

The end of her statement slipped through a smile, her own amusement and delight coloring each word. Her ponytail swished over her shoulders as she leaned to read the tented paper labels in front of the farthest row of pastries.

"So, why did *you* do it?" she asked without letting the pastries out of her sight.

"Hmm?" Aaron managed with a full mouth.

"Why—did you—*do* it?"

Aaron rushed to swallow and cleared his throat. "Why did I...?"

She leaned farther, the seat of her jeans teetering above the stool. "*Do* it!" Her nose turned up at her frustration. "Jumping *to* something? *Away* from something? Playing God, tempting fate...?"

"Uh..."

She jerked upright—poised and alert—all focus on Aaron as her eyes finally raised to meet his. They burned and glittered like hot emerald coals: bright, iridescent green.

"I'm tempting fate," she said, her almond-shaped eyes squinting provocatively, egging Aaron with their intensity, "making sure I'm really alive." She flashed a full smile. "And you?"

Aaron blinked, defending himself from her unwavering stare. "I... me too," he breathed out, then turned away to escape into his doughnut.

"No," she said, every inch of her still. "That's not true. And now... you've got me wondering why you'd lie to a perfect stranger when telling the truth has no conceivable consequence —and I'm being nothing but *perfectly* polite?" She rested her chin in her hand, elbow on the counter. "Unless you're just a compulsive liar. Or—" She turned to face the counter attendant approaching. "I'll have one of those: the smiley heart things with the stuff inside."

"*Un palmier pour mademoiselle,*" the Frenchman behind the counter pronounced impeccably.

Aaron observed as she tilted her head to reply, "The *big* one, please."

The Frenchman answered with a smile, and she returned her attention to Aaron. "Or you don't *like* yourself enough to even admit your own *truth*?"

The Frenchman's face revealed his amusement at her

abrupt accusation as he carefully slid the oversized palmier from his metal spatula onto the perfect square of colored wax paper.

"That's not true," Aaron coughed, feeling the need to clear his throat of sudden tightness.

"Yeah?" she spoke, sliding cash and exact change across the counter.

"I wanted to get back to my doughnut."

"Oh! So, you're a glutton who chooses sugar over social etiquette and personal integrity!" She studied the palmier on the small plate before her. She gently perched it on her fingertips, then took a small bite. "Mmm... my new favorite pastry!"

Her returning smile stretched across her entire face—ear to ear. Her eyes lit up like sunshine itself, and pure joy and delight seemed to emanate out of every pore. She savored the small bite with her whole body, as an experience in and of itself—as if it was the most magnificent discovery of the latest decade of her life.

And Aaron couldn't take his eyes off of her.

"Is yours good?" she asked him.

He nodded.

"Can I try it?"

He reached for the unused fork resting beside his plate.

"Oh, just use your fingers!" she cried with impatience.

He tore off a bite of doughnut, pinched it between thumb and forefinger, and raised it toward the frowning girl. She remained in place; her lips parted.

Daring to hesitate only slightly, Aaron rested the bite on her lower lip and watched it disappear.

"Wow... best doughnut *ever!* That makes Krispy Kreme taste like... like..."

"The cafe at Kmart."

"Yes! That's so disgusting!" Her laughter extended along the entire counter, even prompting the Frenchman to smile by osmosis.

Aaron smiled as well, finding it hard not to join in the laughter as he noticed a pastry crumb stuck to her top lip.

"You've got a..." he said, pointing.

"Oh, thanks." She pouted against her napkin and wiped her smile pristine again.

Her gaze wandered back to meet Aaron's as they shared a private smile. And Aaron noted how each sight of her green eyes seemed to draw him nearer, calm him, slow his ever-racing mind.

"So," she said after another bite of her palmier, "are you going to tell me the truth?"

His eyebrows raised.

"Come on," she urged. "I can see it in there—in your eyes. I have a feeling there's *a lot* in there."

"I was jumping... away, I guess," Aaron answered.

She shook her head. "That's not your own voice. I know the difference, ever since I—" She contemplated the remaining pastry still teetering on her fingertips and rotated it, searching for her next bite—distracting Aaron from the statement she chose to abandon. "I wanna hear the *real* you. You know, the voice in your head. I don't have time for anything else—not anymore."

Aaron leaned forward, into her line of sight. "I've lived..." he said, "a lot. But I've never done anything like what we did today —not quite. And... if this is my *last* life, I don't want to leave anything undone. I want to do it *all*."

She returned his stare, her pastry forgotten. "Okay," she said, her lips left parted in awe.

"I'm not finished," Aaron continued, still holding her full attention. "And today, I wanted to feel a part of it all—like I have before but differently. And I wanted to see... if I really am free.

Find out if fate—or destiny or whatever—has a hold on me, or if it really is all bullshit. Find out if I really am in charge."

He relaxed back onto his stool, facing forward. "But I feel I'm done—done doing the crazy stuff—because it scared the crap out of me this time. I feel... it's already given me all the answers it can." He turned to face her again.

She nodded and said, "I *told* you you'd be fine." She smiled. "And here you are."

Aaron absorbed the words, entranced by everything about her—and everything revealed in such a short moment.

She leaned toward the pastry still in her hands. "I like your voice," she said. "Your real one."

AARON FOUND it difficult to keep up with the pace of the girl chatting away as she walked ahead of him. She didn't seem to notice he continued to fall a few paces behind as they wandered down the sidewalk downtown, still bursting with adrenaline.

"And that's when I died," she continued as Aaron quickened his steps again to avoid missing a single word. "Just like that—no warning. Not really." She tossed her ponytail back over her shoulder, then reached behind her head to pull it tighter, never breaking the rhythm of her steps.

Temporarily at her side again, Aaron questioned her story. "You mean you actually—"

"Yeah. I'm not kidding. I wouldn't joke about that," she said, further confirming her statement with a moment of piercing eye contact. "I don't really joke about anything anymore. I mean, I *can* joke. It's just, I prefer to cut to the chase—you know?—being on borrowed time and all."

"You *died*? Right there, after the surgery, while your grandfather was right at the side of your bed?"

"Yep. White light and all that—what they say is true, you know—I was gone for a full five minutes. Felt like forever to me."

"And you... *remember* it? What you saw?"

"Yeah, like it was yesterday. So perfectly crisp that there's no way it *wasn't* real." She stopped walking for a moment and waited for Aaron to close the few steps between them again. "You know how you just *know* when stuff is true? When... it doesn't matter what it is, even if it's something impossible to explain or convince anyone else of, but every part of you just *knows*?"

Aaron nodded, his eyes still wide as he absorbed every detail.

"And you know you were there," she continued, "because it doesn't feel like a dream, and it's even more than a memory—in more detail than even all this." Her slender arm raised and swept across the air ahead of their path.

Aaron nodded emphatically.

"And you..." She stepped closer to him, the top of her head level with his chin. "You actually believe me. At least... you're not saying it's all in my imagination."

Aaron waited for the surprise confession of her story's untruth, but the girl with dancing eyes only continued to stare at him.

Then, she blinked, suddenly intimidated by the connection. She turned and led their stroll again.

After a few steps, Aaron asked, "What did you see—after the light?"

Staring at the sidewalk, she answered, "Everyone—all the people I've ever known. Well, that would be too many people to see that quickly, but I *knew* they were there, around me—and others too, people that knew me, somehow, people that cared. It was all... *wonderful*, like happiness and support and encouragement coming from everything and everyone." She spun on the toes of her sneakers, almost elbowing a passerby. "From every particle of the air... like it was what everything was made of—the light, the faces, me, *everything*."

Aaron's comment came in a rush. "Like everything was bigger than you ever imagined it and *better*—formed of possibility itself."

She stopped and turned to face him again. "Exactly."

They stood in the center of the sidewalk, facing each other in silence, forcing others to swerve around them, all else invisible to them.

Looking away, she said, "Hey, why don't we grab lunch or something? I mean, what are we gonna do at home—with all this adrenaline? Sit and watch TV?"

"Good point," Aaron answered.

PEERING at each other over toasted sandwiches held over piles of potato chips neither of them had any desire to eat, Aaron's smile was huge as the girl with boundless energy and enthusiasm spoke up again. She carried on the conversation, proving her inability to let more than a full minute pass without saying something.

"What about you?" she asked. "Have you died and come back again?" She picked at her sandwich, stretching and snapping the melted cheese oozing outside the crust.

"Have you always been this forward?"

"Have you always bleached your hair?"

"I don't!" The instant rebuttal surprised even Aaron as it burst out of his mouth.

"*Okay*. It's just a question." She paused to savor her cheesy sandwich. "Sorry. I just say whatever's on my mind."

"I like it," Aaron blurted again, his fondness so obvious that he cleared his throat to audibly detract from it.

"I used to be diff—well, none of that really matters. I've been like this since the accident."

Aaron found himself nodding again.

"Most people find it annoying," she said, locking her eyes on his. "Even my family—especially *guys*."

"I don't."

"I know," she said, releasing him from her gaze. "You're different."

Aaron felt his heart beat faster.

"I knew that when I saw you up there—on the rooftop," she said. "You *acted* scared—to jump—but... you weren't really. It was like you *knew* things, and *those* were scaring you. You're not scared of life or of losing it—like me."

"But I am," he said.

"No, that's not what's in your eyes. It's more." She stared deeply, her gaze penetrating. Her head tilted to the side, her eyes squinting. "There's... *so much,*" she said, still staring. "Too much —it's overwhelming for you. You have to block it out." Her gaze drifted back to her plate. "And that... is what dams everything up and makes you feel scared," she delivered quickly, confidently, just before the sandwich reached her lips.

Aaron drank in the sight of her as she sat across from him: her lip smacking to the way she closed her eyes momentarily with each new bite, as if to capture the full flavor without distraction.

"I don't even know your name," he marveled out loud.

She laughed. "We didn't cover that?"

Aaron shook his head and his smile.

She stretched her arm over the table, holding out her hand in rigid form. She waited to hug his hand in hers.

"Emily," she said, squeezing Aaron's hand more firmly than any other woman—or man—ever had. "Pleasure to meet you."

SATISFACTION PULSED THROUGH *ANOTHER:* a beat breaking into song. He looked on—though it was not his role—and obServed —though it was not yet required of him.

The most basic rites and experiences of corporeality unfolded before his awareness: just two, among many, moving through the dance upon Earth. Their choices—their conjoined path—satisfactorily satiated his intent, serving *his* purpose, though their meeting was not of his intention or influence.

Fulfillment emanated from the pair as he watched them— their miens reaching, intertwining, bonding. Obvious to any with open awareness, the two were tied, connected, for yet-uncountable moments, grounding them in their chosen corpo-reality.

They were preoccupied, distracted with one another— cementing their attachment to the temporal.

As he watched, he radiated with gratification, sound presence, and calculating precision. He found his unknowing contender sufficiently subdued and content to remain in corpo-reality indefinitely.

And his assessment assured The Natural Order of Things to be precisely in line with his own intentions and deepest desires.

2

ALWAYS THE OBSERVER—USUALLY THE QUIET RECEPTOR—AARON found himself also the follower, for one of few times in this life. And he was content to follow—overjoyed, in fact—as Emily so naturally, so fluidly, assumed the lead.

Walking ahead of him again, she served as trailblazer into the hills encircling the city. Her pace was strong and steady—the stride of a born hiker.

As Emily led *this* new adventure in his life, Aaron noticed how she seemed natural in every aspect, activity, and situation he had the pleasure of joining her in. She strode in complete confidence—with an edge of fearlessness. She held fears, but she took extreme pleasure in facing them head on—talking the skeletons right out of their closets.

"Too steep for you?" She smiled at him with a quick glance behind her.

"No," Aaron replied. He worried his constant smile might be suspect, but he couldn't contain it. Every word and thought she expressed rang in his ears as fearless and so refreshing.

He'd felt it all before—in the memories most safeguarded, those he protected and revered with the utmost respect. Still, the whole-self sensation of true connection always arrived and thrived as something impeccably individual, entirely new—like rebirth after the pain of death, no matter how many times the cycle repeated itself.

The morning was cool, allowing Emily to permit her dark hair to cascade over her back. The tomboy-at-first-sight turned fully-feminine goddess—even as she stomped along the dirt path in her well-worn hiking boots.

"Need a break yet?" she called to Aaron.

"If you want," he replied, the phrase just long enough to reveal his shallow breath.

"I thought you said you're a runner," she teased without slowing her pace.

"I am. I just never ran... up here. The trail... is pretty... steep."

"We're breaking." Emily's boots halted. "Your lack of fitness is depressing me," she said with her characteristic, irrepressible smile.

"Wh—!"

To Aaron's frustration, Emily reacted to his pathetic complaint with the widest smile of all. Then, his annoyance vanished as he pondered what might prompt her to smile even larger.

"Your hamstrings ought to be in better shape. Do you just run at a snail's pace? You must have weedy calves and thighs under those jeans—chicken legs, I think they call th—"

"All right, that's enough!" Aaron complained, rushing at her in playful threat.

"Okay, so now I know your soft spot." She held up her hand, folding her thumb and pinky finger in a Girl Scout oath. "I solemnly swear, I will never comment on your weird legs again."

"I don't have—!" Aaron's face twisted up to scrutinize hers. "You never quit, do you?"

"You're endlessly fun to tease, aren't you?"

When they reached the bench carved into the rock face on the cliff-side of the trail, Emily dropped onto the stone seat as if it was covered in cushions. Aaron slowly sat himself, feeling every tendon in his aching legs.

"Oh, look! A little lizard! Over there—just at the edge of the underbrush."

"I don't see it," Aaron said, leaning toward her pointed finger.

"Right there! By that little bitty puddle there."

"I still can't—"

"Are you *blind* too? Right there! You're gonna miss it."

"Is it... right next to that gray rock?"

"They're *all* gray rocks!"

"The one next to the puddle!"

"Yes! Do you see it now?" Her game of teasing forgotten, Emily's face lit up like that of a child caught in the first moment of discovery.

"It's... doing pushups?" Aaron whispered.

"Yeah, looks like it."

"Why do they do that?"

"I have... no idea."

Aaron turned to face her, leaning farther than he realized, his face so close to hers. She instantly noticed his faux pas. He corrected his posture, slowly returning a respectful distance between them. Their eyes remained locked on each other as he moved, and he caught her subtle glance at his mouth.

Tiny shivers tickled up his spine and down again. He leaned toward her—on impulse—his intent obvious as his gaze fell to her own mouth.

"Wait!" she shouted, turning away.

Aaron had no idea the simplest reaction could affect him so deeply, despite all his *experience*. Her reaction *pained* him.

"It's not right," Emily said, still looking toward the point where the trail disappeared around the bend.

Aaron was speechless, internally questioning and second-guessing his decisions, actions, impulses—and hers.

"Come on," she said, jumping up. "Break's over."

Aaron's heart raced even before he started to follow behind her along the steep path. His eyes fell to the ground; looking up at her beauty only made his chest ache more.

FOR AARON, their silence was agonizing, heavier than any possible topic of conversation. The path continued—no end in sight—and Aaron followed Emily without a single complaint, without a single concern raised.

As they rounded the umpteenth bend—twisting to the left and right, always on the dark side of the hill—the sun finally appeared in full glory before them. A blinding beacon of encouragement, it urged them through the final steps to reach the pinnacle.

"*This* is what I wanted you to see," Emily said, waving Aaron to hurry behind her and stand next to her. "There," she said, pointing toward the sun as he stepped near.

He looked out over the city, from a higher point than he'd ever found on his own before. The early morning haze still hung in the valley, capturing and holding the sun's own rays.

"Isn't it *magical*?" she said. "Like a whole 'nother world. Like the city, our little city, is part of something so much bigger, so much more beautiful—as if it goes on forever like..."

"Like *we* go on forever," Aaron finished for her.

"Yeah." She smiled as she turned to face him.

He felt the touch of her fingers on his, her skin soft and warm. His hand wrapped around hers.

"*Now*," she said, speaking so softly, she almost whispered as her gaze extended the invitation—her *request*.

Aaron leaned toward her, committing himself to carrying the movement through to its intended end—no matter what. And he succeeded.

Their lips touched as they squinted at the sun, their faces shutting out the beam of light separating them. Aaron's hand left Emily's as his arms wound around her waist.

He didn't know she'd never been kissed quite like that, that she'd never before heard all of nature sing in symphony for a single moment. He had no idea the gift he gave her—until she closed her eyes and returned the gift to him.

"LIKE CHOCOLATE," Aaron said, his eyes intent on Emily's mouth as he rested beside her on the grass and wildflowers blanketing the hilltop. "A really expensive chocolate."

"You mean, my mouth tastes like vinegar," she said, smiling.

"I like vinegar."

"Oh, stop!" she delivered with a light punch at his shoulder.

"I'm serious."

She faced him, her eyes softer and more feminine post-kiss than Aaron remembered them pre-kiss. "I know you are," Emily said. "It's... really wonderful." Her cheeks filled with a blushing warmth.

She looked out over the city, savoring the view only the two of them were privy to. "I'm so sick of people that aren't serious— like guys who pretend to be serious about football or something, but they're really only into drinking beer, hanging out together, and eating nachos."

Aaron laughed. "I don't even know how to play football."

"That's *awesome*." She smiled again, then ventured, "Tell me something else serious. Something you wouldn't normally tell anyone."

He joined her in drinking in the view, then looked yet higher in the sky above them. "I don't feel—" he said, stopping himself.

Emily turned, cocking her head at him. "Go on."

"It doesn't seem like your name's... really *Emily*."

Her eyes widened. "Wow. That's quite a statement. I could've gone my whole life without anyone telling me I have the wrong name." She smirked at the joke, her mind drifting to other thoughts.

"I feel it's something else," he continued, the depth of his honesty grabbing her attention again. "Something..."

"Like Sabrina? Or Natasha? I thought they were the *prettiest* names when I was little."

"No, something simpler, sort of, but *deeper*. It's like it's on the tip of my tongue but..." She pouted at him, her lips calling to him again. "Maybe... if I kiss you again... I can figure it out."

She giggled as their lips met, Aaron swallowing the sound with his. They both closed their eyes—feeling rather than calculating, *being* rather than thinking.

Aaron ended their connection, leaving Emily poised for more, her eyes still closed.

"*Tela*," he announced, like a boy proudly guessing the secret contents of an unwrapped Christmas present.

Emily opened her eyes. "*Tela*? Where did *that* come from?"

"It's Maltese," Aaron answered before adding, "I believe," to disguise his certainty.

"*Maltese*? How do you know—oh, never mind. I'll consider it one of those mysteries of your strange mind." She started to turn, then her curiosity prompted her again. "What does it mean?"

"Rose," he answered without so much as a blink. "I think," he added as an obvious afterthought.

"Rose..." she repeated. "Very simple, but also... quite complex."

Aaron nodded.

"You're very complex yourself," she said.

―――――――

FOR EMILY, the two syllables that she'd never heard joined together already seemed to belong to her—without explanation, without reason.

For Aaron, speaking his first and foremost thoughts seemed to hold power, freedom, peace—that he'd spent lives trying to find every other way.

And speaking that name itself seemed to infuse the atmosphere with an electricity, an energy—attracting and aligning invisible forms, transfixing events.

3

AARON FLIPPED THE OPEN BOOK OVER HIS LAP AND LET OUT A contented sigh as he gazed at Emily. "As far as I can remember, you're the only woman—that I've *ever* met—who actually reads as much as I do."

She stretched and adjusted her position on the blanket they shared, her loose dress revealing a peek of her peach-colored thighs just above her knees. "That doesn't make your choice in women sound very flattering. And you shouldn't treat a book like that. It weakens the spine."

Aaron quickly turned his book over again, inserting a paper napkin to mark his place as he closed it. "I don't mean just *girl-friends,* et cetera..." He paused to enjoy how Emily's left eyebrow raised at *that* word. "I mean *all* women I've known: my mom, my grandmom, teachers... whomever."

"That's just sad, but I know what you mean."

"This is—"

"And what's the *et cetera* you referred to?" Emily gently closed her own book around a silk bookmark as she sat upright.

"I..." Aaron started without any idea of how to continue.

"I'm waiting."

His mind wandered, theorizing how to make her magical smile return.

"Hello?" she prompted.

"What? Just girls—women. What else is there?"

"You tell *me*... do you have a *baby momma* hidden somewhere you haven't revealed to me yet? You *are* old enough."

"Hardly!"

"Well?"

"No. Of course not."

Emily leaned forward, nearly nose-to-nose with Aaron. "Look into my eyes." He did as instructed. "Say it again."

"No... *Tela*."

Both felt the flow of electricity between them in that moment. Both held themselves back from carrying out their most spontaneous inclination.

Emily leaned back again, folding her legs under her dress. "At least, I always know when you're telling the truth."

"*Have* I ever lied to you?"

She shook her head and smiled. Aaron turned his head and stared into the forest surrounding them.

"Did you hear something? An animal?" she asked.

He smiled, turning his gaze back to her. "No."

"What was it? I haven't seen that look on your face before."

"It's nothing. Just a flicker of light, the sun between the trees —or something." He reached for his book.

"You mean, that kinda looked like a guy's face?"

The book fell from his hands. "What?"

Emily looked in the direction of Aaron's previous focus. "Well, it was just outta the corner of my eye, but I thought... it seemed kinda like an old man's face—a friendly one," she said, ending her description with a tone of light amusement.

"You—"

"Is that what you saw?" she asked.

Habit forced Aaron to open his mouth, preparing a denial. He took a moment to weigh intuition against logic, then nodded.

"He's friendly, right?" she asked. "And you've seen him before? You didn't seem scared or—"

He nodded slowly. "He's..."

"You can tell me."

Aaron's face aged years before Emily's eyes, forming new wrinkles as he drew in a deep breath.

"In your real voice," she reminded him.

"I haven't... told anyone at all—not *who* he is—*no one*."

"That's okay. I like being the first," she smiled. "Hey, in case you forgot, I'm the girl who died and came back to life. Nothing can surprise me."

The corner of his mouth longed to smile, to relax, but he didn't allow it. "He... kind of... watches over me."

"Like a guardian angel."

"Maybe. I don't know. What's a guardian angel like?"

Emily burst into giggles. "I have no idea." The tension of the conversation relieved, she added, "I can feel my uncle around sometimes, you know? Just a sense really—I've never *seen* him. Well, except for when... I was dead for those five minutes. It's like... well, I just feel this extra support around, like... someone's pulling for me—like my uncle used to when he was alive."

Aaron nodded. "I want you to meet my grandmom," he blurted.

"What? From ghosts to your grandmother—just like that?"

Aaron flashed a cheeky grin.

Shaking her head, Emily said, "No one can switch topics as fast as you do."

Aaron shrugged, still smiling.

"So, you think she'd like me?"

"Yes," he said, his eyes full of color, "she's going to be over the moon with you."

———

"AND I WANT you to meet her." Aaron finally breathed after rushing through a barrage of information and events all in one breath.

Maria stopped pretending to wipe down the kitchen counter. "You... you *jumped*... off of a building?"

"Grandmom! That's not what I was saying!" Aaron shifted in his chair at the table, fidgeting like a wind-up toy.

"You said—" She didn't bother to disguise the worry and displeasure on her face.

"Yes, yes! I bungee jumped. It's no big deal—I won't do it again. What matters is that... that I met this... that for the first time, I—"

The coincidental lie pinched his throat, stabbed at his stomach, even before it began. The faces of loves found—and lost— raced through his mind. He felt the dread of dishonoring the dead, then it was gone.

He straightened in his chair while Maria eyed him with curiosity. "I didn't believe," he said, "this would happen—now."

"What would happen?" Maria asked, noticing her grandson's mouth quiver. "*Oh*," she said as her smile broke out—and then, a blush over her broad face.

The latter unnerved Aaron in a new way. He wondered what his words—or lack thereof—actually meant to his grandmother's ears.

Still smiling, Maria turned her back on him, pretending to scrub at an invisible mar on the counter again, her own mind wandering among clouds of happy thoughts. "Well, I'm looking forward to it then. I admit," she said, "I haven't felt up to... meeting people—or *socializing*—but..." She faced Aaron again. "Everything happens for a reason. Maybe this is just what *we* need." She *almost* giggled.

Her belief rang as true as all her words uttered throughout Aaron's life. Some of his grandmother's notions he could verify with fact and experiences of his own. Others were delivered with such conviction that he found himself leaning to her point of view.

For a reason... repeated itself in his mind.

Maria decided to wet the sponge in her hand. "I'll have to clean up. This place is a mess. I've let it get so cluttered. It'll be good to give it a good spring cleaning."

"Umm, actually, she's..." Aaron mumbled, his tone finishing the confession.

Maria spun around, her eyes accusing.

"She's..." he tried again. "I didn't consider... I didn't think you'd mind—"

"Well, let the poor girl inside then! Where are your manners?"

Aaron ran from his seat as Maria's hands planted on her hips, her familiar stern expression returned.

Aaron opened the front door, silently motioned, then his arm lowered out of view, holding another hand as it reappeared again.

Emily looked only at Aaron, trying to hide her embarrassment and fear of his grandmother's disapproval. Aaron walked back into the kitchen and stood before Maria.

"Grandmom, this is—"

Emily turned her head, lifting her face to Maria's. "Emily," she said, holding out her hand.

Maria's eyes darted left to right between them. "Oh, come here!" burst from her as she held her arms out to Emily.

Emily's eyes grew wide and she gasped for air as the vise of Maria's hug squeezed her.

"Welcome! Welcome." Maria let go of the slender girl in her arms, held her at arm's length by her shoulders, and studied her head to toe.

Finally, Maria's eyes met Emily's. She gasped and stumbled backwards. Emily looked to Aaron. Aaron was just as confused.

"Those eyes..." Maria mumbled, stepping farther back.

"Grandmom, be careful." Aaron stepped to Maria's side, leaning her against his shoulder.

"My God," Maria whispered. Her eyes blinked away the threat of tears.

"She's fine," Aaron reassured Emily.

"Mrs. Rivera," Emily whispered, "are you—"

Maria steadied herself, shoving Aaron away. "I'm fine. I'm so sorry." She searched the room for words; she looked again at the girl standing before her.

Emily wore a smile specifically for Maria: a message of reassurance, friendship, respect—and the spark of inner joy.

A smile broke across Maria's face as well, pushing her wrinkled cheeks aside. Even her eyes lit up with acceptance. She slowly nodded.

"You have... *my daughter's eyes,*" she said. And Emily understood the full depth of the compliment.

"You showed her around?" Maria asked when Aaron walked past in the upstairs hallway.

"Mm-hmm," he smiled.

"Good. I want her to feel comfortable here. Did you ask if she wanted anything to—"

"Yep. Getting it now—*if* you'll let me get to the kitchen."

Maria smiled and nodded, stepping aside. "Aaron," she blurted as he headed for the stairs.

"Yeah?"

"She's... *remarkable*—isn't she?" Maria whispered. "So full of... joy."

He nodded, racing down the staircase like a boy on Christmas morning.

4

"IT'S SO BEAUTIFUL OUT HERE," EMILY SAID, HER LOWER LEGS swinging in the air as she flung herself toward the sweeping lower branches of the maple tree. "Such a perfect day."

She swung past Aaron as he sat still in the swing next to her, watching her every movement and expression.

"You don't come out here often, do you?" she asked from the air above him. "It looks deserted—poor garden." She zoomed past him again.

"We haven't," he said.

"You haven't? What do you mean?" She leaned back in her swing, gripping the chains and closing her eyes to focus on the feel of the wind rushing over her body.

"Not..." he started when she was nearest, added to when she swung by again, "since..."

Emily dug her heels into the ground, dragging her momentum to a halt. "Oh, gosh. The—" She looked to the side —at the trunk of the massive tree they sat beneath. "I forgot. You shouldn't have let me—"

"No, it's all right." Aaron forced a smile. "She loved to swing.

The tree..." his voice drifted along with his gaze, "probably misses her."

Emily smiled, letting the seat of her swing rock back and forth a bit. She granted Aaron a moment of silence before she changed the subject.

"My parents are beginning to wonder if I've been adopted. I'm spending so much time over here," she said.

Aaron smiled.

"Does she mind?" Emily asked, beginning to swing again. "Your grandmother?"

"Of course not. She's... happier now."

"Really?"

"Mm-hmm."

"Uh oh," she said, stopping her swing again. "You don't think she's making *plans* for us already?" Her cheeky smile—sporting a single dimple—matched the brilliance of the sun itself.

"Plans?"

"You know... a wedding, grandbabies..."

Aaron started to laugh. "No! No, she's not like that."

"Are you sure?"

Aaron thought for a moment. "I'm pretty sure it would've come up long before now—if she was."

"What, with your *other* girlfriends?"

Aaron started to defend himself, just before discovering Emily's accidental confession. "Wait—are you saying... you're my *girlfriend*?"

"No! That is *not*—"

"That's what you said." Aaron couldn't stop smiling.

"Fine," she practically shouted as she propelled her swing up into the air. "But I'm *not* getting married."

"Who said anything about—"

"I have a life to live. I don't need a man holding me back."

"You *believe* I'd want to hold you back?"

"I don't know," she said on a downswing, passing him. "But I'm never gonna—"

"Well, I'm not either—getting married—then," Aaron shouted to her at the peak of her swing. "*And,* I wasn't even thinking about it," he mumbled to himself.

They continued teasing and taunting—smiling and making faces—as they swung beneath the afternoon sun, in and out of the shade of the maple tree.

MARIA WATCHED from the living room window, catching every smile shared between them—even smiling a bit herself.

AS HE SLEPT, Aaron's consciousness slipped away—more easily than ever before. It receded into the background, almost sleeping itself as his other self reached, searched—and found an old friend.

THE IMAGE of Saig appeared to his mind's eye, no other communication or call necessary. Energy livened around them, imparting their greetings.

I didn't even realize... Tres considered as Saig answered.

You transcend... when you desire—when you... require it.

I'm not sure...

You are—always.

Tres detected his consciousness—his logical mind—alighting, waking with presented challenge.

The Apart, Saig conveyed, *is... a part... of you. As it is... of all. Unlike your corporeal consciousness—your temporal mind's cells and synapses—your true self... is always connected, always alive, always seeking aself-development. It may be denied. Still, it... is.*

Tres toyed with his form, articulating a rainbow of sensation. *We are always... following, seeking fulfillment... of our mien.*

Always.

I'm always seeking freedom. That's why I've come to the Apart.

Saig imparted only acceptance, neutrality, in response to Tres's declaration.

Does that mean I—my true self, Tres asked, his form rippling with the message, *can't be contained in corporeality?*

No aself is. Corporeality is merely... a moment, a choice, an experience—one of so many.

I don't want it to be, Tres imparted, his form undulating. *I want it—this one—to last.*

Of your corporeality's concept of 'time,' it will.

I don't want it to... end.

'End' is a choice, the true self's choice.

Tres's renewed comfort reflected in his hue. *I can see it now,* he imparted. *Every color... within every other color. Light in the dark —darkness in the light. I see—feel—more than my own memories. I know things... I didn't know before.*

You choose to become... aware.

I don't... think about it. It just... happens.

As is natural. Awareness is... most natural.

When I kissed her, I... I saw a name—I felt it. Was it... is it true?

Awareness is the only source of truth.

Her name... is Tela?

Of her true self, yes.

I know... her true... self?

You are... aware.

But how can... why does she have... another name?

Aself has only one... as you are fully aware... Tres.

The obvious impacted even Tres's partly sleeping consciousness. *We all have one true name. One name for our single self—the true self—living many different lives.*

Indeed.

Yours is Saig?

Yes. And I have been called by others.

In your other lives, Tres imparted with the certainty of expanding awareness.

Yes, Saig confirmed.

But... you wouldn't know what they are?

Saig's emanation hovered, condensed, communicating no reply.

Only those selected... are aware, Tres's temporal mind answered its own inquiry, proud with easy assumption. He allowed his form to diminish, color, then phase. *What if it is too much—everything I know?*

Quantification is merely a concept agreed upon by your—

Corporeality.

Indeed.

There's no such thing... as 'too much,' Tres declared with a student's pride, with umber tones.

There is only... what is: awareness, truth... The Natural Order of Things.

5

"It's like we're meant—"

"Shh..." Emily hushed Aaron as they stared into one another's eyes in the dark, sitting so close together that they could feel each other's body heat. "Don't say it," she whispered, turning away, looking up to the stars spread out above in the night sky. "Some things shouldn't—I don't want to ruin it." Her hands smoothed over the cool grass beneath them.

Aaron's entire form—mind and body—focused intently on the brightest star of all, the one who's magnetic pull he'd felt as soon as she'd spoken her very first words to him. "I've never felt anything like it—like what I feel with you."

Emily turned to smile at him, her eyes smoldering in the moonlight. "I know what you mean."

"What do we do... from here?" he asked—as if it was the most important question of all.

"Just... be," she answered—as if it was the most obvious answer of all. "Just *enjoy* it."

She accepted his kiss, enjoying the warmth on her lips, the heat of his breath, and the strength and intent they conveyed.

"I don't want to lose you," he said.

"Shh... you worry too much."

She kissed him again, her smile pressed between them. He traveled into her green eyes, allowing them to carry him away—away from thought, firmly in the moment.

———

THE TWO RUSHED through the front door, giggling and holding hands as they had countless times before. Emily tossed a verbal jab at Aaron, some private joke between them, as he pretended to be upset by it. Their bodies, actions, thoughts, all fit together like the missing pieces to an elaborate puzzle.

"Aaron." Maria's tone commanded their instant attention. As they faced her, she said, "It's Bennett. I'm so sorry, I—"

"What? What happened? Is he all right?" Aaron shouted, still clinging to Emily's hand.

Emily's reaction to the name called up the same level of concern, her mouth forming an O as she held her breath.

"Yes," Maria reassured them both. "Well, no—it's his father. He's—"

"Oh, no," Aaron mumbled. "I wasn't aware—I didn't even know he was back in the hospital."

Maria nodded. "I heard from—well, you should call him. I know you two haven't—"

"Yeah, of course. Where's my—"

"In your pocket—where it always is," Emily answered.

Aaron looked from one face to the other, bewildered.

Emily touched his shoulder. "Just go upstairs, take a few breaths, and give him a call. He needs you now."

Aaron nodded at the floor and stumbled toward the staircase. He looked to Maria, their eyes meeting—exchanging the shared pain of fresh wounds reopened.

EMILY KNOCKED on Aaron's bedroom door.

"Come in," he said. He sat on the end of his bed, staring at his phone.

"How is... are *you* all right?" Emily asked as she entered.

"I couldn't call him. I haven't talked to him in so long. *You* haven't even met him. I—"

"Shh." She sat next to him and slid her arms around him. "It doesn't matter, *none* of that matters—only what you do *right now*."

Aaron's face remained twisted, tight with pain.

"He's your *best friend*," she said. "He's not going to care about all the other stuff."

"What do I say?" Anger edged Aaron's soft tone. "'I know how you feel?' 'Losing someone you love sucks?' That it *still* hurts to think about my own moth—"

"What's all this?" Emily interrupted. "It's not *you*. Whenever you get all worried, it's like a different you takes over. *You* know what to do—whenever it counts, whenever you want to *let* yourself. All the questions and doubt? That's some other guy. And you know which one I... *like the most*."

Aaron looked into her eyes, his face relaxing, his breathing slowing.

"I don't know why you're ever the other guy," she continued. "What are you afraid of? Of knowing everything, of doing everything *right*?" Her tone headed toward laughter. "Of ruining me for any other guy—*ever*—if you actually let me know just how *impressive* you really are?"

Aaron couldn't repress the smiling of his eyes, despite the firm frown under his nose. "Why do you believe in me so much?"

"What else should I believe in?"

His full smile surfaced.

"Call your friend," Emily directed. "*You* know exactly what to say, and..." She stood to leave. "I'm tired of reminding you."

Aaron watched her close the door behind her. Then, he dialed Bennett's number.

"Hey. It's me," he said as he lifted the phone to his ear. "I *hate* that I haven't talked to you in ages. I miss you. And I miss your dad."

6

His eyes glazed with tears, Bennett stood at the lectern nestled in the corner of the small church. His father's body lay in a glossy casket behind him. "My father... he taught me... what true courage is..."

Emily squeezed Aaron's hand where it rested on her lap. She exuded her warmth and support without turning her attention away from Bennett who stood, struggling to speak, before the rows of packed pews.

Aaron flashed a gentle smile in Emily's direction and noticed a slender man standing in the rear of the church. Aaron nodded toward him in greeting that went unnoticed.

"Who's that?" Emily whispered.

"Another old friend." Aaron turned to face the front of the church again, his movement catching the attention of everyone seated behind him. He nodded toward the empty seat next to him.

At an appropriate pause between Bennett's words, Finlay slid into the open seat and caught Emily's green-eyed gaze.

"Emily," Aaron whispered to Finlay. Finlay smiled warmly in her direction.

"How have you been?" Aaron whispered to Finlay without turning his head.

"Great, actually."

"That's wonderful," Aaron said, smiling his reassurance. "Really great. And your mom?"

"Really good. She's... a different woman now."

Aaron drew a deep breath and nodded. All three turned their attention to see Bennett leaving the lectern as the minister took his place.

"If there is no one else," the minister's voice raised, "who would like to speak, then Ms. Carol will—"

Aaron stood, drawing the attention of all. Emily and Finlay's faces reflected their surprise. He squeezed his way down the pew, then the center aisle, patting Bennett's shoulder as he passed his seat at the front. Aaron stepped behind the lectern, the minister receding to the background again.

"I'm..." Aaron began, in a voice his friends and family had not heard before, "a friend of the family. I've known Jim for as long as Bennett and I have been friends—feels like forever." Aaron smiled to himself, catching the glimmer in Bennett's eyes. Maria looked on with approval as she held fast to Bennett's mother's arm in the same pew.

"He was," Aaron continued, "like a father to me. He had the answers for almost everything—even the stuff we boys couldn't ask our mothers." A few chuckles erupted, and each body in the room seemed to relax as if it'd been waiting for permission, needing it like air.

"I could go on all night," the melody of Aaron's calming voice carried over the rows of pews, "about how he was an exceptional man, a model father, a wonderful neighbor, but I believe we all know how... truly great he was. I just wanted to say that, well, that he was *right*. He was an engineer, full of ideas: of how we should live, how we could do it better, how we might all be doing it in the future..."

Veoir... The name materialized in Aaron's mind in that moment. *His... true name means 'to see.' He saw so much that we couldn't...*

The sound of someone clearing their throat drew Aaron's attention back to his position at the lectern before the waiting audience.

"It was as if," Aaron continued, "Jim was from somewhere else and put here with the rest of us just to help make our lives better. He did that, and I can't help but think—no, I *know*—that he's doing the very same thing even now—wherever he is. Nothing else would make sense—scientifically or theoretically. I feel he gave us... all that he could. And now, he's just doing the same somewhere else. And that makes me very happy."

Aaron noticed the smiles in his audience and the peace written on Bennett's face and his mother's. He stepped away from the lectern—prompting the minister to stand again—before he continued.

"And there's something else I know—that we *all* know, if we let ourselves. We—as we sit right here together and mourn our friend and loved one—don't know where someone goes after death, if at all. But... we *feel* it. If we let ourselves, we feel him still with us, very much alive, very much the same. That's not imagination. That's the truth. And... that's something to hold onto, to be grateful for, to celebrate. If he's still *with us*, then he's never truly gone."

Aaron looked over his audience, catching the grins and nods. He stepped to the side; the minister waited for confirmation. Aaron mumbled, "Thanks" and returned to his seat. Emily nodded to him with tears in her eyes.

BENNETT HELD FAST to Finlay's hand as he shook it in both of his own. Finlay smiled in return, accepting the thanks. Bennett turned to Aaron, taking in the sight of Emily.

"Thanks for coming," he said.

"I wish I..." Emily started. "It's nice to meet you," she finished.

"I've been a crap friend," Aaron said. "I—"

"No," Bennett said sharply. "You're just *you*, and... how can I ever be mad at you for that?"

7

BENEATH THE FAR-REACHING BRANCHES OF THE MAPLE TREE, Aaron and Emily listened to the song of its leaves gently stirred by a late-night breeze. The two sat intertwined, staring up at the night sky.

"It's so peaceful," Emily said.

Aaron nodded as his head rested on her shoulder. He lifted his chin and turned to face her, searching for the glistening stars in her own eyes.

"You're doing it again," she said as a wide smile spread slowly across her face. "What do you see?"

"The universe," he said. "Every living thing—all reflected there, right in your eyes."

"Impossible," she said. "They're too small."

"No, not if you really look."

"What else do you see?"

"Besides everything?"

"Any secret messages? Hidden agendas?"

"Past or future?" he said, as she continued to hold the sky in her eyes.

"Stop it!" Emily gently butted his shoulder with her own.

"You want me to tell the truth. You made it *obvious*."

Emily's smile grew even more.

"I don't ever want to deny you *anything*," Aaron said.

She lowered her head to meet his. "Then, don't."

The kiss eased between them, drawing them in, bringing them yet closer together. When they parted, their gaze remained joined.

"I feel," Aaron said, "I really am *myself* when I'm with you. It's so freeing."

Emily answered with a new smile. "Why would you want to be any other way? Any other person?"

"Life," Aaron answered promptly. "Gets in the way—sets the rules."

"I don't believe in rules. I don't believe there's ever a reason to not be yourself—not a good enough reason."

"Sometimes, there is."

"Like what?"

"To protect people."

"By lying to them?"

"Not sharing *everything*."

"Hmm..." Emily's lips pursed as her eyes squinted at the stars overhead. "Are *you* not sharing everything?"

"Not with everyone."

"With me?"

"You *know* the answer to that. You've been *training* me for months now."

"I have not!"

Aaron responded with a twinkle in his eyes. Emily shoved him back against the damp grass beneath them. Her lips pressed against his, daring him to tease her again. Instead, Aaron savored the kiss—and kissed her back.

Their arms wrapped around each other; giggles escaped between deepening kisses. The air around them grew warmer, hugging them, holding them in the moment.

Then, Aaron sat up, Emily still clinging to him.

"What is it?" she asked.

"Sometimes... it's too much."

The hurt appearing on her face pained him more than trying to find those simple words.

"What—?" she started to question.

"No—*inside* me," he said. "In my mind—all around."

"I don't understand."

Aaron's head fell into his hands, held over his bent knees. "It's just... *a lot*. When I'm close to you, it's even more."

"That's..." Emily reached for him. "Perfectly normal—all those feelings and things. I—"

"No, it's different. It's not that. It's..." He paused, seeking his own answers in her eyes. "*More*."

"Aaron, you can tell me *anything*. You know that. Is it something about *us*?"

"No! Yes... no—it's just *me*." He scrutinized her face, his voice growing deeper. "I... get all this information: images, thoughts, ideas, facts..."

"That's... good?"

"It's not *bad*—it's just... overwhelming."

Emily stroked his arm. "Just... take it one moment at a time, one *little* thing, at a time." A grin returned to her face. "Let's try it again." She leaned toward him. Aaron leaned away. "Aaron..."

He looked at her, at the uncharacteristic expression. Then, he kissed her—aggressively but slowly, tenderly—giving himself no other option.

"What do you feel?" she mumbled against his lips.

"You."

"And?"

"Things connecting."

"Things?"

"Particles... matter."

She kissed him again. "And now?" Her lips lingered on his.

"Memories... people."

"Tell me about them," she mouthed between kisses.

"I'm... meeting someone—holding their hand. She's smiling."

"Mmm... interesting."

"Someone else—a man—like a father... a mentor? He's giving me an approving look, and then..." Aaron kissed Emily deeply, seeking something.

They breathed together, held each other, their bodies pressed tight together.

"You..." Aaron said.

"Mmm," Emily moaned.

"With someone..."

"Me... with you?"

"No, someone you knew—long brown hair..."

"Mmm, kiss me," she breathed.

He answered exactly as she wished, and they fell against the ground once more. She curled against him.

"Just *one* moment... at a time," she whispered.

As their lips met again and again, they moved against each other, legs entwined, arms reaching, hands caressing. Aaron fell into the moment—into his life, into his self, joined with Emily—slowing his experience to the essence of each single moment.

His consciousness hesitated—warned—as the images quickened, flowing in a steady barrage: some familiar, some new. He felt his body roll with Emily's direction, laying on top of her, held in place by her arms, by her hips.

"Aaron..." she whispered, her voice wet and deep.

"Emily..." he answered as he pressed against her, every movement a question, each one answered by her hips moving with his.

The thoughts and images wrapped around Aaron like a daze, holding him inside—not frightening but urgent, messaging, filling his consciousness to capacity. He felt a hand reach below his waist, somehow inside his jeans; he pressed his lips harder against Emily's.

He saw her, as a small girl, running over fields of wildflowers, her hair carried on the wind behind her... as a woman, older, smiling over a child cradled in her arms... as a man, proud and imperial, wearing responsibility like a badge... and a man whose features flowed, mingling with Aaron's favorite image of the Emily in his arms. Then, she was an old woman, dancing, on a ship far out to sea. Then, there was another child, holding boy-Emily's hand: a twin.

"I see you. I know *all of you*," Aaron mumbled, his mouth reaching again for Emily's.

"Stay with me," she whispered as their mouths parted. "In *this* moment."

The hand that reached for him, shifted him, guided him, then slid away. Emily moved, so slightly, angling beneath him.

"Right now—*this*—is all that matters," she breathed, her eyes shut against the blinding stars above, her head tilted back, exposing the paleness of her slender neck as she moaned.

Without thought, without self-prompting, Aaron's body moved, his *self* reacted, directing him. Two joined—as close as any two can be—in corporeality.

AARON SLID into a chair at the kitchen table, smiling as he breathed in the scent of weekend breakfast cooking on the stovetop.

"Good morning..." Maria practically sang, sweeping her large body across the kitchen as she laid a plate—piled high —before him.

Aaron eyed her suspiciously before lifting his knife and fork and pointing them at a thick-cut slice of broiled bacon. "Do you have enough for a third?" he asked sheepishly.

"You mean..." Maria trilled from her position at the counter, "for *Emily*, who *stayed over* last night?" With a wave of her arm, another packed plate landed on the table next to him.

"No, she didn't *sleep over*," Aaron argued, stabbing at bacon. "We *fell* asleep, outside—woke up freezing!"

"Oh, okay," Maria giggled, delighting and unnerving him at the same time.

"Hello!" Emily announced, peering through the kitchen doorway. Her hair was perfectly tousled, glittering in the morning light—her green eyes the brightest they'd ever been. Maria noticed the casual graze of Emily's hand over Aaron's shoulder as she sat herself at the table.

"Is this all for me?" Emily asked.

Maria nodded, still smiling as she joined them at the table. Aaron hurried through his breakfast. Then, he looked up to find both women staring at him.

"What?" he asked through a mouthful.

"Shouldn't we wait for your grandmother to eat *with* us?" Emily teased.

"No, no, no," Maria countered. "Eat before it gets cold." Her smile never faded as she watched the two of them, catching every moment shared between them.

"IF YOU'LL EXCUSE ME," Emily asked Maria, handing over the towel-dried plate, "I want to freshen up a bit more."

"Of course," Maria answered, placing the plate in the

cupboard. She joined Aaron in watching Emily bounce out of the kitchen and bound up the stairs.

Aaron turned to his grandmother. "You look... happy."

"I am," she said. "And so are *you*."

He blushed and quickly returned his attention to the glass he scrubbed below the surface of the dishwater. He rinsed the glass under the faucet and handed it to Maria. "Everything's pretty perfect," he said.

PART IX

ACCEPTING

Non est ad astra mollis e terris via.

—— THERE IS NO EASY WAY
FROM THE EARTH TO THE STARS.

1

Saig appeared majestic, serene, as he addressed his student in dutiful guidance—his own constant, joyous energy conveyed with pristine clarity of purpose and intent.

Your instruction continues, Saig imparted, configuring the new lesson in particulate form.

The one... called Tres, his student thrust outward in a gust of sensation, *the other awakened... chooses corporeality, relinquishes all-obServance.* His selected form emanated through all. *I accept... I choose. I am... ANOTHER.*

You... Ciel... continue to seek and serve... your mien, Saig reminded, *even within the Apart.*

Indeed, returned Ciel, radiating an elusive purple hue, vibrant and alive with impatience, manifesting in expansive form even more brilliant than Saig's.

Repression, Saig advised, *only stifles creativity.*

Indeed, Ciel confirmed with flare, imparting pompous satisfaction.

And, it is... creativity... that fulfills, Saig imparted with radiant splendor, *The Natural Order of Things.*

Indeed, answered Ciel as his form dissipated, disconnected and withheld.

CIEL MANIPULATED his form before the Consultation, demonstrating masterful skill, expansive embodiment, and robust creative desire.

I have obServed, he imparted to those gathered at his summoning.

Aself has.

Indeed.

Contributing to aself's... aself-development.

I overSee... all, Ciel imparted by demonstration.

Aself is capable.

Aself is... aware.

It is The Natural Order of Things.

Aself must serve aself's mien, Ciel formulated, seeking confirmation in hue and tone.

Indeed.

It is The Natural Order of Things.

As serves... The Natural Order of Things.

I must seek, Ciel pulsed, *my... aself-development.*

It is The Natural—

And I am selected, Ciel imparted as he illustrated his creativity.

The choice is granted.

And I choose, Ciel imparted, his form rising, dilating, encompassing all aware, *THIS MOMENT!*

A NOTION, charged with desire, propelled by conviction, and

formed by awareness alone, pulsed with energy, amping in electricity, magnetizing. It drew together inclinations, like-notions, and appeals. Particulate matter formed and faded, joining, swelling, growing in capacity and strength, gaining momentum.

Ciel's desire corroborated, compounding in creativity.

A single will—his alone—manifested, tangible, palpable, and carrying intention, implication.

Saig's own awareness alerted, focused. The suggestion of alteration nudged at his essential nature.

The Apart resonated with electrical charge, all-matter synthesizing, forming melodious symphony. Aselves sensed the singular variance reverberating through all.

The Natural Order of Things shuddered.

The ConCentration? aselves questioned, with hesitant, careful celebration and anticipation.

The awareness of each aself honed, searching for the source of the momentous occasion. All vibrated with the prevailing rhythm. All joined in, synchronizing, creating together.

The ConCentration... aselves considered.

All delighted with awareness of impending change, with new creativity, with the spark of initial intention to create a new corporeality.

The OverSeer... conCenters, sung the Apart.

To be replaced by another, aselves alighted.

THE CONSULTATION CONVENED—QUESTIONING, knowing, sensing, awaiting.

The ConCentration, aselves agreed, their conclusions drawn by contradictory methods, all collaborating on a single focal point.

It cannot be...
By force?
Initiated by aself alone.
Never before.
But... now.
All is choice.
The ConCentration is... as all is... The Natural Order of Things.

SAIG'S PULSE expanded and contracted, opening to the flow of new energy—alive and deliberate, unabashed and unforgiving. Light, sound, song pressured, pressed, commanded, compelled.

Vivid memory of what *was* confused with what *will be* and muddled with *all that is.*

Saig's personality broadened, distended, bloated, and contracted, pulsing with the conveyance of all of the Apart.

AIR ESCAPED AARON'S LUNGS. His mouth impulsively gulped for fresh breath, alerting Emily as she walked at his side.

No words came forth, nor breath.

Past, present, and future condensed to one pinpoint moment felt by all choosing to be aware.

THE ONE CALLED Saig filled and fitted, surrounding reigning desire, sensing all communications and concerns. In his lack of readiness, he found readiness as he relied on full awareness to convey the one truth to his own self—to reiterate the *one choice.*

He felt his own totality spread far across the Apart, imbedding in every particle, in every source of energy and self. He continued to expand, flowing on the singular message—the singular lesson—of his own experience.

It is... as all is... The Natural Order of Things.

Saig succumbed, relented—and he chose.

SAIG'S PERSONALITY, his self, conCentered, disbanding as it collated, separating as it recreated itself. His most magnificent creation manifested spontaneously.

Saig burst apart and formed anew.

A new corporeality—a new ConCentration of corporeal life, whole and unique—was born. And so, too, were its first corporeals engendered, full of creative joy and enthusiasm in being the very first to experience the brand-new macrocosm.

AARON'S LUNGS EXPANDED, filling with breath again, his eyes filling with the light of the sun above. He tumbled to the hard ground, his form feeling lighter, empty.

Only a notion remained, a minute sense of something profoundly new. A pinpoint of light, among his inner thoughts and memories, embedded within his total awareness.

His blank eyes—wide and wildly blue—stared at the empty sky above, refusing him any explanation.

CIEL'S INFLUENCE permeated the Apart, announcing itself, claiming its new role, demanding recognition. His desire fulfilled, his satisfaction resonated to and through all—and was accepted without challenge.

All aware recognized and reiterated singular truth. The Natural Order of Things encompasses all—all events, all choices —all in concordance.

The one called Ciel inflated with self-regard. Uncontested, accepted as rooted in the flow of The Natural Order of Things as the new OverSeer, Ciel was free to create unbidden, unquestioned, unhampered—as all are.

"HE'S FINE," Emily mumbled to Maria as she lumbered through the front door. The sweat on her forehead told a different story.

Aaron rested against her, his arms loosely wrapped around her shoulders as she stumbled each step for the both of them. "He just... kind of fainted—or something—for a bit."

"On the couch," Maria directed.

AARON SAT with eyes alert and wide open, his face pale and damp, offering no clues to his condition.

"Aaron. Aaron, what happened?" Maria demanded.

"He hasn't really said anything at all since—" Emily attempted to explain.

"Aaron!" Maria yanked at his shoulders. "Aaron, are you okay? Talk to your grandmom. *Say* something."

Aaron began to shake his head and his unblinking stare. "It's... I don't know... nothing." His attention followed the sound of Maria's panting breaths.

As his eyes locked with his grandmother's, flashing images,

bright and rich in detail and depth, inundated him: men, women, children, all resonating with one characteristic in common, one shared quality among them all. They were—had been, still are—all nurturers, caregivers, or naturally caring in a myriad of ways. They were all *Maria*.

Aaron shook his head at his own thoughts. *No, not 'Maria'— the one called Estre. And there will be more.* Aaron's eyes blinked rapidly. He covered them with his hands, failing to block his inner view.

"Aaron! Are you all right?" Maria's voice resonated.

He forced himself to nod.

"What happened?"

"I've already tr—" Emily stuttered.

"*Tell* me!" Maria shouted.

Fire lighted in Aaron's eyes as he uncovered them, revealing his wild stare—at nothing, into everything. "*You*... don't *want* to know."

Maria stepped back, jerking her hand from his shoulder.

"I'm sorry," Aaron said, diluting the intensity of his stare. "I'm sorry," he repeated for Emily.

He gazed across the room, looking for evidence of what he attempted to describe. "It's nothing—nothing real—just a feeling, a notion. Something's different, but I don't know how... or when..." He turned his stare at his audience. "Can you feel it?"

Emily and Maria looked at each other, then at Aaron.

He lowered his head again. "It's never going to stop," he mumbled.

"What?" Emily asked in a small, careful voice.

"The *knowing*," he answered.

2

CIEL RELISHED HIS NEW ROLE. THERE EXISTED NO GREATER ACCESS to total awareness. To be the seeing rather than *the seen* was Ciel's ultimate impetus.

He remembered all. He was aware of all. He *desired* all.

Though it was his birthright—as a child of the Apart, an aself separate and whole all at once—Ciel extolled his awareness of his complete creative capacity. And he exercised that aptitude with abandon.

As no aself intervenes—OnLooker nor OverSeer nor otherwise—Ciel desired to change, to *affect*. He desired to manipulate, wield, and comprise—that which had *already* been created.

He proceeded to create, flow, learn, and experience—to choose—with a pained, purposeful disregard for his own mien.

"SOMETHING'S... WRONG." Aaron stared into the distance, past the walls of Emily's bedroom, then through the objects near him, into her eyes, and beyond.

Emily reached for him, for her own comfort rather than his. "What do you—you're scaring me. You look so—"

"I can feel it," Aaron said in a deep, unwavering voice, his eyes aglow. "It's changing."

"What's ch—"

Aaron spun around and glared at her. "*Everything!* I don't know how. And you, *you* can't even sense it somehow—at all?"

Emily shook her head, her dark hair sweeping over her shoulders. "But *you're* different," she challenged.

"No. No, I'm the same—with more. Always *more!*"

"Why are you *angry?*" Emily softened her features, coaxing his gentler side.

"Because I don't want to *lose* you."

She stiffened as Aaron's hands rested on her shoulders, despite his genial touch.

"If anything can *change,*" he said, his eyes attempting to project full meaning and implication, "*all* of it can."

The corner of her mouth turned up. "Of course, it can. Anything can change at any moment. That's *life.* That's the beauty of it. That's what makes it all so exciting!"

"No, no! Not like that. Not our lives—the *world!* The universe, what's beyond—*all of it.*" He squeezed her shoulders. "*This—* right *here*—the stuff we're *made* of, the stuff that matters more than anything!"

"Aaron, I know there's truth in that—in what you're saying— I can see it in your eyes, but... you sound *crazy.*"

"Don't *you* say that," he seethed, pulling his hands away. "Not you too. I believed I could tell *you*—"

"Look around!" Her eyes turned toward the window, to the pale blue sky above the tree line, dotted with sparse tufts of cloud. "It's a beautiful day. We're fine. We're alive! Everything's *okay.*"

"I... I don't feel that." He turned and walked away, his pace quick and defiant.

"Aaron! Where are you going? You *can* tell me everything!" she shouted after him, her feet stuck firmly in place. "You're just not *saying* anything!"

THE OVERSEER, imparted a fluctuating form among the Consultation, rocking with subtle vibration.

Alters.

All.

The one... intervenes.

Affects.

Never before.

And now.

It is believed... the ConCentration is...

Initiated.

Hastened.

Is of... persuasion.

Compelled.

Implied.

Beckoned.

By force.

It cannot be... The Natural—

All... is of The Natural Order of Things, one reminded, hovering whole and steady.

Yet, the OverSeer creates...

Without regard.

Aside from true desire.

Aside from aself's mien.

To the extent of the Apart.

Manipulating... entire corporealities.

Yet... it must be...

Indeed, it... must.
It is... The Natural Order of Things.

HUDDLED on the floor of his bedroom, Aaron closed his eyes, wrapped his arms around his knees, and held himself intact as he called upon singular focus, singular intention. His consciousness released its inner image of his corporeal surroundings, transcending one reality to reach another.

WHAT'S HAPPENING? he called on a non-corporeal channel. *Tell me. Something is... everything's wrong,* he compelled as his desire honed in on an imagined image of Saig.

Saig conCenters, returned in answer, the fleeting form of Fei gradually revealed.

He... Tres inquired as he joined Fei in form.

The ConCentration occurs.

Saig... he was my instructor. I need—.

The one called Saig conCenters—as is The Natural Order of Things.

He's... where has he... gone?

He has formed... anew, Fei imparted.

A new...

Corporeality.

I don't know what...

Aself is aware, Fei imparted, whole and hovering. *OverSeer conCenters. It is The Natural Order of Things.*

Saig is... he was... the OverSeer—ObServer of all?

Indeed.

I was selected... Tres undulated, diluted, then subtly resonated brightly again. *I was... to assume the place—the role... of Saig?*

Aself is selected. And... aself remains in corporeal life. Another... is OverSeer.

Another?

As selected. There are two, Fei imparted.

Who...?

The one called Ciel... now overSees... all.

But I... it was... my... choice.

As all is.

It's... still... my choice? Tres asked.

As selected... by The Natural Order of Things.

But will I... I won't be... affected? Can I remain... in corporeality?

It is... aself's choice.

But what's... happening? I feel... things are changing—everything.

The ConCentration occurs.

And that... affects corporeality? And everything in it?

Never before, Fei imparted with certainty.

And... now?

The OverSeer... intervenes.

But you—none of you, none of us—are supposed to—

All is choice. All is The Natural Order of Things.

But something's wrong.

The concept is merely a construction of aself's—

I know. I know! But this—what I sense—isn't... right!

There is only... restriction.

Restriction?

Of sensation... of creation... of awareness... of aself. All are intended to be, to flow... freely and without restriction.

What are you saying?

As OnLooker, aself does not intervene. The ObServed... may... expand aself's own... awareness.

I'm full of awareness! There is no more!

There is always... the choice of expansion—of creativity anew... of continuing aself-development.

3

THE WORLD RUMBLED.

The sky quivered.

The Earth blinked to black, then lit into existence again—as did *all other* corporealities.

Ciel wielded worlds, prancing upon them, articulating within random aspects of unsuspecting corporeals.

And few were aware—if any—as they fixated intently upon their individual corporeal life—seeing, sensing only as they chose to see—as cultures, conceptions of countries, and various corporealities agreed upon together.

With zealousness and over-exuberance transforming into uncontrolled creation—creation *without* joy—the reigning OverSeer overSaw the deliberate *re-creation* of the Apart, the deforming of others' mass creation.

Reality flickered.

4

MARIA FOUND AARON STANDING IN THE HALL, RESTING AGAINST the wall, and gripping at the flaking paint as if grasping for life itself. She rushed to him, wrapping her hands around his shoulders, pulling him back.

"Aaron! Tell me what's—"

"I..." he muttered, lips quivering, "Everything... at once... *changing*. It's all going to—" He stared intently at nothing at all.

"Talk to me!" Maria cried, her voice cracking. "Look at me!" Her words struck him as he felt the sharp pain of his jaw clenched within her firm grasp, drawing his attention to the frantic rhythm of her pleas. "What are you *feeling?* What's going on? Whatever it is, I can't help you if you don't *talk* to me!"

Aaron's eyes welled up with tears. "What if I'm imagining it all? What if... what if I *am* crazy?"

Maria's fingers squeezed harder at his chin. "Nonsense! *You...* you are *not* crazy. The *world* is crazy! Everything that happens... that..." Fresh tears washed over her own cheeks. "I can't make any sense of it. I don't know why it all... but you... *you* are more grounded than anyone else. You're... *perceptive*—like I've never... ever since you were just a *baby*."

Aaron pulled his grandmother's hand from his face and wrapped his arms around her. "I love you," he whispered into her mass of unruly, dark hair streaked with gray. "I'll protect you —like you've protected me."

He peeled himself from the patch of tears left on her shoulder. His eyes were wide and clear once again as he looked beyond his grandmother, beyond their home, to something she could not see nor fathom.

Then, he ran.

AARON REFILLED his lungs with full, deep breaths. His heartbeat slowed as he reached the highest point overlooking the city. Sunlight glimmered over the cityscape, filling the valley, reflecting from windows, steel, bustling cars, and busy lives.

In an instant, for a fleeting moment, Aaron perceived a sudden flicker, as if the world flinched before his eyes and quivered beneath his feet.

How can no one know? The question planted itself within, weighted with worry.

He closed his eyes, rejecting the scene before him as he focused on the gray light behind his eyelids. He opened his eyes again; they glowed vibrantly, refracting the rainbow of color hidden in the sun's white light. He stared into the changing scene before him—and through it.

He permitted the wind its true path. He felt it flow over his skin and permeate his pores, traveling *through* him—atoms adjusting, accommodating, particle flowing with like particle.

Aaron transcended his personal aspect, his perception of individual reality, *corporeality*. He reached beyond, opening to it, joining with it.

And he called to the creator of the chaos.

THE CONVEYANCE TRAVELED through the Apart—a pulse powered with unwavering intention—seeking out its targeted recipient, even as its message was imparted to all.

Ciel... Tres imparted, *I know who you are.*

Tres sensed his self sweeping through perceived distance, visions, variant manifestations—flashing past faces and personalities, all proceeding through their own intentions and choices. The one he named dispersed them all with a single wave of energy, slicing himself into Tres's foremost perception.

And I am... yet more aware... of you... Tres. The articulated voice brimmed with devious delight like a predator lapping at his kill, hesitating before his first bite to savor his own anticipation.

You overstep your bounds, Tres imparted.

There are no 'bounds.' I am... OverSeer. I am aware... of all that I choose.

You... intervene!

I am the first.

You threaten corporeality.

Only one? You... limit your awareness... Tres. And you are... no OverSeer.

I am selected. I have been instructed.

Your instruction ends... as Saig conCenters... as the role of Over-Seer is... fulfilled.

You... do not heed... your... instruction! The OverSeer obServes... without intervention.

The Apart rippled with the voluptuous self-amusement of its OverSeer. *Until now,* Ciel imparted. *And... the overSeeing of the Apart... is no regard of yours.*

All... concerns me.

The darkness permeating the Apart electrified as Ciel

replied. *Your 'concern' resides in your consciousness. It exists in corpo-reality... alone. As... you do.*

The coinciding sensation of entrapment suffocated Tres, strangling his consciousness with the absoluteness of truth.

You dishonor, Tres imparted, regathering his inner conviction, *your predecessors.*

There is only... this moment. I AM OVERSEER... NOW!

Then, obServe. Do not... destroy.

I CREATE!

Without regard.

WITHIN... MY DESIRE! It is of my choice.

And what of... your own development? Your mien?

AND WHAT OF... YOURS?

Tres's focus faltered, images flashed, his consciousness filled with questions, impulsively creating concerns. His attention shifted, imparting a final message to the one overpowering all: *Do not... harm... them.*

DO NOT THREATEN ME, resounded in return.

AARON BLINKED into a subset of awareness, his consciousness registering the scene of the city once again.

Freedom... resonated in mind and senses. *My mien. I have to... how can I... be free?*

How can I free... them?

5

"I WANT TO BE WITH *YOU*." THE WORDS RUSHED FROM AARON'S lips, his eyes wild as they focused on Emily's.

Her instant smile mocked the overwhelming confusion running rampant in his own mind. "You *are* with me," she trivialized.

"No! That's *all* I want—ever. This..." Aaron's line of sight flitted over their surroundings. "*Here*—I don't care about the rest."

Emily frowned her compassion. "I don't think that will make you happy." She recognized the spark in his eyes reflecting his focused attention. "What about all the rest?" she asked. "All the *good* things to happen to you? You can't pin all your happiness on me."

She lightened the truth of her words with a smirk. "Come on, Aaron. What's gotten into you lately? Mid-life crisis?"

He shook his head—against thoughts battling truths, corporeal focus blending with total awareness, against conflicting realization. He looked at her, drawing in her demeanor. Her affection for him was obvious—and how it resonated through all her *self*. Aaron memorized it all.

AARON LAY on his bed in the light of the afternoon, steadying his breathing, calming himself, choosing attention on physical presence over more expansive awareness. He rooted himself within the single moment he *resided* in. He felt the experience that was his alone, filled it, melded with it.

It's all illusion, Aaron's inner voice taunted. *My illusion, my choice,* he clarified in response, even as his physical senses detected an alteration of the surrounding air, an infusion of warming vibrancy—even as the light dimmed by delicate degrees.

REMAIN—WHERE YOU BELONG, boomed a message not at all his own.

Aaron bolted upright, staring straight ahead and across his bedroom. He saw nothing; he felt *everything.*

Accept your existence, Ciel's conveyance thrust at him as it wrapped around his throat. *Remember... everything,* it insisted.

Aaron's heart raced, his memory triggered on command, stabbing at him with precise moments—vivid and painful.

He revisited—remembered—those living shadows hovering over his infancy. He recalled the stranger in the back garden, coldly staring... Finlay's obsession, his bullying... darkness gripping his grandmother, prodding at her, pushing her to distance herself from her grandson at precise moments... Sancha swallowed by the wreckage she drove herself to—.

"You!" Aaron accused aloud, shouting at nothing, lashing out at all. "You *killed* her!"

Impossible, Ciel responded instantaneously—proudly. *Corporeal 'death' is of aself's... choice.*

"No! No, she *didn't.* She wouldn't—"

She has.

"You drove her to it! Somehow, you—"

I merely obServed.

"You... you were there!"

I obServed.

"Why? But you couldn't—"

OnLooker... looks on.

Realization struck Aaron like an invisible bolster slamming against his chest, stealing his breath, rocking him backward.

Your awareness grows... even without instruction, Ciel expressed with amusement.

"*You...*" Aaron's words fell over the resounding external silence, carrying a flow of tears. "You were... supposed to *guide* her."

I did—indeed.

"No!" Aaron screamed, jumping to standing. "It's not possible. You can't. You're forbidden from—"

Who forbids? Aself chooses alone. Aself is free to create. It is The N—

"It's not right! You're not supposed to—"

There is no 'right.' There is merely... what is.

"Then... *bring—her—back.*" The words hung in the air around Aaron, dangling with provocation.

Ciel's contentment only expanded, energizing the atmosphere. *To repeat... a completed corporeal life?* Ciel teased. *It is not... The Natural Order of Things.*

"Neither are you!"

All is natural—as is all I choose.

"You should not be capable!"

Then... neither would... you.

Tres collapsed, relenting—and then, *deliberating.*

6

I APPEAL TO THE CONSULTATION, FEI IMPARTED, STEADYING HIS articulated form against the accelerated flow of the Apart, now fluctuating with continuous re-creation.

The Consultation convenes, confirmed those instantly articulating.

We are three.

And aself... who appeals?

Desires the awareness... of the Consultation and of... no others, Fei answered with a request.

It is not The Natural—

All are aware... who choose awareness.

Awareness permeates... all of the Apart.

I, Fei imparted, compounding energy into focused meaning, *desire—*

Fei's projected form glowed brighter, preparing for the impending arrival all were suddenly aware of. Fei privately admonished his own progression of aself-development now depriving him of the ability to prevent the most natural broadcast of his own impartations.

Ciel infused himself within the Consultation, pressing his

presence upon all. *Aself dares attempt to convey aside from my awareness!*

Aself is free to desire, Fei responded, conforming his articulation as steadfast despite the fluxing environment.

Not, Ciel enforced with limitless potential, *in contradiction... to my own. I—ALONE—AM OVERSEER!*

Indeed, confirmed one member of the Consultation.

The one called Ciel... overSees, imparted another.

I alone am OverSeer, Ciel continued, pressing his individual intentions, *and the other—confined to corporeality—merits no articulation within the Apart.* Ciel's collective articulation permeated all, and all were aware of the one whom Ciel targeted with his disdain.

The one... called Tres, Fei imparted, defying his own mien even as he faithfully served it, *is selected by The Natural—*

I AM SELECTED! Ciel's form inflicted in light and sound. *I AM OVERSEER!*

There is another... selected, conveyed one of the Consultation.

By The Natural Order of Things.

It is so.

It is truth.

There are two.

The instruction... of the one called Tres... continues.

I FORBID IT! rained upon the connected personalities, thrust by Ciel with great desire. *HIS CONNECTION WITH THE APART IS DENIED!*

All is of the Apart, imparted aself of the Consultation.

The Apart is all.

No aself is denied... access.

Awareness.

What is.

UNTIL NOW! decreed Ciel.

7

Aaron awaited Fei's articulation—awaited *any* communication resulting from his own conveyance and requests ushered to the Apart. By every method succeeding before, he failed to achieve access or connection to the reality existing beyond.

When Fei's presence eventually manifested in Aaron's aspect, it was faint, weak, cautionary.

"I can't..." Aaron spoke to the air around him, to the glimpse caught at the periphery of his view. "I haven't been able to reach—"

Connection, came Fei's conveyance, slight and slipping, *is weakened. The OverSeer—*

Aaron cringed, folding in on himself, desiring escape even as he aspired to reach out. "He is *not* the OverSeer! He intervenes!"

Ciel is OverSeer. He is selected. It is—

"It is *not* The Natural Order of Things! This isn't what I was taught! Not what Saig—"

All... is The Natural Order of Things, Fei imparted, as clear as ever before.

"He can't choose—"

All aselves are free... to choose.

"It isn't the way!"

Tres... denial serves no purpose—serves no mien—nor does aself's denial of aself's own choice... of awareness. Fei's form appeared briefly, with a flash of emphasis, before vanishing entirely from Aaron's physical sight. One final communication manifested within Aaron's aspect: *Even as aself denies awareness... all... is... The Natural Order of Things.*

"Then, so is *my* own choice!" Aaron argued aloud, reminding himself.

Aaron was left alone, breathless, his heart pounding—and burning with pure desire.

AARON RAN, fleeing the painfully apparent, the unavoidable. And still, he was unable to block the one message knocking at his consciousness throughout the entirety of his brief conveyance with Fei—the one voice he most intensely desired *not* to accept awareness of.

I WILL DESTROY THEIR ILLUSION, Ciel's desire conveyed to and through Tres.

THEY SEEK UNDERSTANDING, ASELF-DEVELOPMENT— THEY CHOOSE CORPOREAL LIFE. I WILL REMOVE THEIR FALSE PERCEPTION. I WILL USHER ALL TOWARD AWARENESS.

THEY WILL ALL BECOME AWARE... OF ME!

GASPING, red-faced with over-exertion—Aaron reached Emily's home and beckoned her to follow him.

"My parents," she shouted at his back as he turned away

without a word, "think you're crazy!" She struggled to slip her sneakers over her heels. "Hey!" she shouted at Aaron's back. "I can't keep up with you when you're running!"

―――――

As THEY REACHED Aaron's house, he reached over the gate at the side to unlock it and waited for Emily to catch up.

"What..." she said, panting as she reached him. "What do you want... from me?"

"For you to *understand* me," he said, taking her hand in his.

His steps slowed as they entered the back yard. He stopped to look up at the quiet sky turning pink with the approach of dusk, then continued walking, leading Emily to the swing set. He brushed a fallen leaf from the seat his mother used to swing on and directed Emily to sit.

Settling into the swing beside her, he said, "I have to do something." The words spilled easily from him, as if he'd recited them to himself many times over. "I'm not even sure how, but I do know I can't run from it anymore. That's what I've been doing —running, hiding, denying—all this time." He turned from her to face the sky again. "After all these lives."

Emily's nose wrinkled as she studied his face.

"Do you believe we all have a purpose, something we're supposed to do, something we're always chasing?"

"Yeah, I do."

Aaron nodded his relief. "Mine... I've always known, I guess. It was always there—in the back of my mind—no matter *when* I was... but it's just *everything* now."

Emily only nodded in reply, still bereft of words as she searched for the intention behind Aaron's shared thoughts.

He turned his swing toward hers as he reached for her hand and held it tight within his on her lap. "I have to be *free*," he said.

Emily tried to pull her hand away. "Oh... so, that's—"

"It's my purpose, my m—" He cut the word short, forced himself to face her and speak again. "My *mien*."

She gritted her teeth, her lower lip twitching. "Then," she said, whispering. "Go. *Be free*."

Detecting the change in her eyes, Aaron tried to decipher the true meaning of her words. He shook his head. "No, not from *you*." He squeezed her hand. "I have to... I have to be *me*."

"That's what I've always—"

"*Completely*—I have a purpose. I didn't even realize... I've been avoiding it—I can't anymore. I don't know that it's even really possible. I've been fighting it all along. I've—"

"To be *free*? Free from what?"

"From knowing... from what others... from denying it."

"You think that's your *purpose*? Like, your *whole* reason for being here—for being alive? The epitome of all your life experiences—after everything you've gone through, everything that's happened to you..."

His head nodded emphatically.

"*No*, Aaron." Emily placed her free hand over his, tracing his fingers with hers as she tried to collect the right words. "What's that thing you said? The word you used, your..."

"Mien."

"What's that?"

"The *one* thing that makes you *you*, the one thing you're always working toward, doing everything for—even if you don't realize it."

"My *mien*..." Emily turned the word over in her mouth, tasting it. She started to nod, her concentration deep. "Mine, I only realized it... *after*."

Aaron watched her intently, his stare confirming his understanding.

"*My* mien," she continued, "is to *commit.*" She looked up at him, opening her eyes wide, baring her vulnerability.

Aaron's lips moved as he reached for her meaning, wondering if she was toying with him.

"To commit *all* of myself—entirely," she said, "to everything I do—to go *all in.*" She smiled, finding excitement in speaking the knowledge aloud. "Head first," she continued, "worry about the consequences later—if ever."

Her smile was full and heartfelt—committed. "And yours..." she said, now holding Aaron's hands tight within her own, "is *love.*"

Aaron's mouth opened on impulse, forming the words to confirm her misunderstanding.

"*Yes,*" Emily insisted. "You—" Tears began to fill her eyes, surprising both of them. "You *care*... more than anyone I've ever known—about everyone, everything—no matter how much you don't even know it, no matter how much *you* can't see it. You *love*... more deeply, more faithfully, more fully..." Her last words wafted to the sky she peered up at. "No, you don't *say* it, but... I bet you *give* it to everyone you meet, even before they've earned it or you know who they are—even without them realizing it. But *I*..." She sniffled as she wiped at her tears. "*I* know it," she said, looking up again and into his eyes, signaling the end of the thoughts she most wanted to express.

Aaron moved to speak, but she interrupted.

"You see?" she said. "You don't have to *go.* You don't have to run from anything—or *to* anything. You *are* free. And your... mien is to just keep *loving*—like you always have, like you've always known how to do."

Aaron's expression packed every emotion: questioning with discovery, doubt with complete knowing. And his eyes shared her tears. He pulled her to him, holding her tightly as they gently swung beneath the maple tree.

"Emily," he whispered to her, nuzzling her neck, his face buried in the mass of her soft hair. "I wish... I could take you with me."

She moved against his hold, but he only held her tighter, refusing to let go of the moment he knew could not last.

8

"GRANDMOM, SIT WITH ME." AARON PATTED THE COUCH NEXT TO where he sat. The new day, bringing his renewed calmness, was a reprieve for both of them.

"What is it?" she asked, the dust rag poised in her hand as she noticed her grandson's unusual expression.

His smile delivered the reassurance she needed.

"You've been... struggling with something... the last few days," she said for him as she sat herself down, adjusting the throw pillow at her lower back.

Aaron's smile remained resilient as he drew a deep breath. He shuddered slightly as his chest expanded, unable to disguise his own anxiety.

He looked into her eyes as he took her hand in his. The gesture took her by surprise. She glanced down at their hands held together as she fidgeted in her seat, her own worry pouring over her face.

"Are you... leaving?" she asked with trembling voice.

Aaron flinched at her words as he fought to hide his own inner turmoil. "Not..." he started to say in honesty, before his own unanswered questions and uncertainty robbed him of words. "It's..." he tried again—failed again.

Another soothing breath regained his confidence and calm, and he told his grandmother, "I just wanted to make sure... that you know how much you mean to me."

She began to smile—and blush. "Of course, I know—"

"No, *more* than that. You've..." He searched the air for the right phrasing. "It hasn't been easy," he said, looking down at her hand in his: the tiny lines, the freckles from the sun. "*I* haven't been easy."

"Nonsense! You've always been a—"

"No, *you* know what I mean, what I'm trying to say." He looked into her eyes again, emphasizing his straight intention. "*You've* known—all along, before and aside from *everyone* else —that... that..."

"That you're... that you have an important *purpose,*" Maria said with a grandmother's delight.

Aaron's frustration appeared as an uncomfortable smile. "No, I mean, that there's more—"

"That *you*... are more than *this* life," she stated matter-of-factly.

Aaron studied her sudden neutral expression; he spotted that small kernel of knowing. Even if her understanding held a fraction of the full facts of his identity, that was one of the greatest gifts he could be granted.

He accepted her description and tried to deliver the same level of honesty. "And you've *accepted* me—loved me. And you could've... turned me away."

She started to shake her head, her torment twisted in her expression. "Never," she said. "We would n—"

"I know," he admitted, confirming his grandmother's worst fear. "I know... *she* didn't want me—in the beginning."

Even as Maria faced the truth—her mouth hanging open in

fright—she never imagined the infant she once held in her arms could possibly be aware of—or live with—such knowledge. Her lower lip began to tremble; tears welled up in her eyes. She could not stop the thoughts that filled her mind. Her consciousness rummaged for memories of the worst circumstances, comparing them with the new confirmation that the *child* knew all of it. "How..." she mumbled aloud.

At that moment, withholding any answers from his grandmother was not even a possibility for Aaron—not any longer, not from this point forward.

"I was always *me,*" he said, his explanation packed with information no one else—in this life—could ever fully realize. "Since the beginning—*this* beginning." The few words were packed with exponential information.

And Maria's mind recognized what the words offered, even as it chose not to dwell on the complete capacity of their implication. Her intuition instructed her to listen—to accept—above all else.

"And... before?" she asked.

"I was... someone else—*me...* but a different one, another one."

Aaron couldn't determine if her nod revealed belief or only automatic respect for a loved one's point of view. As he opened his mouth to speak again, he feared the result of what he was compelled to say.

"And you... you have also."

Maria began to blink away tears, her body stiff, her hand still curled within his.

Aaron offered, "You've always been *so caring*—a nurturer—a mother of sorts, even when you weren't—" He worked to maintain the last boundary, his outer wall of self-guarding and anticipation of others' abilities to accept complete truth.

And then, it fell—as he ventured to share what so naturally

flowed from him, as he allowed it. His voice lowered—quiet and tentative—as he finished his sentence by saying, "*female.*"

Maria's eyes glittered with intrigue. She made no motion to contradict the revelation.

"And *strong,*" he added. "So very strong."

She blinked at the onrush of emotions, the flood of fantastical thoughts.

"I don't know *how* I know," Aaron said. "I just... *know* things —see them."

She nodded, her voice breaking as she attempted to speak after her long silence. "You always have."

He smiled, enjoying the unusual feeling of real relief and the confirmation of true acceptance for who he was.

Maria adjusted herself on the couch and smoothed her hand over his as she began to speak. "And now?" she asked, still looking at her lap.

"Now..." The word hung in the air, hovering where Aaron left it. "I have to do something—to protect—"

"Protect what?"

"*All.*"

Maria's mind—her remembered experience—could not comprehend any meaning for his statement. She chose acceptance over understanding. "And why *you*?" she asked.

"I'm... it's what I'm meant for," he answered. "Why I... *remember* everything."

She nodded as she stared into the distance, then back at Aaron. "Does Emily... does she know...?"

He shook his head rapidly. "No. How could I... and we've only—"

"But *if,*" Maria said carefully, motherly, "you don't share *who* you are, no one has the chance to fully—"

"She thinks she wants me to be myself—totally—but there's no way she can know just how—"

"Let me finish," Maria's voice broke through. "If you *don't*—no matter *what* it is—you're denying her... the chance to truly *love* you." She broke eye contact and looked down at her lap. "Like *you* love *her*."

Aaron glared at his grandmother, luring her chin up again so her eyes met his. "I haven't even let myself... admit that," he said.

"You should."

"But I'm... I'm not even sure I'm meant—"

"Nonsense. *You* have the largest capacity to *love* that I've ever known. You love... like someone who knows the true *essence* of a person, accepts everything about them, and loves them for *everything* they're made of—good or bad."

He struggled with his grandmother's wholehearted belief and conclusion, with the level of her conviction.

"Don't tell me," she said, "you don't know your own *purpose*."

"I thought," he whispered, almost smiling, "it was... to be free."

A pent-up laugh escaped Maria's mouth. "Free? Free from what?"

Now, the answer Aaron habitually told himself felt dubious, uncertain. "From who I am? How I'm different—*despite it*."

"That's never *anyone's* purpose," she said with certitude. "No, *who* you are—who you *know* yourself to be—is the most natural thing in the world—always." She smiled at him. "Even if it seems completely unique from *everyone* else. Who's *not* different? So, why would it matter *how* you're different?" Her smile faded as her demeanor quieted again. "Why didn't we have this talk ages ago?"

Hearing her own words, Maria remembered her own personal fears, challenged beliefs, and negative associations—all with each new discovery proving her grandson was different than all other children.

"*I'm sorry*," she whispered alongside new tears.

"None of that matters at all—now," Aaron said.

She nodded, grateful for his enduring love, for all of the unnamable things he'd given her.

"And... *I'm* sorry—if anything... if whatever happens..." Aaron couldn't find words for the extent of pain he knew his actions might cause his grandmother, especially as he had no idea of what they might be—the necessary actions *or* their consequences.

"*You know,*" he continued, "that I love you *so much*—and I always will."

Maria nodded. Aaron stood up, straightening himself as he began to walk away.

"You..." she called to him, "you said... you would never leave me."

He turned to face her, with tears in his eyes to match hers. "And I won't. I'll be back," he said.

Maria permitted her smile, her entire body relaxing. "Do you," she asked in her usual light voice, "want to invite your friends—for your birthday next week?"

The question caused more distress for Aaron than Maria could ever know—because her eyes reflected she honestly thought that the answer *mattered*.

And it did—in *her* reality—in corporeality, precisely what Aaron felt driven to protect.

AARON'S STRIDE was slow but deliberate as he walked the distance to Emily's house. His fixation on his mien marched his feet forward, even as his consciousness pondered what the future may hold—guessing and second-guessing.

When he passed Bennett's home, he realized he'd wandered out of his way, taking the less direct route.

He paused before the small house. He noticed how the trees branching over its roof seemed laden with extra weight, as if they too wept in mourning. He couldn't drive himself to walk to the front door, couldn't bring himself to add to his friend's worry. He walked on, never noticing the hand that pulled back the curtains at Bennett's bedroom window nor the eyes following his path.

———

Aaron's arm felt heavy as he reached up to knock on Emily's front door. Her brilliant smile and radiant eyes greeted him.

"Can you talk?" he asked.

"You *never* use your phone, do you?" she accused with amusement.

Aaron shrugged.

"Do you wanna come in? My parents will be out for a while."

He paused to take in the cool outside air and the sensation of expansive space, as if he needed it to breathe easier, to feel firm in his actions. He stepped forward, following Emily's lead.

"I'm glad you're here," she said as they entered her bedroom. "I didn't know, well, *when* I'd see you next—after last time."

When she plopped herself down on her bed, Aaron followed. "I had a nice talk with my grandmom," he said.

"Yeah? Did you... wanna talk about it?"

"It was good." The words came in an exhale. "She..."

"That's really wonderful."

Aaron nodded. "She said some things—well, you and her are a lot alike." He received a glittering smile in return.

"That's a big compliment," Emily said. "I love your grandmother."

"She... you mean a lot to her too." He watched Emily's smile grow. "You two... well, I'm glad you got to meet each other—know each other."

"Yeah, me too..." Emily's words drifted away as her mind wandered. "Aaron, what's up?"

"Oh, the usual."

His flippancy went unappreciated; the look Emily gave him drove him to the most direct speech.

"I want you to know who I am," he said, staring into her eyes.

"Don't I already—"

"No. Not..." he breathed deeply, "there's a lot more. Grandmom says I should tell you."

"What does she know that *I* don't?"

"You know, I'm not even sure, but she... she *gets* it—just enough—or... accepts it."

"Isn't that the same thing?"

"I don't know." And Aaron's face confirmed it. "Everything's so... *life* is so complicated."

Emily nodded, receiving a quick kiss from Aaron before she'd finished.

"What was that for?" she asked, smiling.

"Everything." All else left Aaron's mind as he stared at the girl that had changed him so much since the day he met her, the one he met before *everything* started to change. And he began to doubt, to change his mind—questioning even his own volition.

In that moment, he felt so firmly alive in the *physical* world that he wished he could forget that anything else existed.

"So... who are you, Aaron Rivera," Emily asked.

He blinked, his eyes caught the light from the open window, and he answered, "My name... I am *Tres.*"

"What?"

"My name—the name I've always had."

"And that's... what your grandmother knows?"

He shook his head. "Well, if she remembers. I told her once, when—" His thoughts converged with vivid memories. "And my mom," he said quieter, "a *long* time ago."

"You... *told* them?"

"I knew it—since I was born."

Emily's open, accepting posture closed before his eyes. "What do you mean?" she asked.

Speaking with confidence, he started to explain, "When I was born, I—" And he stopped.

"I don't understand."

Aaron kissed her, chasing her mouth as she impulsively withdrew. He trapped her in shared connection. His arms slid around her, holding her gently, and Emily finally relaxed against him.

In their connection—one *self* melding with another—Aaron allowed himself to slip away, to release the reflexive, corporeal hold on consciousness, and to expand his awareness. He opened to the moment, willing Emily to do the same.

Inwardly, he spoke to her, allowing himself the sense of his physical body giving way, breaking apart, becoming—converging into—the essence of itself. And he called to the essence of hers, warm and willing in his arms.

He felt the expanse of the Apart: infinite support, infinite confirmation—breathing space. His hold on corporeality faded as his articulation within the Apart grew more substantial, solidifying. And he drew Emily with him.

The connection they shared—established in physicality—bridged the non-physical as well, forming a path between them, an awareness, another method of communication. The kisses—opening consciousness to emotion—also opened corporeality to what lay beyond—and within.

What remained of Aaron in corporeal form, *felt* Emily's fear, her reflexive doubt, and her formulating questions.

Instinctively, *Tres* reached for the one called *Tela*.

HERE... Tres expressed with exquisite resonance. *Right here.*

Words were not returned, but moods. She searched, grasped, slid away.

You're with me, he impressed upon her, using all focus to share his sense of safety and security with her. His own awareness encompassed hers, controlling hers, opening her to what lies beyond consciousness.

Like a dream, he imparted. *It's safe. You're with me.*

Dream... he received in a pulse—a pop of colliding energy.

Yes—and we're in it together.

But... she managed to convey as her comfort grew. *We're together...*

Yes.

Kissing...

His self smiled, filling with the thrill of joining with her in the most all-encompassing way—beyond the physical, beyond one limited reality. He desired—so deeply—to express that joy to her.

Are you... smiling? she conveyed, sprinkled with visual static.

He smiled his answer—and felt her smile in return.

Now, let me show you... he imparted with a rush of near-tangible emotion.

He attempted to control the images—the succession of flashing slices of his lives—but they surged with his own eagerness, with his own familiarity with them. Still enveloped in the arms of his corporeal body, she offered no response, no reaction to what she may or may not be receiving.

Tela... he called into the oblivion of all, his self encircled by swirling imagery—fantastic images, dark and joyful, sad and ambitious, frightening and enlightening. He felt he lost his hold on her, then sensed her nearness again. *Tela...*

Tres... she answered, her conveyed thought resounding like a magnificent melody in his awareness. *You...*

Do you see them? he asked in a boy's voice, fearful of the answer. *Can you feel them?*

You are... so much.

And so are you, he impressed upon her, neglecting to block the barrage of new imagery, the intricate visions of all he viewed within *her self*.

Battles—by land and sea... loves lost, tormented, renewed... mothers, fathers, siblings, children... wisdom, seeking, soothing —harm inflicted, regret... birth, solace, discovery.

Tres yanked on the succession of scenes, pulling against his awareness, closing it down, confining it, and protecting her from the barrage.

Tela... he sought, as their surroundings quieted, his awareness blocking hers and setting all aside, leaving only their two selves.

I'm... she imparted weakly.

Full of life, he answered.

Then, he released her, cutting their connection.

TOGETHER, Aaron and Emily opened their eyes to their renewed surroundings. Her bedroom suddenly felt so small— so stifling.

Tears filled her eyes. And Aaron thrilled at the gift of catching her own discovery of them—her embarrassment—as she wiped them away with the back of her hand.

"I..." was all Emily could compel herself to express.

"Are you all right? Did I... do the wrong thing?"

"No," she said, shaking her head. "No, now... I *know* you." She smiled beneath her tears. "You're so... *beautiful.*" She laughed. "*Tres,*" she said, testing it on her tongue. "I even know how to spell it." All the wonder and amazement she felt reflected in her eyes. "And... I feel like I've *known* you... *before.*"

She concentrated on the thought, glancing away, devoting her attention to it. Then, she peered up at him again. She found him crying.

"I can't do it," he said. "I *can't*—" His voice was oddly small and weak.

"Can't do what?"

"Leave you—*this,*" he said. "This world."

"Why would you have to?"

"Because... it's all changing. Something's wrong. It's *hurting,*" he said between sobs, his hand pressed against his chest.

"And... you can *do* something about it?" Her cheeks were dry, the tears vanished. She stared at him with starkly sober eyes.

Aaron shook his head, showing his own disbelief in the possibility. "Maybe. I feel... I'm the only one who possibly can." Tears rushed over his cheeks again. "But it doesn't matter—not anymore. I *have* to stay. I belong *here*—with you."

Emily's eyes flickered with arising anger. She tilted her head, scrutinizing him as he sat—trembling—beside her.

"No," she said, shaking her head. "If *you* can do something— something that you feel needs to be done, *whatever* it is—" She swept her hair out of her face. "If you *don't* go, you're not the man that I... that I *fell in love with.*"

Her stare was intense, accusing—daring. Within her eyes, Aaron recognized the glowing ember of her inner will—its enduring strength. Emily meant every word, *all* implication— like a body means to *breathe* one breath after another, without need for instruction, with only the most natural and inherent intention.

She intended to provoke him, even as she understood completely, whole-bodily, that the consequences for each of them may be more than either could bear.

EVENING FELL as Aaron returned to the home he was raised in and quietly walked inside. He tiptoed up the stairs and past his grandmother's bedroom where she lay sleeping, snoring softly, inside.

He stood in the dark of his own bedroom, facing the window —the moonlight—overlooking the scene of his mother's death. Only the sound of crickets disturbed the resounding silence as they sung their song of mourning.

Too soon, his mind prodded, calling attention to itself.

Ascension... is a choice. All... is choice, the memory of Fei's instruction immediately corrected.

Too soon, Aaron's consciousness argued, recalling the evident delight delivered in Ciel's consequential admission—his confession. And Aaron recalled the undeniable threat, the threat of an expertly conveyed demonstration of Ciel's influence—his intervention—within Aaron's own life.

He forced her to choose, eliminated her choices. And choice... is the greatest ability—awareness—I have, the greatest all aselves are granted.

For a single moment, Aaron felt happiness for Sancha—for the success of her escape from corporeality.

Before it began to change. Before he took control.

Aaron remembered—commemorated—that young girl who'd loved him, saved him, made him feel comfortable in all his oddity, in the agony of repeated childhood—all by being, so beautifully, her most natural self. He envisioned her green eyes that called to him, accepted him, and always drew him back to the moment.

And Aaron thought of Emily's dark eyes: cool and calm, while smoldering with the aliveness of the fire inside her. She was his second savior—and his emancipator.

In an instant, the words of Emily's demand arose within his awareness. And Aaron spontaneously held his breath—in the act of devoting total attention to his *intention*.

He stood, in the center of his room, eyes closed to the moon's glow, feeling the atmosphere around him—warming, moving, exhilarating. He infused himself with his surroundings.

With his breath still held—*withheld*—Aaron ascended.

———

TRES FOUND FEI AWAITING HIM, the friend and tutor's form more clearly outlined than it had ever been—iridescent, awe-inspiring.

Tres willed himself wholly to the Apart, with the Apart, forcing himself to *forget* corporeality to the extent of releasing it completely—allowing it to fall away like a single, translucent layer of just one life once lived.

He aroused all of his own awareness, devoting his whole self to the Apart, drawing on all his segregated strength to one, fine focal point of being.

His corporeal body had drawn its final breath.

PART X

BECOMING

Faber est suae quisque fortunae.

— EVERY MAN IS THE ARTISAN OF HIS OWN FORTUNE.

1

TRES'S ASCENSION WAS UNLIKE ANY TRANSCENDENCE PREVIOUSLY experienced—vastly different from dwelling solely within dream. Distinct from his learned awareness and willed travels to the Apart, Tres was graciously ushered along his passage—accompanied, beckoned, embraced.

Fei articulated at his side. His presence was warm, energizing, benefiting. And there were others.

Pressing at Tres's awareness, following the path of his focus, the images of countless selves transformed before him, coming into view, reaching for him. As they faded into the background again, they remained firm in their own position and worthiness within the Apart.

All aselves present in the Apart gathered around Tres: those residing between their own corporeal lives, serving as OnLooker or with the Consultation, practicing their birthright of creation, or intently honing their own aself-development in other ways. All welcomed the newly ascended with complete acceptance and abiding reverence.

They greeted Tres individually and in unison, recognizing

him as his true self—an aself connected with all, even in his individuality.

And Tres remembered *the rest*.

All was known to him, whole, intricate, and as complete as a rich tapestry with even the finest hand-sewn threads visible at close inspection.

He became aware of his own existence within the Apart—most naturally—as flows to any aself upon their full rejoining with the Apart from corporeal existence. Tres remembered the segments *between:* the lapses between lives, his choices, their reasons. He remembered the gradual, labyrinthine, delightful expression and administration of his mien.

All the divergences he remembered within his own life encounters—every winding path and carefully manipulated experience from one life, beyond, and into the next—merged into a single line within his awareness. His *own* path lay fully apparent before him.

Love glowed in his perception, residing at his core like an interminable heartbeat.

2

ON A CLEAR, DISTINCTLY QUIET MORNING, MARIA DISCOVERED THE body of her grandson. Its lifelessness nearly commanded her own.

The empty shell of Aaron lay collapsed on his bedroom floor. The unnatural positioning disfigured Maria's memory of her vigorous, athletic grandson—his body crumpled like a marionette freed of its strings.

She tumbled on top of it, grasped at it, used all of her strength to lift the weight of the torso. She summoned all of her will to look into her grandson's glazed-over eyes and seek out a sign that what she *knew* was not true.

BENNETT DID NOT HEAR the unearthly wail that escaped Maria as she cried out her defiance.

He felt the piercing pinch of a portion of his own self being immutably severed from him.

As FINLAY KISSED his mother's cheek, soaking in her renewed smile at the start of his day, his vision dimmed, hazing over as he walked across the kitchen floor, forced to steady himself against the counter.

"Finlay?" his mother said as she rose from her seat at the breakfast table.

"I don't know..." he mouthed as the room regained its light, his surroundings solidifying again.

"It's all right now," he declared, smiling away the occurrence and burying his body's indication that something he was connected to had irrevocably changed.

SNUGGLED IN HER BED, Emily held her comforter tucked beneath her chin as fresh tears flowed, washing away those dried on her cheeks during the night.

Still asleep, she wept for the love she'd known, for the love that still lived within her, and for all the experiences, joys, and discoveries the far reaches of her consciousness knew would now never be.

When she later awoke, she would forget every realization as it instantly faded, embedding itself into another part of her self-awareness.

IT'S DIFFERENT. TRES'S FORM FLOURISHED WITH NEW VIGOR, WITH full force of vitality, as the complete composite of himself.

And... as is always, confirmed Fei, delighting in finding the ordinarily pleasant task of welcoming a returning ObServed to be especially satisfying.

Tres fluttered, sensing his self lighter, more energized, brimming with full capacity.

You adjust heartily, Fei imparted in compliment.

I feel... as... more, Tres conveyed, aglow with discovery.

As you are. The subtlety in Fei's presented self was not unnoticed by Tres.

And so, Fei continued, *my obServance... ends.*

You... you are no longer... my OnLooker...

As the term colored, forming in expression in a new way, the full breadth of its function within The Natural Order of Things blossomed in Tres's awareness.

Fei's pleasure—his predominant feeling of fulfillment— emanated as bubbles of laughter. *Indeed,* he confirmed. *And you... are aware of the full capacity of the role, its full meaning within the Apart—and of yours.* Fei hovered on his delight, dispersing his

form to impart his joy. *My obligation ends—as you have ascended...*
transcended in full.

Me?

Indeed.

I'm on my own now?

As always. OnLooker does not intervene.

But I... feel so connected to you.

As... all... are.

Tres understood—through sudden, sparking awareness,
through memory of existence with and in connection to the
Apart rather than from memory of corporeal experience.

And you... Tres imparted as his awareness continued to
expand, *you were also my... in another life—and in yet another...*

Tres's excitement slowed, his conveyance halted as he sensed
Fei's surprise, Fei's spontaneous reminder that none—other
than the *selected*—are gifted with any knowledge of their own
corporeal existences.

You have served me well, Tres expressed instead—and with
the same meaning.

YOU... ARE HERE.

The communication stretched across the Apart, carrying
every embedded intention and accusation.

YOU CHOOSE... UNWISELY, Ciel's conveyance resonated
through all being and matter.

4

FEI... TRES REACTED, HIS PLEA CAREFUL, GUARDED. *WE MUST STOP him. We must... contain... his insurgent creation.*

No aself may restrict another, Fei imparted in reply. *Creativity is aself's expression, the choice of all aselves.*

The OverSeer... intervenes—with all!

All that is... is The Natural Order of Things. As is... is truth.

Matching the tone of the Apart itself, Ciel's interruption severed all communication, all awareness: *I AM... THE NATURAL ORDER... OF ALL.*

The avowal reverberated throughout all, imparted in a permeating stream of sense-distorting phenomena.

I AM THE ONE—THE ONLY—WHO OVERSEES... ALL.

But there are two. Tres's reflection arrived on impulse—unbidden, uncontrolled, nonprovocative while infused with significance.

A MISTAKE! Ciel declared to all.

Simultaneously, the forms of Fei and Tres flickered with the truth they were wholly aware of, the truth both sensed through experience: *There are... no 'mistakes.'*

Ciel burst into more immediate awareness, articulating

himself before the two—before all. He hovered— reaching—as a heady umber haze.

ONE... OVERSEES! THE OTHER... IS MERELY A STUDENT— AND NOW... WITHOUT HIS TUTOR.

Saig... taught me well, Tres imparted in reply with cool tone and neutral dimension. *As he taught you. And you, the one called Ciel, deny your own instruction. You dishonor the role granted you by The Natural Order of Things. You dishonor all those before—all those of this moment.*

I DENY ONLY LIMITS! I MASTER CREATIVITY. I EXPRESS WITHOUT REPRESSION. I—

Sharpening his focus, combining all senses, Tres formed communication capable of interrupting the voice carried by all. *YOU INTERVENE!*

BECAUSE I AM ABLE! IT IS... MY... CHOICE!

Tres condensed, reconvened, harmonized himself. *And what of mine... what of the choice of all others?*

The dark-hued haze that was Ciel expanded, glowing and growing, as tentacles of motion spreading throughout the Apart, touching all, enforcing a single will on all—and integrating itself *within* Tres.

You will... destroy, trembled through Tres, pushing against the embedded, electrified fingers of Ciel's will now dwelling within him, *all that is created.*

Ciel's laughter erupted, spewing a bombardment of force and inclination, repulsive and suffocating.

Tres's senses reached for awareness of Fei—finding none— before altogether stifled. His awareness dwindled to *none* at all— not even of his own form—none except for Ciel's overbearing intention.

YOU, Ciel conveyed across the Apart, *FEIGN CONCERN FOR ALL OF CREATION, EVEN AS YOU, STUDENT, FAIL IN TOTAL AWARENESS OF IT. YOU... ARE CONCERNED SOLELY WITH*

MAINTAINING ILLUSIONS... WITH THOSE YOU AMUSED YOURSELF WITH IN MERE CORPOREALITY.

Stillness.

Muted tones.

All appeared to pause before the most pervasive perception bombarded all awareness yet again.

I...WILL UNVEIL THE ILLUSION. ALL... WILL BE REAC-QUAINTED... WITH THE TRUTH, Ciel imparted.

The illusion, Tres conveyed in spurts of energy drawn from his inner source now diminishing, *is truth. The illusion... creates experience. Experience... is a self-development. It is The Natural—*

I AM... THE NATURAL ORDER OF THINGS!

No, Ciel... you are merely... of its selection.

I AM OVERSEER!

But not... of all. The truth presented itself abruptly—in Tres's own awareness, even as it conveyed itself to all.

OVERSEER OVERSEES... ALL!

But you... do not... overSee... my self.

The accusation—the suggestion of limited power and ability —enraged Ciel, vibrating his umber core, energizing his acrimony, displacing light with dark, creation with void. Tres's fading form—his remaining sense of his dissipating self— detected a new invasion: Ciel's revised attack directly on Tres's very identity.

Tres's form oscillated with an array of panicked, random projections. Ciel injected himself deeper, widening the breadth of his evasive incursion. His awareness penetrated, rooting itself within Tres, seizing his essence of self.

Reaching, Ciel bludgeoned his awareness against abrupt,

impenetrable impediment. The OverSeer, the selected, could not *overSee* within Tres himself.

My lives are my own, Tres imparted in reaction—and in gratitude for his own realization. *My intention is mine alone to know.*

I AM OVERSEER!

Ciel thrust himself at the center of Tres, at the unforeseen blockage, at the discovery of the slightest—yet most irritating—limitation of his own awareness.

You do not... overSee... me, Tres reverberated in complaint and in unrelenting agony.

IT CANNOT BE!

I... am also... selected, Tres imparted the reason for his assumption, wrapping it in conviction. *I alone hold total awareness of... myself. No other may obtain awareness. No other may overSee.*

I... OVERSEE... ALL! Ciel squeezed, wrenching the sinews of Tres's self apart, tearing at his very existence. And he found that he *could not.*

FOR A SINGLE MOMENT, all was still.

The Apart awaited.

All waited.

THEN, the OverSeer declared his intention. And, by desiring it, he made it so.

I WILL... TAKE THEM ALL... FROM YOU.

Ciel's overbearing intention refocused, declaring new, dominating priority—consequently losing its grasp on Tres.

Tres floundered in form and awareness, non-particulate. In another moment, he was recollected. He pulled energy and assistance—the Apart itself—toward him as he healed himself, reconvened himself.

Tres's own anger reformed—and with his anger, fear returned. And in the company of fear, awareness faded; the truth slipped away.

Is it possible? Tres asked himself, asking all. *Can they... be removed? Can he destroy... aselves?* Tres repositioned, defended, undulated in his doubt. *But... there is no 'death,'* rose from within him as a glimmer of truth.

I... MAY INTERVENE, Ciel clarified with renewed confidence and soaring intention. *AS I HAVE... BEFORE.*

Sancha... sensed Tres as a sigh, a whimper, of his own memory. *But she chose. She was... ready.*

I LEFT HER... NO OTHER CHOICE. Ciel's pride reverberated, tickling at all, reproducing itself.

And Tres felt the ache—the wrenching convulsion—that Ciel so willfully intended. Tres's whole self sensed the pang of fury; his anger expanded into rage.

You looked on... yet, you neglected your role, Tres imparted in conjunction with his own realization. *You neglected her, as OnLooker. She was always... a child—always... a lost soul. She had no direction; she was left... unguided.*

IT IS NOT... OF MY RESPONSIBILITY.

She was... your responsibility! You were her OnLooker!

I AM SELECTED... FOR GREATER AWARENESS.

Then, you neglected your own training. You denied your own experience—your own self.

DID I? Ciel delivered with great force and abundance, with self-amusement and exhilaration. *I APPLIED MY INSTRUC-TION. I PRACTICED—MASTERED—THE MANIPULATION OF CORPOREALITY!*

By forfeiting your chosen role... your own aself-development.

BY CREATING WITHIN IT—IN SPITE OF IT! IN SPITE OF... MY OBSERVED.

I CREATED, Ciel's conceited confession continued, *WITHIN... HER.*

Inwardly asked, the question arose within Tres as a mere posit of possibility, an inflection of a yet-to-be-formed idea: *what did you do...?* Tres, did not suppose—nor desire—an answer.

Despite the hesitancy of his intention, the answer was delivered—with immense, grossly-gestating pleasure.

I... CREATED... YOU.

WITHOUT INVITATION, the newly unleashed memories of Tres's *complete* existence—those granted him as he ascended from corporeality and assembled wholly within the Apart—now saturated his awareness. They begged his attention as they assimilated themselves, rising as realization.

Tres recalled his *choice*: the sudden opportunity to return to corporeal life again, to begin anew. He remembered his desire for the challenge and the aself-development to be obtained. He had returned to corporeality as an *unwanted* child. He had chosen the experience of an infant altogether unprepared—for a life dedicated to teaching those he was born *to*, as much as to accepting their influence in teaching *him*.

He was born to Sancha, to Maria, and at that exact moment, granted full awareness while in corporeality: full conscious realization of all lives formerly lived. He remembered *everything*.

And he was simultaneously selected, by The Natural Order of Things—*while* in corporeal existence, at the beginning of his *new* existence. He was the first.

The first now redirected his attention to the one who created him.

YOU... a meandering, memory-wandering Tres managed to

impart. He recalled the vague mentions, the slivers of facts he'd been able to extract from his mother and grandmother about his origins. Sancha seemed to dream the one who seduced her —*that* relationship, that event. And *he* was left a mystery of fleeting existence—indefinable, unknowable.

He—Tres's progenitor—had not been... *corporeal.* He was Sancha's OnLooker.

AND IT WAS EASY, Ciel's conveyance burst through. *A DISAPPOINTMENT—TO DRAW HER... TO CONNECT WITH HER... WITHIN DREAM. SHE GAVE HERSELF... SO FREELY.*

All apportionment of Tres incited with fury. Gaining clarity from indignation, he regained awareness and matched Ciel's own conveyance.

YOU STOLE HER LIFE! Tres accused, fueled by his newly formed desire to inflict his will outside of himself.

I GAVE HER LIFE! Ciel's self-pride imparted, *YOUR LIFE.* His projected form undulated, permeating all, mocking creativity itself.

AND YOU, TRES, Ciel continued, *WERE NOT... INTENDED. YOU... ARE AN ACCIDENT—A MERE CONTINGENCY—I DO INTEND... TO CORRECT.*

YOU DEFY! YOU INTERVENE! Tres accused, reminding all of the Apart. As his own anger grew, so did his vulnerability. As his desire for retribution welled up, his will also weakened.

Tres infused with hatred, with spite. He fooled himself into believing he could satiate his most dangerous desire, abate his new hunger. *YOU DO NOT DESERVE... TO BE!*

YET, I AM—AS YOU ARE—OF THE NATURAL ORDER OF THINGS.

Ciel's capacity surrounded Tres, dancing with delight, delivering sensory data, inundating Tres with truth unsought and undeniable.

The OverSeer, Tres imparted, weakening, *does not intervene. All aselves are free to choose. All is choice.*

EVEN, Ciel's conveyance vibrated, *AS I LEAVE THEM ONLY ONE.*

THE MOST VIVID memory to flare in Tres's consciousness that moment was the sensation of corporeal form, of existing in body. Ciel's desire clenched Tres's being—as a hand wrapped around a vulnerable human neck. It confined and constricted, choking away his very existence.

TRES SENSED HIMSELF SLIPPING, sliding from self, desperately desiring to escape.

He reached for his memories of *life*: drive, motivation, inspiration. He remembered relationships, friends, foes, family. He recalled successes, failures—all serving purpose, intention, choices he himself had made *before*.

Still, he continued to descend, to fade, to sputter out of self—to ponder the possibility of utter non-existence.

He desired the freedom to *forget*.

BUT THE MEMORIES REMAINED, holding fast, flashing through awareness—as if imparting a message of their own.

Tela's shining green eyes appeared in Tres's perception as memory morphed, manipulating. So recently extracted from corporeality, Tres's awareness incorporated all the senses of temporal form. He recalled them, re-experiencing them.

His awareness was vibrant and alive—instantly, expertly creating precisely what he most desired—even while he remained too disconnected from his *self* to realize the activity naturally arising from mere intention.

His message transcended through and beyond.

The vision of Tela's eyes expanded in lucidity as she manifested in form, articulating within his awareness. And she was joined by others.

Tres's own form, faint and nearly forceless, perceived their faces. He sensed their smiles and support, their identities conveying abiding strength.

As he perished, he was not alone. As he despaired, he was joined. As he desired, all came to be.

Tres... wafted into his awareness: the voice of one and of all. *You suffer.* Their realization was his own. His sense of suffering spread from him, mixing with like energy, locating the same permeating from the Apart.

Another voice, one Tres once owned, wandered through his surrendering self. *There is no 'pain.' Suffering is perceived only... as aself denies aself's mien.* The voice belonged to Fei—and to Saig—to Liet, and to all within the Apart.

Tres... imparted the shared voice of all those Tres loved within the corporeal life he left so recently.

You love... you do not hate, resonated Tela with Saig with Rien with Liet with Veoir with Fei with Leal with Estre.

And Ciel laughed at all.

You love, insisted Tres's inner voice, only to himself. *It is your core. It is your... mien.*

I do... love you, Tres imparted—only faintly, weak of feeling—to those who came to his aid.

And the Apart convened, drawing on its collective self. All aselves answered, taught, imparted at once and together to Tres: *Aself's mien—aself's true mien—is impartially... undeniably... inclusive. Mien... excludes none.*

Tela, Tres proclaimed. *Estre and Veoir,* he remembered. *Liet,*

Rien, and Leal, he realized. *I love you all. I will miss you all. I am sorry... I could not save you—your corporeal selves—as you saved me.*

Aself does not love... all, the collective Apart conveyed. *Aself denies aself's mien.*

I cannot love... to any greater extent, Tres imparted as his sense of self faded.

It is... aself's choice, the Apart reminded. *And aself's mien.*

And so, you do not love... me... Tela's identity imparted with singular provocation, *if you cannot love... all.*

Suffering tightened its grip. Pain etched through Tres's awareness. His self reached, grasping at all, touching nothing.

I do love, he cried from his essence, choking on his own lie.

The collective voice rose and fell, undulating with pulse, commanding awareness, focus, realization. *Love all... include all... fulfill your mien.*

Tres desired to, but he sensed no remaining capacity.

Be the one... I know you to be, came Tela's request: simple, honest, and filled with affection.

With failing ability and waning awareness, Tres sensed the presence of the *one* excluded, the one who dared intervene within his corporeal life, and with Sancha's—the one called Ciel.

IT IS... YOUR CHOICE, the OverSeer imparted as he prodded at Tres's overwhelming desire to leave all suffering behind.

With purpose and curiosity arising from desperation, Tres searched the path of his own memories—of his lives and of his most recent corporeal existence. He reflected on his singular experience, the challenge that his most recent life had been: his delight despite his agony and the multitude of magnificent moments despite all pain and suffering, of worry and despair, of feeling excluded from what that life should have been for him.

And Tres chose to shower that boy, from infancy through

manhood, with love—with respect and gratitude, with honor and joy.

Tres openly thanked all for his last life, and he thanked himself for choosing it. And in thanking his existence, he thanked its creator—*his* creator. He thanked his father.

Tres felt love, unabashed and unhindered—for himself, and so, for all. And he felt it returned from all in existence, all created before and since.

The Apart smiled upon him—as it always is, even as aself denies the awareness.

Tres filled with love, with awareness, with the acceptance of The Natural Order of Things. And he sharpened his focus, concentrating his being on a single focal point as he expressed his full, unadulterated gratitude and love toward the one called Ciel.

YOUR LOVE... OFFERS ME NOTHING, Ciel returned. *MY INTENTION REMAINS. MY DESIRE IS REALIZED.*

As it offers me... all, Tres imparted, *complete acceptance of my own mien, my purpose, my path, my aself-development—as it serves The Natural Order of Things.* His strength grew with true intention—gaining support from all of the Apart and all created—as his mien was served, recognized, honored.

Tres's own awareness and self-ability reached a crescendo sensed by all.

As it is... indeed, the collective voice of the Apart conveyed in song, *The Natural Order of Things—for all is... creation. All is love manifest.*

As I am, Tres glowed, lighting all darkness, coloring all perception with heartfelt delight, *so are you... Ciel. You are created in love—as all is.*

IT IS... OF NO CONSEQUENCE... TO ME! raged Ciel, battling the light.

Yet... it is you... and you are it, Tres imparted with intrinsic wisdom. *And so, you must follow your own mien. Your self yearns for it.*

I YEARN... ONLY TO ALTER! TO AFFECT! TO CHANGE!

And so, imparted Tres, synchronizing in song with the aselves he was bonded with, through life after life, and with all of the Apart, *you may only find your peace—the ultimate success that awaits you—as you... include yourself. Your true self yearns, Ciel... to develop, to change... yourself. It is... your mien.*

No reply was offered—none that did not resonate to the core of all of existence.

Ciel ruptured with venomous denial, particulating in pulse, embedding the shrapnel of his protest within all. And all corporeality acknowledged the sensation, returning abiding love and acceptance, reverberating with the impenetrable solidity of creativity.

Ciel was inundated with the obvious—with the truth he knew but had long denied all awareness of. Ciel ached for change, for the new, for the full and ultimate challenge of his own creative capacity. And he felt the respectful nudge of the one he'd invested so much of his creative effort into controlling.

You are OverSeer, Tres congratulated, honored, and reminded. *You alone—of all that exists, all of creation, all of the Apart—hold the ability to... conCenter.*

The ConCentration... Ciel's conveyance vibrated, mild and inquisitive, integrated with innocent delight.

To create... Tres reinforced, *corporeality—individual, unique, anew—and of your own, singular creation.*

An entire corporeality... Ciel's true self considered.

Of your own manipulation—the re-creation... of your... own self.

The Apart and all within joined in tone and intention, combining energy with support, reaffirming Ciel's renewed awareness of his own inner joy—restoring his self's inherent sense of wonder and curiosity, of *naturally* desired creativity.

Ciel's form revised, subdued and sensual. *The ultimate alteration... the mastering of creativity.*

Tres integrated his own awareness, his own joy and delight. *Alteration—transformation—of aself... mastering oneself.*

THE VIBRATION—AT first, low and rhythmic—whirled within the Apart, gathering support from all, gaining momentum, encircling in waves of intention and driven desire. Ciel's form transformed itself, pulsing and motioning, manipulating all that immediately adjoined, then expanding in wake and reach.

Ciel expertly, delightedly, focused all his individual skill, motivation, and mastery—impacting a single moment with supreme ability and manifestation.

In an instant, Ciel commenced his conCentering. He transformed into a magnificently rendered recreation resonating through all, integrating with all, dispersing across the Apart. He separated, reorganized, then condensed and conCentered himself—into a *sui generis* corporeality, unique and perfect.

He became the ConCentration of experience for newly birthed corporeal lives and their self-chosen paths of aself-development.

5

TRES ADMIRED THE SUBLIME, EXALTED DISPLAY OF THE BIRTH OF A new corporeality. He delighted in the awe it inspired within him. As he absorbed the lighter, more joyful energy abundant in the Apart, he too transformed.

Tres metamorphosed—just as naturally, most intuitively—as the new OverSeer of the Apart, ObServer of all that is. The new role, his more expansive identity, established in the same instant and at the most minute metaphysical levels.

The ConCentration glared in vibrancy, ushering a sense of wellbeing to all, inciting simultaneous amazement and compelling sympathy, inspiration, and motivation. Tres was overwhelmed with total-self compassion. It vibrated throughout his being and extended to all existing outside of him. His self wept, smiled, and loved all in one instant.

As OverSeer, Tres's final barriers—those barring his self against absolute awareness—fell away. He allowed the ultimate, infinite expansion of his own awareness. The new capacity flourished within and without him, tethering him to all activity throughout the Apart. Tres felt the instantaneous nature and existence of all events and each experience: multiple roles, perceptions, and progressions in aself-development all happening *now*.

He felt surrounded by endless support and energy: his personal connection to all. He sensed the origins of each and all, the lives contributing abundant experience to all, and the existence of infinite corporealities.

He was aware of the corporeality Saig established—became —and that of Ciel. Tres felt the new temporal lives birthing from them: creatures so different from Earth's inhabitants he'd known throughout his own lives. They, too, were connected and intimately related with *all*.

And he realized that no aself is alone. He sensed the continuously propagating, ever-nourishing *family* each and all are a part of: all connected, all communicating, none less so than any other.

The inherent, self-cultivating perfection of the Apart, the sublime organization of The Natural Order of Things, confirmed itself in his awareness. It fueled him as he existed alongside it.

And he brimmed with the fulfillment of his own mien. It radiated from his essence, energized his creativity, communicated with all aselves.

Tres realized his own full capacity and boundless ability. And still, he did not yet acknowledge his own severance— informal and absolute—from corporeal life. Residual longing— attachment—remained as a thorn embedded in his new, infinitely expansive self-awareness.

6

THEY FEEL LIKE A DREAM, TRES IMPARTED, DIRECTING HIS perception toward Fei while unintentionally communicating to all choosing to include the OverSeer's ponderings within their own awareness.

Every life of my own, Tres conveyed, *every person I've known... they're like dreams now... subtle, imagined diversions from my true existence in the Apart.*

Thus is... the corporeal, Fei imparted. *Dream—within corporeality—exists as aself's eternal connection to the Apart and true self.*

My connection... to Estre, Tela—the others—is still strong.

The connection... fades in awareness—as OverSeer's all-awareness... matures.

Tres's desire resonated throughout the Apart with unrestrained intensity. *I must see them. I must be with them again. They won't—*

OverSeer cannot.

I have to. I... left too soon. I had to protect them. And now, they need—

OverSeer does not return to corporeality. Your final corporeal life... ends.

I am OverSeer. I have all-awareness, all-ability.

OverSeer... does not intervene. Fei's message resounded with the strength of its truth, the truth of its expansive implication.

I cannot... desert them. I promised—

A corporeal concept, Fei interrupted, his skilled conveyance absorbing the vibration of Tres's. *As aself... desires, so manifests.* Fei tempered the vividness of his conveyance. *Your corporeal 'promise' is upheld... as OverSeer applies... intention.*

Tres calmed, in form and energy. *I am OverSeer. I can never return. My own cycle of corporeal lives ends.*

As those of aselves continue... as aselves fulfill their own choices, realize the lessons aself-selected.

I can't... go back.

OverSeer does not.

It is... The Natural Order of Things, imparted Tres, the Over-Seer. And he *felt* the same, alive and thriving within him.

MARIA AND EMILY wrapped themselves in the other's arms, allowing their tears to flow as they huddled against everyone on the outside—those that could not know *him* in the ways that they had. They soothed one another, shared their pain, exchanged all the reasons why life is sometimes, so often, unbearable.

And they convinced one another that one day, they would wake without first thinking of him, might live an entire day without every detail of their experience reminding them—first and foremost—of the one who called himself *Tres*.

7

"HE'S... WHERE HE BELONGS," MARIA WHISPERED, ALMOST impulsively, as she sat with Emily and gazed into the back garden. "Out there," she pointed with her eyes toward the sky.

Emily tried to sense the same, tried to gain peace through Maria's wisdom—but she could not. "Do you think," she asked, "there's... a heaven?"

Maria shook her head as she continued to stare at what Emily could not see. "I have," she said. She pondered the admission, then said, "Maybe I still do, but... that just doesn't seem *enough*, for someone like... *Tres*."

Emily reacted to the name and the fluid sound of its single syllable. The tiny hairs at the back of her neck stood on end. "So, you *do* remember."

"He told me—us, Sancha and I—after... I was sick."

"He told me about that—about you being so close to..."

Maria nodded. "So much happened. Every day was a surprise with him." She grinned at Emily, then turned to face the window again. "I... I *asked him* who he was."

"You did?"

Maria nodded, solemn and focused on the moments

embedded in her memory. "I don't know why—when I think about it now. Sometimes, with him, I would forget that he was just a child sitting in front of me. There'd be moments when, he felt like *more*. The questions just came out."

Emily nodded.

"I don't know what I was expecting," Maria continued. "I learned to never *expect* anything with him. He just... answered my question. He *told me* who he was, what his name was."

"And what did you—"

"I locked it away. I never used it—as if he never even risked so much just to share it." Maria's face twitched with pain. "I should have, I think. No, I *know* it. I was afraid—afraid of him— even after he saved my life."

"I don't think you were *afraid*."

"I was," Maria insisted, the volume of her voice lifting. "For so long, so much about him seemed so... *unnatural*. And now..." She paused, brushed the first tear from her eye. "Now, I know he's the most *natural* one of us all."

The idea wrenched Emily's emotions as well. She would've nodded her agreement—if she wasn't distracted by the flow of her own memories of him.

"I should've told him," Maria said, choking on her own words.

"No. He knew," Emily said. "He knew... everything that needed knowing." She smiled delicately, lifting her shoulders in a slight shrug.

Maria looked at her, the girl seated across from her—at the life in her face, the glow of inner joy that could not be stifled by anything at all. Maria envied her—and loved her. And she was grateful for Emily being a part of *him,* a connection Maria could still touch and see and hold.

8

EMILY WALKED FORWARD, WILLING HER FEET TO TAKE ONE STEP after the next, the murmur of strangers' voices a discomforting din at the edge of her attention. Her hands reached for the edge of the open casket, gripping with white knuckles. Her fingers smoothed over the satin inlay.

She didn't recognize the face of the body tucked inside. Its eyes were closed, its tenant undeniably absent.

Maria's large hand—as cold and subtly trembling as Emily's own—rested on her shoulder. "I can't," Emily mumbled, inhaling additional strength. "I can't even *cry*."

Maria nodded. "I can't make myself look."

"It seems like..." Emily continued, feeding her need to communicate and connect, "I woke up this morning feeling like I was..."

"*With* him," Maria finished for her.

A sudden shiver exposed Emily's surprise. She turned to face Maria. "I guess... I've done all my crying already."

"And you know," Maria said, "that you're only crying for yourself, that *he*... is okay."

Emily permitted herself one more glance at the pallid shell

lying in the casket. "Of course, he is," she said, "I can't imagine... anything else."

A SMALL GATHERING surrounded the burial plot. Maria and Emily stood arm in arm next to Finlay and Bennett, nearest the now-closed casket containing their friend, grandchild, or lover.

"You know, it's..." Bennett whispered to Finlay, "his birthday."

Finlay nodded, his gaze focused on the white casket perched precariously over its final resting place. "It's strange, isn't it? Saying goodbye to a box."

"Do you think it's what he... would've wanted?"

"No idea. It doesn't even feel like he's really *gone*."

"No," Bennett agreed too quickly, his mouth opening to speak of a dream before he decided against it. "I'm glad," he said instead, "that we have each other—I mean, others that knew him... the way that we did."

"The whole thing—all those years—feels like a dream."

"Yeah. And now, it will be a different one."

Bennett's words—almost uttered without conscious thought —resonated in Finlay's mind, ringing true in some way, by some feeling. A pang of discomfort, deep and affecting, rose in his chest—a longing, or the inner realization of a connection now lost.

In their shared grief, Bennett and Finlay found themselves drawn to each other, forming a friendship without their intention—through the deeper connection they shared but would never be consciously, *temporally* aware of.

THE ONE CALLED TRES obSERVED, aware of all, overSeeing all.

From within the Apart, without articulation—without intervention—he looked on, unnoticed by those invested in corporeal form.

He watched, regarding those assembled for the viewing and the burial of the temporal form he once embodied. He absorbed every word spoken, every glance made, every emotion conveyed.

And he mourned with them.

He grieved the loss of the sensory experience he would never again share with them. He mourned the excruciating truth that his keen awareness delivered to him.

Their true selves, once ascended from their corporeality, would—most naturally—*forget* him.

9

ASELF'S INSTRUCTION... CONTINUES, IMPARTED AN ASELF OF THE Consultation, extending the reassurance to Tres.

As aself's role begins.

As OverSeer.

Abruptly.

It is... a first.

The only.

All aselves aid.

The Consultation offers guidance.

Indeed.

And welcome... once more.

The three of the Consultation shaped and sinewed singularly, synchronizing their sensory show of gratitude, honor, affection, and enduring support.

And an opportunity...

Arises.

As OverSeer...

Is invited.

To aid... in the selection.

Of OnLooker.

For the first... corporeal life.

To arise.

To begin... anew.

Tres, the OverSeer—exuberant and exhilarated with love and compassion and the full realization of the breadth of all existence—accepted the honor. And he celebrated (the honor) in both concept and in reflection upon his own memories of lives formerly lived.

The first new corporeal life, he imparted with veneration.

As I am the first... to have awakened in corporeal life. Tres considered, delighting in and appreciating the never-ending curiosity—the spontaneity, the surprise—that is all existence, that is The Natural Order of Things.

Indeed, imparted one aself of the Consultation.

The only.

The exception.

The exception... revered Tres, in awe of all possibility—in awe of all that had been and all that would be. *Nulla regula sine exceptione...* he recited, as confirmed by all his experiences and every memory. *There is no rule without exception.*

Indeed, affirmed the aselves of the Consultation in unison, embossing the truth with a burst of golden light.

It is...

As all is...

The Natural Order of Things.

Tres impulsively resonated with the same understanding, his form alight with new awareness—and with new awareness, renewed hope.

There is no rule without exception...

SHE CURLED IN HER SLEEP, the soft tendrils of her dark hair

pooled around her, her cheeks flush with the warmth of deep dream.

Tela... her subconscious received.

My Emily... translated the latent ability her whole-self-awareness held.

The voice embedded its message—its immense intent— from the expanse beyond, from the reality *apart*. It emanated from the only self with singular, total awareness and all-capability.

Emily... remember me.

Do not stand at my grave and weep
I am not there; I do not sleep.
I am a thousand winds that blow,
I am the diamond glints on snow,
I am the sun on ripened grain,
I am the gentle autumn rain.
When you awaken in the morning's hush
I am the swift uplifting rush
Of quiet birds in circled flight.
I am the soft stars that shine at night.
Do not stand at my grave and cry,
I am not there; I did not die.

— MARY ELIZABETH FRYE

ACKNOWLEDGMENTS

FIRST AND FOREMOST, I OWE A LIFETIME OF GRATITUDE TO MY biggest supporter, my best friend, my husband, Devon, without whom this story would not have been uncovered, from wherever stories waft in from, and would never have been told. "Write your novel now. Don't wait any longer" was his request I found no reasonable excuse for denying. I'm also in his debt for braving the role of *first reader* for every story I write and being forced to defend himself as my *first critic*. And, for respecting and protecting my "writing time" even more than I do, he is a significant contributor to anything and everything I happen to write.

Thank you, Sam, for choosing—and sometimes insisting on —being my companion during the writing of this story and even dressing up for the occasion in your sleek gray suit and coordinating white cravat. It was always reassuring to have you there at my desk side, especially when I was writing the spooky bits. No doubt, the story's stronger for your silent influence. And thank you, Becks, for your companionship and volunteering to *overSee* my work during the editing process. Your authoritative presence assured me I was on the right track. Without the both of you, writing a novel would be as lonely as it could be. It's much more fun when I'm alerted for every ground squirrel, fence lizard, hummingbird, or dark-eyed junco in view.

Rachel Smith, you are a godsend for authors, publishers, and authorpreneurs who are fortuitous enough to discover and enlist your literary publishing and marketing expertise. I doubt there are any in the industry savvier than you—or more downright pleasant to work with.

Thank you, Stephanie Larson and Jessica B., for delving into this story and offering your unadulterated comments and suggestions for improvement. Your meticulousness and every editing note have been invaluable.

I am very grateful to my team of dedicated technical advisers, Gary Boward and Matt Boward. Thank you both for addressing each unsolicited question about American high school track. And thank you, Gary, for verifying my memory of static line jumps and correcting the rock climbing lingo not at all in my vocabulary.

Finally, I'm compelled to acknowledge Benedict Ajax Spencer who happened to be conceived in the same year as this novel (it's true!), or maybe it's more appropriate to refer to his being born in the year of this novel's publication. You were the first infant I held after creating the story of Tres, the infant *beginning again*. You unknowingly instigated a magical moment for me as I realized I'd created a character that felt very much alive, and I wished everyone reading his story would be as moved by it as I am. Or perhaps... you, Ajax, were very much aware? I hope the world and beyond never lose their wonder for you. And I hope you realize how lucky you are to be born to two exceptional human beings. Then again, perhaps you *chose* them for yourself...

(This novel was written and edited near Los Angeles, California —and also edited in England, Japan, South Korea, and the skies between. Thank you to the flight attendant on Korean Air who whipped up a recipe for an amazing mocha coffee—the perfect jet-lagged writer's fuel!)

ABOUT THE AUTHOR

JUSTINE AVERY IS AN AWARD-WINNING AUTHOR OF STORIES LARGE and small *for all*. Born in the American Midwest and raised all over the world, she is inherently an explorer, duly fascinated by everything around her and excitedly noting the stories that abound all around. As an avid reader of all genres, she weaves her own stories among them all. She has a predilection for writing speculative fiction and story twists and surprises she can't even predict herself.

Avery has either lived in or explored all 50 states of the union, over 36 countries, and all but one continent; she lost count after moving 30-some times before the age of 20. She's *intentionally* jumped out of airplanes and off the highest bungee jump in New Zealand, scuba dived *unintentionally* with sharks, designed websites, intranets, and technical manuals, bartered with indigenous Panamanians, welded automobile frames, observed at the Bujinkan Hombu Dojo in Noba, Japan, and masterminded prosperous internet businesses—to name a few adventures. She earned a Bachelor of Arts degree that life has never required, and at age 28, she sold everything she owned and quit corporate life—and her final "job"—to freelance and travel the world as she always dreamed of. And she's never looked back.

Aside from her native English, Avery speaks a bit of Japanese and a bit more Spanish, her accent is an ever-evolving mixture of Midwestern American with notes of the Deep South and indiscriminate British vocabulary and rhythm, and she says "eh"—like the Kiwis, not the Canadians. She currently lives near Los Angeles with her husband, British film director Devon Avery, and their children. She writes from wherever her curiosity takes her.

Avery loves to connect with fellow readers and creatives, explorers and imaginers, and cordially invites you to say "hello"—or *konnichiwa*.

www.JustineAvery.com
Twitter: @Justine_Avery
Goodreads: JustineAvery

ALSO BY JUSTINE AVERY

Visit www.JustineAvery.com for the complete list of currently available titles and those coming soon.